I0699754

ALONG ABOUT MIDNIGHT

ALONG ABOUT MIDNIGHT

RAVEN'S HOLLOW BOOKS

Cover design by Stefanie Fontecha
Interior design by www.helpingauthorseveryday.com
Illustrations by Caitlin Cox
Edited by T.L. Beeding

Library of Congress Cataloging-in Publication Data

Sinnott, Dorian J.
Raven's Hollow Publishing

ISBN: 979-8-9883557-3-1

Printed in the United States of America
10 9 8 7 6 5 4 3 2 1

*This book is dedicated to the lost and the lonely. To those left behind. To those who cling to the past. To memories. To ghosts. **You are not alone.** You are not forgotten. You are loved.*

*Even in the darkest hours, your inner **light** still shines. Never let it go out. One day, it will guide you **home.***

1.

The autumn gray hung heavy over Oakridge late that October. And with it, came a chill that couldn't be shaken. One that clung deep—down to the bone. Beneath the vibrant amber and gold foliage, a thick fog rolled in, brushing against the tree trunks and damp, decaying leaves. In the early mornings, it stretched its way from the park at the edge of town through the neighborhoods nestled in the hollow. But as evening set in, it extended its reach, creeping to the gates of the Chapel Hill Cemetery at the far end of town. The cemetery where local teens spent the majority of the month. Sharing their secrets. Waiting for shadows to set. Longing for ghosts.

1 

Peter Harlow leaned against the cold iron gate, lighting a cigarette. He took a long drag, exhaling a cloud of smoke. The scent of the tobacco was heavy, one he wasn't necessarily fond of. Yet, it was relaxing.

He took another puff, the ash burning his tongue as he shut his eyes. Pressing his head against the gate, he inhaled the crisp air of evening. He remained silent, taking in the night, as the sound of crunching leaves rose up nearby. It was soft at first, but gradually became louder. Harsher. Peter squinted through the shadows, trying to make out who was headed his way. It was late, he thought, and the cemetery grounds were closed. Surely it wasn't a visitor.

Blowing a final cloud of smoke, Peter dropped his cigarette to the ground, mashing it into the pavement. He kept his attention on the sounds down the sidewalk, calling out in a raspy breath.

"Hello?"

But there was no answer. Peter chewed his lip as he stared off down the street—towards where the rustling had come from. The shadows grew thicker by the minute, and even with the streetlamps illuminating patches of sidewalk, it was hard to see. He waited a moment longer, still and silent, until he heard it again. This time, however, he could make out a shape slowly approaching him.

Its silhouette loomed across the pavement. Creeping. And then, a reflection of yellow. What appeared to be eyes, watching him. Coming closer. Peter tensed, heart racing as it drew nearer.

Only when it became close enough, touched by the faint streetlight, did he see what it was. A cat. Long and slender. Its silky black fur shone beneath the lights, yellow eyes glinting. It chirped softly, trotting over to him.

Peter sighed in relief. "It's only a damn cat..."

The cat looked him over—inspecting him. It chirped again, brushing against his leg as he winced, trying to shoo it away. But it paid him no mind. After circling his legs, it stopped and sniffed the air. Taking in the chill and scent of damp leaves. And then...something else. Its ears flattened, tail beginning to twitch—gazing off into the cemetery. With a low growl, it hissed. Peter glanced behind him, through the iron gates and shadow. Into the steadily darkening graveyard. All he could see was the fog, lingering around the base of the silhouetted trees and headstones. But something felt off. A weight heavy in the pit of his stomach. As if someone were out there.

Watching.

2

CEMETERY

Once more, the rustling of leaves came up behind him. Crunching. Footsteps approaching. A pale hand reached from the darkness and touched his shoulder. He jumped, letting out a gasp of surprise.

"Whoa, hey! Peter, it's just me."

Peter breathed in relief as his eyes met the teenage girl—Sam Vanderpool—appearing from the shadows. "Geez, Sam...what are you trying to do? Scare me to death?"

"At least you're in a good spot if I did." She motioned to the cemetery behind them with a wink. "They wouldn't have to carry you far."

Peter scoffed, reaching into his pocket for another cigarette. He placed it between his teeth before offering one to Sam, but she shook her head.

"You know that's not for me."

Lighting the cigarette, Peter inhaled sharply, letting the ashy taste linger on his tongue. He turned back to the sidewalk where the cat had been, only to find it gone. As if it had never been there at all.

"What is it?" Sam asked.

"Ah, nothing..." Peter took another puff. "Just a cat. Probably one of the local strays."

"Cat? I didn't see a cat."

Sam tucked a strand of violet hair behind her ear, facing the cemetery. The night was slipping into its darkest hours now, and it was harder to make out the silhouettes of headstones in the shadows. Returning her gaze to Peter, she looked him up and down in scrutiny.

"Did you bring your pumpkin?"

Peter exhaled a stream of smoke, glancing at her. Sure enough, in her arms was a plump, round jack-o'-lantern. Carved out and ready to light. Adjusting the soft gray beanie on his head, he groaned.

"I completely forgot."

"Don't sweat it," Sam said. "Besides, knowing Ritchie and Theo, they probably forgot, too."

Peter managed a weak smirk before dropping what was left of his cigarette to the ground, crushing it under his foot. "That is, if they show at all."

"They better hurry up." Sam hugged her pumpkin to her chest. "It's almost midnight. And we *both* know the police patrol this place like crazy around Halloween."

"I'm sure they'll be here soon. You know how Ritchie is. Always dragging his feet. And besides, his dad's a cop, remember? So don't worry."

Sam shook her head. "Yeah. *His* dad's a cop. That doesn't stop him from busting *us*, though."Peter parted his lips to respond, but was interrupted by the sound of deep laughter carrying down the block. He and Sam looked towards the silhouettes of two teens at the far end of the street—near the lights. They were bulky with broad shoulders—voices growing louder as they approached. Sam rolled her eyes once they came into view.

"And speak of the Devil. About time."

Ritchie Buchanan and Theo Williams, the school's quarterback and wide receiver, were sporting their varsity jackets—the only real attire they'd worn since the start of the season. Theo could have been the poster child for any football team, having the right build and charisma. Ritchie, on the other hand, fit the bill for simply being popular. He had a well chiseled face and bright eyes—with fiery auburn hair and freckles to boot. And, as far as Sam was concerned, his attitude often matched his role. A jock.

Their boisterous laughter continued as they made their way over to Peter and Sam, jack-o'-lanterns in hand. At the sight of them, Peter's gaze dropped to the browning leaves at his feet. He stuffed his hands into his pockets, leaning back against the gate until Ritchie and Theo were beside them.

"Took you long enough," Sam said as she eyed them over.

"Hey, I had to wait for my dad to head out for the night." Ritchie tucked the carved pumpkin under his arm. "You know he works the midnight patrol."

"And don't forget, you had us *carve* these jack-o'-lanterns. Between that and getting my Physics homework done...it takes time," Theo chimed in.

"Well, at least we're all here now," Sam said.

Ritchie turned to Peter. He still hadn't stepped away from the gate, focus remaining on the decaying leaves that scattered the sidewalk. Seeing that his hands were in his pockets, Ritchie scrunched up his nose.

"Where's *your* pumpkin?"

Peter sighed heavily, smoothing the dark bangs poking out from beneath his beanie. He averted his gaze, shifting his feet.

"I forgot."

"Forgot?" Ritchie echoed. "We literally have been talking about this for the last *week*. And you *forgot*?"

"Hey, it's fine, okay?" Sam said. "We have three. That'll be enough. Now come on, it's late. Are we doing this or not?"

5

"I didn't sneak out for nothing," Theo replied, shrugging. "Besides. I don't know about you, but I'm down for finding out if what they say about this place is true. And the only way we're gonna is if we go in."

"Haunted or not..." Ritchie flashed a toothy grin. "It's spooky season. Everyone's looking for some kind of scare. And where better than an old cemetery at midnight, hm?"

"Of course." Sam smirked. "Now, let's go before someone sees us."

Ritchie scoffed before pushing past her, through the cemetery gates. Theo silently joined him at his side, listening to the dark air around them. The only sounds that came from within were their feet along the pavement. The crunching gravel under their shoes. The rustling leaves. Peter raised his head to Sam.

"You ready?" she asked.

Peter nodded. With a soft smile, Sam looped her arm through his as she led him through the old iron gates of Chapel Hill.

"There's a legend about cemeteries, you know," Sam said as they walked amongst the shadows, gripping their jack-o'-lanterns tight. "To keep trespassers away."

Ritchie turned his pocket flashlight on, illuminating the path before them. He'd waited until they were out of sight from the road, in case anyone had been nearby. Keeping watch. He took a cautious breath, allowing the light to stray to the gravestones lining the pathway.

"You ever hear of Grims?" Sam asked.

Peter kept his gaze on the faint ray of light. "Like the reaper?"

"Not entirely," Sam said. "These are more like...guardians."

The path went on for what felt like forever—winding through the thick groves of stone. Hardly any were new—all from the turn of the century. Ancient, crumbling things. Shrouded in shadow and fog.

Peter kept his hands buried deep in the pockets of his jeans as he walked, glancing from one side to the other. Making out the faint silhouettes of the stones. How they felt like eyes in the night, watching every step the group took farther into the cemetery. Up the hill. Towards the old chapel. And though he knew it was vacant, the idea of something waiting out there amongst the headstones ate away at him.

His fear subsided, however, as the group reached their destination at the base of a tall, dead tree. Where the grave markers became fewer. The night air colder.

Though it bore no leaves, its branches remained outstretched to the skies. Its bark was twisted, coiling around the trunk like tight cords. And while it no longer fed off the soil, it still glistened in the moonlight. Appearing as alive as any other tree in Chapel Hill. Perhaps, even more so.

Ritchie gestured the group to the base of the tree with his flashlight before taking a seat. Theo joined him, gazing up through the bare branches at the dark skies and moon peeking through the clouds. Peter was hesitant at first, but then motioned Sam to join him as he sat beside Ritchie. The ground was cold and damp, but they made do as they got situated around the twisting trunk.

"You know the story about this tree?" Theo asked. "My grandad used to tell me they hanged witches from the branches. Those accused of stealing away children. Said they cut out their tongues to prevent them from speaking spells. Cursing the town."

"Those are just old fairy tales," Ritchie scoffed, but Theo continued.

"That's what they *want* you to believe. But why do you think the tree still thrives even in death? Though their tongues were gone, they managed to bewitch it. Let it survive long after everyone who wronged them were gone. As a reminder to the town," he said. "That's why the bark's twisted. Just like the old ropes they used to hang them."

"Isn't this the tree people claim they've *seen* them hanging? Their ghosts anyway?" Peter asked.

"Precisely the one."

"It's sad," Sam said, "how even to this day, society *still* finds it more acceptable to shun and destroy those who are different, rather than embrace them. Get to know them. See who they really are."

She placed her jack-o'-lantern on the ground, staring at the hollowed out eyes and jolly smile. Pursing her lips, she shook her head.

"Being the *witch* was the crime...not hanging them."

"It's a shame how little we've changed," Peter added.

Ritchie set the flashlight down in the center of the group. He cleared his throat, turning back to Sam.

"So, these *Grims* you mentioned. Go on."

Sam let her eyes fall to the light. "Oh. Right. So, basically, they protected the grounds from thieves back in the olden days."

"Are they...ghosts?" Peter asked quietly.

"Spirits, yes. But not human."

The three boys watched with interest as Sam adjusted herself beneath the tree. She rested against the trunk, motioning out through the shadows of the cemetery. Midnight had fallen hard, making it impossible to see any shapes in the darkness.

"Way back, they used to bury a dog in the cemeteries before any human bodies were laid to rest," Sam explained. "People believed that the soul of whatever was buried first would be tied to the land, unable to leave. Unable to rest. They thought a dog was a good choice for that. Dogs are loyal, after all."

"So, they just killed a dog for the sake of it and buried it?" Theo asked.

"Buried it *alive*," Sam corrected him.

"That's sick."

"There's a lot of sick things people have done to animals out of superstition," Sam said, disgusted. "Look at cats. For how long did people believe they were witches? I'll bet you *they* were hanged as well."

"And then what? With the Grim?" Peter asked.

"Well, there are a bunch of different myths," Sam continued. "But, the main story is that the spirit does, indeed, remain in the cemetery. Patrolling the grounds. Guarding the dead. Keeping the Devil out. Some say if it spots you trespassing, it'll chase you into an early grave."

She looked between the boys seated around her, a smile tugging at her lips. They all gazed into the darkness, searching for any signs of movement.

"You'll know the Grim is around by its unholy howls and glowing red eyes. If you see them, though, you're too late."

Silence fell among the group. The cemetery itself was still, only the chirping of crickets echoing in the distance. Ritchie exhaled deeply, reaching for the flashlight.

"Is that why we brought these pumpkins out here? To try and find some *dog*?" he asked.

Sam's smirk grew. "Not quite."

Reaching into the bag at her side, she removed three tea light candles. She placed the first inside her jack-o'-lantern, before holding the other two out for Ritchie and Theo.

"Do you mind, Peter?" She motioned to him.

He tossed his lighter to her. With a spark, a small flame ignited from it. She lit the wick of her candle, and then passed the lighter to Theo, instructing him to do the same. Once he and Ritchie had their pumpkins burning softly from inside, she resituated herself, getting comfortable. "Alright. Turn the flashlight off, Ritchie. We need it as dark as possible." Ritchie did as instructed. In an instant, everything became pitch black, save for the faint flickering coming from inside the jack-o'-lanterns. Running her fingers against her soft stockings, Sam smiled.

"So. Are you ready for a *real* ghost story?"

The silence was practically deafening as Sam began her tale. A tale passed down by many throughout Oakridge over the years. A tale that lured countless teenagers to the very spot she and her friends sat—beneath the old, twisted tree. The candle flames from inside the carved pumpkins continued to flicker as she gazed upon them, clearing her throat.

"You ever hear the story of how jack-o'-lanterns came to be?" she asked.

The boys shook their heads, trying to make out her facial features in the shadows. It had become nearly impossible to see.

"Long ago, there was a poor man who was always down on his luck. John Barker. No matter what he did or how hard he worked, he never seemed to get anywhere. *Everyone* looked down on him. The town shunned him, made him an outcast. It eventually got to the point where he could no longer pay his bills. He'd become too far in debt. It drove him mad. Drove him to drink. And that's where this story *really* begins. With a man looking for a way out. Looking for a second chance. A man stuck wandering an old cemetery,

drinking his sorrows and worries away," Sam said. "But what he didn't know was that he *would* be given a second chance. A deal. But not one he necessarily wanted, or expected."

Sam leaned in closer, gesturing across the shadows of the cemetery. Across the crumbling stones. "It was Halloween night and John was drunk out of his mind. He was on his way home from the bar, staggering through the streets. And somehow, in his stupor, he ended up here. In this very cemetery."

"Bull*shit*," Ritchie said, but Sam quickly cut him off.

"John wandered between the graves—much newer than they are now. Blubbering and cursing his life. His misfortunes. He was out here for hours, walking circles up and down the hill. And, in time, he became tired. On the last lap around the chapel, he saw it. A gravestone shaped like a chair. A throne. John sat upon it, resting his feet and mind," she said. "But, while he sat, a mist rolled in. One deeper and thicker than any he'd seen before. And from it emerged the Devil. He asked John why he was so sorrowful. Why he looked so broken. In his drunken state, John told the Devil everything about his life. How he was destitute. Desperate. How no one showed him respect. The Devil smiled, offering John a hand. He told him that his wish could be granted. His wish to be a King—and all the riches and glory that went along with it. So John, of course, agreed. He drank down the last bit of whiskey he had and fell asleep in the chair, thinking it was all a dream. But, the Devil was very real. And he had made out better than John had with the deal. He claimed another soul—just what he wanted."

A gentle breeze rustled through the surrounding trees as the friends huddled closer together. Their jack-o'-lanterns flickered with each touch of wind, but stayed lit. Sam bit her lip as she smirked.

"When John awoke the next morning, hungover, he realized what he had done. Realized he made a deal with the Devil. A deal promising riches in exchange for his soul. And, of course, he wanted out of the contract. After all, no matter how tempting the offer, *no one* wants to make a deal with the Devil."

"So what happened?" Theo asked, intrigued.

"John spent all morning looking for the Devil, calling out for him amongst the graves. And after much searching, he finally found him. In this here tree. The Devil's Tree." Sam tilted her head towards the branches above her. "You know, Theo, that's why they say they hanged the witches here. They claimed that by doing so, they were sending them back to Hell. Back to the Devil they believed they worshiped."

She continued staring into the dark, bare branches. They were just barely visible, even after her eyes adjusted to the shadows. The boys followed her gaze upward, peering through the darkness.

"After John found the Devil, hiding in the hollow of the tree, he begged for his soul's freedom. For the Devil to take back the deal. But, obviously, the Devil didn't accept. Once a deal is made, it's made for all eternity. John pleaded over and over again, until he finally asked the Devil if there was anything he could do for just three days of freedom. The Devil, feeling pity, told John that he would honor his offer in exchange for a simple candle. A candle to light the dark shadows of the hollow. One to seal the deal when lit. So, of course, John agreed. He went out and found the Devil a small, white candle. He left it in the hollow of the tree, on the condition that his soul remained unclaimed for three days. And, should he die within that time, it would rightfully return to Heaven. Delighted, the Devil agreed with no qualms. After all, John was a healthy and fit young man. Three days were enough to spare. But, John knew how to trick the Devil."

Sam turned back to her friends. They sat there, still. Silent. Gripping their jack-o'-lanterns. Hanging on to her every word.

"On the last night of his freedom, just before the stroke of midnight, John strung himself up from the branches of the Devil's Tree. Laughing as he did. Crying out *I'm free! I'm free!* But, he wasn't free. Not in the slightest."

The branches above creaked in the wind, shadows snaking across the dark ground. Dancing across the jack-o'-lanterns. Sam's fingers caressed her pleated skirt as she continued.

"When John arrived at the gates of Heaven, he was turned away. He'd made a deal with the Devil, and whether or not it was to be upheld, it was unforgivable. And so, he was cast back down to Earth. At the base of the tree. Beneath his swinging corpse—left for the vultures to eat. Sure enough, on the next day, the Devil stirred from the hollow and found him, strung up in the branches. John begged that the Devil have mercy and take his soul, as Heaven wouldn't have it. But the Devil sneered. He'd been cheated. Fooled. And for that, he no longer desired John's soul. Instead, he trapped him in darkness. Between Heaven and Hell. In limbo. Unwanted. Unclaimed."

Sam pulled her pumpkin onto her lap, watching the candlelight flicker. The face she carved didn't seem as joyful as it once had been.

"John was left to wander alone between realms, lost to the shadows. Given only the candle he had retrieved for the Devil—a reminder of his betrayal—to light his way. If it ever went out, it would leave him in eternal darkness. So, he carved out a pumpkin, to make a lantern and keep his candle safe from the wind. And he carried it with him—through the mist and shadow. Through the void. Searching for a place to rest. A place to find peace for his soul."

She cast her gaze across the dark graves and pitch black landscape before them. Again, the branches creaked overhead as her fingers pressed into the thick orange flesh of her pumpkin.

"Some say on Halloween night, when the veil is at its thinnest, when the dead come back to walk the Earth, you can see him out there. Wandering amongst the graves. Jack-o'-lantern lighting his way. But, if you *do* see him, never follow, or you'll suffer the same fate. Lost in an endless loop out there in the void. In the darkness. With only your jack-o'-lantern to guide you."

Sam got to her feet, keeping her pumpkin tight against her chest. The boys watched the light inside of it flicker. Theo pulled his pumpkin closer as Ritchie scoffed, standing as well.

"Cool story," he said. "But come on. You really brought us out here for *that*? I was expecting something a little more...*scary*. And true."

"Oh, it's true," Sam said. "Who said I was finished, by the way? Now, get your pumpkins and follow me."

"Where are we *going*?" Ritchie groaned.

Peter stood and flicked his lighter on, the feeble flame dancing in the night air. Sam stayed close by him, in case it went out, so her pumpkin could light the path for him. With a smile, she glanced back at Ritchie.

"To see the throne."

The outer rim of the cemetery lacked clear cut paths and felt darker than the rest. Yet, the friends trudged on, holding their jack-o'-lanterns, using what little light came from them to see. They walked in perfect precession—a line of glinting candlelight that hovered between the graves. Like ghost lights.

"It's not much farther," Sam said as she scanned the headstones.

It was difficult without a true, strong light source, especially when everything in the darkness all appeared the same. But as they continued up the hill, past the old chapel—locked up and abandoned—Sam spotted what she was looking for on the outskirts of the cemetery property. Away from the rest of the headstones. A grin slipped across her lips as she ventured towards it, calling out for the others to follow. They hurried along at her heels, avoiding stones and roots, until they made it to where Sam had stopped.

Only when they were close enough could they make the old grave out—if one could call it that. It wasn't a typical headstone at all. It was a chair—a *throne*. Carved out of limestone. Like many of the other markers, parts of it were worn away with time. But still, its shape remained, frame strong and sturdy. Once the friends were all standing before it, Ritchie raised an eyebrow.

"What *is* this?"

"The Devil's Throne," Sam said with a smile. "The very one John made his deal on that fateful Halloween night."

"The Devil's Throne?" Peter's voice was low.

Sam placed her jack-o'-lantern at the base of the stone, motioning Ritchie and Theo to do the same. They hesitated at first, but then followed suit. The group looked on as the light behind the carvings flashed, perfect offerings at the foot of the throne.

"So, this is where it happened, huh?" Theo asked, crossing his arms for warmth.

Sam nodded. "And could happen again."

"What do you mean?" Peter asked softly.

"The legend goes on to say that, just like John, anyone can summon the Devil. You just have to wait until Halloween night. If you sit upon the throne at midnight, the Devil *will* appear to you. He'll search your deepest desires and offer to grant you a wish. Whether you accept or not, you have to stay seated in the throne all night. Until sunrise."

"What happens if you leave?" Ritchie asked.

"The Devil claims your soul."

"And if you stay?" he pressed again.

"You best hope the first light of day doesn't reach you. If it does, they say the portal beneath the throne will open, and you'll be dragged down to the depths of Hell. Down with the Devil."

"So, you have to stay there until sunrise or the Devil gets your soul... but if sunrise reaches you...I mean, doesn't that sound like a lose-lose situation?" Peter asked.

"You only have a split second," Sam replied. "That blink of an eye to rise up and leave the throne. To trick the Devil. Just like John did—in that brief moment before the stroke of midnight on his third day."

Ritchie pursed his lips, staring at the withering limestone. The faint candlelight from the pumpkins danced through the shadows as he tilted his head in thought.

"So. Who's down to come back on Halloween and give it a go?"

"Absolutely not, man," Theo said, holding his hands up in surrender. "Do you know how many cops are out here on Halloween? They have this whole place practically on lockdown."

"And? I'm sure my dad will let us sneak in. What do you say?"

"I don't know, Ritchie..." Peter averted his gaze. "Is it really worth getting busted for?"

"Then how about right now?" Ritchie crossed his arms. "We're all up here. Let's see if it works."

"Did you not hear Sam? She literally just said on *Halloween night*," Theo replied.

"The less chance of getting dragged to Hell, the better, right?" Ritchie motioned to the throne before them. "So, who's gonna do it?"

"You *can't* be serious." Sam rolled her eyes.

"Oh, I am, though," Ritchie replied. "We were promised a scare. And nothing about some fool who made a bad deal is remotely scary, okay? So, I want to test your story and see if we can conjure up some *real* frights tonight."

"Fine. Then why don't *you* do it, Ritchie?"

"Because," he grinned, "*I'm* not a fool."

Sam shook her head. Pointing his finger at each of them, Ritchie raised his eyebrow. He waited for someone to step forward, offering themselves to the throne. Once more, Theo put his hands up, not interested. But Peter, who had been standing off to the side, finally shrugged.

"Alright, why not."

"There we go!" Ritchie exclaimed. "See, Peter's not afraid of some dumb superstition."

Peter stepped over the pumpkins blazing at the base of the throne, climbing up into the seat. He dragged his palms across the cold stone, the rough texture grating against his skin. He shifted slightly as he gazed out into the dark depths of the cemetery. Into the fog that rolled up the hill. At his feet, the jack-o'-lanterns flickered.

"So tell me, Peter," Ritchie smirked, "what do you desire?"

14

Peter pursed his lips in thought, brown eyes focused in the distance. He let the sounds around him amplify—echoing through his mind. He heard the crickets chirping near the gate and the leaves rustling in the breeze. The branches creaking. The night stirring. Across the back of his hand, an ant scurried, drawing his attention back. Flicking it away, he grunted, glancing at Ritchie.

"Being honest," Peter chuckled, "to pass my Chemistry test on Friday."

"*That* would be a miracle," Theo replied, snorting.

"Hey," Peter shot back, "just because *you* got put into Physics doesn't mean it's as easy as you think."

"Never said it was easy," Theo smirked. "Just said it would be a miracle if you passed."

"Imagine selling your soul for a Chemistry grade," Sam said, letting out a laugh. "Though, I'm sure someone out there would."

"Yeah," Ritchie said, gathering a handful of leaves. "*Peter.*"

He dropped the pile of damp, decaying leaves atop Peter, laughing as he flinched. They fluttered down, collecting on the open stone of the seat around him, catching on his plaid flannel shirt and beanie. He brushed them off, adjusting his bangs as he glared at Ritchie. His friend bowed deeply in mockery.

"All hail the King."

Peter managed a breathy chuckle as he slid off the cold stone. "It's getting really late. We should probably start heading home."

"Yeah," Theo said, "my mom will have a *cow* if she knows I've been out this late on a school night."

Sam picked her jack-o'-lantern up, holding it against her chest. "Ready?"

Ritchie nodded, pulling his pocket flashlight back out. He turned it on, allowing the bright beam of light to cut through the darkness. As he, Theo, and Peter began heading towards the dirt path down the hill, Sam called out to them.

"Wait! What about your pumpkins?"

"Leave them for Old John," Ritchie said. "Besides, from what you said, he needs them more than we do."

Sam was silent as her friends descended beyond the chapel, into the shadows. She waited until only the flashlight could be seen before following along. Leaving Ritchie and Theo's jack-o'-lanterns to flicker atop the hill.

The dirt pathways were nearly impossible to see, even with the flashlight. Much of the light bounced back on itself in the fog, a stark contrast against the shadows that spun around them—lurking just beyond the shroud of white mist. Sam rubbed her arms, attempting to keep warm. Even through her thick sweater, the chill still bit.

"Anyone know what time it is?" she asked as the group reached the forking path at the center of the cemetery.

Theo glanced at his watch, the digital numbers glowing softly. "Going on one thirty."

Ritchie shined his flashlight towards where the paths connected, illuminating a sign: THIS WAY OUT. He motioned his friends to follow, down the marked road.

"Have we really been out here that long?" Sam asked.

"You know what they say," Ritchie said. "Time flies when you're having—"

"Did you hear that?" Peter asked, tensing as he stopped in his tracks.

"Hear *what*?" Ritchie returned.

Peter remained still, listening hard. Yet, he heard nothing but ordinary night sounds echoing off the graves. He shook his head, starting down the path once more towards where the iron gates waited. But as he took a step, he heard it again. The rustle of leaves out amongst the graves.

"There it is again," he said just above a whisper.

"Where?" Ritchie inquired.

"Over there."

Ritchie swung the flashlight where Peter pointed. But there was nothing there. Only lonesome headstones protruding from the damp earth. Scanning the area one last time, Ritchie turned the light back on the path before them.

"I don't see anything," he said. "It was probably just the wind."

As Peter was about to disagree, he spotted something behind the group, emerging from the billowing gray fog. Standing in the middle of the path.

A dog.

Although dark, its features stood out against the night. They were wispy—almost like the fog itself. Its body was large and muscular. Eyes a deep red. They burned through the shadows, fixated on the four friends. Its jowls were turned up, exposing sharp, white fangs—dripping with hot saliva. Its hackles raised, a low growl rattling in its chest.

No one dared to move.

"The Grim..." Theo whispered.

"No way," Ritchie said. "It can't be. That's just a story...right?"

The dog took a step forward. Its growls grew louder, teeth gleaming. Bared into a chiseled crescent-moon grin. The group hesitated for only a moment before instinct kicked in. Turning on their heels, they ran down the forked path towards the cemetery gates.

Their shoes thundered against the dirt as they hurried for the exit, hearts pounding. Behind them, leaves crunched violently. Claws scraped against the ground. Vicious snarls echoed off tree trunks. But they pressed forward, determined to make it through those large iron gates.

As soon as they reached them, however, they let out an alarmed gasp—stopped dead in their tracks by the blinding beam of a flashlight. Once their eyes adjusted, the fear in their guts sunk deeper.

"*Shit*." Ritchie swore under his breath.

Officer Buchanan stood before them, shaking his head. Radioing headquarters, he kept his eyes on the group of teens.

"Yeah, it's just a couple of kids at Chapel Hill. We've got it covered. Over."

He sighed in disappointment, turning his attention to Ritchie. The boy was trembling—knees weak from his adrenaline filled sprint. Hearing the leaves rustle behind him once again, he glanced over his shoulder. Fearful of what he'd see.

But it was only another officer and a member of the K-9 unit. The German Shepherd sniffed the ground thoroughly, both on and off the path. Searching. The friends breathed a collective sigh of relief.

"What are you kids doing out here?" Officer Buchanan demanded, aiming his question towards Ritchie.

"Just hanging out, Dad," Ritchie explained. "Telling scary stories, you know? We weren't vandalizing anything, if that's what you're thinking."

17

"I never *said* I thought you were vandalizing. That aside, how many times have I told you? You shouldn't be out here after dark. Especially with all that's going on."

"What do you mean?" Peter asked, rubbing the soft flannel against his arms to try and keep warm.

"Another kid's gone missing," Officer Buchanan said solemnly. "Billy Barone."

Everyone was silent. Officer Buchanan sighed as he looked between each of them.

"That's the fourth one this week," he said. "There's a curfew in place for a reason. To keep *you* safe."

"I know..." Ritchie muttered.

"Now, consider this your warning. And *don't* let me catch you out here again. Understand?"

The group nodded.

"Good. Now get yourselves home. It's late," Officer Buchanan said.

As he headed back to his squad car, Ritchie's shoulders slouched. His flashy demeanor completely extinguished. Glancing at his friends, he managed a weak smile.

"Well, it was fun while it lasted," he said.

"Could have ended worse," Theo replied. "Be glad it was your dad out here tonight."

"Legit," Sam said. "Especially if what he said was true. Did another kid really go missing?"

"At this rate, they'll be canceling Halloween all together," Theo replied, gazing off to the blue and red flashing lights beyond the gate.

An older man stood beside the car, talking to Officer Buchanan. His greasy hair hung in long, stringy strands across his head as he cast a glare at the friends. A scowl lined his lips before he turned towards the old stone house beside the cemetery. The groundskeeper's home.

"You think it was him that called?" Peter asked softly.

"It wouldn't surprise me," Theo said.

Officer Buchanan's voice carried out, calling to his son. With a sigh, Ritchie ran his fingers through his auburn hair. Then, he flashed a quick toothy grin.

"Well, at least tonight ended up being exciting," he said. "It'll be one to talk about for years to come."

"No doubt about that," Peter said.

"Anyway. My dad's waiting. See you at school."

Ritchie headed through the cemetery gates and over to his father's squad car. He opened the door to the back seat, climbing in. Once he was settled, Officer Buchanan flashed the lights atop the car with one *woop* of the siren, before pulling away.

"Well, I better be getting home myself," Theo said. "Gotta get up early tomorrow. It was a good time, though. Thanks for the scares."

He didn't wait for a reply as he headed down the sidewalk, towards the streetlamps that illuminated the corners. Peter and Sam stood in silence for a moment, before they, too, were ready to head home.

"Here," Sam said, holding out her pumpkin.

Though it had dimmed, the candle inside still flickered. Giving off a gentle glow. Peter raised an eyebrow as he hesitantly took it from her, staring at its jolly carved face.

"You've got a farther walk than I do," Sam said. "I figured you could use some light to guide you home."

Peter managed a weak smile. He watched as Sam gently tucked a few strands of hair behind her ear before glancing up at the night sky. The moon was even brighter now—stars visible as the clouds began to dissipate.

"Looks like the moon's here to help, too." She smiled. "Be safe getting home, okay?"

Peter nodded. "Yeah. You, too."

He didn't bother moving until Sam made her way down the street, vanishing from sight. Then, he glanced over his shoulder, back through the iron gates of the cemetery. Into the pitch black darkness.

All was still. Silent.

Yet, he felt as though something was in there watching. Patrolling the grounds. Staring back at him. Peter returned his gaze to the pumpkin in his grasp, hesitating only a moment before heading down the street towards his neighborhood.

Again, he swore he heard the crunch of leaves beneath light footsteps, trailing behind him. But he didn't bother to look back. Something in the pit of his stomach forbade him. As he crossed the street, the sounds stopped.

But in the middle of the road sat that skinny black cat. Fur shining beneath the dim streetlights. Yellow eyes glinting. Watching Peter intently as he made his way back home—guided only by the jack-o'-lantern's light.

II.

THE STREETS WERE PACKED the morning of the thirteenth, cars lining the interstate. Eager for the news. It wasn't every day that Trapp & Co. was bustling with visitors. Though mainly a toy company, manufacturing everything from dolls to cars and bikes to block sets, they made sure to put out a new costume every October. And with only a little over two weeks until Halloween, parents were rushing to see the latest they'd released in anticipation for the big night. Hoping to snatch them from the corporate showcase before they made it to shelves.

In years past, they'd produced witch hats and over-the-head ghost costumes that were far from exciting. But according to their press releases in the late summer, they were convinced they'd made the hottest costume on the market. One every child would be begging for.

Paul Trenchard looked out the large glass windows of his office, overlooking the street. The block was swarming with parents and children alike, waiting impatiently for their turn into the building to view the products themselves. As the Director of Sales, he was satisfied with the outcome. Trapp & Co.'s annual profit was down, but he knew that the fourth quarter push would be enough to get them safely into the new year. And with Christmas coming, he was certain the extra holiday sales would guarantee everything to come up green on their final reports.

He continued gazing out over the street, taking in the multitude of people lining up. Filled with amazement. It was only when he heard a soft knock against the door that he drew his attention away.

His assistant stood in the doorway, clearing her throat. "Mr. Trenchard? They're ready when you are."

Paul nodded, smoothing his tie. "Thanks, Angela. Let them know I'll be there momentarily."

"Yes, sir."

Her heels clicked down the hallway as she headed towards the lobby. Shutting his eyes, Paul took a deep breath, composing himself. While there was always an ounce of nervousness when publicly presenting a new product, this time it came with relief. All the sleepless nights he and his team had endured with planning and testing would finally pay off. He just had to make it through his presentation. Once he was ready, he followed Angela towards the crowd gathered at the entrance.

The lobby was bustling as he made his way into it, pushing through the sea of spectators eagerly awaiting the official release. Their chatter was loud, making it difficult for him to instruct Angela to take her place at the product table. Paul was nearly shouting his words back and forth with her. Once he was situated at the podium, however, the crowd went silent. They turned their attention to him, waiting for the announcement.

"I want to thank you all for joining us today for the unveiling of our latest product," Paul said, allowing his gaze to pass from face to face. "We at Trapp & Co. have worked hard this year to put together something fun and unique for the Halloween season. As a young boy, it was always one of my favorite holidays. The memories made with friends while trick-or-treating... I'm sure you all have a similar fondness."

He paused to take a sip of water. He could see parents nodding in agreement, smiles lining their lips. Clearing his throat, he continued.

"And I'm sure with those memories also come those of your own parents, warning you of the dangers of Halloween. Telling you to always carry a flashlight so you'd be easier to see. Or cutting the eye holes on your masks larger so *you* could see where you were going at night. One of the things we take pride in here at Trapp & Co. is safety. *All* our products are always tested before hitting the market, and every design we implement is with your child's welfare in mind. That's why I'm so pleased with our final result—and I hope you will be, too. Ladies and gentleman, I present to you, our Light-and-Glow Pumpkin Masks."

Paul motioned to the covered table beside the podium. As the crowd turned to look, Angela pulled back the sheet that had been laid over the product—revealing a set of four masks. They were about the size of an actual large pumpkin, sleek and shiny in their coat of fresh paint over rubber and latex. Each one had a different face carved into it—from cute to generic to scary. It was obvious from their appearance that they were high quality. Made with fine attention to detail.

"There are four pumpkin masks to choose from. We have a happy pumpkin, a scary pumpkin, a sad pumpkin, and a silly pumpkin. All made to fit the mood of Halloween," Paul said. "So, now you may be asking yourselves...how are these masks made with safety in mind? Well, for one, we made sure that they weren't too constricting. As I'm sure you all know, the problem with most masks is they get hot wearing them. They're uncomfortable. *Our* masks fit properly, and do so with ease. We've added a special coating of paint on the *inside* to prevent that wet rubber feeling against the face and neck. It provides for easier ventilation, as well."

Paul picked one of the masks off the table. The sad pumpkin face stared up at him pathetically as he looked it over, before holding it up to the crowd.

"But we didn't stop there. We used a special fluorescent paint mix that allows the masks to glow in the dark. A helpful way to be seen more easily at night. And, if that isn't enough...we came up with *another* solution."

Slipping his hand inside the mask, Paul flicked a small switch at the back along the neckline. Yellow light poured from the eyes, nose, and mouth carvings—flickering softly, like a real jack-o'-lantern. The crowd murmured in admiration.

"We added the option to illuminate the masks so they become even more visible. As you can see, these lights give off a realistic glow. You can bet that alone will make them a conversation piece around school and parties. And don't worry. The lights are on a separate panel above the eyes, allowing a full field of vision for the wearer. In fact, during testing, our subjects stated that the added light acted almost like a flashlight for close distance."

Paul set the mask on his podium, its face twinkling. He took another sip of water before continuing.

"For those of you wondering, based on how there looks to be no eye holes at all...they are made of a protective surface that allows for full sight, while giving off the realistic glow effect. As I stated before, safety is our priority. We put as much care into the production of these masks as we could to ensure your child has fun, looks cool, and is completely protected."

Paul nodded to Angela. She bowed her head with a smile, lifting boxes of masks out from beneath the table. They were overflowing with the new product—fresh from the manufacturing plant. The first batch to make it to the public.

"If you could please form a single file line, Angela would be happy to get a mask for you. And don't worry. There's enough for everyone, so we kindly ask for your patience as we get them sorted. Thank you," Paul said.

The crowd did as he instructed. As Angela dug through the boxes, handing parents the masks they asked for, Paul stepped down from the podium.

"You have this under control?" he asked her softly.

Angela nodded. "I should be good. I'll get an inventory report sent up as soon as everyone clears out. Just so we have an idea which design is most popular, and what to restock and get sent out to shelves this week."

"You're the best, Ange," Paul said with a smile.

Snatching the pumpkin mask off the podium, he breathed a sigh of relief. Listening to the eager crowd select their masks—excitement in their voices—he headed back down the hallway.

When Paul returned to his office, he was surprised to find one of his staff members, Jim, waiting for him—report in hand. He held his clipboard out, clearing his throat.

"How did it go?"

"Just about as well as I expected," Paul said, taking the clipboard and skimming the data recorded. "Though we may need to place a larger order before the weekend. I have a feeling these are going to fly off the shelves."

Jim nodded. "Doesn't surprise me. As soon as kids start wearing them to school and showing their friends, everyone is going to end up wanting one."

"Exactly." Paul took a seat at his desk. "Word of mouth is the best marketing tool there is. And it's free."

Jim stifled a chuckle. "Mr. Trapp's favorite word."

"No kidding."

Paul set the pumpkin mask on his desk before fingering through the stack of paperwork. Old test reports, product descriptions, and inventory logs. When he found an order form for the manufacturing plant, he removed it, setting it aside to fill out once Angela's numbers came back. As he

continued reviewing the other documents, Jim glanced over to the mask. Its illuminated, sad expression made him purse his lips in thought.

"You planning on sending *that* one to the stores?" he asked.

Paul looked up at him. "What? Oh. The mask? Not this one. This is one of the test models. Still has a few kinks here and there, I'm sure. It's not finalized like the others."

Jim paused. "What's going to be done with it, then?"

"Probably just end up in one of the showcases or get put in a storage closet somewhere. With the rest of the old prototypes...you know how this place is," Paul said. "Why do you ask?"

"Just wondering, since Halloween is coming up and all. My son doesn't have a costume yet. It's probably his last year trick-or-treating...senior year, you know? He keeps saying he doesn't want to go out and doesn't want to dress up, but I'm trying to persuade him. Get him to enjoy being a kid for one last year. I'm sure you understand," Jim said. "I figured it would be something for him to wear that wasn't over the top. And it would offer the company that free marketing."

Paul picked the mask up and held it out to Jim. "Why not? It'll get more use having your boy wear it for one night than it will here."

"Thank you, Mr. Trenchard." Jim smiled happily.

"Not a problem."

Jim squeezed the mask, the rubber and latex folding in his hands. Dipping his head in departure, he wished Paul a good evening before heading out of the office. Once he was alone again, Paul addressed the stack of papers one more time, a smile slipping across his lips. Even though he wasn't in the lobby, he could hear the distant chatter. The excitement. A complete success.

Signing his name on the order form for Angela to send to the plant with her numbers, he approved final production. The last step needed before the official release to stores. The guaranteed green on their profit report. And the promised raise he'd been longing for.

The skies were dark late that afternoon as Paul left the office. A light drizzle fell, dampening the ground and fallen leaves—heightening the scent of decay. The smell of autumn. Of summer's dying breath. Yet, even in its somber light, there was the promise of spring. Somewhere beyond the bitter winter—approaching sooner than anyone had prepared for.

Paul pulled into the parking lot of the local grocery store, exhaling a relieved breath. Getting out of the car, he tugged the collar of his overcoat up, deterring the cold rain. Thankfully, he only needed a gallon of milk. A quick in and out. Shrugging the evening chill from his shoulders, he hurried inside, gathering what he had come in for.

As he headed back towards the front of the store to check out, the gallon of milk tucked securely under one arm, he spotted a bin of pumpkins just beyond the produce section. Paul hesitated at first, but then decided to look them over. See if any were decent. The perfect shape for carving. He'd promised his son he would find a pumpkin soon for the two of them to carve Halloween night, and he knew the longer he waited, the less of a choice he would have.

The pumpkins varied in shape and size—crammed together in the large bin. Some had blemishes: warts, scars, and broken stems. Others were oddly proportioned. But then, there were others that were pristine. The perfect poster child on every Halloween greeting card. Paul's hand brushed one of them, looking it over before he felt another's touch. Long, wrinkled fingers nudged against his own. He quickly glanced up, catching the gaze of an elderly woman standing beside him, admiring the pumpkins.

"Oh, dear," she said, yanking her hand away. "I'm so sorry. I didn't mean to—"

Paul waved her off, picking up the pumpkin he had been inspecting. "No worries. It's that time of year. Everyone's getting their pumpkins."

The woman smirked, exposing her crooked and yellowed teeth. Brushing a stringy gray strand of hair from her face, she returned to the bin, pulling out a disfigured pumpkin. It was covered in bumps, stem lopsided and bottom uneven. Still, she looked it over before nodding, holding it against her chest.

"Are you...carving?" Paul asked, nodding to her odd choice.

The woman shook her head. "Oh, no! These old hands couldn't dream of it. I use them for baking. Lots of yummy recipes for sweets this time of year. And fresh baked pumpkin seeds."

Her eyes scanned Paul's pumpkin—the perfect pick. She licked her lips, allowing her gaze to meet his.

"And you? Carving?"

Paul nodded. "Well, my son anyway. I just help out. He's still young, so he just draws the face and has me cut it out. You know how it is."

He chuckled. The old woman's smile drew wider in agreement. Before she could continue conversation, however, Paul glanced at his watch, motioning towards the registers.

"I should be on my way. My wife's probably wondering what's taking me so long. You have a good rest of the night. And a happy Halloween."

The woman watched as he stepped away, walking over to the express lane. Running her fingers against the bumps on her pumpkin's skin, she responded quietly.

"Happy Halloween."

The evening went by quickly after Paul returned home. He greeted his wife and boys happily, eager to share with them the news of the day. Over dinner, he explained how the success of the masks would pull Trapp and Co. out of the negative and allow a more promising path for products in the coming year. And, of course, all the rewards and benefits it would have for the employees.

"I'll be sure to get one for you, too, Andy," he said across the table to his youngest son. "You wanted the silly pumpkin face, right?"

The little boy's eyes were wide with excitement as he nodded. Paul smiled back before turning to his older son.

"What about you, Alex?" he asked. "You know I can get a mask for you if you'd like one."

The teen shook his head. "Nah, that's alright. They sound super sick, but they're not my thing, you know? Besides, I've already got my costume picked out. For the big party, remember?"

Paul nodded. "I guess I forgot."

"Get one for Andy, though," Alex said. "He'll be the coolest pumpkin head on the street."

Andy beamed at his brother. Then, his gaze passed to the pumpkin seated beside him at the dinner table.

"Can we carve the pumpkin to look like the mask?" he asked.

Paul smirked. "Of course. You can carve whatever face you'd like. But remember—we have to wait until Halloween."

After dinner, he helped his wife gather and wash the dishes, putting on a seasonal and family friendly film to wind down. The stillness of the early evening was comforting—accompanied by the chirping crickets in the yard. Their melodies echoed softly through the house, counting away the hours. Soon, it was nearing 10 p.m., and Alex was ready for bed. He bid his parents a good night before climbing the stairs, grogginess heavy in his voice. Not long after he departed, Paul, too, felt exhaustion setting in.

"I've got another early day tomorrow," he told his wife. "Do you want me to put Andy to bed?"

He motioned to the young boy who had fallen asleep on the couch. His chest rose and fell with each gentle breath he took—still gripping the popcorn bowl as he dozed. His wife smiled as she watched him, shaking her head.

"That's alright," she said. "He's comfortable. I'll let him stay down here until I'm ready to turn in."

Paul leaned down and planted a kiss against her lips. "Goodnight."

"Night."

Undoing his tie, he began up the stairwell to the master bedroom. Exhaustion was kicking in—more mental than anything. He couldn't wait to crawl into bed and fall asleep. Catch up on the lack of it from working late on the prototype masks and writing the perfect pitch. For the first time since early that summer, he could relax. Undisturbed. Embraced by the comfort that awaited him between the sheets.

At around 3 a.m., he saw them. Clear as day in the darkness, standing beside his bed. Two little boys and a girl, no older than Andy. They loomed over him —eyes full of hate. At first glance, they looked like ordinary children. That was, until Paul noticed one glaring factor.

Their faces were melting off.

One boy's skin was bubbled and burnt, open sores oozing pus. It spread across the entire right side of his face to his nose, peeling back what little flesh remained. The other's hair was singed on the left. As if a chemical burned it clean off. His eye was disfigured—like yellowed jelly in the socket. The skin around his mouth was eaten away—lips disintegrated and exposing his teeth down to the jawbone. The girl looked the worst, though. Her entire face was covered in open sores, pooling blood. One of her ears was missing— cartilage devoured. Loose flesh hung in patches from her cheeks. Peeled off. Dangling.

At first, they didn't speak. Paul wasn't so sure they even *could*. But their presence was enough to terrify him. Break him into a cold sweat. It all felt too real. So real that Paul swore he could smell the heavy stench of chemicals. The burning of flesh.

"Look what you've done..."

The voice hissed from the throat of the little boy covered in pus. He vacantly stared through Paul as he inched closer to the bed. Once more, he heard the voice, this time, more forceful. Heavy against his ear.

"Look what you've done!"

That was when Paul awoke.

He tried to adjust to the darkness around him, but everything was spinning. The shadows flickered like static—stench still heavy from his dream. It lingered. Burned into his mind. And even as he started to calm himself, he felt uneasy. Disturbed.

Reaching for the lamp beside his bed, he struggled to turn it on. Yet, as he felt for the turn key, his heart stopped. Beside the bed stood a small boy.

The child's eyes glinted through the shadows, skin ripped back on his face. Bubbled. Bloodied. Just as it had been in his nightmare. Without hesitation, Paul clicked the turn key two notches, flooding the bedroom in light. He had to suppress a scream when he realized that the child was still there.

It was only Andy. Paul's heart pounded against his chest as he heaved a sigh of relief. His wife stirred awake beside him, noticing his distress and her son standing in the room. Rubbing her eyes, she sat up.

"Hey...what's going on?"

"Andy...just startled me is all," Paul lied.

He pressed a hand to his chest, heart rate slowing to normal. Taking another deep breath, he focused on his son.

"What are you doing up, Andy? What's wrong?"

The little boy looked at him, eyes flooded with tears. "I had a bad dream..."

Paul pursed his lips as he scooted over in bed, patting the mattress—inviting Andy to join them. The child wasted no time climbing under the covers, nestling against his father. He didn't dare close his eyes, however.

"It's alright," Paul said. "I know it was scary, but just remember...it was only a dream. Nothing can hurt you."

Andy was silent for a moment, but then he spoke quietly. "But they wanted to hurt *you*..."

Paul didn't know what to say. He felt fear sinking in again as he gazed down at his son. The child gripped the blanket tight, staring off into nothingness.

"They looked so scary," Andy whispered, "with their putty faces. All gooey."

Paul's heart dropped. That feeling in his stomach clenched tighter at the realization that his son had dreamed the same thing. Had seen those disfigured, melting children. Watching him with singed and drooping eyes. But he knew he couldn't say anything about it. And he certainly couldn't confess to Andy that he'd seen them, too. Wrapping an arm around his son, Paul pulled him close, planting a kiss on his forehead.

"Well, they're gone now. Don't worry about them, okay? We'll keep the light on tonight. Just in case. But, you get some sleep. Mommy and I are here. So is Alex. And I promise...we won't let anything happen to you."

32

Andy nestled tighter against his father, eventually finding sleep as his eyelids grew heavy. It wasn't long before he was fast asleep again, safe and secure beside his parents. Yet, Paul didn't dare turn the lamp off. He kept its glow on high, illuminating every shadow in the bedroom. He wasn't about to take any chances. Not for himself, and not for his son.

But no matter how bright the lamp burned, Paul couldn't fall back asleep. The faces of the children ate away at him. How real they looked. How painful. And Andy's words of their "putty faces" made him even more uneasy. The longer he thought about it, the sicker he felt. And so, he tried to get comfortable beneath the covers. Staring up at the ceiling.

By 5 a.m., the drowsiness finally kicked in. Paul was unable to fight it, no matter how hard he tried. And so, for the first time in his position as Sales Director, he made the decision to call out of work. Too exhausted from the sleepless night. Too shaken from his dreams.

As much as he knew the news and excitement was sure to be joyous at the office that morning, the last thing Paul wanted to do was think of those masks. Those silly, bright pumpkin masks. Faces smiling. Lit up bright. Set to release to stores in a matter of days.

III.

CHRISSY CRINGED AT HER REFLECTION in the mirror. The cheaply made exotic gown clung to every curve of her body—both wanted and not. She turned sideways, unsure if she even wanted to see. Upon catching a glimpse of herself, she groaned, pinching the little flab that formed around her belly. But before she could slide the outfit off, a knock on the dressing room door stopped her.

"You almost done in there, Chrissy? Hurry up and let us see!"

She sighed in aggravation, parting the doorway and peering out. "No way, Linda. It looks awful."

"Oh, come on. It can't be *that* bad," the girl outside the door replied.

She gave the handle a sharp tug, rattling the stall. Chrissy huffed, folding her arms across her chest, trying to hide any unsavory rolls that may have become prominent.

"Stop being a baby," Linda jeered. "I'm sure you look fine."

Chrissy groaned again. "Fine. But *don't* laugh."

She slowly opened the door to the changing room, cautiously stepping out. Her eyes scanned the store, making sure no one else aside from her friends were looking. As soon as she was out—costume fully visible—Linda clapped her hands together.

"Shut *up!*" she exclaimed. "Chrissy, you look gorgeous!"

Chrissy shook her head, shielding the parts of the costume that made her uncomfortable. "It accentuates things I just…"

"Oh, stop it," Linda said, waving her off before turning to the girl beside her. "Tell her, Tasha."

"I think you look great," Tasha replied with a smile. "It fits you perfectly. And the colors bring out your eyes. I totally think you should get it."

"I don't know…" Chrissy stammered uneasily.

"Look, we've been in here almost three hours," Linda said. "You're going to find something that you don't like with everything you try on. Trust me. We *all* do."

She walked over to her friend, reaching out and gently taking her hands. Giving them a squeeze, she offered a small smile to Chrissy.

"But, also trust us when we say you look *damn* good, girl."

"Legit," Tasha added. "And so what if you have a little bit of a belly? Literally *everyone* does. If someone gives you a hard time about it, you give *them* a hard time right back."

"This world is so against anyone over a size zero," Linda scoffed. "But, I'll tell you one thing. What they can't stand more than a little flab is confidence. So wear those rolls with pride, girl!"

Chrissy's face flushed as she managed a smile, lowering her arms. No longer hiding behind them. Once Linda knew she was comfortable, she wrapped an arm around her shoulder.

"See? You feel better already."

"Now all you need is a tiara," Tasha said. "And I'd say you're all set."

She pulled one from the rack beside the changing rooms, sliding it over Chrissy's thick blonde curls. The silver shimmer caught in the fluorescent lights above, bringing together her costume. Tasha nodded in approval.

"Perfect."

"Come on," Linda pressed. "Let's get this stuff paid for so we can get out of here. I've been dying for a bubble tea since we got to the mall."

The friends changed back into their clothes, neatly folding the costumes they had chosen before paying. The hardest part was over. Now, it was just waiting out the anticipation for Halloween night.

"You ask anyone to Homecoming yet?" Tasha asked as they made their way down the sidewalk, back to Chrissy's house.

The gentle breeze was cool, but felt good late that afternoon. It shuffled the leaves in the trees lining the street, their bright colors turning over with each breath. It was a shame that by Halloween night, the branches would be bare.

"Isn't that the *guy's* job?" Linda snorted.

"Well, if they aren't doing their job and asking..." Tasha shrugged. "Someone's gotta."

"Leave it to a woman to have to do everything," Linda replied. "Typical, huh?"

Chrissy managed a weak smile. She didn't respond, watching Linda twirl a finger through her pin straight brunette hair.

"Anyway. *I'm* obviously going with Ritchie Buchanan," she said.

"Of course," Tasha rolled her eyes. "What a surprise."

"He asked me last week during lunch," Linda continued. "We planned matching outfits and everything. It's the only way to do it, honestly. What about you?"

"Doug Feeney," Tasha said proudly. "Haven't asked him yet, but I doubt he'll say no."

"*Doug Feeney*?" Linda's voice was a shrill shriek of laughter. "The *Poindexter*? You've *got* to be kidding me. He's a total dweeb!"

"Well, not all of us have a taste for pretentious jocks," Tasha replied sharply. "Besides, Doug's slated to be valedictorian this year. I'll take brains over brawn any day."

"You do you." Linda waved her off. "What about *you*, Chrissy? Anyone catch your eye yet?"

Chrissy tightened the grip on her bag as she stammered. "Well, I... really haven't given it much thought, to be honest."

"Haven't given it much thought? Chrissy, the dance is only a few weeks away," Linda said.

"I know," Chrissy replied. "I've just been so busy with everything else this month, it's flown by. I can't believe the year is almost over already. And then, before we know it, it's going to be summer. We're going to have graduated."

"It still doesn't feel possible," Tasha said. "I swear it was yesterday we were in Mrs. Sawyer's fifth grade class."

"Time keeps going but it never slows down," Linda said. "But seriously, Chrissy. I can hook you up with someone. Evan Hofstadter? Drew McCaffrey? Jeremey Kiernan?"

Chrissy felt her face flush in embarrassment. "I'm sure I'll find someone closer to."

As they rounded the corner onto Cedar Street, they were distracted from their talk of school dances and potential dates. Instead, they became focused on what stood in the middle of the sidewalk. Batting at a leaf.

A skinny black cat sat in their path, chirping as he continued to play with the fallen foliage. At first, he paid the girls no mind. But once the leaf blew out of his reach, he turned his attention to them. Once more he chirped, tail shooting into the air as he trotted over to greet them. The friends couldn't help but coo once he was at their feet, throwing his soft body against their legs, purring loudly.

"Where did you come from, little guy?" Tasha asked, reaching down to scratch behind his ears.

The cat tilted his head upwards, leaning in and accepting her touch. He closed his eyes, purring intensely as his whiskers twitched. Chrissy looked to see if there was any identification on him—a collar or tags—but there was

none. Pursing her lips, she stroked his back, feeling his sleek fur beneath her fingers.

"You really shouldn't be out here," she said. "Especially this time of year. There are crazy people who hurt cats—particularly black ones—around Halloween."

"Isn't that just a rumor made up by the media?" Linda asked. "Like the whole razor blades in the candy thing?"

Tasha shook her head. "Oh no. My dad's told me stories about cats going missing around Halloween when *he* was a kid. Awful things. People used to take them up to the cemetery on Chapel Hill and torture them. It was horrible."

"Your dad's full of it." Linda waved her off. "He probably just wants you to stay away from the cemetery because people go out there to do drugs at night. Believe me. *No one's* hurting cats. And you know how I know?"

"How?" Tasha asked, crossing her arms.

"Because you know that crazy old lady who lives by the quarry? She's got a ton of them. And she lets them wander all over. Never hear anything about *them* going missing."

"I'm surprised, honestly," Tasha said. "She's up on the mountain trails. Cougars are *everywhere* up there."

"She'd cause a riot if it ever disappeared. I'll bet this is one of hers."

"Either way," Chrissy said, removing her hand from the cat, "he shouldn't be out here. People hurting cats on Halloween or not...in town, cars are a serious problem. Especially at night."

"She's right," Tasha cooed. "You should go home, little baby."

The cat's tail flicked as he stared at the girls. He remained where he was for a moment before glancing at one of the houses across the street. The porch light flicked on, catching his attention. He darted across the street and through the front yard, leaping onto the windowsill. His tail beat harshly against the siding of the house as he stared inside—meowing loudly.

"Well," Linda said. "That must be where he lives."

"If that's the case, at least he doesn't wander too far from home," Chrissy said with relief.

They gave the cat one final look before continuing down Cedar Street, crossing over to Hemlock Avenue. They were only a few blocks from Chrissy's house where they would be spending the night, and they wanted to make it there before the shadows fell. The first touch of dusk.

"Did you get any snacks for tonight?" Linda asked as she tied her hair up into a ponytail. "You *do* know I plan on staying up all night, right?"

"I mean, that's the point of a sleepover, *duh*," Tasha sassed back.

"I got a few bags of chips and some pop," Chrissy said, tying her plush bathrobe shut around her waist. "I'm sure we have candy lying around, too. But, I don't know how much you'll want...you know. So you don't get candied out by Halloween."

"Who's ever gotten candied out before?" Linda laughed. "Is it the good stuff at least?"

"*I* think it's good," Chrissy said.

"Okay. Candy. What's your favorite?" Tasha asked. "Mine's got to be Skittles. Hands down."

"Milky Way," Linda said. "Nothing better than a full sized one of those."

"*Anything* full sized is good. No complaints from me there," Chrissy said with a smile. "I think Snickers are mine."

"You and literally everyone else on this planet," Linda replied. "But, for real. They're pretty good."

"Honestly," Tasha said as she leaned back against Chrissy's bed, "there's probably only a handful of candies that I don't like."

"That cheap stuff," Linda said. "You know what I'm talking about. Peanut butter taffies and that wax stuff. Yuck."

"Yeah, no thanks," Chrissy said.

"Why do people even give that stuff out? Does *anyone* think it's good?" Tasha asked.

"The people who give it out either have no taste, are too cheap to buy the good stuff, or hate kids. Just saying," Linda replied.

She glanced down at her manicured nails, pursing her lips while Tasha and Chrissy finished brushing their hair.

"So. Real talk. What are we planning on doing tonight?" she asked.

"Well, let's see," Tasha said, "we already talked about Homecoming and boys, so I guess that's out."

"Oh, please. There's so much more I could say. Besides, Chrissy still hasn't figured out who she's asking." Linda snapped her fingers in thought. "That's it! Get out last year's yearbook. We'll narrow it down and find her the perfect match."

Chrissy shook her head. "Really...I'm not worried about it."

But Linda didn't wait. Getting to her feet, she walked over to Chrissy's desk, rummaging through the drawer where she knew it was kept. After a moment, she found it, fingers clasping the dark green cover with golden letters: OAKRIDGE HIGH YEARBOOK. She brought it back to her friends, plopping it on the bed before flipping to the then junior class.

"Let's see," she said. "Who do we have to choose from..."

"Steve Acker?" Tasha inquired, pointing to the first boy's picture.

"Nah. He's already going with Stacy Quinn. Everyone knows they've been together since freshman year," Linda said, skimming the pages. "Kevin Anders. Lee Ashland. Brian Baker. Henry Brown. Ritchie Buchanan...who, of course, is going with *me*."

"Believe us," Tasha replied sarcastically, "we *know*."

Linda waved her off before returning to the yearbook, continuing to read the names of the boys in their class. Chrissy had already tuned her out, shaking her head at all of them. No matter how Linda tried to push her, she stood firm with the fact she was busy with schoolwork and wrapping up projects for the month. She'd worry about Homecoming when she was ready.

"This is boring, Linda," Tasha said after a few more pages of Linda's browsing. "There's got to be something else we can do."

"I have some board games," Chrissy replied. "I can get a few if we want to play them."

"Board games? Come on. What are we? *Twelve*?" Linda scoffed. "Think of something *fun*."

Chrissy remained silent as she looked between her friends. Linda tapped her foot impatiently, arms folded across her chest as she waited for a response. Tasha, on the other hand, bit her lip in hesitation.

"Well," she said after a moment, "I have an idea. But I don't know if you'd be up for it."

"Hit us," Linda said. "It can't be any more boring than just sitting here."

Tasha scooted across the bed, voice barely above a whisper. "Wanna play something scary?"

41

"Scary?" Chrissy asked. "Like what?"

"Like, a ritual. To try and summon something."

"*Summon* something?" Linda asked. "What do you mean by that? Like, occult shit?"

Tasha shrugged. "I mean, it's Halloween time, right? What better way to celebrate than to scare ourselves silly."

"What kind of summoning?" Chrissy asked, voice low.

"Just some mirror ghosts," Tasha replied. "You know...like Bloody Mary and stuff."

Chrissy rubbed her arms as she chewed her lip. Though scary sleepover games had always been a thing brought up over the years since Junior High, she never partook in them. Even though she knew that they were just superstitions to keep everyone up late and unable to sleep, she didn't want to take any chances.

"I-I don't know..." She stammered.

"We can always do other mirror games if you're not up for that one," Tasha said. "Some that are way less scary. Like... Oh, hey! The one about lighting a candle around midnight and seeing the reflection of your true love. That's a good one, right?"

Linda smirked. "Yeah, Chrissy. Maybe it'll show you who you need to hurry up and ask to Homecoming."

Chrissy smiled meekly. When she still didn't budge or give a definitive answer, Tasha got to her feet, walking over to her. She gently took Chrissy's hands, giving them a squeeze.

"Nothing scary, okay? Unless you want to."

There was another moment of hesitation before Chrissy sighed, giving a nod. "Alright."

Tasha struck a match, watching the feeble flame hiss to life. She quickly drew it over to the wick of the candle, igniting it. It flickered on the bathroom

42

counter as the friends gathered around, positioning themselves before the vanity mirror.

"So...how do we play this game?" Chrissy asked quietly.

"The true love one?" Tasha asked. "That one's easy. You just light a candle, turn off all the lights, and stand in front of the mirror. You count to ten and stare at your reflection—but you can't look away. Once you get to ten, legend has it you'll see the face of your true love appear in the mirror. And he'll stay until you're ready to end it. When you want to say goodbye, just blow out your candle and turn on the light. Simple, right?"

"Do you really see the reflection of your true love?" Chrissy asked. "I mean...wouldn't your mind just make up shapes and patterns in the darkness? Form features over your own reflection so it looks like you're seeing someone else?"

Linda groaned. "Does it really matter, Chrissy? Whether it's really the face of our true love or our minds playing tricks...so what? The point is, it's fun."

"You ready?" Tasha asked.

Chrissy nodded slowly, heart pounding as her friend moved to the light switch on the wall, flicking it. The bathroom was instantly shrouded in shadow—except for the burning candle flame.

Clearing her throat, Tasha motioned to the candle. "So, who wants to go first?"

"Chrissy should," Linda said. "After all, she's the only one without a potential date. Let's see who fate has determined is her perfect match."

Picking the candle off the counter, Tasha extended it to Chrissy. She didn't budge at first, eyeing the flickering light uneasily. Then, with a sigh, she reached out and took it, holding it against her chest.

"Now what?" she asked softly.

"Just approach the mirror," Tasha said. "And then count to ten. See if you see something."

"That's all I have to do?" Chrissy asked. "Just count to ten? Nothing else?"

"Not from the legend I was told."

Chrissy took a deep breath. Doing as Tasha instructed, she approached the mirror, pressing herself against the counter. She blinked back the light and shadow, eyes attempting to adjust to the darkness. Hot wax dripped against her fingers, running across her knuckles, but she didn't move. Her gaze remained fixated on the mirror before her—where only her faint image and bright candlelight was reflected.

43

"One, two, three," she started slowly. "Four...five...six..."

She could see the outline of her face, barely lit by the flame. More than anything, it was the paleness of her skin that stood out. Like a harrowing ghost inhabiting the glass.

"Seven...eight...nine..."

Taking another deep breath, she leaned in, forehead nearly touching the mirror. She didn't dare look away as she called out the final number.

"Ten."

The candle flickered. Chrissy stared hard and deep at the dark glass, hoping to see the shadows stir—conjure up shapes. But they never did. All she saw was own her face—washed out by the flame.

"Well?" Tasha asked from behind her. "What do you see?"

Chrissy squinted as she scrutinized the glass. Checking to see if something had moved—been summoned. But there was nothing.

"Just my reflection," she said disappointedly. "I don't see anything."

Linda chuckled. "Well, I guess you're destined to be alone then, Chrissy."

"Maybe we need to actually do it on Halloween," Tasha said with a shrug. "I just thought it'd be cool, you know? To try out and see. No harm done, I guess."

"It would have been nice to see something," Chrissy said. "Even if it's our minds creating it. I wonder if the candle is too bright. Maybe it has to be darker."

"Or maybe it's just bogus," Linda jabbed. "Another total waste of time. Thanks, Tasha."

She moved to turn the light back on, but Tasha stopped her. Her voice was quiet.

"I...do have another one. But it's not as innocent."

"Oh?" Linda crossed her arms. "Go on."

"Have you ever heard of Wanderin' Jack?"

Chrissy and Linda shook their heads. Turning towards the mirror, Tasha gazed into it, fixated on the candle flame. It danced in the darkness, barely illuminating her face as she spoke.

"They say if you call upon him, he'll appear in the mirror—looking for candlelight. Some say he'll let you ask a question, which he has to answer truthfully. But, in exchange, you must give him the light of your candle. Once he takes it, you have to immediately turn the lights on to send him away. If you don't, he'll climb out of the mirror and put you in his place. And then,

44

you'll be stuck behind the glass forever—wandering in search of candlelight. Waiting for someone to come and awaken *you* in their reflection."

"Does it...really happen?" Chrissy's voice trembled.

Tasha shrugged. "According to the legend it does."

"What does Wanderin' Jack look like?" Chrissy asked. "Is he a man, or...?"

"Oh, what's it matter?" Linda asked. "The scarier the better, right? Like you said—it's Halloween time. Might as well wake old Jack up and see what he's got to offer."

"But if we don't turn on the lights in time...?" Chrissy pressed.

"We will," Tasha said. "Believe me. Of all the people who've passed this down, no one's mentioned anyone getting dragged into the mirror. And besides! If that were the case, we wouldn't see him, would we? No need for him to be hiding if someone set him free. Traded places with him."

"I'm sure it's just another gimmick," Linda said. "Like the whole true love thing. But, you never know, right?"

"What do you say?" Tasha looked at Chrissy.

She gripped the candle tightly, continuing to gaze into the glass. Her heart pounded against her chest as she focused on the shadows—watching them morph around her pale reflection. She only looked away to ensure the light switch was close enough, should it be needed. Sighing, she nodded.

"Okay. Let's do it..."

The candle flickered as the friends gathered, shadows stirring around them. Swallowing any trace of light that didn't come from the lit wick. Down the hall, the grandfather clock chimed its hourly tone. Midnight.

Chrissy exhaled a shaky breath, allowing her gaze to pass back to the mirror. Like the room around them, the reflection was dark. Barely illuminated. Turning to Tasha, she spoke softly.

"What now?"

Tasha motioned for the candle. "Here, give it to me. I'm the one leading, so I should hold it."

She took it from Chrissy, making sure it stayed lit. Then, she faced the mirror, staring into the glass. Her focus remained on the small flame as she ushered Chrissy and Linda closer. They pressed themselves against the sink, leaning in. Ensuring they could see everything happening in the shadows.

"Remember, take this seriously," Tasha whispered. "No fooling around. And, if we see something, don't freak out. Just ask a question...and then, if it's true and works, I'll give him the candle. As soon as I do, turn the light on. Got it?"

Chrissy and Linda nodded. Taking a deep breath, Tasha returned her gaze to the flickering flame. It danced in the mirror, putting her into a trance-like state. Composing herself in the calm and quiet darkness, she spoke. Voice barely above a whisper.

"Wanderin' Jack, all alone;
Left to shadow, far from home.
Wanderin' Jack, lost in the night;
In search of guidance, morning light.
Wanderin' Jack, we call your name;
We offer you, our candle's flame."

Chrissy stifled a gasp as the candle in Tasha's hand sputtered violently. The flame dimmed, and then regrew. Larger and brighter than ever. But she remained silent. Keeping watch on the light before them. The reflection in the mirror. Waiting to see if anything manifested behind the glass.

"Wanderin' Jack, all alone;
Left to shadow, far from home.
Wanderin' Jack, lost in the night;
In search of guidance, morning light.
Wanderin' Jack, we call your name;
We offer you, our candle's flame."

Tasha repeated the chant once again. And, as before, the candle flashed. This time, however, it sparked blue. Chrissy's heart thudded as she gripped Linda's arm, not daring to look away from the mirror.

"Did you see that?" Linda whispered. "Do you think...?"

"Shh," Tasha hushed her. "Come on. We all have to say it. One more time."

She faced the mirror again, staring at her reflection. Their faces shifted in the candlelight, morphing. Resembling hellish ghouls. A trick of the light, but enough to startle them. Chrissy and Linda reached out and took hold of

Tasha's arms, gripping her tight. Swallowing hard, they nodded, joining in with the final chant.

"*Wanderin' Jack, all alone;*
Left to shadow, far from home.
Wanderin' Jack, lost in the night;
In search of guidance, morning light.
Wanderin' Jack, we call your name;
We offer you, our candle's flame."

There was silence. Stillness. This time, the candle didn't flash brightly. Didn't spit its flame. The girls scoured the glass for any sign that their summoning worked. But as they waited, nothing happened. After a while Linda sighed, leaning against the sink.

"So," she said, rolling her eyes. "Another dud, huh?"

She reached to turn the light on, but Chrissy stopped her. "Wait! Not yet..."

Chrissy squinted to get a better look through the darkness. Beyond the glare the flame cast. Deep in the mirror, something moved. Something that hadn't been there before. Tasha turned to her slowly, gripping the candle.

"Chrissy? What is it?"

"Do you see that?"

Tasha looked closer at the reflection. Into the shadows around them. She could just make out a low hanging fog behind the glass. Swirling. Illuminated white. Glowing beneath what looked to be the moon's soft light.

"But...how can that be?" Tasha asked.

The images started to become clear. Old, rotting trees, devoid of leaves. Overturned tombstones. Spider webs—catching the light of the silver moon. And then, they could hear it. Wind through hollow branches. Leaves scuttling across dirt paths. The sound of footsteps approaching. The buzzing of flies.

The candle flame flickered in Tasha's trembling hands. Her shoulders quivered as she stared into the mirror—into the realm beyond the glass. She shook her head as a figure took form in the shadows.

"Please tell me you're both seeing this," she said.

Chrissy nodded. "Yeah..."

"You're sure it's not the light playing tricks?" Linda asked.

"There's no way we'd all see it if it were," Tasha replied, swallowing hard.

47

The friends backed away from the sink, eyes still fixated on the mirror. On the approaching figure. Once it reached the glass, it stopped. Looming in the shadows and mist, features indistinguishable.

"Wanderin' Jack?" Chrissy's voice came out in a weak whimper.

"Aren't we supposed to ask a question?" Linda asked. "That's what you said, right? If he appears, we get to ask him a question...and he has to answer truthfully."

"Who gets to ask it?" Tasha asked, watching the figure before them.

"You should," Chrissy said. "You're the one who called him here. Just so everything is done right."

Tasha nodded. The candle flame danced wildly at the wick as she raised it in offering.

"I don't know what to ask," she whispered.

"Ask *anything*." Linda groaned.

Tasha was silent. Her head spun as she stared into the depths of the glass. Into the fog and shadow. Far beyond the twisting trees and tombstones. Then, she centered her gaze on the figure standing before her. Silhouetted. With a trembling breath, she parted her lips.

"Why do they call you Wanderin' Jack?" she asked.

The figure stood still and silent. But something moved behind the glass. Across his face. A gleam where his eyes should be. And then, Tasha felt it. Eating away at her like fire. Burning in the pit of her stomach. Her soul. She clenched her jaw to try and numb the pain, leaning against the sink, candle barely in her grip.

She saw flashes of long forgotten memories, playing on repeat. She saw the gray skies of autumn, the withering leaves. Old gravestones in the cold and gentle rain, covered with moss. Then, a man—young. Walking through the leaves, towards something dark. Desolate. Something he knew he shouldn't. The flashes became faster, racing before her. The young man. The decay. The stones. The fire. The bones. The shadows. The dirt. The ants. The flies.

Faster and faster the images played. Tasha grew lightheaded as they spun—her stomach turning. She tried to brace herself, hold tight against the sink, but it was useless. Her body gave out from faintness, knees buckling as her face came down against the porcelain with a loud *thwack*. She hit the floor, blood pooling from her nose.

"Tasha!" Chrissy cried, hurrying to her side, attempting to shake her back to consciousness. "What happened, Tasha? Are you okay?"

But she didn't respond. Her body remained limp as Chrissy turned her attention back to the mirror. She could still see the flickering candle, but now, it was behind the glass. Taken by the figure. Knowledge for light. Chrissy's heart sank into her stomach as she looked at Linda.

"Turn on the light!"

"He didn't answer the question," Linda said, eyes narrowing.

"Linda, *please*!"

"*No*," Linda snapped back. "He *didn't* answer the question."

She stepped forward, pressing her palms against the sink as she glared into the glass. Chrissy continued to try and wake Tasha, but to no avail. All the while still begging Linda to turn the bathroom light on. But she wouldn't. Not until she got the answer. Heard it for herself.

Leaning in as close as she could, she glared at the silhouette. "What *are* you?"

The candle hissed, going out. Engulfing the bathroom in pitch darkness. Chrissy gasped, pressing her face against Tasha to shield herself from the shadows as Linda looked around. Trying to let her eyes adjust. Once again, Chrissy pleaded that she turn the light on. But as Linda felt her way towards the switch on the wall, the flame reappeared in the mirror. Brighter than before.

Screams built in the girls' throats, fear rising from the pits of their stomachs. The light of the candle danced across the face of the figure—illuminating its pale features. His eyes were sunken in—deep and hollow. Lost. And his skin was mottled, pulled tight against the bone. Like that of a corpse. His lips were curled up in a hellish grin, exposing rotten teeth barely hanging from blackened gums. Flies poured from in between his teeth, swarming the glass.

Hot tears ran down Chrissy's cheeks as she released Tasha, getting to her feet. Linda was frozen in fear, trembling as she gazed upon the decaying man in the mirror. Chrissy frantically felt for the light switch, sobbing pitifully. But before she could flick it on—bathe the room in white light—something grabbed her. Something tight, twisting around her wrist. Digging in.

A black vine snaked up her arm, shooting from behind the glass where he stood. His grin grew wider as Chrissy screamed, leaves tearing through her skin, down to the bone. She tried to fight them as their pull became stronger, yanking her towards the mirror.

It was only when Linda began to feel them, too, that she cried out. Shaken from her shocked state. They wound their way up her body,

entangling her legs. Both girls screamed for help, begging someone to hear them—but they were met with silence.

With a sharp tug, they flew forward—hard against the porcelain sink. But still, they fought back. Clawing and screaming. Trying to tear through the thick, rope-like vines pulling them closer to the mirror. Closer to him.

Yet, their strength wasn't enough. As more vines bound them, they felt themselves being lifted. Up over the sink. Towards the cold, unforgiving glass. Tasha's limp body followed behind, dragged along by more black vines. Leaving nothing but a trail where her blood had pooled. Chrissy and Linda cried out once more, throats raw. But their voices faded as they jolted forward. Through the glass.

The house fell into silence after that. Shadows crept heavily through the empty bathroom. And with them, a lingering odor of decaying leaves and mud. Remnants of the deep autumn night—devoid of stars. Of guidance. Nothing but lost souls, searching for light.

IV.

A WAKE OF VULTURES CIRCLED CHAPEL HILL CEMETERY early that morning. Back and forth they soared, searching the grounds for any trace of fresh meat. Carcasses of small animals left behind. At first, they kept to the gravesites—shadows dancing across headstones and fresh plots. But then, they headed down the hill, to the back of the groundskeeper's house. Circling the pond tucked away beneath the old willow trees.

As soon as the groundskeeper, Horace Johnson, saw them landing in droves beside the water's edge, he hurried outside. The morning air was crisp, dew heavy and mixed with rain from the night before. It made the ground

53

slick, causing him to lose his footing halfway through the yard. He cursed aloud as he went down, the muck soaking through his jeans. The stale stench of autumn leaves clung to the earth, in browning piles where they collected against the trunks of bearing trees.

Horace brushed himself off and got back onto his feet. Reaching into his pocket, he pulled out a peppermint, unwrapping it and clenching it between his teeth. With a grunt, he headed onwards towards the pond, watching the vultures continue to land. Even from a distance, he could see them gathered near the water, dark feathers ruffled as they plucked away at a carcass. Red blood stained their beaks, tugging strands of flesh from their find. At first, they paid Horace no mind as he approached. But once he was able to see what they were devouring, he shooed them away. Cursing them.

They spread their wings, hissing as they hopped along the muddy ground. And then they took flight, landing in the barren trees surrounding the property. Still eyeing Horace and their disturbed meal.

The limp carcasses of two mallard ducks were torn open at the water's edge. Bloodied feathers plucked clean and scattered. The vultures had done a number on the flesh and innards, and Horace had to cover his nose and mouth against the stench of death rising from the bodies. Turning away from the carnage, he balled his fists.

"Those goddamn kids." He growled under his breath. "Always sneaking around, up to no good, out here all hours of the night. Now they've gone and killed my ducks."

Horace shot a look to the vultures perched in the branches. His brow furrowed as he glared at them. Watching their wings open wide in a mocking dance.

"Scavengers."

As he headed back towards his home and the cemetery gates, he could feel them still watching. Perched in the trees. Never once taking their beady eyes off him.

Once Horace had made himself a pot of coffee, he was off on his daily duties, shovel in hand. The sun peeked through gray skies, spreading a gentle glow across the damp grounds. Grounds that were still slippery and slick— especially the farther up the hill Horace went. He surveyed the landscape, eyeing the plots and gravestones that lined the pathways. Checking for any signs of trespassers. Troubled teens looking for a scare, hiding amongst the stones and trees—smoking and drinking. He'd taken pride in catching them before, and he certainly would again. Especially after his discovery out by the pond. Once he was confident no one else was on the grounds, he continued on—checking the pathways for footprints in the mud. Any trace that someone had been lurking after hours—when the rain fell in the night.

But still, he found nothing. Just the untouched, damp earth. Groaning at his lack of evidence, Horace rested a moment, contemplating his climb to the top of the hill. He leaned against the trunk of one of the old oak trees, gazing out through the groves of timeworn stone. Decaying leaves rested at the bases of many of them—the plots no longer visited. Yet, it wasn't their vacancy that caught Horace's attention. He squinted for a better look, spotting something he hadn't before, nestled against the headstones of century forgotten graves.

Pumpkins.

The bright orange gourds stood out against the gray and brown bleakness of autumn. He was unsure how he hadn't seen them before, planted at every grave. A garden of them spreading up the hill.

Horace's first thought was that someone had brought an excess supply of the pumpkins, decorating the lesser loved plots. But, he knew everyone who came and went. He watched them from his window every day, overlooking the cemetery. And while a few families placed small pumpkins on the graves of their dearly departed, it was never *this* many.

"I'll bet it was those troublemakers." Horace hissed through yellowed teeth. "Up here after dark with their pumpkins. Probably throwing seeds. Littering the grounds. Now there'll be pumpkin patches growing all over the hill!"

He snatched his shovel up, storming over to one of the headstones. With a grunt, he drove the sharp head through the gourd, splitting it open. A stream of bright orange goop spilled from inside, landing across the fallen leaves. And Horace didn't stop there. Again, he brought the shovel down, mashing the pumpkin until it was nothing more than a pile of squelchy innards and seeds. Wiping his brow, he glared at the mess. His attention was turned away as branches creaked behind him—feeling watchful eyes on the back of his neck.

Turning, he glanced into the trees, spotting the vultures. They'd left the comfort of the pond where they'd had their morning meal, now perching alongside the hill. Their feathers ruffled as they stared down at him, shifting on their feet. Horace gripped the shovel tighter, attempting to ignore their presence.

"Damn kids," he muttered, gazing across the pumpkin-covered plots. "It's going to take *weeks* to get these dug up."

Every gravesite had one growing, sprouting from tangled vines at the base of the headstones. And the farther up the hill he went, the larger they became. The more abundant. Fresh from the soil. With each step, he cursed them aloud. The pumpkins. The vultures. The teens. Anything he considered an inconvenience. A detriment to his work and peace.

As he made his way towards the top of the hill, mumbling under his breath, his eyes met the little old chapel—overlooking the fields of graves. The stone edifice had been weathered over the years, but it still stood sturdy and erect. Horace normally wouldn't have thought anything of it, but he stopped in his tracks upon the sight. For the first time in years, the doors were open.

The mid-morning breeze scattered fresh fallen leaves about the entrance, blowing them inside across the wooden floors. Against the pews. Down the aisle towards the altar. Horace grunted, setting his shovel against the cold stone before stepping inside. He ran his dirt covered fingers through the greasy strands of hair hanging in his face. Morning light streaked through the windows, exposing fragments of dust that shimmered in the air. Aside from the rustling leaves, all was quiet. Yet, Horace remained on guard as he approached the altar.

It was covered in layers of dust from years of abandon—just the same as the pews. Cobwebs stretched across it, collected in their own grimy film. Cornstalks lined the reredos, their husks adorning the altar. Pumpkins sat beside them—plucked from the patches growing amongst the graves. A perfect picture of harvest. Horace licked his lips, glaring angrily at the display.

"*Blasphemy.*"

As he went to remove the pumpkins and husks from the altar, he heard movement beyond the chapel door. Leaves crunching. Padded paws across the earth. With a startled breath, he turned to the doorway, only catching a glimpse of leaves scattering in the breeze. Yet, he felt someone watching. Turning away from the altar, he hurried down the aisle and back outside, scanning the cemetery.

He was only met with the sounds of the vultures and rustling leaves on the trees. Sunlight filtered through the golden and amber canopies, dappled across the gravestones and pumpkins. But that was all. With a gruff grunt, Horace retrieved his shovel before digging through his pockets for the chapel key. One he hadn't used in so long.

As he closed the door, fidgeting with the lock, rustling came up behind him once again. Soft footsteps across the damp soil. Turning, he was met by an elderly woman. His grip on the shovel tightened as he stepped back in alarm.

"Oh, my apologies! I didn't mean to startle you." She laughed, brushing the clinging leaves from her skirt.

Horace sighed in relief. Flicking his head to get the few strands of long, greasy hair from his face, he gave a chuckle of his own in return.

"Not to worry, ma'am," he said. "Forgive me if I seem on edge. I've been cleaning up after a group of pesky teens all morning. Haven't seen them around, have you?"

"Teens?" The woman shook her head. "Couldn't say I have."

"Well, if you *do*, be sure to find me," Horace said. "They've been nothing but trouble the last few weeks. Once autumn hits the air, they're like flies to rot. Up here doing drugs and terrorizing the place."

"The disrespect of this generation is shameful."

"You're telling me. It's because they're undisciplined. They think they can get away with whatever they want. That they're above the law. *Royalty*. Wait until reality hits them."

"It's a hard truth, for sure."

"And they get worse by the year." He gestured to the doors behind him. "I just found the chapel vandalized. And my ducks! The mated pair was killed."

"Oh, my." The woman's eyes widened as she covered her mouth with a wrinkled hand. "That's awful. I'm terribly sorry."

Horace shrugged. "Like my Pappy used to say...anyone who has the gall to harm an animal, would just as soon do the same to a person."

"How horrifying, especially with all the children going missing in town." The woman pursed her lips at the thought.

"You can't trust *anyone* these days," Horace said. "I don't want to think those kids would be involved with all that. I *pray* not, anyway."

He turned his attention back to the graves, scanning the oversized pumpkins sprouting from them. His eyes narrowed as he motioned towards them.

57

"And they planted pumpkin patches overnight," he said. "Whatever joke *that* is they're trying to pull."

The old woman followed his gaze across the landscape of gray and orange. Stone and pumpkins. She took in how large they were. How plump. Putting a finger to her lips, she shook her head.

"These *couldn't* have grown overnight," she said.

"What?" Horace raised an eyebrow. "Well, of course they did! They weren't here yesterday."

"A patch this thick and full...why, it would take *months* to grow."

Horace gritted his teeth. "You calling me crazy?"

"Not at all," the woman said. "Just pointing out a fact."

She drew her attention down the hill—towards the entrance. Morning was slipping away by the moment. As she adjusted her dark shawl, the old woman glanced back at Horace.

"Before I'm on my way, if you don't mind my asking... You haven't seen a cat around here, have you?" she asked.

"Cat?"

"A slim black one. Terribly sweet. Loves attention."

"Can't say I have."

With a nod of discouragement, she started down the path before her. The breeze tossed her skirt and shawl, causing her to pull it tighter around her shoulders.

"I'll keep my eye out," Horace called after her. "For your cat."

The woman smiled sadly. "And I for your teens. Have a good day."

Horace stayed put, watching her in silence. Once she disappeared beyond the gravestones and trees, he started towards the first pumpkin he saw, driving the head of the shovel through the thick skin. It split open with ease, bright orange guts and seeds spilling from the sides. And then, he started for the next one.

Sticky pumpkin guts littered the old stones as he made his rounds. Smashing and splitting every one he could.

By the time noon rolled around, Horace's hands were cracked and blistered. They ached as he drove the shovel into the large pumpkin before him, just barely cutting it open. He winced as the blade made contact—pain searing through his palms and fingers. With shaky hands, he pulled the shovel free, resting it against the soft mud.

From the trees, the leaves rustled. Vultures stirred in the branches as they watched, eager for a bite of freshly destroyed pumpkin. Horace glared up at them as he retrieved his shovel, wiping the dripping sweat from his forehead.

"That's enough for today," he mumbled aloud, staggering back through the grove of graves.

His boots sloshed through the slick sod, focused only on returning to his house at the far end of the cemetery. Its cozy warmth. Yet, as he made his way down the hill, he spotted something from the corner of his eye. Something he hadn't on his way up earlier that morning. Positioned beyond the pathways—out amongst the headstones—were three scarecrows.

They were nothing like scarecrows Horace had ever seen, however. They were old and worn, covered with dirt and leaves. Mud clung to their tattered burlap faces and damp clothing. And from their bodies, tightly fastened to wooden stakes, thick pumpkin vines sprouted. They wrapped around the necks and arms—jutting out from behind the burlap masks. Horace exhaled as he approached them.

"Where did *you* come from?"

He could only get so close before turning away, gagging. The stench of decay was heavy under the layers of burlap. Its musty, damp scent permeated the air, buzzing with flies. Horace waved them off, backing away. Rain water had soaked deep—clearly over many months. He prodded at one with the head of the shovel, feeling the stiff body shift. Full of old straw and leaves. Rotting away beneath the fabric.

Horace couldn't understand how he hadn't seen them before. His daily patrols of the cemetery would have garnered their discovery long before autumn. Especially in their condition. His conclusion, as with everything else in the cemetery that day, was simple.

"Delinquents."

He spat at the ground beneath the scarecrows, giving them one final look of disgust before heading towards his home. Tuning out the vivid pumpkins lining the way, peeking from between the headstones.

In the trees above, the vultures remained perched, eyeing him. They shifted on their feet, ruffling their feathers in the bitter breeze that wafted through the cemetery. Watching. Waiting. Hungry. And even as the shadows of afternoon slithered across the graves, still they sat. Ravenously awaiting their next meal.

V.

IT WAS THE CAT THAT AWOKE PETER early that morning. The same one that had for the entirety of the week—pawing at his bedroom window. His sleek black fur was barely visible against the shadows of morning, but his drawn out mewls were enough for Peter to know he was there. Frantically begging to be let in.

Peter pulled a pillow over his head with a groan. He tried to drown out the sounds beyond the glass, but the longer he ignored them, the louder they became.

"Leave me alone!" Peter hollered, voice muffled beneath his pillow.

But still, the cat carried on. Pawing the glass. Yellow eyes burning bright in the faint light of day—slowly peeking over the horizon. Again, he let out a long yowl, adamant on entering. Peter scrunched his nose, throwing his pillow to the end of the bed as he sat up, glaring at the skinny black cat. Only when their eyes locked did it stop, giving Peter a high-pitched chirp before rubbing against the glass. Getting to his feet, Peter ran his fingers through his mussed, dark hair.

"Stupid cat."

He grabbed his clothes from the chair beside his bed—faded black jeans with the knees torn and an old gray flannel shirt. Unfolding them from their messy heap, he gave them a whiff before changing. They could stand another day, carrying only the lingering scent of cigarette smoke. Once he was dressed, he combed through his hair with his fingers and slipped his beanie on —covering what he could of the dark mop atop his head. Then, he grabbed his messenger bag, heading out of his room. Away from the prying cat, still watching from beyond the glass.

Peter pushed through the kitchen doorway, eyes weary as they remained fixed on the floor. He shuffled past the table, bag bumping one of the chairs and getting snagged. With a groan, he tugged it free. As he started towards the door again, however, the voice of his father stopped him.

"Hey, Petey. You're up early. What's the rush?"

Jim Harlow was in his usual spot at the table, reading the daily newspaper. He peered over his glasses, watching his son stop beside the refrigerator. Peter merely grunted, yanking the door open. The light inside hit him, stinging his tired eyes. He skimmed the sparse interior, sighing when he found nothing of interest. Nudging the fridge shut with his foot, he adjusted his messenger bag before heading over to the table. He snatched a lightly buttered slice of toast from the plate in the center, biting into it in dissatisfaction. It was dark—burnt, in his opinion—and flaky. More his

father's taste than his own. Still he stood there, intently chewing, not bothering to speak.

Jim folded the paper, setting it aside. "Alright. What's going on?"

"It's that cat," he said, mouth full of bread. "It keeps me up all night. I hardly get any sleep."

"Still?" Jim pushed his glasses up on his nose in thought. "When did you say it started coming around?"

"About a week ago," Peter replied, pouring himself a glass of orange juice. "It must have followed me home."

"From where? School?"

Peter hesitated. "Yeah. School."

He took a sip, averting his gaze from his father. Once the tart, citrusy flavor hit his tongue, he pulled the glass from his lips, gagging.

"*Uck*. Pulp."

"You should ask around and see if anyone near the school is missing one," his father said. "Especially with Halloween coming up. You know what crazies do to cats."

"Yeah..." Peter gripped the strap of his messenger bag.

"Actually. Speaking of Halloween..." Jim took a sip of coffee before standing. "Stay there. I've got something for you."

Peter rolled his eyes as his father walked past him into the living room. He set his half-eaten slice of toast back on the plate, heaving a sigh. Rocking on the heels of his shoes, he glanced at the clock on the wall. 6:27 a.m. Jim finally reentered the room, a brightly painted pumpkin mask in hand. Peter sneered at the sight.

"What's *that*?" he asked.

"Remember how I told you my company has been working on some pretty cool costumes this year?" Jim waved the mask at Peter. "Check it out. The Light-and-Glow Pumpkin Masks—sure to be an absolute hit."

"Neat," Peter said, shifting on his feet, sneaking a glimpse of the clock again.

"Isn't it? I talked to my boss and he was fine with me taking this one. It's a prototype, so it may not be completely up to snuff like the mass market ones, but I figured it wouldn't matter." Jim offered the mask to his son. "Here."

Peter hesitated, reluctantly taking it. His lips tugged into a frown as he ran his thumbs over the latex. The sad face of the pumpkin stared up at him pathetically.

65

"I figured since it's probably your last year trick-or-treating with your friends, it would be cool to have. And, besides, they're set to be the popular thing this year. Everyone will be wearing them!"

Peter shook his head. "I'm not going trick-or-treating this year, Dad."

Jim's grin quickly diminished. "What?"

"I'm not a little kid anymore. Besides, half the town gets nasty if they see anyone over ten asking for candy." He held the mask back out to his father. "And also, if *everyone* is wearing them this year...I'd rather pass."

"Oh, come on, Petey," Jim pleaded. "Don't grow up on me just yet. Enjoy your last year of school. Be a *kid* just a little longer."

Peter clenched his jaw. With a heavy breath, he pressed the mask to his father's chest, forcing him to take it. Adjusting his messenger bag, taking some weight off his shoulder, he turned to the doorway.

"I gotta go."

Jim lowered the mask to his side. He watched as Peter reached for the doorknob, stopping him by clearing his throat.

"Aren't you forgetting something?"

Peter bristled. "Come on, Dad..."

Jim made his way over to his son, wrapping an arm around his shoulders. Peter stiffened beneath the touch. As Jim pulled away, however, he scrunched his nose, looking Peter up and down.

"You're not still smoking, are you? You *know* how I feel about that, Peter..."

Peter tugged the door open. "I'm gonna be late."

Jim raised an eyebrow. "We'll talk about this later. Have a good day. Love you."

"Yeah," Peter said, stepping outside. "You, too."

The morning air was crisp with mid-October chill. Fog hung dense and low over the street, obscuring anything beyond the lawn. Everything was painted in somber gray, an ode to oncoming winter. Peter hunched his shoulders, shaking off the chill that crept through him as he made his way down the sidewalk. He removed a pair of over the ear headphones from his bag, sliding them atop his head. Loud, heavy music spun like static from them, buzzing around Peter as he walked. He shoved his hands deep into the pocket of his jeans, focused only on the ground ahead and the metal in his speakers.

From the windowsill, the cat watched him. Its long, skinny tail swayed as it chirped, hopping down onto the sidewalk. It scurried through the fallen

leaves lining the path, hurrying over to Peter. He nearly tripped as it brushed against his leg affectionately.

"Get out of here." Peter groaned. "Go home."

He gave it a gentle, but firm, nudge with his foot, making his way to his bicycle against the garage. Dragging it down the driveway, he glanced back at the cat before mounting. It watched as he turned his attention to the road, pedaling towards the high school. With a chirp, it sat in the middle of the driveway, listening to the leaves rustle in the wake of morning.

The sun was warm in the schoolyard that afternoon, reflecting off the aluminum bleachers. Given the dreary, gray morning, it was beautiful. The vibrant ambers and golds of the trees stood out bolder than ever against the bright blue sky—leaves fluttering in the soft breeze that swept across the football field. All was silent, until the high-pitched referee's whistle sounded, followed by the violent clashing of helmets.

Sam adjusted her earbuds, flipping through the pages of her Economics textbook. She paid no mind to the heavily padded bodies rushing down the field, tuning out their grunts and the coach's demands with her music. She tucked a few strands of violet hair behind her ear, bobbing her head in time with the beat. Lost in the melody. Only when Peter approached the bleachers did she pause, returning to reality.

"Wasn't expecting to find *you* here." Peter chuckled. "Don't tell me you're into football now."

"Absolutely not," Sam replied, tugging her right earbud free. "I have no interest in sportsball of any kind. It's all just a hyper masculine, beefed up testosterone fest."

Peter smirked. "It's the spirit of the school."

"That doesn't surprise me." Sam closed her Economics book. "They're complaining about not having enough funding, but are willing to cut the art programs to keep the sports. All that talk about a bigger and better football

field in the next few years... Ridiculous. There's nothing wrong with the one we have now."

"At least we'll be long gone from this place by then," Peter said.

He sat on the bleacher seat below Sam, gazing out across the field. The vibrant green and yellow uniforms of the Oakridge Cougars were blinding in the sunlight. Squinting, he attempted to make out Ritchie and Theo in the sea of glinting helmets, but it was impossible. From a distance, everyone looked identical.

"I may not know a thing about it," Sam said, leaning forward, "but from what I've heard, we have a pretty decent team this year."

"Well, at least it'll make Homecoming more eventful for Ritchie and Theo," Peter said. "It's all about the jocks and cheerleaders anyway."

He fumbled through the messenger bag at his side, removing his pack of cigarettes. Giving it a shake, he tugged one from the box, placing it between his teeth. As he searched for his lighter, Sam frowned.

"Hey!" She slapped his shoulder. "Not on school grounds. Do you *want* another referral?"

Peter snorted. "That was sophomore year. And besides, Principal Wendell's had a vendetta against me since day one. You know that."

Sam reached out, yanking the cigarette from his mouth. Shaking her head, she waved it at him.

"Eight months," she said. "That's all you've got left to put up with this place. Don't give them reason to make it less."

The referee's whistle blared across the field again, this time drawn out. The coach clapped his hands together, calling the team over for a huddle. Peter and Sam watched as the burly bodies hurried to the sidelines, now full of boisterous chatter.

"Don't forget. The big game next Thursday is against Springfield." The coach's voice echoed to the bleachers. "We have a rough history with them, and I'd like to see you change that."

A few pointers were given in preparation for the game later in the week, followed by highlights of the practice. At the top of the hour, the team was dismissed. While most of the players returned to the school, eager for the locker rooms to shower and change, Ritchie and Theo headed for the bleachers.

Ritchie slid his helmet off, auburn hair sweaty and tousled. Dirt dusted his face, camouflaging his freckles beneath it. He tugged the towel draped around his neck free, dabbing his cheeks and forehead. When he was

done, he offered it to Theo. Taking it, he, too, removed his helmet, wiping the sweat from his brow.

"Think we're ready to face Springfield?" he asked, tossing the towel back to Ritchie.

"As ready as we're going to be. If Coach Harrison doesn't like it, tough shit." Ritchie smirked before turning his attention to Peter and Sam. "Fancy seeing you two here. I thought you didn't give a damn about sports."

Sam managed a chuckle. "Only for you, Ritchie."

He flashed a bright, toothy grin. "That's what they all say."

Running his fingers through his hair, he took a seat on the bleachers. Theo joined him, stretching his legs as he leaned back. He glanced at Sam with a smile.

"You coming to the game Thursday night, then?"

"I'll think about it," Sam said. "Don't forget, I have this Economics test on Friday. It's been the bane of my existence for the last two weeks."

Ritchie cringed. "I'm so glad I'm in Government this semester. Economics is math. And math and I do *not* mix."

"Tell me about it," Sam replied.

"Oh, hey. *Speaking* of tests..." Ritchie turned his gaze to Peter. "How'd that Chemistry test go, *Your Highness*?"

Peter scoffed, crossing his arms over his knees. "The worst it possibly could have."

"Did you flunk it?" Ritchie pressed.

"And *then* some."

"Well, damn." Ritchie pursed his lips. "I guess even after sitting in his throne, the Devil said fuck you."

Peter scowled. He glared at the empty space on the bleacher below him, focused on the blinding light that reflected from the surface—watching a couple of ants dart back and forth. Ritchie let out a burst of laughter, clapping Theo on the shoulder.

"Would you shut up?" Sam snapped at them before turning her attention to Peter. "It's just one test. You'll be fine."

Peter shook his head. "I'm already lined up to fail this quarter. And not just Chemistry. You know I'm a straight C student *at best*."

He ran his hands over his face, pushing his fingertips into the dark bangs poking out from beneath his beanie. His palms caressed his eyes as he managed a sigh.

"I just...I really don't see myself graduating."

"Whoa, man," Theo said, resting a hand on Peter's knee. "It's only October. You have the whole rest of the year to catch up on your GPA. Don't sweat it."

"It's not just *this* year," Peter said. "Since freshman year, I've been teetering between Cs and Ds. You know how many times I flunked finals. I spent my whole summer making up classes to even get this far. I just…"

He groaned. Tugging his beanie down over his eyes, he leaned back against the bleachers. His lips drew into a shaky frown as he remained still, deafened by his friends' silence. They looked between each other, until Theo found words of encouragement.

"High school's just four years of your life," he said. "So what if you're not a straight A student? All that doesn't matter in the long run."

"You're forgetting these four years are the most important years of *life*, though, Theo." Peter mumbled. "They're the foundation for *everything*. My career. My entire future. And what do I have to show for it?"

"I'll say it again," Theo said adamantly, "you still have time to apply yourself and get those grades up."

"Theo's right. You're smart, Peter," Sam said. "I think it really just comes down to your focus."

"That's easy for *you* to say. You've all got it planned out… Sam, you're moving in with your dad across the country after graduation. Ritchie, you're heading up north to the police academy. And, Theo, you've already got a ton of scholarships." Peter shook his head. "All *I'm* going to be good for after graduation is flipping burgers at McFuckholes."

"You mean that *fancy* Scottish restaurant?" Ritchie chuckled.

"Shut *up*." Sam glared at him. "There's nothing wrong or shameful about working at a fast food joint. *I* work there. You know that."

"Yeah, *part time*," Peter said softly. "It's not your *career*. You're just saving up for when you get to New York. So you can go to college. Better yourself."

He glanced away, out across the football field as a gentle breeze began to blow in. The chill stung his eyes as he sighed, shaking his head.

"All my life, that's all anyone's ever said I'll amount to." He managed a defeated chuckle. "And they're right."

"So prove them wrong," Ritchie said. "Spite is the best motivator. Put your all into the rest of the year and bring your GPA up. Then, when you're living out *your* dreams, they won't have anything to say."

Sam pursed her lips. "I don't think you've ever told us… What *are* your dreams, Peter?"

He was silent for a long while before closing his eyes. "I don't even know anymore..."

The wind picked up, rustling through the surrounding trees. Sam kept her lips tight, watching Peter intently. Only when she cleared her throat did he turn his focus to her. She rummaged through her bag, pulling out a small cardboard box. As old and worn as it was, the bright yellow exterior wasn't faded. The word TAROT across the side caught Peter's eye.

"Here," Sam said, removing the deck of cards and shuffling. "Pick one."

She fanned them out, revealing backings just as vibrant as their box. Peter raised an eyebrow.

"What for?"

"A reading of your future."

Ritchie snorted as he got to his feet, scooping up his helmet. "Oh get *real*, Sam. You can't seriously believe this mumbo jumbo."

"If you're not interested, then go somewhere else," Sam said, not bothering to glance up at him. "Now, go on. Pick one."

Peter's fingertips hesitantly brushed against the gilded edges of the cards. They glided back and forth a few times, until he felt a tingling sensation—like a spark. He pointed to a card towards the end of the pile. Sam removed it, flipping it over and setting it on the bleacher seat so its title could be read.

THE FOOL.

The jester-like character depicted on the card stood at a cliff's edge, head tilted upward towards the radiant sun. A dog trailed at his heels on hind legs, leaving behind the path they had strayed from. A smile tugged at Sam's lips as she motioned to the card.

"The *Fool*?" Ritchie sneered, elbowing Peter playfully in the side. "Well, Peter. Looks like the cards aren't wrong."

"That's *not* what the Fool means, Ritchie," Sam snapped.

Again, she motioned to the card, making sure Peter's attention was only on her words—not Ritchie's. She picked it up, its edges glinting in the fading afternoon sunlight, offering it to Peter. He paused, but then took it.

"New beginnings. *That's* what the Fool is about. A fresh start. Leaving behind the path you've walked for so long. Ready to make the jump into something new. Changes."

"But what if I'm not ready for change? What if—"

She wrapped her hands around his as a soft smile returned to her lips. "You just have to have faith."

Peter glanced down at the card in his hands. He tried to convince himself that Sam was right. The Fool, even in his jester attire, was basking in the sun. Unafraid of the plunging cliff before him. Of going on alone. Yet, his heart panged as he ran his thumb across the number "0" at the top of the image. The feeling of nothingness returned.

He extended the card to Sam, but she held her hand up, stopping him. Shaking her head, she smiled.

"I've got plenty of other decks at home," she said. "Keep it. Maybe it'll serve as some positivity for the rest of the quarter."

Gathering her bag, Sam got to her feet. The smell of oncoming rain lingered in the late afternoon breeze, becoming heavier by the moment. She pulled up her hood, bidding her friends farewell as she hurried home. The boys remained at the bleachers for a short while longer before they, too, went their separate ways. Theo and Ritchie returned to the school, to change in the locker room before the janitors forbade them access. Peter, however, stayed seated, looking over the card. When he finally felt the first drops of rain, he slipped it into his bag, retrieving his bicycle and pedaling home for the night.

The rain fell hard throughout the evening. It pounded against the pavement, soaking the fallen foliage that scattered across the ground. Though dreary, there was a sense of peace to the night.

Peter left his window cracked. The cool air drifted in, fluttering his curtains. Outside, the rain *pitter-pattered* against the windowsill in rhythmic tempo. The soothing ambience helped Peter drift into a deep sleep—one he hadn't had in what felt like weeks. He kept his comforter pulled up to his chin, wrapped tightly around him to keep the creeping chill from his bones. And soundlessly, he slept.

The cemetery was darker than Peter remembered as he made his way through the snaking paths. The mud was thick from the rain , making it difficult to navigate. All around him, he could hear rustling in the distance. Could feel eyes watching from the trees. His heart beat against his chest as he headed farther in—towards the old, twisted tree.

A faint, amber light flickered at its base, flashing between the headstones. Peter squinted, unable to make out much in the darkness. Through the mud he trudged, not daring to look back, even as the feeling of eyes from above became heavier. The rustling louder. Peppered with avion-like hisses.

The walk seemed longer than usual. But as he drew closer to the tree, the light grew brighter, and he began to hear music. A procession of bells. Drums. Trumpets. His breaths became softer as he approached, attempting to quiet himself. Unsure of what awaited ahead.

Leaves fluttered around him, carrying whispers on the wind. With every rustle from the branches above, he could hear it. Soft. Breathy. Calling his name.

Peter...

Peter glanced up into the trees. Between the shifting dirty golden hues, he saw them. Vultures. Hundreds of them. Big, bulbous black bodies, stark against the leaves. Their beady eyes watched him intently as they hissed—whispers growing louder.

Peter, Peter...

The flicker of firelight danced across the twisted trunk of the old tree, pirouetting with shadows that made the bark seem to pulse. As Peter approached, ducking behind a large headstone, he was able to make out the source of the music.

A clowder of cats.

At least, that's what Peter took them to be. They were long and sleek like the one that came around his house—chirping in the same manner. Yet, unlike that cat, *these* walked on two legs. Circling a large bonfire before the tree.

Round and round they went, slender bodies dancing beneath the moonlight. The flames reflected in their eyes, like gold and green sparks. But stranger than their movements were their instruments. Some cats carried small drums, beating upon them in ritualistic rhythm. Others carried tiny horns, tooting bright and brassy notes to the wind. But as cheery as it sounded, Peter was unnerved. The music and twirling bipedal cats filled him with nausea.

His head spun as he stared at the tree, spotting an immense garden of pumpkins around the trunk. All were carved with leering faces—candlelight blazing inside. Louder and louder the music became, practically static now. Peter's ears rang as he turned his focus on the flames, blazing brighter by the moment.

Then everything flashed white.

When the light faded, the music had stopped. All was silent except for the smoldering embers of the extinguished fire. Darkness flooded the cemetery once more. As Peter's eyes adjusted to the shadows, he saw something swaying in the branches. Something small. Dark. One at first, but then many. Squinting for a better look, his heart stopped when he finally made out the shapes.

They were the cats, strung up in the branches of the tree. Their lifeless bodies were no longer shiny, but matted and skeletal. Tight rope cut deep into their necks, wearing away the fur. Their jaws were pried open, unhinged, exposing bloodied mouths. Tongues removed. Their lifeless eyes bulged wide, staring out through the cemetery as their corpses swung in the wind— dancing in the tree.

Peter stumbled backwards as he attempted to flee—watching their dead gaze snap to him. He landed hard on the muddy ground, wincing as his tailbone made contact with a low grave marker. Biting back the searing pain, he pushed himself onto his knees. Turning for one final glimpse at the tree, he found a beady black pair of eyes blocking his view. Staring him down. A large vulture was perched on the headstone before him, wings opened wide. It hissed, surveying every part of him. Gaze searing deep. Craning its neck towards Peter, the vulture emitted another sound. A whisper.

What do you desire?

Peter's heart raced as he awoke to the mewling of the cat on his windowsill. His pillow was soaked through with sweat, hair hanging into his eyes in thick, damp strands. The faint light of dawn painted his walls as he sunk lower beneath his comforter.

"It was just a dream…"

He slowly sat up, head throbbing. Holding a hand to his temple, he groaned. As he let his arm fall back to his side, however, he noticed it. Sticky blood upon his fingers. Peter swallowed hard, hands trembling as he stared at his stained skin. Then, a fresh drop of blood fell—splashing on his sheets. Peter's eyes widened as a warm, wet sensation ran down his upper lip. Touching his face, he breathed a weak whimper as he found his fingers coated in bright red.

"*Shit.*"

He pinched his nose, tilting his head forward to ease the bleeding. Only then did he see the already dried stains down the front of his t-shirt. His pillow also had wet droplets coating it—still fresh. Once he was certain the bleeding had stopped, he wiped his nose on the back of his hand, frowning at the red streak left behind.

Preparing to clean himself up, he heard another yowl. Peering at the window, he saw that skinny black cat again—pawing at the screen. Peter groaned, getting up and shutting the glass. The cat continued to pace on the sill, whiskers erect as it begged for his attention. Peter stared at it long and hard before pursing his lips. Then, turning to his bed and the damp, bloodstained pillow, he had an idea.

The pillowcase swung at Peter's side as he pedaled his bike down Alder Avenue. From inside, the distressed, but curious, meows of the cat echoed. It pawed against the fabric, adamant to be released. Yet, no matter how hard it pushed and tugged, Peter kept his grip tight. He was just as determined as the cat. And he hoped this would be the end of it.

As the iron gates of the Chapel Hill Cemetery came into view, Peter breathed a sigh of relief. The sun had just barely risen, silhouetting them in the early morning light. He pedaled inside, stopping beyond the entrance. The pillowcase continued to sway as the cat moved around inside, yowling louder than before. Peter dismounted, lowering the case to the ground before opening it. The cat hurried out from its confinement, stopping once it realized where it was. It sniffed the crisp morning air, chirping as leaves fluttered from the trees. When it caught sight of one scraping across the ground, it took off—eager to hunt it down.

With the cat distracted, Peter hopped back on his bike, tucking the bloodstained pillowcase inside his messenger bag. As he pulled out of the cemetery gates, however, he could sense someone watching him. From the groundskeeper's house on the corner.

From the upper window, Horace Johnson stared out. Like a timeworn apparition behind the glass. Silent. Stern. Watching as Peter crossed the street, pedaling through the damp morning mist.

VI.

BILLY BARONE COULDN'T WAIT FOR HALLOWEEN. He'd been contemplating his costume for months—changing his mind nearly every week, much to his mother's dismay. At first, he wanted to be a spaceman. Then a werewolf. Then an alien. His mother encouraged him to settle between the three: an alien werewolf in space. But, by then, Billy had already moved on to his latest fascination.

"I want to be a cowboy!"

His mother had to admit she was relieved by his final decision. The costume was of little cost, comprised of a pair of blue jeans and faded flannel

shirt Billy already owned. The hat and boots were the only expense—acquired at the seasonal Halloween store—and she managed to find an old, red bandana amongst her accessories to lend him. Billy was ecstatic. With his already eager anticipation for the end of the month and his newfound obsession with cowboys, he begged his mother to let him wear the outfit early. Promising he wouldn't dirty it.

She was hesitant, trying to persuade him to wear anything else. She even aimed for leniency with having him wear *only* the shirt, jeans, and bandana. But Billy was stubborn. He couldn't be a *real* cowboy without his hat and boots. And so, after many debates, she finally gave in.

Billy wore his costume everywhere he went. To the grocery store, to school, and to the park at the end of town. Everyone he met acknowledged his attire, playing along that he was straight out of the westerns he watched on TV. And the more the townsfolk addressed him as such, the more he came to believe.

Thus, little Billy Barone became the cowboy of Oakridge.

It was warmer than usual when Billy decided to play by the train tracks—out by the quarry. There was no breeze throughout the day and the sun rivaled the heat of summer. Though hot in his flannel shirt and jeans, he ignored the discomfort. He was, after all, a cowboy in his mind. And he knew how hot it always looked in westerns.

As he walked alongside the tracks, he kicked a stone, humming to himself. In the distance, he could make out the looming figures of old train cars—rusted and worn from years of abandonment. An iron graveyard. He'd been told countless times to stay away from the tracks and the trains and the quarry, but Billy was curious. His mother's words fell on deaf ears.

Once he made it into the trainyard, he gazed in awe at all left behind. Dilapidated. Beneath their coats of rust, Billy found the engines and boxcars intriguing. Plucked right of the wild west. He'd seen numerous heist scenes in his shows—outlaw gangs racing along the tracks on horseback, firing their

pistols into the air. Steam billowing from the engine as Sheriff Daggett had a shootout atop the speeding cars. Those parts were always his favorite. In fascination, he wandered deeper into the remains beside the tracks.

Gravel crunched beneath his boots as he slunk around each car, peeking inside. Fearful of finding members of one of his western gangs hiding amongst them, pistols drawn. Billy patted his pockets at the thought, realizing his mother forgot to include a cap gun with the rest of his outfit.

"Dang it," he muttered under his breath.

He would have to remind her when he got home to pick one up from the costume shop. After all, he thought, just like the hat and boots, he couldn't be a *real* cowboy without a pistol. And he certainly couldn't stop the bad guys without one either. Once he made it to the last car near the edge of the quarry, he exhaled in relief.

No outlaws.

Straightening up, he looked the rusty exterior of the car over, running his fingertips along the groove of the iron wheels. He hesitated, but then formed his fingers into a faux pistol, closing one eye and aiming it up at the car.

"Reach for the sky, Boxcar Bart!"

His words slurred into a poor attempt at an old western drawl. His hand drew back as he puffed out his cheeks, expelling a loud *pkew* sound. Pretending to mount a horse, he galloped between the cars, imitating the sound of hooves. Back and forth he went for minutes, yelling a slew of phrases from his shows as he carried on—pretending to chase down the outlaws. That was, until he reached an abandoned car set off from the others.

It was overgrown in weeds, vines wrapped around the wheels and climbing the sides. Like the others, it was decayed. However, this car was open, revealing its dark interior. Pulling back on invisible reins as he came to a halt, Billy drew silent. He swallowed hard, trying to peer through the shadows within the car. He didn't remember it being open when he had passed before. But, he told himself, he was too busy looking for train robbers to probably notice.

As he was about to back away, something inside the car creaked. Billy's heart raced as he swallowed again, listening to the *pitter-patter* of feet. His shoulders trembled, knees growing weak as he tried to convince himself to be brave. To be like Sheriff Daggett. Taking a deep breath, he pursed his lips in determination, drawing his finger gun upwards. He pointed it at the entrance to the car, closing one eye as he took aim.

Before he could faux fire, Billy was startled by a large orange and white cat—bounding from inside the train car. It landed at his feet, blinking up at him with amber eyes. It took a moment, but Billy caught his breath, managing a smile at the feisty feline.

"Oh, hi, kitty," he said, crouching down.

The cat's whiskers twitched as he stared at Billy. He tilted his oversized head, emitting a deep, drawn out meow before scampering beneath one of the other cars. Billy watched as he left, unaware of the footsteps approaching behind him.

"Are you lost, little one?"

Billy spun around, gazing into the face of an elderly woman. Though rigid in many of her features, her expression was soft. Billy pushed the brim of his cowboy hat back before shaking his head.

"No. Just playing."

The woman nodded. "I see. Although, this isn't the safest place to play, you know? The trains are old and not so sturdy. And the quarry there... you don't want to fall and get hurt, do you?"

Billy shook his head.

"Now then. Where are your mom and dad?"

"At home," Billy murmured.

"Do they know you're out here?"

Billy scuffed the toes of his boots through the gravel, guilty gaze falling to the ground. Light clouds of dust blew up, coating his feet. Now, he didn't feel like Sheriff Daggett at all. He felt like one of the outlaws—being interrogated.

"That's no good," the old woman said. "I know. Why don't you come back to my house? We can call them to come get you."

Billy pressed his lips together. "Mmm...my mom says I shouldn't go with strangers. She might get real mad."

"She would be madder if you ended up getting hurt out here without her knowing." The woman motioned towards the quarry. "The ground is weak near the edge. The stones don't hold up well. I've seen quite a few children slip and fall. Break bones. That's why this area's off limits, you know."

"But," Billy began, glancing at the woman, "I wasn't playing near the edge. Just by the train cars...looking for bad guys."

The woman looked Billy up and down, inspecting his cowboy costume. She paused in deep thought, pursing her lips and nodding with a smile.

"Of course you were!" she exclaimed. "You are a very brave sheriff."

Billy's eyes lit up. A smile tugged at the corners of his mouth as he tilted his head to her. The woman crossed her arms with a nod.

"I have a secret," she said. "I know where their hideout is."

"You *do*?"

She nodded again. "But, you'll need a horse. Without one, they'll outrun you for sure."

"A horse?"

"That's right. After all, *real* cowboys have horses."

She wasn't wrong, Billy thought. Every cowboy—good or bad—rode a horse. A living, breathing horse. Not one of their imagination. His bright expression quickly faded into a frown.

"But...I don't know where to get one," he admitted.

The old woman beamed wider, exposing her yellowed teeth. "Not to worry. I have plenty of horses in the pasture by my house. You're more than welcome to have one, Sheriff."

"*Really*?" Billy's eyes grew wide in awe.

"Of course. And while we're there, why don't we call your mother, hm? Let her know you're safe and sound and to come pick you and your new horse up."

There was a moment of hesitation from Billy, but then, he agreed. The woman smirked, holding out her wrinkled hand to him. He took it, skipping along at her side as they made their way out of the trainyard, beyond the tracks leaving town.

The old woman's home was set back in a grove of oaks and firs—nestled on the mountainside. It was a small cottage, surrounded by ferns and freshly fallen leaves. A few toadstools lined the pathway, withering and gnawed away by nature. A perfect backdrop of autumn. Billy trailed behind her, taking in the quiet afternoon. In the distance, he heard birds chirping and trees

rustling. But as he approached the cottage, his heart sank. There was nothing but forest surrounding it. No pasture for his promised horse to be. The woman sensed his disappointment as she made her way up the front steps, fumbling for her keys.

"Not to worry," she said. "I'll get the horses rounded up in a bit and let you take your pick."

As she opened the door, the sweet scent of warm, baked pumpkin billowed from inside. It was heavy with cinnamon and nutmeg, and just a hint of vanilla. Billy couldn't help but draw nearer, stomach growling.

"I've got a pie on," the woman said. "Why don't you come inside? It should be ready any minute."

Billy didn't hesitate. He pushed his cowboy hat back on his head and followed the woman inside.

The taste of sweetened pumpkin was alluring. Billy couldn't help but take bite after bite of the pie. He wiped his mouth on the back of his hand, glancing around the kitchen. Everything was antique. Rustic. As he took another forkful of pie, he forgot about the horses in the pasture. He forgot about the outlaws and the trainyard. And he forgot about being a cowboy. At that moment, all he cared about was the dessert before him.

The old woman made her way back into the kitchen, carrying a heavy pumpkin. She grunted as she set it on the table with a *thud*. Heaving a sigh as she caught her breath, she smiled at Billy.

"I gave your mother a call. She said she'll be on her way soon," she said. "In the meantime, how would you like to help me carve some pumpkins?"

Billy took another bite of pie, looking the pumpkin over. "Sure!"

"I've got plenty of other treats to make. Muffins, cookies, more pies... This pumpkin should be enough for most of them," the woman said.

She dug through her kitchen drawer, pulling out a sharp knife. Looking it over, she nodded in satisfaction and returned to the table. She pressed the tip of the blade into the top of the pumpkin, cutting deep around the stem. Once she completed her circular cut, she set the knife aside and twisted the stem—rocking it back and forth. After a few attempts, it came loose—a string of pumpkin goop hanging from it.

"Digging around in there is hard on these old hands." The woman laughed. "Think you can get all the guts out for me?"

Billy nodded with a grin. Every year, his father carved a jack-o-lantern on Halloween night. Billy drew the face while his father cut, and then, he would get to scoop out the goop inside. It was his favorite part.

Pushing his hands into the pumpkin, Billy felt the cold, wet insides slosh around his fingers. Taking a handful of innards, he gave them a squeeze. They squelched in his grasp. He tugged out fistfuls of the bright orange guck, plopping it on the table beside him. And then, back he went, elbow deep inside the gourd. Digging away at the sticky goop.

The woman watched, a smile tugging at her lips with each pile of orange slop Billy removed. She slipped her hand into one of the wet piles. Feeling around, she gathered a few seeds, pulling them free. Dabbing them with a cloth, she rubbed her thumb against the still moist shells. As Billy set another fistful of innards down, he stopped, watching her in wonder.

"Have you ever tried pumpkin seeds?" the woman asked.

Billy shook his head. He placed his hands on the table, sticky pumpkin guts coating his fingers. The woman's grin drew wider, flashing yellowed teeth and dark, rotting gums. Billy felt a twinge of uneasiness as she held out the pumpkin seeds, urging him to take them.

"Oh, my!" she exclaimed. "Why, they're the best part of carving pumpkins. Little treats to eat while you work. Go on, try them. They're rather tasty."

Billy was hesitant, but took the offered seeds. After all, the pie the old woman had baked was delicious. If something so good could come from a pumpkin, surely the seeds wouldn't disappoint either. He popped the handful into his mouth, slimy goop still clinging to them as he bit down. They were hard to break at first, but once he was able to get through the shells, he could taste their earthy flavor.

He scrunched his nose as he chewed, mashing the sharp edges of the shell, trying to dissolve the stringy pieces of pumpkin. It took a few moments, but eventually, he swallowed.

"Well?" she asked.

"They're...okay," Billy shrugged.

The woman chuckled, wiping her hands on her apron. "They're much better when they're roasted, of course. With a sprinkle of garlic, salt, and paprika. They have a nice crunch to them, and so much flavor."

She headed for the sink, turning on the faucet and letting the water run. And then, she began to hum. Billy paid her no mind, returning his focus to the pumpkin. He pressed his hands back into it, feeling through the goop. His fingers brushed against more seeds—their flat edges rough to the touch. Yet, still he worked, cleaning out what he could of the gourd, until he felt it.

A burning. A twisting.

Billy winced as pain gripped his intestines, slithering up and down his abdomen. It was sharp. Jarring. Like knives turning in his stomach. Sweat beaded on his forehead as he undid the bandana around his neck, using it to dab the drops away. He pressed it tight to his skin to relieve some of the pain. But it kept coming in waves, each one stronger than before. Leaning against the table, Billy groaned.

The old woman turned off the faucet, sipping water from the glass she had poured. Facing the young boy, she watched as he writhed and whimpered, tears pricking at his eyes. A smirk tugged at her lips as she made her way back over to the table. Billy's cheeks were flushed, sweat matting his hair as he struggled to breathe. Sticky hands gripped his stomach, nails digging into his flannel as he begged for the pain to stop.

The old woman placed a gentle hand upon his back, hushing him. "Now, now...it'll all be over soon."

Billy pleaded for help, but she merely stood by and watched. Watched as his body began to convulse. He retched, vomiting a pile of pie and pumpkin seeds onto the table. It reeked of bile and rot, its consistency the same as the goop he had been scooping just moments before. Billy wheezed as he stared at the vomit, feeling his innards twist again. Nauseating heat seared through his guts, as though his insides were being torn apart. Another putrid stream of bright orange expelled from his throat—littered with rotting leaves and bits of twisted vine.

He attempted to beg for help again, but was stopped by thick pressure in his throat. He couldn't swallow, feeling the churning moving up through his chest and towards his mouth. Twisting. Closing his eyes, he fought back tears as the burning tore through him—finally giving him the strength to scream. A scream that was quickly silenced as thick vines erupted from his mouth.

The old woman stood there, smirk growing as a brown tabby jumped onto the counter beside her. He purred softly, nudging his head against her as

she stroked behind his ears. Sliding the pumpkin over to her, she inspected it before turning to the cat.

"What do you think?" she asked. "Another perfect pumpkin for carving. My, how beautiful the patch will be this year."

VII.

THE NEW LIGHT-AND-GLOW PUMPKIN MASKS were all little Greg Feeney talked about. He'd begged his mother and father for one since seeing the televised ads in August. They looped on replay every commercial break, displaying the set of four exciting faces. Greg was adamant on being the jolly pumpkin for Halloween, and he wouldn't settle for anything else.

Though pestered by his younger brother's constant blabbering about the mask, Doug was determined to make him happy. He knew they would be pricey. Everything at Trapp & Co. over the last few years had spiked in price, with the cost of materials and overall demand rising. But still, he saved what he could of his allowance to surprise his little brother with the costume he longed for.

Doug did his best to drown out the boisterous chatter echoing through the Oakridge High cafeteria. Fifth Period was always the busiest lunchtime, and while he normally spent it in the library, his hunger wouldn't allow it that day. He reluctantly gathered his lunch tray, inspecting the crowded tables around him. Everyone had their own cliques—tables pre-planned. And most certainly weren't keen on hosting "outsiders" like himself. When he spotted a vacant seat at the far end of the cafeteria, away from the noise and excitement, he headed there, plopping his tray down.

He peeled open his milk carton before picking at the sticker on his apple. Though hungry, it didn't abate his disappointment in the quality of the school lunch. Like many others in his grade, he agreed it had been on a steady decline. But, at least for the seniors, it would be the last year they'd have to endure it. Doug took a bite of his flat, square slice of pizza, grimacing at the cool temperature and barely melted cheese. A texture comparable to soft cardboard. Swallowing in dissatisfaction, he reached for his apple and took a bite.

"Well, shit."

The shrill voice of Ritchie Buchanan was unmistakable, even through the noisy cafeteria. Doug pushed his glasses onto the bridge of his nose, glancing up as a lunch tray dropped on the table across from him. Ritchie swung his legs over the low stool, seating himself with a grin.

"Is this really Doug Feeney I see?" He rested his elbows on the table, cupping his face in his hands as he inspected Doug. "FYI...you're at *our* table."

Doug gripped the edges of his tray, averting his gaze. Before he could answer, however, three more classmates sat beside him: Theo Williams, Sam Vanderpool, and Peter Harlow.

"It's *fine*," Sam admonished Ritchie, before turning her attention to Doug. "It's not often we see *you* here. Is the library closed?"

"No," Doug replied softly. "I woke up late. Forgot to grab breakfast. I-I can leave if you want. I didn't mean to intrude, I just—"

"Hey, man, don't sweat it," Theo chuckled. "Ritchie's just pulling your chain. You're welcome to sit with us whenever you like."

"Yeah," Ritchie said, gently nudging his elbow into Theo's ribs. "Just because I'm a jock doesn't mean I'm an *asshole*."

"Not all the time, anyway." Theo quipped back with a smirk.

"*Get a room*," Peter teased, picking at the sandwich on his tray.

Doug glanced between the friends, unsure of what to say. As Ritchie leaned across the table again, he merely watched, listening to the conversation.

"Okay, so, Thursday night. We still doing this?"

"Thursday?" Peter asked, taking a bite of his sandwich.

"Yeah. *Thursday*. Don't tell me you forgot already," Ritchie snorted.

Peter chewed his mouthful of food slowly before swallowing. "Hey, I've got a lot coming up so you'll have to remind me."

Ritchie scanned the area to make sure no one could overhear him before speaking through gritted teeth. "*Chapel Hill*."

"What?" Peter leaned in, unable to hear over the loud chatter.

Rolling his eyes, Ritchie brandished a chicken tender at him. A drop of barbecue sauce flung from it, hitting Peter on the upper left cheek. He flinched, closing one eye as Ritchie spoke again—louder this time.

"The *cemetery*."

Peter sat back on his stool, reaching for a napkin, but Sam beat him to it. She gently wiped the splatter of sauce from his cheek, thumb brushing against the dark mole below his eye. She smiled at him softly and then turned back to her salad.

"Midnight, right?" Sam asked.

Ritchie nodded. "Yeah. My dad's on traffic duty that night. He usually leaves around eleven, so that'll give us time for him to be out of the area."

"You picking us up?" Theo asked, sipping his milk.

"No way," Ritchie said. "If the car's missing, my dad will be suspicious. He'll never let me borrow it again. Besides, rolling up and parking a car outside a *closed* cemetery at midnight? Come on now. We're walking."

He bit into his chicken tender, chewing it in thought. After a moment, he snapped his fingers and pulled out his cell phone, waving it at his friends.

91

"Also. No phones," he said. "GPS tracking and all that. Leave them at home."

"What if there's an emergency?" Sam asked, raising an eyebrow.

"There won't be," Ritchie said. "We're just going to be sitting around and telling ghost stories. Besides, if anything gets sketchy, we'll leave. It's not *that* far from home."

Sam rolled her eyes. She dug her fork into her salad, gathering leaves of spinach onto the tines.

"Anything we should bring?" Theo piped up.

"Pumpkins," Sam replied. "Carve them out. We'll need them, so please don't forget."

"You hear that, Peter?" Ritchie asked. "*Pumpkins. Midnight. Thursday.*"

Peter's nose wrinkled as his eyes narrowed. "Yeah. I heard."

Sam glanced at Doug. He sat in silence, eating his lunch, continuing to listen. Chewing her lip in thought, she cleared her throat.

"If...*you're* not doing anything on Thursday, Doug," she began, "you're more than welcome to join us, too."

Doug's face flushed as the conversation turned on him. He shook his head with a meek smile.

"Thank you," he stammered. "But, it's really not my thing."

"Why not?" Ritchie pressed. "You scared?"

Doug tensed. "No. No, I just...I've been trying to spend time with my little brother as much as I can lately. I've been reserving my evenings for him."

"Your little brother?"

Doug nodded. "I got accepted to a university out of state next year. I know it's going to be rough on him, not having me around, so I've been setting aside as much time as I can with him before then."

"Congrats, man." Theo grinned. "You should be proud of yourself."

"Thanks," Doug replied, "but I still feel bad for Greg, you know?"

The apple crunched as Doug bit into it, droplets of juice spraying across his tray. He chewed, deep in thought, before turning to Peter.

"Your dad works for Trapp & Co. right?"

"Yeah? Why?" Peter responded around a mouthful of mustard, slopped from his sandwich.

"Speaking of my brother...you know the new product line for Halloween? The pumpkin masks? They're all Greg's been talking about," Doug said. "They're supposed to launch some time this month, but I haven't

been able to find anything about it. Do you know when that's scheduled for?"

Peter scoffed. "Honestly, I had no idea they were working on masks this year. I don't pay much attention to what my dad does work-wise. Sorry."

He twirled the straw in his carton of milk, raising it to his lips. His eyes remained fixed on the table—not once making contact with Doug. The disappointment in his voice told Peter his hopeful excitement had diminished.

"Oh..."

"I mean, he's *mentioned* something about the thirteenth I think? But I really couldn't tell you," Peter remarked. "Though, if you're in any classes with Alex Trenchard...his dad's pretty high up there. He'd probably have a better idea."

"Alex Trenchard. Isn't he throwing a big Halloween party this year?" Ritchie asked.

"If he is, *I* haven't heard anything about it," Theo said.

"I'll find out," Ritchie replied. "Because if he *is*...that's one we *don't* want to miss."

Ritchie held his hand up, rubbing his thumb and index finger together. He waggled his eyebrows with a toothy grin, Theo shaking his head in response. Peter watched them, finishing what was left of his sandwich before leaning back on his stool.

"I'll ask Alex, then," Doug said. "And if you hear anything more, please let me know. It would mean so much to Greg."

"Sure," Peter said.

"Are your parents going to the product release?" Theo asked.

"I'm planning on going myself," Doug replied.

"*You*?" Ritchie scoffed. "If it's the thirteenth, that's a school day. You'd really give up your perfect attendance since Kindergarten for a stupid *mask*?"

"It's important to Greg, so it's important to *me*," Doug said determinedly.

"Well, if you need any excuses for not being in class, Peter *will* have the info on *those*." Ritchie snickered.

Peter shook his head, folding his napkin over his tray. "Really, though, I can ask my dad and see if he can get one or something. That way you don't have to miss school."

"I appreciate that, but this is something I've already committed to," Doug said. "I just really want to make it special for Greg, you know? I want him to know I care. That going away to college next year isn't me leaving him

for good. So, I'm doing all I can to help him understand that. I imagine the worst feeling in the world is being left behind. Believing you're forgotten. I don't want that for him."

Peter's gaze dropped to his tray. He fell into deep silence as Doug piled his garbage together.

"Greg's really young," he said. "It's hard for him to comprehend everything. I need him to see that me going away doesn't mean I don't care about and love him dearly. Or that he was a burden. I'm just growing up and moving on. It's a part of life. And I want to make the change as easy as possible for him."

Peter sighed heavily, getting to his feet. He fumbled in his pocket, tugging out a single cigarette. Gripping it between trembling fingers, he glanced between his friends, voice shaky.

"I'll see you next period," he said. "I'm...just going for a quick smoke."

Peter hurried into the hall, passing between the cafeteria tables. Sam's eyes softened as she took in his abandoned lunch tray. Doug's smile faded.

"Good luck." Ritchie sneered after Peter. "He's going to get his ass busted again. Where was it last time? In the locker room bathroom during Phys Ed?"

"Was it something I said?" Doug asked sheepishly, looking at Sam.

She shook her head. "No, it's not you."

Sam turned towards the doors to the hallway, staring. Waiting. But Peter never returned. The friends were silent for the remainder of the period, finishing their lunches. Only when the bell rang—vibrating off the concrete walls—did they speak.

"It was nice having lunch with you, Doug," Sam said.

"Yeah, man," Theo added, "you should join us more often."

Doug managed a weak smile. "Yeah, sure."

"Alright," Ritchie said, picking up his tray. "Off to math. See you later."

He flashed a grin before heading for the cafeteria doors, Theo following close behind him. Sam scooped up Peter's tray in addition to hers, walking it over to the garbage can and emptying it. She waved farewell to Doug, before becoming one with the sea of students hurrying to their next class. Doug waved in return, watching until she was no longer visible. Taking a deep breath, he slouched his shoulders, waiting in silence until the cafeteria emptied. Leaving him forgotten amongst the vacant tables and trays.

It was nearly impossible getting into Trapp & Co. on the morning of the thirteenth. Cars lined the streets, and the once neatly filed line turned into a much larger gathering by late morning. While Doug was expecting a big turn out, he hadn't expected *this*. He stayed in the flow of the crowd, managing to get inside and make his way towards the front. The air was hot from how packed it became, his glasses beginning to fog. Slipping them off, he wiped the lenses clean on his shirt, before turning his attention to the podium as the room drew silent.

Paul Trenchard and his assistant Angela greeted the curious crowd, taking their places at the podium. The introduction to the masks dragged on, but it was full of information on their features, safety, and variants. Doug paid attention to as much as he could before his mind began to wander. He glanced across the crowd, focusing on faces and minute details in the corporate building's architecture. Anything to keep his impatience at bay. After a long while, Paul finished his speech—finally presenting the masks.

Doug's eyes lit up when he saw them. As intricate and high-quality as they appeared in the commercials, they were much more exciting in person. Their paint was glossy in the overhead lights, and the glow feature was bright. Realistic. They could have easily been mistaken for an actual jack-o'-lantern. He skimmed the options available: jolly, silly, scary, and sad. When it was time to line up for purchasing, he hurried into the happy mask's queue.

"That'll be $59.95."

Angela presented the cheerful mask to Doug, turning it over and showing off its features up close. It was fresh from the box, still strong with the scent of paint and latex. He looked it over with a nod before pulling a wad of cash from his pocket. He handed it to Angela as she smiled, giving him the mask.

"If you have any questions or concerns, please utilize our feedback line," Angela said. "And we're always in the office Monday through Friday, should you need to stop by."

"Thank you." Doug smiled. "These masks are awesome. My brother is going to be so excited."

He held the mask out, stretching it to see its full display. The material was smooth and soft beneath his fingers. Everything was perfect. Everything, except the heavy scent of paint that became stronger now that he was holding it. Doug glanced at Angela.

"Should I be concerned about the smell?"

Angela pushed her glasses up on her nose, shaking her head. "Not at all. This batch just got back from production this morning. They're fresh off the line, which is why they've still got that new smell to them. Give it a few days to air out and it'll be fine. Certainly by Halloween, anyway."

Doug nodded. "Thanks again."

Tucking the mask inside his backpack, he pushed his way through the crowd still vying for their spots in line. Once outside, back into the chilled autumn air, Doug took a deep breath. His heart pounded in adrenaline fueled excitement. He did it. He got the mask. And missing school for it was worth it.

Now Greg had what he wanted most.

"Is that *real*?"

Greg's voice screeched across the dinner table that evening. The bright, jolly pumpkin mask stared at him from the center—eyes and mouth glowing bright. Doug nudged it over to him, a wide smile spreading across his face.

"Yes, it's real, buddy," he said with a chuckle.

Greg snatched it up, hugging it to his chest as he bounced in his seat. His focus was no longer on his dinner plate, or anything at the table for that matter. All he was interested in now was the mask, gripped tightly in his little hands.

"How'd you manage to get one?" their mother asked suspiciously, setting her fork down.

"I went to the product launch," Doug admitted.

"The launch? When was that? After school?"

Doug shook his head. "Don't be mad. I just...I *had* to do it for Greg."

"*Douglas.*"

Doug's father placed a hand atop their mother's. He hushed her, motioning to their youngest and the joy that had overtaken him.

"Don't worry," Doug said. "I had some classmates take notes for me. Right now, this was more important."

"It's just one day," Doug's father agreed. "Besides, do you know how many times *I* skipped school growing up? Doug's at the top of his class. He has nothing to worry about."

His mother sighed. "I know, I know."

Glancing between her sons, she managed a smile. Greg continued to play with the mask before hopping down from his seat. He hurried over to his mother, eyes bright.

"Mama, can I try it on?" he asked.

"Of course." She watched as Greg hurried towards the living room. "But be *careful* with it, please. Your brother went through a lot of trouble to get that for you. Don't ruin it!"

The front door opened and closed, Greg's squeals of excitement echoing inside. Doug smiled and shook his head, taking another forkful of his dinner. His father patted him on the back, giving him an approving nod.

"You did good, son," he said. "I know you're worried about going away for school next fall...but I promise Greg knows how much you love him. And I can assure you, he loves you just as much."

Doug gazed out the kitchen window, watching his younger brother slip the latex pumpkin mask over his head. His squeals continued as he darted back and forth, scampering through piles of fallen leaves.

"Thanks, Dad."

The air was crisp that evening as Greg played in his front yard. Yet, his mask kept his face warm—shielding the breeze that drifted through the trees, rattling their branches. He dove into a pile of freshly fallen leaves his father had raked earlier that day, sending them scattering across the lawn. His voice trailed throughout the neighborhood—hoots and hollers vibrating off nearby houses. A few times, his mother reminded him that there were others in the neighborhood and to keep it down, but his father stopped her.

"Let him be a kid," he said.

And so, Greg kept up his antics. Caught up in the wild imagination that he was an old scarecrow—searching for his straw hat.

Again, he dove into the leaves, kicking them around. Rummaging with every twist and turn of his body. He'd rise up from the pile, shimmy through it, then throw himself back down—covering himself in the brown, decaying leaves. They were damp, heavy with the scent of mildew. But Greg was unable to smell it. The odor of the paint coating the latex was too strong. To the point that after a while, he felt lightheaded. He pounced into the leaf pile one last time before nestling within them, trying to regain his focus.

The longer Greg laid amongst the pile of leaves, the more everything swirled. Felt dreamlike. Surreal. His head spun, everything swimming as he scanned the front yard. He caught the faint light glowing from inside the house—the flickering television in the living room. But everything felt so far away. A world in slow motion. The sounds of evening began to fade, lost in the distance between himself and reality. All that felt real—close—was the smell. The chemical odor of paint burning his nostrils. Making it hard to see. To hear. To breathe.

That's when the warmth inside the mask became unbearable. Sweat beaded across Greg's forehead, dripping down his face. He tried to pull the mask off, but the condensation made it stick to his skin. Shrink against his neck.

His breaths became panicky as he tugged harder. The more he sweat, the heavier the stench of the paint became. He tried to call out to his mother for help, but his voice was stuck in his throat—smothered by the heat and fumes. The world turned upside down through the eyeholes. His head ached, his throat stung, and his lungs burned.

And then his skin began to burn, as well.

The latex clung tighter as he fell back into the pile of leaves. He gasped for air, feeling the mask folding in on him. Now, it wasn't just his neck it was stuck to. It was his forehead. His nose. His cheeks. And the longer it stayed there, pressed wetly against his skin, the hotter everything became. Searing his flesh. Greg clawed the sides of the mask, yanking as hard as he could as he flailed around in the leaves. When he finally found enough air to scream, it broke through the sickly heat in his throat. Raspy and weak. Filled with fear and pain.

"Mama!"

By the time his parents made it outside, Greg was convulsing. Thick white froth oozed through the mouth hole of the mask, tinged with pink. Doug watched from the porch in horror as they held his little brother in place, prying the mask off him. And though he couldn't see what they did, their screams were enough to send him into his own spiral of fear.

Greg's face was an oozing mess. Blood coated the sagging flaps of skin, slopping in singed layers down his chin. What hadn't been burned away was left inside the mask—clinging in goopy strings to the latex. Ripped clean off when the mask had been removed. Greg wheezed, struggling to find breath. His lidless eyes bulged, staring upwards to the sky.

"*Call 911*!" His father's voice cracked.

Doug did as instructed. His entire body trembled as he waited to be connected to the emergency line, swallowing down the nauseous guilt that engulfed him. When the dispatcher answered, his voice came out monotone. Sullen.

He couldn't look at his parents. Couldn't look at Greg. His eyes remained fixed on the pumpkin mask, discarded in the leaves. It stared back at him—eye and mouth holes glowing in the fading light of dusk. Bloodstained. Dripping with remnants of flesh. Grinning that big, wide jolly pumpkin grin.

VIII.

THE ONLY SOUND IN THE CEMETERY was leaves crunching beneath Peter's feet. They lined the dirt pathways, heavy in piles beneath the bare branches of trees. Darkness blanketed the landscape, making it impossible to see the gravestones in the distance. But still, Peter pressed on. Up towards the flickering light atop the hill, coming from within the old chapel.

His eyes were fixed on it, drawing him closer. An unseen force luring him to the orange glow. The air was cold—thick with the breath of oncoming winter. Peter's teeth chattered as he rubbed his arms for warmth, but comfort didn't come. And while the night was frigid, part of the chill came from the eyes watching in the trees. Those beady black orbs gawking at his every step—hissing into the wind.

Peter, Peter, pumpkin-eater.

Peter swallowed around the lump forming in his throat, peering through the shadows. The darkness stirred, growing thicker as the fog rolled in. His shoulders trembled as he stopped in the middle of the path, the light from the chapel no longer burning. Now, it was silent. Dark. All he could hear was his quivering breath, heavy in the fog. Until, once again, the whispers met him.

From his head, he fed the seeder.

The leaves on the path behind him shifted. Peter held his breath, careful not to make a sound as he slowly glanced over his shoulder. But once more, he was met with only darkness. Shadows.

They crowned him with a pumpkin-shell.

A low growl echoed down the path. In the distance, Peter was able to see them. Two red eyes shining through the black of night. They locked on him as he exhaled, chest heaving in fear.

And dragged him off to rot in Hell.

The trees shook violently as the vultures took off from their branches. He flinched as they circled, eyeing him like a fresh carcass. Gnashing his teeth, he swept his gaze up and down between the path and the sky—eyes surrounding him from all angles.

Peter, Peter, pumpkin-eater,
From his head, he fed the seeder;
They crowned him with a pumpkin-shell,
And dragged him off to rot in Hell.

Padded feet scampered through the leaves. The shadows grew thicker. Colder. Closing in. And in the darkness, all sound vanished. The leaves. His breath. There was nothing in the void. Nothing, except a small flame—flickering at the fringe of the blackness. Relaxing his shoulders, Peter watched it dance.

Peter, Peter, pumpkin-eater...

He took a step forward.

Peter, Peter...

His eyes grew wide as he felt himself pulled along—tugged towards the flame. But this time, there was no fear. There was only peace. A sensation of rest. Once he was close enough to make the candle out—white wax dripping down the sides—he reached for it. It moved towards him, offering itself.

Peter's fingers wrapped around it as another voice called from the void. This one closer. Raspier. Causing the candle flame to flicker with its breath.

What do you desire?

Peter awoke to the sound of glass shattering beside his bed. His tired eyes fluttered open as his arm hit his nightstand, knocking something off. He sat up, blinking back the bright light of late morning that doused his bedroom. A picture frame lay on the floor, fragments of glass sticking out from beneath it. Sighing, Peter picked it up, shaking the photograph free of the frame.

A picture of three smiling faces stared back at him. Loving. Happy. They were positioned before a cake, covered in sparkling candles. Jim stood to the left of the photograph, head turned towards a just turned eleven-year-old Peter in the center. He hardly recognized his younger self as he gazed at the photo. His brown eyes were wide with wonder, dimples prominent as he grinned, clinging tightly to the woman on the right-hand side of the image. Her smile was infectious as she embraced young Peter, pulling him close. He stared at her features, chewing his lip. After a moment, he cleared his throat, setting the photograph on his nightstand—face down, so the words on the back could be seen: MARCH 3rd - PETEY'S 11th BIRTHDAY.

Peter heaved a sigh as his gaze fell on what was set beside the picture—the painted face of the Fool. He didn't bother picking the card up, but he didn't look away. He took in every last detail, down to the rays of sun bathing the joyful Fool. His attention was only drawn away when he heard that familiar meow again. Coming from his window.

The skinny black cat was perched on the sill, staring at Peter as he had done for weeks. Peter groaned, gritting his teeth. His attempts to return it to where he first encountered it had failed. Clearly, there was nowhere else the cat would rather be than at his house. Pawing to be let in. But Peter wouldn't have it. Getting to his feet, careful to avoid the broken glass, he closed the curtains.

"Not today..." He growled.

As he turned back to his bed, however, Peter noticed a large carpenter ant hurrying along the inside sill. Its legs and antennae twitched, black body sleek in the light. Sneering, Peter smashed it with his thumb, feeling its thick body pop beneath the pressure. The ant writhed for a moment before it shriveled and became still. Peter wiped his hand on his pajama pants, staring at the lifeless body of the insect in disgust. Where there was one, there were certain to be more. Cursing, he gathered his change of clothes and headed towards the living room.

"You're up late." Jim closed the cover of the book he was reading as he leaned back in his armchair. "Still not sleeping well?"

Peter stood by the front door, eyes on the floor as he shook his head. He ran his fingers through his hair, tucking a few unruly strands behind his ear. He felt his father's concerned gaze from across the living room—grating on him.

"What's wrong?"

"Just nightmares," Peter replied. "I keep having them. And that damn cat. He's still coming around."

"He followed you back here *again*?"

Peter nodded. "I don't know what to do anymore."

"Have you tried melatonin?" Jim asked. "I *do* have sleeping pills in the cabinet if you need them. Not on a school night, of course...but maybe on the weekends try and see if they'll help."

Peter's lips drew into a hard frown. "So, medicate me again. Got it."

"No, not *medicate* you, Peter. I'm just trying to find ways to help you sleep. You look like a zombie crawling around here anymore."

"Perfect. Halloween's next week. Lay me out on the lawn." Peter sneered sarcastically.

Jim placed his book on the stand beside him, pressing his glasses up against the bridge of his nose. He breathed a heavy sigh.

"How about drinking some chamomile tea before bed, then? It's supposed to help."

"Yeah. Sure."

Jim didn't say anything more on the matter. He kept his focus on his son, watching as he plucked at the cuffs of his flannel shirt. Peter still didn't make eye contact, gaze lost across the room at the ticking grandfather clock in the corner. Managing a defeated smile, Jim stretched and got to his feet.

"Waiting for something?" he asked.

"Ritchie," Peter said. "We're going to the diner. Sorry. Thought I already told you."

"No, it's alright," Jim replied, approaching Peter. "I just like to know where you are. With everything happening right now—all those kids going missing—I want you to be safe, Petey."

Peter bit his lip. He tensed as his father wrapped an arm around his shoulder. Jim passed him a sad look, patting his arm gently.

"No secrets. We promised each other that, right?"

"Right..."

As they stood in silence, Peter's gaze slipped to the wall beside the clock. The black body of an ant scurried across it. His eyes narrowed as he shrugged his shoulder from his father's touch, pointing towards it.

"There's an ant," he said. "I found one in my room, too."

"They're probably coming in from the rain." Jim shook his head. "I'll set some traps out. We don't need those eating away at the woodwork. They're destructive in hordes."

Beep, beep, beep.

Peter turned to the doorway, spotting the familiar black Mustang convertible parked by the road. Ritchie and Theo took up the front two seats, Sam in the back. With the top down, he could hear their laughter even from inside the house, followed by Ritchie's shrill voice.

"*Hey, Peter!*"

"I gotta go," Peter said.

"Be careful. Love you."

Peter didn't respond. Slipping his dirty and worn Converse on, he hurried out the door. The crisp air was a relief as he took a deep breath, leaving the stuffiness of his home behind. Pushing his hands into his pockets, he started towards the car, spotting the black cat still perched outside his window. It stretched in the late morning sun, lying down on the sill. Peter ignored it as he approached the car, hopping into the back.

"I see your dad let you take the *good* car," he said with a smirk.

Ritchie chuckled. "He knows I wouldn't be caught *dead* with the jalopy."

"Be grateful he lends you a car at *all*," Sam remarked, twirling a strand of hair around her finger.

Ritchie waved her off, checking to make sure Peter was buckled before putting the car into drive. As it rolled away from the house, the cat on the windowsill sat up—tail twitching. It watched as Peter glanced back to it, their eyes locking before the vehicle disappeared down the street.

The diner was littered with cheap Halloween décor. Bat and pumpkin garland was strung across the walls, coupled with black and orange streamers. Dollar store ghosts hung from the vents—twirling with each blast of heat. Even the counter was fully decorated. A light up jack-o'-lantern was situated beside the register, stringy polyester cobwebs stretched sloppily across the front. From the speakers, the radio churned out seasonal songs—an old mix of every Halloween party's standards.

While the diner was packed, the group of friends managed to find a booth in the back corner. Away from the noisy families out to lunch. When their food and milkshakes arrived, they clinked their glasses together—toasting the weekend. And Oakridge's big win against Springfield.

"Coach Harrison can chill out for the rest of the season now." Theo chuckled.

"You're telling *me*," Ritchie said. "He's been up our asses all month."

He took a sip of his strawberry shake, eyeing the orange and black spider sprinkles atop the whipped cream. Licking his lips clean, he glanced at the other tables and booths.

"They really decked this place out, huh?"

"I'm glad. Too many places are cutting back on Halloween anymore," Sam said, picking one of the fries from her plate and dipping it in her vanilla shake.

Peter watched her from the corner of his eye as he sucked the thick chocolate shake through his straw. Ritchie scoffed at Sam's comment, grabbing the ketchup bottle beside the window.

"This whole *town* might be cutting back if things keep going the way they are," he said.

He gave the glass bottle a whack, splashing a pile of ketchup over his fries. Grabbing a forkful, he stuffed them into his mouth and chewed in annoyance.

"Is your dad talking about an earlier curfew this year?" Theo asked.

"Not just a curfew," Ritchie said around a mouthful of food. "Canceling Halloween all together."

"*Fuck* that, man."

"Do you think they'd really do that?" Peter asked, reaching for the ketchup bottle.

"From what I've been hearing, absolutely." Ritchie leaned forward, keeping his voice low. "Did you hear about Chrissy, Linda, and Tasha?"

"The cheerleaders?" Sam asked.

Ritchie nodded. "They all went missing. No one's seen them for days."

"The cheer squad could hardly do their routines Thursday night," Theo said. "That's how we found out. They made an announcement if anyone's seen them to let the police know."

"I'll bet it's cougars." Ritchie snorted.

"*Cougars*?" Theo raised an eyebrow. "I've never heard of them coming into town before."

"That doesn't mean anything," Ritchie said. "There have been more sightings of them up the mountain this year than usual."

"I don't know, man." Theo muttered.

Peter took a bite of his cheeseburger, chewing thoughtfully. His eyes strayed across the table, fixing on Ritchie's varsity jacket, taking in the conversation. The talk of more kids going missing—now from their class.

"Weren't you and Linda supposed to be going to Homecoming together?" Sam asked, turning to Ritchie.

He shrugged, taking a long sip of his milkshake. "Yeah. I mean, no disrespect to her...I hope she's okay and I hope they find her...but, to be honest, I'm relieved."

Sam raised an eyebrow. Silence befell the table as Ritchie glanced at Theo. He let it linger for a moment before turning back to Peter and Sam, shrugging again.

"Everyone expects the quarterback and cheer captain to go to Homecoming together, you know? At least, now I don't have to put on an act."

Theo twirled the straw in his chocolate shake, pursing his lips. As Ritchie stabbed another forkful of fries, Sam placed a hand atop his, lowering it back to the plate.

"You shouldn't *have* to," she said softly.

"It's school politics," Ritchie shrugged. "Tradition. You have to play along to survive. You know how it is."

"Like hanging witches..." Peter said, gaze lost beyond the window—amongst the traffic of Saturday afternoon. "How little we've changed."

He cleared his throat, blinking back the tired haze in his eyes as he returned to his plate. Picking up a single fry, he took a bite. The chatter throughout the diner grew louder, becoming more lively as more patrons made their way in for lunch. Peter drew his attention to the other tables, trying to pick out idle conversation. A cue he could borrow to lighten the mood. But Sam beat him to it. Her fingertips brushed across his knuckles, causing him to flinch.

"You look tired," she said worriedly. "Is everything alright?"

"I'm still not sleeping," Peter replied. "My nightmares have been getting worse."

"It's been a few weeks now, hasn't it?" Theo asked.

Peter nodded. "Ever since we came back from the cemetery that night."

Ritchie grabbed a toothpick from the holder on the table, scraping it between his teeth. When he was done, he pushed it to the side of his mouth, flicking it with his tongue as he smirked.

"Oh?" He rested his elbows on the table. "Maybe it's the Devil. You should ask him for a refund, since you bombed that Chemistry test. Tell him he only gets a quarter of your soul."

Peter rolled his eyes. Peering out the window again, he watched the breeze scatter browning, decayed leaves down the street. Cars honked in the distance, echoing through the brisk afternoon air. With a sigh, he faced his friends again.

"And that cat keeps coming around."

"Cat?" Theo raised an eyebrow.

"Yeah. The night we went to the cemetery, while I was waiting for you guys, this black cat came out of nowhere. It wanted attention but I shooed it

off," Peter said. "Ever since then, it's been hanging around my house. It must have followed me home."

"So, why don't you just dump it at the cemetery then?" Ritchie asked, twirling the toothpick with his tongue.

"I tried," Peter said. "But it's back again."

He ran his fingers through his hair, closing his eyes. They were heavy, full of exhaustion. The corners of his mouth turned down into a harsh frown as he shook his head.

"It's either the cat waking me up every night or my dreams."

"What are your dreams about?" Sam asked after a moment.

"Lots of things," Peter said. "Cats. Vultures. The cemetery..."

"I'll bet you it's fear," Ritchie said, crossing his arms and sitting back in the booth.

Peter parted his lips, watching him pull the toothpick from his mouth, setting it on his plate.

"Going out to the cemetery. Listening to scary stories," he continued. "Is that it? Got Old John and the Devil on your mind?"

"You know I don't give a—"

"Hey," Ritchie interrupted, snapping his fingers. "How about we go back up there?"

"*Now*?" Sam asked, cocking an eyebrow.

"Yeah. Before the sun goes down," Ritchie said. "Maybe it'll help get Peter's mind off everything. Being back up there in the daylight should calm his nerves."

Sam looked at Peter. "Is...that something *you* want to do?"

He ran his fingertips against the tines of his fork, thinking of his dreams. Of the vultures circling. Of the fire on the hill. Of the dancing cats. He thought of the words whispered to him. Words that echoed through his waking mind. *What do you desire?* Darkness began to swim at the corners of his vision, a chill tingling across his skin. His breath grew rapid, a cat's meow filling his head, causing him to flinch.

"Peter?"

Peter, Peter...

"Peter?" Sam's concerned voice broke through his thoughts, snapping him back to the diner. "Are you okay...?"

He swallowed around the quivering lump growing in his throat. "Yeah. Yeah, no. I'm down. Let's go."

"Are you *sure*?"

Peter nodded, avoiding her gaze. He got to his feet, stepping out of the booth. With a sigh, Sam pushed her plate to the center of the table. Settling the check and leaving their tips, the friends headed back to Ritchie's car. As it pulled away from the little diner, towards Chapel Hill, Peter's stomach churned. In the distance, a wake of vultures circled.

Ritchie parked the car outside the old, rusted gates of the cemetery. Beyond them, the bright colors of autumn shimmered vibrantly in the trees—a welcoming array of dirty gold and amber. In the daylight, it was nothing like the shadowed, stony void night made it appear to be. Stepping out of the car, the friends breathed in the crisp air, listening to the leaves rustle in the breeze.

They headed through the gates, down the dirt path, until they reached the fork in the center of the cemetery. Peter came to a stop in the middle, looking down each path before him. Wind tossed the leaves as he listened, waiting for a haunting whisper to join in. The whispers from his nightmares. But he was only met with the peaceful sounds of autumn. He tensed, watching Ritchie ascend the hill towards the chapel and the old tree. With a trembling exhale, he followed.

While much of the cemetery looked different under the sun, the friends noticed something that hadn't been there weeks prior. From the withering stones sprouted thick vines—pumpkins protruding from the earth. They were at every gravesite. Bright. Plump. Peter's heart raced as he stared, tracing them up the hill—to the base of the twisted tree.

"What's with all the pumpkins?" Theo asked as he, too, peered across the endlessness. "It looks like a full on *patch* up here."

"These weren't here before...were they?" Sam asked, voice low.

"How should *I* know?" Ritchie snorted. "It was dark. The only pumpkins I gave a rat's ass about were the ones *you* made us bring up here, Sam."

"They couldn't have grown *that* fast..." Sam muttered. "It's not possible."

Ritchie took a seat beneath the tree, resting his head against the trunk. He gazed through the bare branches, admiring the blue skies above. How much brighter they appeared against the colors of autumn. As his friends gathered around, getting comfortable, he smirked at Peter.

"So, feeling any better?"

"Not really." Peter mumbled, lighting a cigarette and sticking it between his teeth.

He took a long drag before exhaling a thick cloud of smoke. The ash burned his tongue, but the rush of nicotine eased his tense shoulders. Puffing again, he turned his attention to Ritchie.

"I feel like I'm cursed." He managed a weak laugh. "It's so stupid."

"It's not stupid, man," Theo said. "I mean, you said all this started happening after we were up here, right? I know it's supposed to be just a story, but...you *were* the one who sat on the throne."

Ritchie cocked his head. "You said you wanted to pass your Chemistry test. Heaven knows you didn't... Did you wish for something else?"

"What?" Peter covered his mouth, choking on smoke.

"Of course he *didn't*," Theo said. "We all heard him loud and clear."

"No," Ritchie said, eyes locked on Peter. "To *himself*."

"What on earth would I wish for?" Peter asked. "Besides, you don't believe this stuff. It's all a joke to you."

"It's not about what *I* believe," Ritchie said. "It's about what *you* believe. So. *Do* you believe? I know Sam does."

"I believe there's truth in superstition. Fate. Magic. *Ghosts*. But the *Devil*?" Sam shook her head.

"Well I'll be damned." Ritchie flashed a toothy grin. "And here you dragged our sorry asses up here, making us think—"

"You don't think the Devil's real?" Theo interrupted him softly, turning to Sam.

"Not the Devil, no. The Devil is something humanity created to cast their blame on. Their fears. A scapegoat, if you will. See, the problem with humanity is we can never own up to our flaws. The wrongs we did. We only take credit for the good. We want the praise. But we look for any excuse to not have to answer to our sins. To not have to face up to accountability. We're so quick to blame things on the Devil. To blame those we believe to be *of* the Devil. But really, he hides among humanity itself. So, no. I *don't* believe in the Devil. But I *do* believe in the story of Old John." Sam gazed up into the branches of the tree, admiring the twisted bark. "I believe John, in his drunken state and down on his luck, did something he regretted. But he couldn't own up to it. And I believe that, yes, he said he saw the Devil. But the Devil was just a mirror of himself. A manifestation of his guilt. His fear. A truth he couldn't live with—of being the town fool. One which led him to his fate that night."

She ran her fingers through her violet hair, tucking a few strands behind her ear. Then, she turned her attention to Peter. His lips were pressed together, cigarette burning to ash between his fingers.

"It's a scary story to tell around Halloween. A parable on guilt. Fear and all of what happens when we let it eat away at us. It drives us to the darkness. Makes us wallow and wander alone in the void. How empty and devastating it is." Sam shook her head. "But, that's all the Devil is. A lesson."

"See." Ritchie snorted. "I *knew* it was bullshit."

"Not *all* of it," Sam retorted. "What happened to John Barker is very real. He *was* the town fool, so overburdened by it that he drank himself stupid. That he came up here on Halloween night and hanged himself from this tree. There's always fact in fiction, Ritchie. Stories change over time, but they're never forgotten. You just have to dig through the dirt to find the truth."

Theo clapped Peter on the back, causing him to flinch. He looked up at his friend, watching as he sat against the trunk beside Ritchie.

"Well, there you have it," he said. "Maybe Ritchie is right. It's fear that's got you up at night. Guilt, even. Because we almost got busted big time."

"It's not that," Peter said. "You all know me... When in my life have I *ever* given a shit if I got caught?"

"Then what else did you do?" Ritchie asked, leaning forward. "Come on now. Whatever it is must be pretty bad."

"I didn't *do anything*!"

Peter got to his feet, dropping his cigarette and crushing it beneath his shoe. The exhaustion in his eyes was prominent now—lined with puffy red bags. His breath trembled as he glared at Ritchie. The smile on his friend's face vanished.

"I just want to know who *damned* me." Peter choked.

Sam reached up and gently touched his hand. For the first time, he didn't flinch. She locked her fingers with his, guiding him to sit back down. Before her, laying across the tree roots, were a fan of tarot cards. These cards, however, were different from the ones she had the week prior. She bit her lip, looking Peter over intently, before pulling four random cards from the pile.

"Relax," she whispered to him, turning them over one by one.

THE WHEEL OF FORTUNE.

9 OF SWORDS.

5 OF CUPS.

THE FOOL.

Peter stared at the imagery on the cards. The Wheel was, for the most part, bright. Winged animals adorned the corners, hovering in ethereal skies. It took him a moment to notice the bright red Devil that held the Wheel on his back. Upon seeing it, he shifted his gaze to the next. A young man sat up in bed, surrounded by darkness and nine blades above his head. He wept uncontrollably into his hands—tormented by shadows. The next was a simple card. A figure cloaked in black stood in a barren wasteland, five empty and shattered chalices at his feet. He looked broken. Hollow. The final card made him pause, clenching his jaw as he spotted the familiar Fool reaching towards the sunlight. The Fool that sat on the nightstand beside his bed. Ritchie snickered when he saw it.

"Oh, look. It's Peter again."

"*Shut up*," Peter snapped.

Sam pondered each card, from the Wheel to the Fool and the cloaked man and the sobbing man. Readjusting the order of them, she laid them out to illustrate.

"So, looking at this," she said, "I think they're meant to be read backwards."

"Backwards?" Peter asked.

Sam nodded. "Right. So, we *start* with The Fool. That's you. That's your journey. New beginnings. Then, we have the 5 of Cups. This one is about loss and sorrow. Being stuck in the past, unable to move forward. Something holding you back."

Peter stared blankly at the card. He pursed his lips as Sam moved on to the next.

"Then, the 9 of Swords. Nightmares. Distress. Things plaguing your wellbeing. And finally, the Wheel of Fortune. Fate. The future. A crossroad."

"And, what does that all mean?" Peter asked.

"That you worry too much," Sam said. "You're under a lot of stress this year. Graduating is the big one. You have the potential to do great—to get to that cliffside. To feel the sun. But, you're letting the past drag you down. Hold you back. You're caught up on things that are over and done, things out of your control. Thoughts of not being good enough, of being trapped in this town. Never moving on, never amounting to anything. You're not letting yourself have the future you deserve. But, the thing is, *you* get to spin that wheel. You can either repeat the past, stay stuck here forever, or head towards the hill."

"But it's all the same in the end. Whether I graduate or not, I'm still stuck here. Left behind to rot in this godforsaken town. I'm not going *anywhere*. But, *you* all are..."

"And *you* can, too. You just have to have faith. There's light out there in the darkness, you know. You just have to let it in."

Peter locked his gaze on the Fool. Sam gently took his hand, giving it a light squeeze.

"Bottom line...you're losing sleep because you're overthinking."

"And you *really* needed *cards* to tell you that?" Ritchie scoffed.

"Better than you blaming the *Devil*, Ritchie."

He raised his hands in surrender. Getting to his feet, he gazed out across the crumbling headstones and pumpkins growing around them. The breeze rustled the leaves of nearby trees, branches creaking overhead. As he turned back to his friends, about to speak, a brash voice echoed from the dirt path. The friends tensed as a figure rose over the hill.

"*Fuck*," Ritchie breathed.

Horace Johnson was drenched in sweat, visibly shaking as he approached the tree. His greasy hair was slicked back, eyes bitter and blazing. He glared at each of the teens, stopping as his gaze fell on Peter. Gnashing his teeth, he stabbed a crooked, trembling finger towards him.

"*You*." He hissed. "I *knew* you were trouble."

"Hey now," Ritchie said, approaching Horace with his hands up. "We're not doing anything, okay? We're *allowed* to be here. Your hours are posted on the gate."

"Quiet yourself, Buchanan," Horace snapped. "Or I'll have your father up here in a heartbeat."

"For *what*?" Ritchie scoffed. "How do you know I'm not paying respects? Are you going to deny me my grief?"

Horace ignored Ritchie's sarcastic comments, turning his attention back on Peter. His arms were now wrapped around his knees, peering out from behind Sam.

"I knew I should have called the police when I saw you the other morning," Horace said. "Riding your bike out here at sunrise. *Trespassing*."

Sam turned to Peter with a raised eyebrow. His lips were drawn into an uneasy frown, a lump forming in his throat. He tried to swallow it, searching for words.

"I...I didn't do anything," he said weakly.

"Didn't *do* anything?" Horace snarled, hands curling into fists. "You killed my *fucking ducks.*"

"*No I didn't.*" Peter spat in defense, eyes narrowing.

"Don't lie to me, you little *shit.*" Horace stepped towards Peter.

"Hey, man. Let's chill for a second," Theo said, stepping between them. "Peter wouldn't kill *anything.* I think you've got the wrong kid."

Horace shook his head. "I know a *hoodlum* when I see one."

Peter rose to his feet, knees trembling. He rubbed the dirt from his palms against his jeans, watching the groundskeeper carefully. Again, he pointed his finger at Peter—this time, angrier. Sharper.

"And not just my ducks. That cat, too."

"*Cat*?" Peter's voice cracked.

"I saw you bring it here the other day, stuffed in a bloody pillowcase," Horace said. "It's been missing, you know? The old woman by the quarry? It's one of hers. She was out here looking for it and I told her I'd let her know if I saw anything. And, sure enough, I did. And not something anyone would *ever* want to see."

"What do you *mean*?" Peter choked. "It's been at my house every day for the last few weeks. It was there *this morning*."

"Cut the shit," Horace said. "I *found* that cat on my morning patrol the other day. Found it *hanging* in this tree. Strung up by its neck."

Peter's heart pounded as hot, angry tears burned his eyes. He parted his quivering lips, shaking his head in disbelief.

"That's...that's not poss—"

"Its *tongue was cut out*!"

The tears spilled over. A few ran down Peter's cheeks as he shook his head violently, gritting his teeth. His breathing grew erratic as Sam wrapped an arm around his shoulders, pulling him in, trying to calm him. But it was useless. All he saw were flashes from his nightmares—the dancing cats. Circling the tree. And then, their lifeless bodies, swaying in the branches.

"That's not *possible*..." He blubbered again.

"And I know you've been out here at night. I've heard footsteps, seen fires by the tree. By the chapel. Found all these *fucking* pumpkins." The veins in Horace's neck bulged as he shoved Theo out of the way, getting into Peter's face. "Lie all you want, but this place has eyes. And you can't hide from what they've seen."

Peter swallowed a quivering breath as his gaze slipped to the branches of the surrounding trees. The leaves rustled as black shapes shifted—feathers

117

ruffling. Talons scraping. Beady eyes peered out from between the amber foliage. Watching.

"I've already filed a report with the police," Horace said. "They can't do much without solid proof, but they'll be questioning everything. And every time I catch you up here, I'll be calling. You can be sure of that."

Clenching his fists, Horace backed away. He returned down the path towards his home, not looking back. When he was out of sight, Ritchie spat on the ground, turning to Peter. Sam's hand tightly gripped his arm, Theo joining and placing a hand on his shoulder. His eyes were puffy and redder than before, still wet with anger. Frustration.

"Don't sweat it," Ritchie said. "My dad knows you're not that kind of person. Let that greasy asshole spew his empty threats and waste the police's time. They're not going to be happy about it."

"I didn't kill *anything*..." Peter mumbled.

"We know you didn't," Sam assured him. "You would never."

"It was there this morning," Peter said, eyes glazed over as he stared across the cemetery. "The cat. It was there this morning, outside my window. It has been. *Every single day*."

He pressed his fingertips to his forehead, brushing his dark, tousled bangs to the side. His stomach turned as he thought of its slender body soaking up the sun before he left. Whiskers outstretched. Mewling for attention. And then, the thought of its mutilated body swaying from the bare branches. An image from his nightmares. Closing his eyes, he choked back a sob. His friends embraced him, holding him close.

"I didn't do it..."

No one spoke as they made their way back down the path, towards the fork marked THIS WAY OUT. Peter's head spun as he dragged his feet, wanting nothing more than to go home. To try and sleep the rest of the day away. Sleep as much as his nightmares would let him.

The blue skies turned to gray as the afternoon went on, bringing a deeper chill with it. On the horizon, the smell of rain lingered. The friends picked up their pace with the change in the wind, hurrying through the groves of stone and patches of pumpkins. Ritchie stopped, however, when he caught the scent of something putrid. It wafted in on the breeze, causing him to wrinkle his nose in disgust.

"Do you guys smell that?"

Before the others could answer, Ritchie spotted something he hadn't before. Not their first night there, nor on their way up the hill earlier. Three scarecrows, posted amongst the graves. Tattered. Rotten. Buzzing with flies.

"*Blegh*!" He gagged, plugging his nose.

The others stood back, faces contorted in repulsion as he slowly approached his discovery. The flies grew louder—mixed with the sounds of churning maggots and ants. His stomach lurched as he dry heaved, unable to get any closer.

"What the *fuck*."

"Are those...scarecrows?" Sam asked, covering her nose and mouth.

"They smell like *corpses*." Theo stifled.

"I wouldn't be surprised if they *were*," Ritchie said, waving away the flies that swarmed the air.

The burlap covering the scarecrows was coated in dried mud and mildew. It was frayed, insects wriggling through the material, gnawing away at it. Ritchie could make out rotten pumpkin guts oozing between the layers—stringy and hanging. Covered in moldy seeds. He wrinkled his face and stepped back, shaking his head.

"These things are rotting from the inside out," he said. "They look like they were made from pumpkins. I'll bet someone put them up here last month and the crows have been feasting on them. With all the rain we've had...they've gotten moldy and decayed."

"That's what Horace *should* be concerning himself with," Theo said. "I know it's a cemetery, but that doesn't mean it has to *reek* like death."

Sam glanced at Peter, noticing he wasn't paying attention to the scarecrows. His eyes were fixed on the ground, empty and glazed over. Even the smell didn't seem to bother him. She rested a hand on his upper arm, frowning as he yanked it out of her grasp.

"Come on. Let's get out of here," she said to the others, starting towards the exit.

Peter and Theo followed behind, but Ritchie took another look at the scarecrows. The flies swarmed their large, burlap covered pumpkin heads. But the more he looked, the more he swore one looked familiar.

"*Linda?*"

As he leaned in, attempting to get a better look, a high-pitched hiss erupted from the head. From the burlap and rotting pumpkin slithered a centipede—legs twitching as it crawled through the infestation of flies. Taking a heavy breath, Ritchie stepped away, following his friends to the cemetery gates.

"Try not to think about it," Sam said to Peter as they stepped onto the sidewalk.

"For real, man. You know Horace Johnson is just an angry old man looking for any excuse to take it out on us," Theo added. "Besides, Ritchie's not going to let his dad do anything to you. Everything's going to be okay."

Peter said nothing. He shoved his hands into his pockets, shoulders slumping. The clouds were darker than before now, leaves turning themselves over in the trees. He could feel the storm approaching.

"I'll see you later," he said softly, not bothering to look back at his friends.

They stood in silence as he crossed the street, slow and somber. Sam gripped the strap of her bag tightly as she sighed. Bidding Theo and Ritchie farewell, she, too, headed home. Once she had crossed the street, out of sight, Theo turned to Ritchie. Both of them remained still, mulling over their thoughts.

"Do you think...?" Theo trailed, staring up into the storm clouds.

"What? That Peter actually did it?" Ritchie asked. "I mean...he said he hasn't been sleeping."

"And the groundskeeper *did* say he heard footsteps at night. Seen fires. Seen *Peter*... You think he's sleepwalking?"

Ritchie chewed his lip. "Maybe."

Theo took a deep breath. "You know...I never saw a cat."

"Hm?"

"Peter said he saw it the night we were first up here. Has seen it every day at his house since. Saw it this *morning*." Theo shook his head. "But I didn't see a cat today. Did you?"

Ritchie stared at him. "No."

"If what the groundskeeper is saying is true, there definitely *was* a cat. But I know for a fact I didn't see one when we picked him up."

"So...you think Peter's lying?"

"I don't *want* to think such things, but..."

"But what if he *did* do it?"

The two stood in silence, a few drops of cold rain falling on them. Rubbing their shoulders for warmth, they ventured back to the car. As it pulled away from the curb, Horace Johnson watched from his window. Eyes as dark as the skies.

Peter hurried to the bathroom when he returned home. He tore open the medicine cabinet above the sink, rummaging through pill bottles until he found the one he was looking for. SLEEPING PILLS. Peter twisted the cap off, hands trembling. The little, oval pills spilled out, *clanking* in the sink as he cursed aloud. Gathering what he could and returning them to their bottle, Peter popped one into his mouth. Washing it down with a glass of water, he headed for his bedroom.

"Petey?"

Jim's voice carried down the hallway, but he was met with bitter silence. Seeing Peter's door shut, he didn't bother to try for conversation. Heading back to the living room, he left his son to the quiet and privacy of his bedroom.

The rain fell hard against the windowsill, the darkness of the storm bleeding across the walls. For once, however, Peter found the shadows

inviting. They eased the tiredness behind his eyes, luring him towards sleep as the pill kicked in. Rhythmic drops beat against the glass, losing him in their symphony. Yet, somewhere out there, in the *pitter-patter* of the rain, he swore it was calling his name.

Pe-

-ter

Pe-

-ter

Pitter-patter.

Peter-Peter.

His eyelids grew heavy. Darkness tunneled at the corners of his vision as he nestled beneath the covers. He pulled the comforter up to his chin, burrowing into his pillow and sighing in exhaustion. Still focused on the rain.

Pe-

-ter

Pe-

-ter

It wasn't long before his eyes closed and he drifted off to sleep. A sleep he had been without for nights. Yet, even as he fell under, he found himself searching. Listening. Hoping to hear the scraping of tiny claws. The tapping of padded paws. The adamant mewls. Any sign of that skinny black cat that tormented him night after night.

But for the first time in weeks, it never came.

IX.

PAUL TRENCHARD WAS BAFFLED by the number of cars lining the streets outside Trapp & Co. that morning. The sidewalk and lobby were almost as full as they had been only days prior—at the launch of the Light-and-Glow Pumpkin Masks. But as he stepped out of his car, making his way inside the building through the crowd, the excitement from the thirteenth wasn't there. This crowd was sullen. Inconsolable. Angry eyes and bitter words pelted him.

"*You* did this!"

"You promised our children would be *safe*!"

125

Paul made his way through the sea of outraged parents, breaking past the security point and beelining for his office. His head spun, the nasty words following him down the long hallway until he reached the elevator at the end. Scanning his keycard, he swallowed his anxiety and stabbed the Floor 3 button. The doors shut, muffling the buzzing crowd as the elevator ascended.

"It's the paint," Angela said solemnly, clicking her pen repeatedly against her clipboard.

"The *paint*?"

Paul kept his head in his hands, elbows resting upon his desk. Floors down, he could still make out the hollers and demands of hysterical families. He shut his eyes, taking a deep breath before glancing at Angela.

"What exactly happened?"

"Some children were hurt by the masks," she said softly. "They were burned. Some sort of chemical reaction or something. Most of them are alright. They were treated quickly enough... But a few of them..."

She bit her lip and looked away. Her glasses slid down her nose as she tried to collect herself, gripping her clipboard tightly.

"Some are in awful condition," she said. "Their skin completely melted off. And one little boy..."

Angela shook her head. Paul watched on in horror as she turned to face him, tears welling in her eyes.

"He didn't make it..."

Paul sat back in his seat, wilting. The room spun as he tried to gather his thoughts and drown out the sounds downstairs. They grew louder with demands to speak to the CEO. Demands to speak with *him*. Swallowing the growing lump in his throat, he passed his gaze back to Angela.

"And you said it's the paint?" he repeated. "I want to be sure I'm hearing that right."

"Yes," Angela nodded. "I don't understand it, though. We sent the prototypes in and had them tested. There was no reaction to them. Employees tried them on. Test subjects... It just doesn't add up."

Paul sat in deep thought. "And that's the paint we used on the final product, yes?"

"It has to be," Angela said. "We didn't approve anything else. I mean, unless Mr. Trapp changed something after the order was placed. But, why would he?"

"Cost."

Paul got to his feet, turning his back on her. He stared into the gray skies out his large windows, lips drawing into a frown as he sighed.

"Can you run me an order report?" he asked. "Get all the details and specifics. Find out *exactly* what was ordered for the prototypes, and what was ordered for the mass production. I want to see if there are any inconsistencies."

Angela nodded. "Of course."

She hurried out of the office to retrieve what Paul requested. He took a heavy breath before picking up his desk phone. Dialing the extension, he waited until the voice at the other end answered.

"Get me Fred."

The conference room was dim as the executive staff gathered to discuss their findings. They kept the overhead lights off, staying as secretive as they could in case anyone happened to come by. Happened to break past security. Once seated, Angela handed her file to Paul, lips tight.

The room was silent as Paul opened and read the report. From what he could make out, the prototype order and final production order mirrored one another. They were from the same molds, the same latex, and the same paints. He couldn't find anything that stood out. Anything that could have caused such horrific damage. As he scanned the report once more, however, he stopped as something *did* catch his eye. Not the latex. Not the paint.

It was the sealant.

The original order for the prototypes was more costly, but it was one that was standard. Guaranteed for safety. The order for final production, however, was a far cheaper option—one combined with paint thinner to allow it to smooth and seal. Paul held his breath, clutching the papers in his hands. He frowned at Fred Lazzaro, the Chief Compliance Officer.

"Corners were cut," was all Paul could say.

Fred heaved a sigh. "The paint?"

"The *sealant*. From the report, it looks like a cheaper alternative was used. It required a combination of chemicals to get it to have the same effect. It must have caused a reaction."

The staff looked between one another, whispering urgently. Fred pinched the bridge of his nose, contemplating the situation. Even from the conference room, the wails of grieving and angry parents reached their ears. Paul stared on, empty.

"What should we do?"

"I addressed the matter with Mr. Trapp." Fred cleared his throat. "He is well aware and is blaming the mistake on the company we chose to go to production with."

Paul blinked, mouth falling open. "Pardon?"

"He says that the prototypes were tested and safe. They caused no reactions or side effects of any kind," Fred shrugged. "He wants the media to know that the *production company* chose to use a cheaper material, which resulted in this devastation. Not Trapp & Co."

"But the order reports are going to show otherwise," Angela argued from across the table. "If it makes it to the news and *that's* the story... They're going to come after *us* for defamation. And they'll have clear proof that the request for those materials came from us directly."

"Not unless Mr. Trapp can pull up another record somewhere," Frank replied.

"We *have* to address this," Paul said, stiffening. "I need to know *exactly* what you want me to say."

The room turned to Fred. He pursed his lips, reaching for his phone. Choosing redial, he waited for the CEO to answer.

Paul struggled to reach the podium in the lobby. The sea of outraged consumers swarmed him, shouting and grabbing. Security held them off as Paul cleared his throat, tapping the microphone to ensure it was on. Once he was able to compose himself, he cleared his throat, calling for the crowd's attention. At first, no one listened. They kept hollering, shoving against the security guards and others around them. But finally, after a few attempts, he was able to get the noise down to a droll murmur.

"I thank you all for your cooperation," Paul said, swallowing the shakiness in his voice. "I am here today to issue our deepest condolences for this devastating turn of events due to our latest product. As a parent myself, I can not *fathom* the amount of anger and grief you are feeling. You placed your trust in us, and we have failed you. There is nothing I can say or do that will earn you our trust again."

A few shouts broke through the crowd as Paul scanned the papers at the podium. He skimmed the few notes he had taken on what to address, sweat beading on his forehead and neck. He loosened his tie, clearing his throat once again before returning his gaze amongst the lobby of angry faces.

"In reviewing our order log, it has come to our attention that there had been a change of material without our knowledge. Our prototypes, as you had all seen here the other day, were crafted with the immense care we promised all of you. However, it appears that in our mass order, the production line switched to using a cheaper material, which resulted in the disastrous aftereffects. We were not made aware of the change, as our order logs had remained consistent with that of our prototypes." Paul took a deep breath. "Due to this, going forward, we will *no longer* be working with this production company. Our past products have always been topnotch, but with a slip up this great, we will *not* take any second chances. Any risks. As addressed in our product launch, *your* safety...your *children's* safety...is our greatest concern."

The noise of the crowd amplified. Paul could make out a few comments cursing him. Cursing the company. But he kept his composure, gripping the stack of papers in his trembling hands.

"There is nothing that can undo the damage and pain you and your families have suffered," he continued. "I personally wish I could take it all away. But, to uphold our promise of safety, we will be pulling *all* Light-and-Glow Pumpkin Masks from the market immediately. We will be issuing a statement about the materials used, which have been proven to cause severe chemical burns, lung damage, and other devastating side effects. We also will be publicly removing any associations to that production company, and advising our fellow companies who have used their services to cease. We simply ask that, in return, you allow *us* to handle it. To prevent mass hysteria. To prevent falsified claims. And to further protect your family from the prying media."

The hollers didn't stop. Growing voices shook the lobby as Paul turned to security. They nodded, escorting Fred to the podium.

"After speaking with our CEO, we have decided to come to a settlement agreement. A cash payout to all families who have been affected by this grievous mistake. Our Chief Compliance Officer, Mr. Fred Lazzaro, would be happy to explain in further detail. Once more, we thank you for your concerns, and we *deeply* apologize for any harm this has caused. From Trapp & Co. and from my heart personally, I am so very sorry."

Paul stepped away as Frank took over the microphone, spewing legal jargon to the crowd as they gathered closer. He reiterated the topics Paul had brought up, assuring the families that Trapp & Co. had not been aware of the change in materials. The blame returned to the production line—the outsourced company that prepared and produced all Light-and-Glow Pumpkin Masks. There was more legal jargon, more apologies, and then, the final mention of the hush money. Astronomical figures that, while they would damage the income of the company significantly, would protect its image. Paul returned to his office to gather his belongings, stomach churning at the thought. Knowing the damage was irreversible. Knowing there were lies to cover it up.

Knowing it was all their fault.

A gentle knock on his door drew Paul away from his focus. Expecting Angela or Fred, he was taken aback when he found Jim Harlow standing there, clipboard in hand. The corners of his mouth were drawn down, eyes weary as he stepped into the office. Paul managed a weak smile as he snapped his briefcase shut.

"Ah, Jim," he said softly. "Is there something I can help you with?"

Jim leveled his gaze. "What exactly is going on with the masks? We've heard some talk, but..."

"It's confidential," Paul replied quickly. "Mr. Trapp is adamant that nothing be brought to the public and no information be shared. Anyone who goes against orders will be terminated immediately."

Jim frowned. "Understood. But, if I may ask... I took one home for my son. Remember?"

"A prototype, right?"

Jim nodded. "I believe so."

Paul ran his fingers through his slicked back hair, sighing heavily. "It was the sealant, of all things. It wasn't used in the prototypes, only the final products. Your mask should be safe. But I wouldn't blame you if you disposed of it."

"I couldn't imagine something like that happening to Peter," Jim shivered. "What others are saying they've heard about those kids... The images I see in my mind..."

He clutched his clipboard to his chest as Paul slipped his coat on, heading for the door. He glanced back at Jim one final time, expression stern.

"Don't mention any of this to your son. Please."

Jim silently agreed. Hanging his head in thought, he stayed behind as Paul headed down the hallway towards the elevators. Prepared to face the unruly crowd in the lobby once more.

The afternoon skies were dull and gray as Paul made his way to his car at the end of the street. Behind him, the echoes of voices still rang from inside Trapp & Co. While they had died down substantially from earlier that day, he couldn't help but listen. Pick out words tossed around as security continued to usher people out.

Only when he reached his car did he no longer try to eavesdrop. He fumbled for his keys, attempting to leave the vicinity as quickly as possible. His mind whirled from the events of the day, wanting nothing more than to be at home with his family. His sons. To hold them close. Be thankful he hadn't invested in a mask for little Andy.

As he unlocked the door to his car, tugging it open, he heard a voice call to him. His shoulders stiffened as he turned, surprised to see a teenage boy standing there. His eyes were red and puffy behind his thick glasses, cheeks tear-stained as he stared at Paul. In his trembling hands, he gripped an envelope, holding it out to him.

"My brother..." His voice was hollow. "Look what you did to my *brother...*"

Paul froze. He stared at the envelope, too fearful to take it. He wanted to say something, but words failed him. When he didn't budge, the teen tore the envelope open, brandishing a stack of photographs at him.

"*Look!*"

All were of a young boy—elementary school age—with chemical burns covering his face and neck. The skin had boiled off, flesh hanging in strings from his cheeks. His jawbone was exposed on one side, bubbling pockets of blood and ooze weeping through open sores. With each photo the teen flipped through, the carnage grew worse. Paul stifled a gag as he took a step backwards, gripping his car door.

It wasn't from disgust, nor from guilt. It was from knowing. From things he had seen. The photographs, as brutal and gruesome as they were,

were nothing in comparison to the children from his dream. Surrounding him in the darkness, staring at him in his bed. Their faces bloody. Melting off.

Putty faces...

Paul released a quivering breath, shaking his head. Tears pricked at his eyes as he held a hand out to the teen. But he refused to take it. He simply glared back, lips drawn into a hard and unforgiving frown.

"I am *so sorry*." Paul whimpered. "Truly. If I could take away the pain, fix it...I would."

"He's dead because of *you*," the teen said. "And I'll never forget. I'll *never* forgive."

Another tear ran down his face as he lifted his glasses, wiping it away. He stuffed the photographs back inside the envelope, watching Paul climb into his car, shutting the door. He rolled the window down a crack, about to speak. But before he could, the teen cut him off.

"You don't even care," he snarled, face wrinkled in anger. "*None* of you do. You get to go home to your families. Pretend like nothing happened. But *my* family? We have to go home to an empty chair. A silent bedroom. We have to go home to face the truth while you all hide behind your little lies. Little lies and goddamn *hush money*."

Paul frowned, chest aching. "It wasn't my call. And I swear to you, we didn't know. *Had* I known...those masks *never* would have gone to market."

The teen glared at him as he started his car. Gripping the wheel, he sat in silence for a moment before sighing.

"What is your name?" Paul asked. "Please."

"Doug Feeney," the teen growled through gritted teeth.

Paul nodded. "Doug. Please offer my condolences to your family. I'd give anything to make it right. *Anything*."

"There's nothing you ever *could* give," Doug bit back.

With nothing else to say, Paul rolled up the window and slowly drove away. Doug stood there, silent and broken, watching the car until it was no longer in sight. Tears pricked at his eyes again as he removed his glasses, using his shirt sleeve to dry them. From behind him, a soft, raspy voice caught his attention.

"An eye for an eye," it breathed. "A tooth for a tooth."

Doug glanced over his shoulder, taken aback by the elderly woman approaching him. She staggered as she walked, wrinkled hands gripping a wooden cane for support. As she shook her head, she clicked her tongue against the roof of her mouth.

"A *son* for a *son*..."

"What?" Doug asked, slipping his glasses back on.

"How cold and cruel these corporate clowns are," the woman said. "They use their money to silence. To withhold any accountability."

Her milky eyes stared up at the glass building before them. The last of the parents were leaving, security tight around the doors. Curling her lips up, exposing her rotten teeth, she spat.

"And they'll do it again," she said. "Over and over. A vicious cycle. A cycle where no one learns. No one suffers the consequences."

She turned to Doug. More tears pricked at his eyes as he tried to hide them. Frowning, the old woman reached out, running one of her long, crooked fingers along his cheek, brushing the tears away.

"Only the families of those afflicted."

"I don't know what to do," Doug said through shaky breaths. "My parents...they took the money. That's all they *could* do. We can't talk about it. It's just...brushed under the rug. We're supposed to act like nothing happened. Just move on with our lives. But that's not fair to Greg. There's no amount of money that *ever* could be enough to fix what they did. Fix the pain they caused us. The pain they caused *him*."

"They deserve to *know* that pain," the woman agreed, holding Doug's face in her hands. "Know how helpless it is to watch their children suffer before them. Suffer as they stand by and can only *watch*."

"Come home to an empty chair..."

Another tear rolled down Doug's cheek. Once again, the woman brushed it away. Her grin grew wider, yellow teeth fully exposed as she looked Doug in the eye.

"They *can*, you know..."

Sliding her hand down his face, she gripped her cane. Yet, her gaze never strayed from him. From behind his misty stare, he, too, didn't look away.

"An eye for an eye."

Doug's eyes darkened. Sniffling one final time, his lips drew into a prominent frown. Gripping the envelope tighter until it crushed beneath his grasp.

"A *son* for a *son*."

X.

ANTS INFESTED THE ROOM. Thousands of them. Their little bodies trailed from the door to the foot of the bed—rustling up the mattress and across the sheets. Chattering as they paraded in perfect precession.

Peter, Peter...

The body lying on the bed was engulfed in them. They darted up the legs and across the torso, pooling at the chest and neck. Beneath the skin, white maggots wriggled—churning through the flesh. The window was covered in flies—buzzing wildly. But the head was where they swarmed the worst.

Peter, Peter...

The insects nibbled away at tender flesh. Crawling inside the ears and nose, plucking at closed eyelids. Pouring from the mouth, coating the tongue in a writhing heap. The black mass of ants shifted in the dark. Ever-growing. Scurrying across the helpless body beneath them. Still. Stiff. Until the eyes fluttered open—knocking away the curious and hungry horde. Straining to scream as more erupted from the throat.

Peter shot up in bed, covered in sweat. His chest heaved as he struggled to catch his breath, shoulders trembling. His skin itched—crawling with invisible ants and maggots. Working their way through his hair, his nose, his ears. Chewing at his eyes. His mouth. Saliva dripped down his chin as he gasped, holding back the sob that threatened to break from his throat. He gritted his teeth, rocking back and forth as he tried to shake away the images of the insects. Shake the feeling of their tiny feet crawling over him. Infesting his pores.

"It's just a dream." He palmed himself hard in the forehead. "It's not real. It's *not real*."

But it felt real. As real as any other nightmare he'd had over the last few weeks. Every one had been eerie, awakening him with a flood of unease, but they were growing unbearable. Keeping him up at night, afraid to fall back asleep. Afraid of what may be lurking in the shadowed corners of his room. Creeping along the walls. Along the floor. Peter slid his hand beneath the sleeve of his sweatshirt, scratching the skin of his arm until it was raw. Yet, even then, he still felt the writhing bodies. The little legs.

In the silence, Peter finally broke. Tears welled in his eyes as he tried to stifle his sobs, but it was to no avail. His shoulders shook as the first wave came, sharp and sniveling. Then, it rose to audible blubbering. More saliva pooled from his mouth as he wept, mucus dripping from his nose. His eyes burned and his head spun and his skin crawled. All around him, the shadows

stirred, conjuring shapes in the darkness. Eyes watching. Taunting his fragility. Peter did his best to ignore them—until they reached his windowsill.

The curtains fluttered in the breeze blowing in from outside, the light of the moon catching upon them. They moved like ghosts with each gust. As he stared at the billowing fabric, he noticed a shape beyond the window shift in the night. A silhouette. The sound of tiny claws scratched against the sill, followed by the all too familiar meow that had plagued him each and every night. Allowing his gaze to fall on the glass, he saw it. That skinny black cat. Standing just outside the window.

But tonight, it was different. It stood upon two legs, head pressed against the glass. Its saucer sized yellow eyes burned in the dark of the night— like faint candles. Its jowls were turned up into a wide crescent moon grin, exposing pinpoint white teeth—and a missing tongue. Its tail swished as it gawked at Peter, not taking its eyes off him.

Peter's heart raced against his chest. His breaths became ragged as he began to hyperventilate. And though he wanted to look away, he couldn't. He was paralyzed in fear. Stuck staring into the eyes of the cat. With each second, they grew larger. Wider. Contorting the features of its face until it hardly looked like a cat at all. Peter shut his eyes, lower lip trembling as he wept.

"It's not real..."

When he finally glanced back to the window, the cat was gone. All he was met with was early morning fog, and the darkness of dawn not yet ready to break. Sniffling, he wiped his nose on the back of his hand, letting the last of his tears spill. Mourning another sleepless night.

Peter stared solemnly into the mug of coffee before him. The steam brushed against his face, earthy scent of the dark, unsweetened roast lingering in the air. His fingers laced around the edges of the mug, keeping his hands warm, but he couldn't bring himself to sip. His brown eyes were vacant—lined with heavy bags. Though he longed to drown the night out with caffeine, he didn't have the strength.

"Well, someone pinch me!" Jim's voice was full of surprise as it carried through the kitchen. "I've never seen *you* put on a pot of coffee before."

Peter sneered at his father's comment, pulling his mug closer. His hands trembled as he raised it to his lips, forcing himself to take a sip of the black coffee. Its flat, bitter taste burned his tongue, causing him to wince in disgust. Jim watched his son as he filled his own mug, stirring in sugar and cream before taking a seat at the table. Peter didn't bother looking up.

"Come to think of it...you're never awake this early on a weekend, either," Jim said. "What's wrong?"

"It's nothing. I'm fine."

Jim sipped his coffee. "You don't look fine. Are you sick?"

Peter shook his head. "I didn't sleep."

"*Again*?"

"Nightmares."

"Did you try—?"

"The pills didn't work."

Peter's grip on the mug tightened. He stared into the dark coffee, raising it to his lips again. This time, he took a swig, biting back the cheap flavor. Jim set his mug down, reaching across the table and gently resting a hand upon his son's. Peter flinched at the touch.

"What is it? You can tell me, you know?" Jim encouraged softly.

Peter remained silent, closing his eyes. Jim gave his hand a light squeeze before pulling away. He took another sip of coffee, watching his son before clearing his throat.

"Mr. Matthews called the other day. He said you fell asleep in class. The third time in the last two weeks."

Peter blinked his eyes open, lips drawing into a frown. He returned his gaze to his mug, hands trembling. Jim took notice, softening his voice.

"I'm not *mad*, Petey. I just want to know what's wrong."

"I *told* you. I'm having *nightmares*. I'm not *sleeping*."

"Do you want to talk to someone about it?"

"*Talk* to someone? You mean like a shrink?" Peter scoffed. "No thanks. I'm *not* doing *that* again."

"Peter."

Jim looked at his son with sincerity. He pushed his glasses up on his nose before sighing and shaking his head. Peter pressed his lips together, brow

furrowing as he averted his gaze across the table—refusing to look at his father.

"I just want to know you're okay," Jim said.

"I already told you. I'm *fine*."

Exhaling sharply, Jim stood. He went to the counter, rummaging through a stack of papers before returning. Slapping an opened envelope before Peter, he motioned to it.

"Your progress report came," he snapped. "Don't tell me you're *fine*."

Peter's eyes slowly drifted up to his father. His grip on the mug weakened, expression of annoyance quickly dissipating into one of worry. The glaring comments marked with "In Danger of Failing" stood out on the white paper—bold and screaming. Peter bit his lip, chewing it nervously.

"And I *know* you're smoking again," Jim said. "I smell it on you every time you come home. Your whole room *reeks* of it, Peter."

The vacant expression returned to Peter's face. Though his gaze was aimed at Jim, his vision became clouded. Spacey. Blurred from building tears. Tears he didn't dare let fall in front of his father.

"Is it about Mom?" Jim asked. "It's alright if it is. You can tell me."

"What's this have to do with *her*?" Peter demanded, voice low and quivering.

"I'm just trying to find some answers, that's all," Jim said. "I want to *help* you, Petey. After everything with Mom, that's when your grades started slipping. I know that's when you started smoking. Things were better for a little while...now they're not again. Is that what it is?"

"*No*." Peter gritted his teeth, the tears stinging now. "And either way, what's it matter? Do you think I'm a failure, too, Dad? Is *that* why you're bringing this up?"

"You are *not* a failure, Peter."

Peter's words cracked from the lump forming in his throat. "Do you think I'm a fool?"

"No. You're *not* a fool, either."

His shoulders trembled as a quivering breath escaped his lungs. With a whimper, the tears began to roll down his cheeks. He tried to stop them, but it was no use. His voice was soft and quiet when he was finally able to speak.

"Do you blame me?"

"No..." Jim wrapped his arms around his son, pulling him close. "No, Petey. I wouldn't *ever* blame you."

His fingers tangled in the tousled strands of Peter's dark hair. His own tears pricked at his eyes as he tried to blink them away. They caused his glasses

to steam as he exhaled a shaky sigh. For the first time in forever, Peter returned the hug. His eyes were closed tightly, body quivering as he sobbed.

"It's all my fault..."

"It is *not* your fault." Jim pulled Peter from him, shaking his shoulders. "Your mother wasn't well. She wasn't herself anymore. And none of that had anything to do with *you*. She *loved* you, Petey..."

"She told me she *hated* me. That's the last thing she ever—"

"She was very sick. She didn't know what she was saying. She didn't know what she was doing. She was deteriorating. Rotting away. But I *swear* to you. She *loved* you."

A single tear rolled down Peter's cheek. Snot clung to his nose again, dripping down to his lips. He wiped his face on the back of his shirt sleeve as Jim pulled him in for another hug, rocking him gently. This time, Peter didn't return the embrace. He simply stared across the table at the faint rays of sunlight streaking across the kitchen floor.

"I did something wrong..."

Jim pulled away, taking in his son's face. "What do you mean?"

"No secrets, right?"

"Right."

"That cat..." Peter closed his eyes, choking back another wave of sobs. "It *didn't* follow me home from school."

Jim raised an eyebrow, pushing his glasses up. He watched Peter wipe his nose on the back of his hand, sniffling and averting his gaze. Shaking his head, he gritted his teeth, releasing a pained whimper.

"It came from the cemetery."

"The *cemetery*? You mean Chapel Hill?"

"We snuck out there a few weeks ago," Peter said. "At midnight. We were just having fun, telling scary stories and hanging out. We didn't do anything wrong, I *swear*."

"*Peter*..."

"It followed me home after that. And then...all this started."

Peter rested his cheek against his father's shoulder, heart throbbing in his chest. He did his best to quell his sorrow, but the waves hit harder with each breath he took. After remaining in silence, allowing his father to hold him, he blubbered.

"I just want the nightmares to stop..."

As the month slipped closer to October's end, most of the leaves had already fallen. They lay crumbled in decaying mounds along the sidewalks and lawns. But for the few that hung on, clinging to their branches, they were vibrant. Gold, amber, and red. They flickered in the breeze, bright against the gray afternoon skies as Peter pedaled his way down the block. The tires of his bike ran through scattered piles, crushing them. They crunched as he sped to the corner, crossing into the next neighborhood.

The air was brisk—growing closer to winter's frosty breath by the day. Peter sniffled as he pedaled, blinking back the wetness still in his eyes. They stung from the cold breeze beating against his face, slowing him down. For the first time that season, he took in the homes on the surrounding streets— all decorated for Halloween. Jack-o'-lanterns lined porches, skeletons sat upon hay bales, and fabric ghosts hung from trees. Some yards were made into makeshift cemeteries, crawling with zombies and foam tombstones. Others were more jolly: sporting rubber black cats and smiling scarecrows.

Inhaling the crisp scent of the fallen leaves, Peter's mind raced. Fixated only on the images in his mind. Jack-o'-lanterns. Scarecrows. Tombstones. Black cats. But they weren't décor. They weren't seasonal joys to litter the lawn with. Upstage the neighbors. They were real.

Peter pedaled farther than usual as he tried to clear his thoughts. Tried to ease his nerves. Taking a back road, he found himself riding near the quarry—the popular hangout for delinquent teens. He pumped the brakes as he entered the trainyard, tires scuffing in the gravel. He rubbed his eyes with the back of his shirt sleeve, gazing out at the old, rusted engines before him. Their black, towering frames were somber against gray skies. Haunting. Ghosts left to wallow in their steel and iron graveyard. Kicking his bike stand out, Peter dismounted, sulking over to one of the empty boxcars.

He climbed up into it and took a seat, slinging his legs over the side. Staring across the crumbled rock and overgrown tracks, he lit a cigarette, inhaling his first puff sharply. He let the smokey ash linger on his tongue longer than usual, then expelled the cloud through barely parted lips. The silent stillness of the quarry eased him, an ease he hadn't felt in weeks. He lightly kicked his legs, smoking his cigarette down to the filter and letting his eyes fall closed. He hadn't been near the quarry in over a year. Back when he would sneak out after dark to make shady purchases.

It wasn't often Peter smoked weed, but when he did, it was amongst the train cars. Fellow classmates with older siblings or college students returning home on breaks would often sell their stashes there. Dispersing it to teens looking to buy. Peter had smoked there many times before—losing himself in euphoric highs. But, lately, he found the substance made him drowsy. Unmotivated. It brought a greater sense of sorrow than ecstasy. And so, he'd stuck to cigarettes. Far easier to obtain, and quicker to ease his troubles.

Flicking the cigarette butt into the gravel, Peter exhaled the last cloud of smoke slowly. He watched it billow from between his lips, floating away and becoming one with the gray skies above. He sighed, leaning back on his palms and staring out into the distance. Far across the quarry. The sloping mountainside was ablaze in the colors of autumn, contrasting the thick, deep greens of the conifers. Picturesque. Peter didn't move, simply taking in the quiet around him. The cool of the afternoon. The beauty of the leaves. And for once, in that moment, he felt that euphoria again. Coming from deep within.

Peter stayed there for a long while, in his peace, until he heard a rattle in the back of the car. He stiffened at the sound, peering over his shoulder. It was hard to make out much through the shadow, but when he heard the sound again, followed by the *pitter-patter* of tiny paws, he sighed. A rugged white and orange cat strutted from the back corner of the car—awoken from its slumber and now interested in Peter. Its head was too large for its body,

eyes small and squinted. Its cheeks puffed as it approached Peter, letting out a deep and questioning yowl.

Peter was hesitant as the cat nudged its big head against him, purring for attention. With a trembling hand, he gave in. His fingers gently scratched behind the cat's mite-infested ears, a sad smile meeting his lips.

"Hey, buddy..."

The cat chirped as it leaned into his touch, tail swishing. Peter continued to stroke it—along the back and under the chin—feeling hot tears prick his eyes again. He sniffled softly, wiping his nose on the back of his hand.

"You shouldn't be out here," he said to the cat. "There are awful people that would do horrible things to you. Go home."

The cat sat and stared up at him, blinking its squinted amber eyes slowly. As Peter sighed again, it jumped down from the train car, yowling at him in appreciation before trotting down the tracks. Peter remained seated, watching until the cat disappeared into the quarry. His lips drew into a frown as he thought of the black cat outside his window. Of its soft purrs as it rubbed against his leg. Of its body hanging in the tree—mutilated. Taking a deep breath, he gazed out at the horizon. At the road beyond the tracks. Beyond the quarry. The road seldom traveled—into the mountain hills. Leading up to a little cottage his conscience wouldn't let him avoid.

The bike trembled as Peter pedaled up the long dirt trail, avoiding exposed roots and rocks. There was a stillness in the air as he made his way through the woods, thick and heavy. He could feel it out there in the hemlock and old oaks. Out amongst the foliage and rotting leaves. Something alive. Something watching. Watching from the dark between the trees. Still, he pedaled on, stopping only when he reached his destination at the end of the road. Deep in the thick grove of trees.

The cottage looked cozy against the autumn colors. Thick ferns lined the mossy path, chanterelle mushrooms sprouting beside them. From the chimney, puffs of sweet-smelling smoke spewed—blanketing the yard. Peter gripped the handlebars of his bike as he took a deep breath, collecting himself. Sliding from his seat, he propped the bike up and headed towards the front door.

Cats lined the yard everywhere he looked—all shapes, sizes, and breeds. Some sat in the windowsills, others beneath the trees. Others still remained on the lawn, curled up and bathing in the fading midday light. As he walked up the cobblestone pathway, their eyes turned on him. Inspecting him curiously. But none greeted him. They remained where they were, watching from afar.

Peter took another heavy breath, relaxing his shoulders as he stopped at the wooden door. Tightening his lips with a nod, he found the courage to knock. When there wasn't an answer, he tried again—rapping his knuckles harder this time.

"Just a minute!"

He stiffened at the raspy voice from inside. Wringing his hands, he ran over potential words in his head—things he could possibly say. Swallowing a lump of fear, he composed himself as the doorway parted.

"Yes? May I help you?"

"H-hi," Peter stammered. "Are you, uh, are you the one who lives here? I mean..."

An elderly woman hobbled onto the doorstep, leaning on her wooden cane for support. She squinted, looking Peter over as his words caught in his throat. Her lips turned up in a grin, revealing crooked, yellowing teeth.

"I-I'm sorry," Peter stuttered again. "I don't mean to be a bother."

"Oh, nonsense!" the woman exclaimed. "It's not very often that I have visitors."

Peter smiled back sadly, watching as she tapped her cane upon the doorstep. Her eyes, though milky, continued to stare at him. Looking over each of his features. Prying deep. He drew his attention away from her, however, when he heard a long, drawn-out meow from his side. A slender gray and white cat trotted over to the woman, rubbing against her leg. She cooed to it, bending down to stroke its head before clearing her throat.

"What's your name?" she asked.

"Peter..."

"Peter," she repeated with a nod. "Well, it's nice to meet you. I'm Grýla. What brings you out here?"

"Well," Peter began, dropping his gaze to the cat. "It's about one of your cats..."

"Oh?" Grýla straightened herself, fully focused on Peter now.

"A black one," he said. "That hung around the cemetery."

The woman tightened her grip on her cane. Her mouth drew into a deep frown as her eyes fell to the ground. Sorrow lined her face, evident in each of her wrinkles. Peter sighed, mirroring her expression.

"I'm so sorry," he said. "I'm sure the groundskeeper told you what hap—"

"He did," she said. "My poor little deary. How cruel people are. So full of hatred."

"I'm so sorry..." Peter repeated.

He hung his head, lost for words. There wasn't much more he could say. He knew Horace Johnson blamed him, and no amount of trying to say otherwise would change that. And he was certain it would be the same with the old woman, too. She leaned against the doorway, mulling over her own thoughts before clearing her throat.

"Why don't you come in," she said. "I've just put some soup on. And a delicious pie in the oven."

"Oh." Peter stammered. "Actually, I have to be getting home soon. I don't think my dad wants me out too late."

"But you came all this way," Grýla said. "A quick bite to eat won't hurt. It's been a long while since I've had company."

Peter breathed a sigh, running his fingers against the back of his neck. "Alright."

The old woman grinned as she held the door open, motioning inside. Peter was hesitant, but slowly made his way up the steps. The heavy, alluring aroma of pumpkin and cinnamon wafted from inside. With a weak smile, Peter entered the cottage, the cats trailing in behind him.

The kitchen was dim, lit only by flickering candles and oil lamps. The afternoon sun barely made its way through the window—blocked by the vibrant leaves of the bigleaf maples. They set the space aglow in a dreamy golden hue. Peter sat at the large oak table, watching as the cats swarmed around Grýla's legs. They mewled for food and attention, whiskers and tails twitching.

"Pumpkin soup?" she asked Peter. "It's an old family recipe."

"Sure," he responded softly.

Grýla poured him a steaming bowl, humming as she slid it over to him. Its light orange color was swirled with white cream, pumpkin seeds decorating the top. The sweet smell that rose up from it was inviting—holding hints of cinnamon and clove. He picked up his spoon, stirring the soup as the old woman sat across from him. She broke off a piece of freshly baked pumpkin bread, taking a bite. Her eyes were fixed on him, waiting for him to taste. Peter blew on the soup to cool it before giving it a try. The flavors were strong against his tongue—sweet, with just the right amount of spice. He gave Grýla a nod, taking another spoonful.

"It's really good," he said with a sad smile. "It's been a long time since I've had anything homemade... Thank you."

"My pleasure," the woman replied, stirring her own bowl. "Feel free to have as much as you'd like."

Peter took another bite, letting the creamy texture and flavor linger on his tongue before swallowing. He remained silent as he ate, eyes drifting to the wooden cuckoo clock on the wall. A reminder that his father was at home waiting.

As he went for another taste, one of the cats leapt onto the table, hurrying over to him. He set his spoon down, running his fingers behind the plump tuxedo's ears as he smiled softly.

"You have a lot of cats," he remarked.

"They're like children to me," Grýla replied happily. "They keep me busy, that's for sure."

"How many are there?"

"Thirteen," the woman said before pausing. "Well. No. Twelve now."

The tuxedo cat nudged its head against Peter as his gaze dropped to the bowl of soup. He continued to stroke behind its ears, taking a deep, weary breath.

"Again, I'm sorry..."

"As I said before, people are cruel."

Peter frowned. "Your cat...he had been coming around my house for a while. I didn't know he was yours. I would have come by sooner if I had."

"He was always wandering off," Grýla said. "Most of them stay around the vicinity of the house. They'll explore the woods here and there, but they don't go into town."

"I brought him back to the cemetery," Peter said after a moment. "He'd followed me home from there one night. I couldn't sleep. He kept me up, wanting to be let in. So, I took him back. I thought maybe he was lost. Maybe he'd find his way home from there. But..."

Peter ran a hand through his mussed hair. He chewed his bottom lip, taking another spoonful of the soup. Swallowing it hard, he shook his head.

"I can't help but feel responsible..."

He put his face into his hands, taking a shaky breath as Grýla watched from across the table. She didn't speak, but kept her full attention on him. When he finally glanced up again, eyes wet as he blinked back tears, he trembled.

"But, I *swear* to you. I didn't do *anything* to your cat."

The old woman nodded, gathering her bowl as she pushed away from the table. Peter dabbed the back of his sleeve against his face, drying his eyes as he gazed into his bowl. The creamy orange soup still steamed, pumpkin seeds submerging. As he took another bite, Grýla spoke, carrying her dishes to the sink.

"Are you sure about that?"

Peter held the spoon suspended over the soup, turning to her slowly. She didn't look back, placing her bowl in the basin as water began to run from the faucet. She scrubbed away the remnants of soup and bread, humming lightly. Peter's heart pounded as he swallowed a nervous lump, feeling a wave of guilt wash over him. Guilt he felt in the cemetery when confronted about the cat. Guilt he knew he shouldn't feel, but did. As he glanced back down to the tabletop, he became lightheaded.

The room spun, flickering candlelight creating hazy orbs that drifted across his vision. He dropped his spoon with a clatter into his soup. Putting a hand to his head, he squeezed his temples as he closed his eyes. But the dizziness didn't go away. It only made his heart beat faster—like a panic induced high—and his breathing became unsteady. The old woman's humming grew louder, grating on his ears as he leaned forward, pressing his forehead to the table.

Peter, Peter...

149

He gradually opened his eyes, everything tilted and blurry. A soft moan gurgled from his throat as he held his stomach. He could barely make Grýla out as she continued to scrub the dishes, raspy voice replacing the humming.

"*Peter, Peter pumpkin-eater,*" she sang. "*From his head, he fed the seeder.*"

"W-what?" Peter breathed weakly.

"*They crowned him with a pumpkin-shell,*" she continued before turning back to him. "*And dragged him off to rot in Hell.*"

Her features became blurred and distorted as she approached him, the flickering candlelight burning his eyes. Tears began to build as his stomach lurched, head pounding—sending pain into his temples and face. Again, he questioned her, receiving a wide grin.

"Shh," she hushed him. "No need to get yourself worked up."

She took his face in her wrinkled hands. Her thumb caressed his upper left cheek, brushing his mole as she smirked, forcing him to look upon her. His pupils were dilated, eyes dark and vacant. His breathing grew short and panicked as she shook her head.

"My little deary told me *everything* about you, Peter," she cooed. "Where you live. Where you sleep. What you dream. What you *desire*."

Peter parted his lips, but no words came. The room continued to spin, everything wavy and distorted. The colors, the light, the sounds. He whimpered as Grýla sneered.

"You sat on the throne," she said. "You made a deal with the Devil."

"N-no..." Peter's voice cracked.

"And not just the night my deary followed you home," she said, pursing her lips. "No. You sat on that throne *many* nights. Staring off into the darkness. Lighting candles. Whispering wishes. *Desires.*"

Peter shook his head slowly. "W-what...what do you mean?"

Grýla tilted his chin up, staring into his dreary eyes as she smirked. "You think you were dreaming, don't you?"

Peter blinked uneasily, visions from his nightmares flooding his mind. But now, they felt real as they flashed before him, causing his head to ache. He could feel the wet earth beneath his feet, the cold breeze in the dead of the night. He could see the fires flickering under the old tree, the cats gathered around it—dancing. And overhead, he could see the vultures, hear them whisper his name through the rustling branches.

Peter, Peter...

150

And then, he saw the stone throne. The withering graves. He saw himself seated upon it, eyes heavy and vacant, staring out through the shadows. Jack-o'-lanterns flickered at his feet as his lips mouthed silent words, answering the circling vultures surrounding him.

What do you desire?

He heard the trumpets and the drums. He felt the ants crawling up his legs. The flies buzzing around his head. He smelled the decaying leaves beneath the rain. And he felt the soft, black fur of the cat as he scruffed it by the neck. The handle of his pocket knife as he sawed through muscle. And he heard the screeching mewls and hisses—before all went silent. All except a sickening *crack* as its body swung limp in the tree.

Hot tears ran down Peter's cheek as he shook his head, breath quivering. "I-I didn't...I didn't..."

"But you *did*," Grýla said with a grin. "And there's nothing to be ashamed or afraid of. It's all part of the plan, you see? Just how the legend goes."

"L-legend?"

"Oh, don't be daft, boy. You know the story of Wanderin' Jack."

Peter tried desperately to focus. His hands gripped his stomach as it lurched—hot and bubbling. Sweat beaded on his forehead as he winced.

"W-Wanderin' Jack?"

"Wanderin' Jack...John Barker..." The old woman shrugged. "It's all the same. Different stories told around town to keep foolish children on their best behavior. Keep them out of the cemetery at night. But, you see, every version always gets it wrong."

Grýla turned to a plump pumpkin in the center of the table. Grabbing a butcher's knife, she drove it into the top, carving around the stem. Once she had completely circled it, she yanked up, exposing the stringy guts—littered with seeds.

"Jack was desperate. *That* part was right. A young man foolish enough to call upon the Devil. Make a deal. And of course, the Devil abided, taking Jack's soul in exchange for his desires. After all, one must give in order to receive. Nothing in life, or death for that matter, is free. Sounds familiar, doesn't it?" Grýla reached inside the pumpkin, pulling out a wad of wet goop. "But, *this* is where the others get it wrong. You see, the Devil wasn't just looking for a soul to steal. He was looking for a *vessel*. A body left empty to wander the shadows, searching for helpless and despairing fools willing to give anything for what they desire. And that's just what he did."

Emptying the pumpkin of all its seeds and guts, the woman scraped it clean with the blade. Then, she drove into the thick, orange flesh, carving away until a triangle for an eye was made. She continued on to the second, all the while staring at Peter. The candlelight stung his eyes as he sat there, mouth slightly agape. Too weak and dizzy to move.

"The Devil trapped Jack in the darkness, in an endless void—lost amongst the shadows and fog of the cemetery. And then he mocked him, lending him only a candle in a hollowed out pumpkin. He told him there was no need to fear being alone. He would now be King—but only to the pumpkins. The pumpkins left to carry his light. Keep it protected from the wind. The rain. Jack's body was claimed by the Devil, but his soul was bound to the earth. Bound to the darkness. Lost. Forever wandering aimlessly, looking for the way home. Searching for light." Grýla set the butcher knife down, gazing upon the freshly carved pumpkin. "Waiting for another to come along on some late night. Another down on their luck. Desperate and foolish. Foolish enough to sit upon the throne and utter their desires."

Peter gritted his teeth, expelling quick, harsh breaths. Sweat dripped down the sides of his face, drenching his hair and neck. He shook his head again, feeling the room tilt. Watching everything continue to spin. Spiral more and more out of control.

"Some girls were naive enough to give dear Jack fresh light recently," Grýla said, lighting a tea candle within the pumpkin. "They called upon him in a mirror, reciting an old spell. Offered him a new candle. Offered him *freedom*."

Her milky eyes returned to Peter. She smiled as she turned the pumpkin to face him. Its carved expression was sinister—mouth drawn up in sharp, jagged teeth. The light from inside flickered violently, making Peter wince.

"And *you*, Peter," she said, grin widening. "*You* gave the Devil your deepest desires. Offered your body, just as Jack had. And now, he's come to collect it."

Peter shook his head, eyes wide. He gasped for air as he felt his throat clench, stomach gurgling and tightening. As the room swirled in his drugged state, the face of the pumpkin moved, as well. Eye holes gliding upward— light watching him. Searing through his soul.

"The pumpkins are waiting," Grýla said. "They want their new King. Can't you hear them?"

Peter dug his nails into the wood of the table. All around him, the eyes of the cats leered. Just as the vultures in the cemetery had. Their mouths opened, tongues lolling as the breathy whispers from his nightmares spilled out.

> *Peter, Peter, pumpkin-eater,*
> *From his head, he fed the seeder;*
> *They crowned him with a pumpkin-shell,*
> *And dragged him off to rot in Hell.*

Peter closed his eyes, shoulders trembling as he whimpered. Tears streamed down his cheeks, heart pounding against his chest until it felt as if it would burst. He panted, blubbering as drool dripped down his chin.

> *Peter, Peter, pumpkin-eater,*
> *Bound in vines, he was a bleeder;*
> *They spoke the words and read the spell,*
> *And crowned the Fool to rule in Hell.*

The wooden chair Peter was seated on gave way, falling backwards. He winced in pain as the back of his head hit the hard floor with a *thud*. A gasp escaped his lungs, vision clearing as his body quivered. The cats crept closer, licking their chops as Grýla sneered.

> *Peter, Peter...*
> *Peter, Peter...*

Pushing up from the floor, Peter bolted for the doorway. His head still spun, but he managed to yank it open, hurrying onto the steps. With an audible sob, he forced his index and middle finger down his throat. He leaned over the edge of the step, spewing bright orange vomit into the herb garden beside the house. Retching, he choked as his insides writhed in pain. The bitter taste clung to his tongue, causing him to spit as he wiped the puke from his mouth. Everything slowly began to return to normal. His vision no longer spun, head no longer ached.

Gathering himself, Peter glanced down into the herb garden at the thick pile of vomit. The remnants of tainted soup. But as he found the foul smelling goop, his eyes locked on something else sprouting from the garden. Vines. Except, they weren't growing from the soil.

They were covered in flies, swarming around what he thought at first to be a rotten pumpkin. But the closer he looked, the clearer it became. A weathered cowboy outfit, buried beneath vines and weeds. Tiny hands. Small fingers, stiffened into curls of agony. His lips quivered as he saw through the piles of ants and flies—realizing it was the lifeless and decaying body of missing Billy Barone. Where his head once was, however, a large pumpkin now grew—thick and plump.

As Peter began to back away, eyes wide in disbelief and shock, a thin tabby pounced on top of the gourd. It stared at Peter, hissing. He quickly darted down the steps and over to his bike, mounting it. Kicking the stand up, he pedaled as fast as his legs would allow, leaving the cottage to the darkening evening.

"It was *her*, Sam... The old woman on the mountain. Beyond the train tracks."

Peter trembled on Sam's bedroom floor, still covered in sweat. He reeked of fresh vomit and mud, eyes wide and empty. Sam sat beside him, dabbing his face with a cold, wet washcloth. She shook her head, trying to piece together everything she had just been told.

"Start over," she said softly. "And slow down. What about her?"

"The woman with the cats," Peter replied. "She knew about John and the Devil. She knew we were up there."

"Well, duh," Sam said. "It's a town legend. I'm sure *everyone* knows it. And, also, if the groundskeeper told her about her cat, of *course* she's going to know we were there."

"It's not that." Peter clenched his teeth and shut his eyes. "I...I can't explain it. She *drugged* me. She made me eat this soup. It was like the worst trip I've ever had, Sam. Everything was spinning, and there were weird colors and it was loud and...I saw things."

"*Saw* things?"

Peter pressed his lips together. He glanced at her, weary eyes red and puffy. Reaching up, he took her hand in his, stopping her from wiping his cheek.

"Maybe I really *did* kill that cat..."

"*What*?" Sam whispered, eyebrows raised.

155

"I don't know. I just. My nightmares…" Peter held his head. "I don't know… I feel like something's coming for me. I've felt it for a while now, but after today…"

"What do you think is coming?" Sam leaned forward, touching his cheek again.

Peter hesitated, lost in thought before replying in a whisper. "The Devil."

"Come on, Peter," Sam said. "We *literally* just had this conversation. It's a story. Just a legend made up in the town centuries ago. The Devil's *not* real."

"But what if he *is*, Sam?" Peter looked into her eyes. "What if I really *did* make a deal with him? Sold him my soul?"

"Over a *Chemistry test*?"

"No…"

Peter closed his eyes. Taking a deep breath, he tried to quell his thoughts. His lower lip quivered as a tear ran down his cheek. When Sam noticed, she quickly brushed it away with her thumb.

"Peter…"

"I just want to be happy, Sam."

She wrapped her arms around his neck, pulling him close. He rested his chin upon her shoulder, desperately fighting the rest of his tears. Pushing her fingers through his dark hair, Sam sighed.

"And you deserve to be," she said. "*No one* should ever have to be unhappy."

"I'm getting tired, Sam," Peter said.

"Have you tried sleeping pills?"

"No," Peter whispered, more tears coming. "Not like that. Tired of *existing*. Of wandering around here…hollow. Broken. I'm nothing but a burden. A disappointment. To everyone I've ever known. I saw it in my mom's eyes when she left, and I see it on my dad's face every day. I'm constantly reminded. Reminded how everyone would be better off without me. I keep having dreams that Death is coming. I hear it call for me at night. I see it in the vultures. In that *damn cat*. I can feel it getting closer. It wants me… And, maybe *I* want it, too…"

"Have you talked to anyone about this?" Sam's brow furrowed in concern.

"I'm talking to *you*."

"Yes, but…"

"Just promise me something," Peter said, wiping his nose on the back of his hand. "Promise me that you won't miss me when I'm gone. Promise me—"

Sam shook her head. "No. No, Peter, *stop* that."

"I feel it coming," he said again. "It's getting stronger every day. And I'm tired. I just...I just want to be happy again."

"You *will* be..."

"No. I'll be *forgotten*. Like always," Peter said. "Face it, Sam. I'm flunking. I'm not going to make it to graduation. You and Ritchie and Theo? You've all got plans. You've all got futures. You're going to move on to better things. *Brighter* things. You're not going to be trapped in some washed up town in the middle of nowhere. You're going to meet so many new people, make so many new friends. You won't need to hold on to me. I'm not *worth* holding on to... I'll just be a memory. A memory of a fool you once knew. One you should live without."

"How do you expect me to forget you, Peter?" Sam asked sadly.

"Because people always *do*. Look at my mother. She walked out. Like I never existed. It was better for her that way, I guess. And if *my mother* can forget me...then of course *you* can."

"I'm *not* your mother, Peter. And besides, she was *sick*."

"*She left me...*" Peter choked back fresh tears. "And soon, you're all going to leave me, too..."

"Peter..." Sam tightened her embrace.

"Everyone always has," he whimpered. "Everyone always will..."

"Time and distance mean *nothing*. You don't know what could happen. Where we end up being," Sam said, gently stroking back his hair. "So what if we all go separate ways? That's *life*. That's growing up."

"Then I don't want to grow up..."

"Do you really think I'm *ever* going to forget you? You're my *best friend*. And whether or not that means forever, in this very moment...in this very *memory*, you will *always* be my best friend. I can't promise that's what twenty-year-old me has to say. Thirty-year-old me. *Forty*-year-old me. But I assure you, in every memory, in every story I will *ever* tell...*seventeen*-year-old me has a best friend they *adore*. A best friend they couldn't *dream* of life without. A best friend named Peter. And I won't *ever* forget him."

Peter nuzzled into her shoulder. He let his breathing slow, trying to focus on something positive. Sam bit her lip as tears pricked her eyes.

"You are *so* loved, Peter," she said. "Don't ever think that you're not. Don't ever think you're a burden. A waste. A disappointment. Your dad loves you. Ritchie loves you. Theo loves you. *I* love you. And we'd *all* be lost without you."

She lowered her forehead to the back of Peter's neck, feeling his shoulders tremble beneath her.

"I want to be able to remember the Peter I grew up with," she said. "Not the Peter who *never* grew up..."

Sam's phone vibrated, screen lighting up as a message displayed across it. A group chat, sent from Ritchie: *CONFIRMED: PARTY AT TRENCHARD'S, BITCHES! HALLOWEEN. 7 P.M.*

Sam dabbed her eyes, reaching for her phone. "Now's not the time, Ritchie..."

"No, wait," Peter said, pulling away from her. "Message him."

"What? Why?"

"That old woman... Remember all those kids that went missing?"

"What about them?" Sam asked.

"Billy Barone. The kid in the news? The one whose mom said he was wearing a cowboy costume? I found him..."

"You *what*?"

"He's dead, Sam," Peter replied, eyes fading back to their empty state. "She buried him in her garden. Covered him in weeds. Used his body for a pumpkin patch."

Sam stared at him. "*What*?"

"I'm serious, Sam... Please."

"You're not shitting me, are you?" Sam asked, gripping her phone tightly. "Like, you're *sure* this wasn't something you saw while you were *tripping*, right?"

"It was *real*," Peter said. "You *have* to believe me. *Please*, Sam."

"You're *sure*?"

Peter nodded. "We have to get the police up there. Text Ritchie."

Sam took a deep breath before pulling up a private message, sending Ritchie a quick text. Once she saw it was delivered, she set her phone down, turning back to Peter. She gazed into his dark brown eyes, still glazed over and tired. Brushing back his bangs, she sighed.

"I just want you to be okay..."

"I'll be okay," Peter said through tight teeth.

"*Promise* me. *Promise* that you'll be okay. That you won't let go. That you'll *stay*. *Promise me* that you'll find your happiness. Even if we're not together to see it. *Promise me*... So when we *do* find each other again, in another time, another place, another *life*, we can say you did it. *Promise* me."

"I promise..."

Sam hesitated, drawing a quivering breath before leaning in to Peter. Their soft lips touched, but only for a moment. Peter pulled away, trembling beneath a warm, static pulse that raced through his veins. A jolt of adrenaline. *Happiness*. Sam touched his cheek, running her fingers across his tear-stained skin before leaning in again. This time, however, he returned the motion—their lips locking. They held against each other for what felt like minutes, until Sam gently backed away. The stale taste of cigarettes on Peter's breath hung in her mouth, but she didn't mind. Tangling her fingers in his hair, she gazed into his eyes.

"*Swear* it."

He rested his head in her lap, exhaustion finally hitting. Breathing softly, he cleared his throat.

"I swear it..."

Sam gently ran her fingertips down his back as he steadily dozed off. The tears had dried on his cheeks now, but their traces were still heavy. Taking a shaky breath, Sam was about to shut her eyes, too, until Peter's soft voice stopped her.

"Sam?"

"Yeah?"

"Can you pull one of your cards for me?"

"Of course," Sam said. "What for?"

"The future," he said quietly. "Just to know what's coming."

Sam dug through her bag, removing her tarot deck. She shuffled the cards, glancing at Peter as he drifted off into a light sleep. As she went through, cycling the cards, one of them fell out—landing on Peter's back. She blinked as she set the deck aside, slowly reaching out and taking it. As she turned it face up, her stomach dropped.

Staring back at her was a terrifying, winged creature: half man, half goat. It sat upon a throne, between Heaven and Hell. Chained on either side of it was a man and a woman. Prisoners. Lost to the void between the light and the dark. And while Sam knew the meaning of the card wasn't one to fear, the name stood out to her. Bold. Blaring.

THE DEVIL.

A LOUD *SPLASH* ECHOED FROM THE POND beyond the cemetery gates. Crows in the nearby tree scattered at the sound, cawing as they dispersed up the hill. Evening fell hard, sending dark shadows across the paths and between the stones. From the water's edge, the faint ray of a flashlight flitted across the pond. And then, a trio of hushed voices rose.

"Be *quiet*." Emily, a girl in her preteens, rolled her eyes.

She tucked one of her long braids behind her ear, rummaging through the thick grass that grew along the water. The two boys with her, Michael and David, looked on in silence. Michael was short for his age—timid. David, on

the other hand, was tall and bulky. Not afraid to be vocal. He crossed his arms, staring at Emily with a huff.

"It was just a *rock*," he snapped.

"I know that, *dipshit*," Emily shot back. "But do you *want* that old fart to find us?"

"Just hurry up." David groaned, rubbing his arms. "It's freezing out here."

Emily unzipped her backpack, motioning Michael closer. He bit his lip, shining the light in the direction she gestured. Sure enough, sticking out beneath the foliage and weeds were five lonely duck eggs. They were cold to the touch, emitting a strong sulfuric odor. Emily gagged as she carefully grabbed them one at a time, placing them into the bag.

"*Shit*." David spat. "Those things *reek*."

"Well, they're rotten," Emily said as she closed the backpack, slipping it over her shoulders. "What do you expect?"

"Where are the ducks?" Michael asked, shining his light across the water. "Why'd they leave the eggs unattended?"

"Who knows." Emily shrugged. "Maybe a fox got them."

"They're going to be so *sick* on Halloween." David cackled. "We still need to decide whose house to bomb with them."

"I've got a list," Emily said. "It'll be total payback. They won't be able to get rid of the smell for *weeks*."

The trio giggled and snorted as they gathered their belongings. Emily kept the backpack steady, as to not crack the eggs while they crept across the lawn. They ducked behind trees as the porch lights of the groundskeeper's home turned on. They flooded the yard, causing the preteens to curse aloud. Keeping low, they scurried off the property and through the cemetery gates.

Horace Johnson huffed as he made his way down the steps. His eyes met the silhouetted figures hurrying down the street, causing him to grimace. The cemetery had been closed for well over an hour—when dusk settled upon the hollow. And now, just days before Halloween, he knew the number of troublesome kids on the grounds would be growing. Gathering a lantern from his porch, he headed out amongst the graves, searching for any trespassers on his nightly routine.

The cemetery was dark as he made his way through, guided by the faint light of his lantern. It swayed as he shone it along the pathways, looking for any sign of vandalism. Yet, everything was silent. Untouched. Horace grunted as he stepped over an exposed root, listening for any sounds that may have drifted from the hilltop. But aside from the chilly breeze, he was met with stillness. As he ventured through the lower plots, scouring for any teenagers hiding behind stone, he was about to turn in for the night. That was, until he spotted the faint firelight up the hill. Near the chapel.

He gritted his teeth as he directed the lantern up the pathways. While it was difficult to make much out in the shadows, Horace was certain he saw the amber light. The hill seemed to glow from it, twinkling within the looming fog.

"Damn kids," he cursed beneath his breath.

He picked up his pace, trudging through the darkness and damp earth. As he approached the crossroads at the center of the cemetery, he heard it. A whisper on the wind, blowing through the treetops. But he paid it no mind, drowning it out with humming. Still, he felt the eyes. Tiny black things watching from above. Prying. Only when he reached the center of the fork did he stop, staring up the path before him. Towards the feeble fire flickering in the night.

For a moment, he thought about turning around. Heading back to the warmth of his home—assessing the damage at dawn. But the idea of trespassers on the property kept him going. He knew the repercussions of not intervening; it would mean finding countless mutilated animal carcasses and graffiti in the daylight. Gripping his lantern determinedly, he ascended the hill.

Leaves crunched behind him—sounds of padded feet echoing off the headstones. Raspy whispers from above coaxed him to carry on. To go to the chapel. Shining his light towards the noises, however, he saw nothing. Horace stiffened, mumbling to himself as he carried on. Blaming delinquent teens.

When he reached the upper cemetery, he stopped. His mouth fell open as his eyes widened, staring out at the scenery. It was covered in pumpkins, far larger than they were weeks prior—vines heavy and thick. There wasn't a gravesite that didn't have at least one sprouting from it. But their multiplied numbers wasn't what troubled him. It was their glow. The candlelight flickering inside.

Every single one of them—*thousands*—had been carved and lit.

Horace lowered his lantern, its light failing in comparison to that of the jack-o'-lanterns. Their faces varied in expression—some cheerful, others sinister. But all of them were turned and facing the path. Facing Horace. *Staring* at him. He swallowed hard as he gazed across the graves and blazing jack-o'-lanterns.

"What the—?"

The tree branches creaked above him. Once more, he sensed the eyes watching. Staring down his neck. The breathy whispers returned, this time as avian hisses.

Hanged Man, Hanged Man...

Horace shone his lantern up towards the trees. Nothing but pitch blackness met him. His heart raced as he gritted his yellowed teeth, listening to the leaves rustle. The bodies shift. The words echo—drifting up the hill.

Hanged Man, Hanged Man...

He kicked one of the pumpkins along the path, smashing its face in with his boot. The candlelight inside quickly vanished. Horace grunted as he stomped chunks of pumpkin flesh from his foot, cursing aloud.

"Show yourself!" He hollered.

He waited in silence for a response, for any movement beyond the graves. But all remained as it was. Just the rustling leaves, the creaking branches, the flickering pumpkins. Horace tightened the grip on his lantern

as he stiffened, hearing the voices again. This time, they were louder. Brushing against his ear.

Hanged Man, Hanged Man...

Vultures scattered from the trees, their large black bodies taking off towards the chapel. Horace flinched as they soared, circling the steeple. But it wasn't their haunting, aerial dance that caught his attention. It was the light bathing from the windows. The door parted wide. The orange glow flashing within—bright like fire. Its steeple bell tolled, echoing across the dark cemetery. A sound not heard in ages. Horace's shoulders trembled as he lowered his lantern, mesmerized by the ringing bell.

Ignoring the whispers on the wind, he started towards the top of the hill. He dragged his feet along the dirt path, lined with the light of the pumpkins. Watching him. Grinning. A crowd of candlelight guiding his way.

Horace knew he had locked the chapel earlier that month. He recalled it being the morning he ran into the elderly woman from beyond the quarry. The elderly woman looking for her missing cat. The cat he had found tongueless, swinging by the neck from the old tree. But once again, the doors were open—flooding the hill in amber light.

He cautiously stepped inside, surveying the area. The chapel was empty, just as it had been on his last visit. Except, unlike before, the decorations and offerings had multiplied.

Carved pumpkins lined the pews, aglow and facing the altar. The candelabras were lit as well, along with what appeared to be hundreds of smaller candles around the reredos. Dried cornstalks still adorned the sanctuary, this time, however, wrapped in thick vine. It stretched across the altar, up the stained glass windows and around the giant cross in the center. In the chancel, three scarecrows were erected—flies buzzing about their worn burlap faces. Scarecrows Horace knew he had seen before—amongst the graves.

He tread carefully, taking in all of the additions. Looking for any sign of trespassers. And while frustration lined his face at the sight of what was clearly vandalism, fear also riddled him. He swallowed back a lump forming in his throat, peering across the nave. Waiting for movement. He let out a gasp, recoiling as a cold gust of air whipped past him. A vulture, soaring down the aisle.

It perched at the pulpit, black beady eyes staring across the pews as it spread its wings. Shifting on its feet, its beak parted as it looked at Horace—gaze searing through him. It hissed, pink tongue lolling from its mouth, whispers from the graves returning.

Hanged Man, Hanged Man...

The sound of heavy paws echoed through the chapel. Leaves scattered, shifting across the wooden floors as Horace tensed. From behind him, a low growl rose. The vulture hunched, tilting its head towards the doors. Following its gaze, Horace glanced over his shoulder.

A large black dog filled the entryway, red eyes gleaming through the dim shadows. Its long, pointed ears stood upright on its head, jowls dripping in hot hate. It raised its hackles, snarling at Horace—tail low. Horace's heart thundered in his chest as he gripped his lantern, the only weapon he had. As he backed away, the dog took a step closer, making its way into the nave. Its white fangs were fully exposed, drenched in thick saliva. With each step forward it took, its growls grew louder. Deeper.

"Go on, *get*!" Horace hollered.

In a panic, he grabbed one of the jack-o'-lanterns from the pews, hurling it at the dog. It hit the ground beside the animal, smashing upon impact. But instead of causing a distraction, Horace only made it angrier. The dog's ears flattened against its head as it lowered itself, creeping between the pews.

"No..." Horace quivered, snatching another pumpkin. "*Get away!*"

Again, he threw it. This time, it should have made contact with the animal's back. But instead, the pumpkin fell to the ground—slipping through the dog's dark, spectral silhouette. Horace's blood ran cold. The dog's jowls drew up into a crescent moon grin—teeth glinting in the candlelight.

Horace shook his head, sweat beading on his face and neck as he trembled. He dropped his lantern, the light inside extinguishing as the glass shattered. With one final attempt to save himself, he backed against the wall.

"*Stay back!*"

The chapel went dark, as if a gust of wind had blown through. Putting out every candle. Every jack-o'-lantern. Horace held his breath, heart racing as he remained still. The shadows around him stirred, his eyes unable to adjust. Everything was pitch black, twinging with the static of the void. That was, until a pair of glowing red eyes appeared—blazing through the darkness—mere inches from his face.

A low growl vibrated around him as he screamed. It only lasted a moment before it became trapped in his throat, overpowered by vicious snarling. And then, all fell silent.

From the pulpit, the vulture watched, wings wide and haunting. It bobbed its head to the sounds of night returning through the chapel—stopping only when another figure appeared in the doorway. It was silhouetted in shadow, features indistinguishable in the dark. The sound of scuffing feet echoed down the aisle, steadily approaching the altar. Only when they stopped before it, admiring the offerings of harvest, did the vulture hiss, bowing its head in deference.

All hail the King.

XII.

The darkness stirred as Peter opened his eyes. Heavy, static music softly fed into his ears through his headphones. It was his last-ditch effort to fall asleep—stay asleep. But, just like every other attempt he made over the month, it failed. The nightmares overpowered the music, gnawing at his thoughts. Prying at his eyelids.

Peter paused the metal vibrations of guitars and drums—throaty growls and bitter angst—sliding the headphones from his ears. They rested around his neck as he peered through the shadows of his room. With the curtains pulled tight, all was darker than usual. Though it was hard to make out any definitive shapes, sound radiated off the walls. Buzzing. Loud in the blackness.

What sounded like a swarm of flies.

Peter gradually sat up, squinting across the room—trying for a better look. He didn't dare turn his bedside lamp on, for fear of what he would find. He remained still, blankets tight around his lower half. His shoulders tensed as the buzzing grew louder. Closer.

A single fly landed on Peter's cheek, crawling towards his eye. He choked out a gasp, swatting it away in disgust and alarm. It flew to his nightstand, resting on the tarot card still there. On the face of the Fool. Sweat formed on Peter's brow as he watched it, matting his hair. His breaths became labored—panic boiling through his chest and into his throat. He tried to quell it, but the putrid stench in the shadows only fueled it.

It was a mix of mud and decay, heavy like the scents in his dreams. Like the reek of the scarecrows Ritchie found in the cemetery. He retched as it grew stronger, flies swarming frantically. Circling his bed.

Across the room, a faint flicker caught Peter's eye. It danced like candlelight, illuminating the dark corner. Only then was Peter able to make out the silhouette of a figure. Tall. Pale. Although hard to see through the shadows, its features were prominent. Its face was gray—skin pulled tight over bone. Long, slender fingers gripped a single white candle—wax landing in droplets on the floor. Where the eyes should have been were only dark, empty sockets. Yet, Peter felt them watching. Staring through him. Craving his soul.

He trembled as tears pricked at his vision. He wanted nothing more than to burrow beneath the comforter—hide between the sheets of his bed— but he was frozen in fear. His chest heaved as his heart raced, drool dripping down his chin in panic. He shut his eyes, shaking his head and cursing aloud.

"*It's not real,*" he repeated. "*It's not real.*"

But when he opened his eyes, the figure was still there. Closer now. The buzzing flies became louder, invading his bed. Peter swatted them away as his tears fell. A wheezing sob escaped his throat. The figure continued to stare at him, blackened teeth exposed—lips curled into a hollow grin. The stench of rot was stronger now, burning Peter's nostrils. He whimpered as his name was called from across the room, echoing in a raspy hiss.

Peter, Peter...

"What do you *want*?" Peter choked out.

His lips quivered as snot ran from his nose, coating them. The figure didn't answer. It only drew closer, the candle glowing brighter. Peter shoved himself backwards in bed—pressed flat against his headboard. His panicky breaths were rapid now.

"*Leave me alone!*" He wept.

Pulling his headphones over his ears, he turned his music back on. Aggressive metalcore blasted through the speakers as he cranked it to full volume. He flinched, gritting his teeth, trying to focus on the lyrics. The guttural lows and high-pitched screams. He closed his eyes, wet tears running down his cheeks. Senses heightening as the fetid odor drew nearer. Wafting against his nostrils.

"It's not real!"

The music cut out, static crackling through the headphones. And then, that low, raspy voice screeched through Peter's ears.

The pumpkins are waiting...

Peter snapped open his eyes, finding the figure looming over him. Its body pressed down against the bed, the candle mere inches from his face. Flies swarmed around its rotten head, pouring from between its teeth as it grinned. A hollow, jack-o'-lantern grin. Peter screamed, reaching for the lamp on his nightstand and turning it on.

His bedroom was flooded with light. As the shadows dispersed, so did the figure. And so did the flies. The blaring music returned through his headphones as he sobbed, frantically searching for any sign of the entity. But it was gone. Lost to the light. As if it had never been there at all. Peter grabbed his pillow, hugging it to his chest as he rocked, wailing into it.

The door to his room opened, Jim rushing inside. He rubbed the sleep from his eyes, adjusting his glasses before addressing Peter—who was shaking violently. He didn't notice his father, too drowned out by the music and fear.

"Petey?" Jim approached the bed. "Petey, what's wrong?"

He gently rested a hand on Peter's shoulder, receiving another scream in return. A panicked, wild gaze. Jim flinched, but softened as his son began to tremble again, spilling tears. Peter pressed his face tight to Jim's chest as he fought to steady his breath. Jim tangled his fingers in his son's hair, stroking it back as he took a seat beside him.

"Shh," he hushed him. "I'm here. It's alright. I'm here."

He held Peter until his sobs died down into weak whimpers, assuring him there was nothing to be afraid of, and that he wasn't alone. As Peter's shoulders eased, body slumping tiredly against his father, Jim found himself staring at the bed. At the old and worn comforter, coated in fresh mud.

XIII.

THE AFTERNOON AIR WAS CRISP on Halloween, weather perfect for trick-or-treating later in the evening. The sound of excited children echoed up and down the street, preparing for the night. Peter slumped, watching them from his bedroom window. He opened it wide, resting his elbows on the sill as he took a long drag on a cigarette. His eyes were lined with dark, heavy bags, thicker than ever. His head spun, littered with anxious thoughts of his nightmares and Grýla's words as he took another puff.

Ashy smoke swirled around his tongue as he kept it trapped in his mouth, closing his eyes. It burned lightly—but the feeling refreshed his dissolving nerves. Parting his lips, he blew the cloud of smoke out his window. His shoulders eased, the rush of nicotine setting in. As he went to take another drag, his phone buzzed with a group message, screen lighting up beside him.

Ritchie set his nickname to Ritchie BOOchanan.
Ritchie set the nickname for Sam to Sam VanderPIRE
Ritchie set the nickname for Theo to Theo KILLiams
Ritchie set your nickname to Peter HarlowEEN
(Ritchie): *Happy Halloween, bitches!*

Peter rolled his eyes and stuck the cigarette between his teeth, picking his phone up. Texting a single *pumpkin* emoji, he waited for the others to reply. He took one last puff, mashing the cigarette butt against the sill before flicking it into the bushes.

(Theo): *Creepy nicknames. Nice!*
(Sam): *Happy Halloween! What's the plan tonight?*
(Theo): *Gotta take my bro n sis trick r treating but good after. We partying?*
(Ritchie): *Duh.*
(Theo): *Trenchard's right?*
(Ritchie): *Yep. What time u free?*
(Sam): *I'm down whenever. Just lmk.*

Peter sat on the edge of his bed, thumbing his phone. It vibrated as he replied: *Same.*

(Theo): *8 good? Gives me time to get home n ready.*
(Sam): *Works for me.*
(Peter): *Yea*
(Ritchie): *Cool cool. YO wait til u see my costume. It's GREAT.*
(Sam): *Oh I bet. See u at 8*
(Theo): *Ttyl*

Peter sent a *thumbs up* emoji. He slouched his shoulders, staring at his phone as the group message went silent. Biting his lip, he took a deep breath, opening a private message with Sam. His thumb hovered over the keyboard hesitantly before sending a quick text: *Can I call u?*

He waited a moment, staring impatiently at the chat before Sam wrote back: *OFC.*

Again, he hesitated before hitting the call icon. The dial tone rang twice on the other end before Sam picked up.

"Hey, Peter," she said. "Happy Halloween! What's up?"

"I just need to talk to somebody," he said quietly.

"What's wrong?"

"I had another bad night. Really bad dreams."

"The same stuff?"

"Worse."

There was silence. Fidgeting with his lighter, he shut his eyes. His chest ached as the anxiety returned—washing over him. From the other end of the phone, Sam spoke softly.

"Peter?"

"I'm scared," he said, tears welling in his tired eyes.

"Of what?"

A pause. "Dying."

"You *don't* have to worry about that, Peter," Sam said sternly. "Not for a long time, anyway."

"No." Peter shook his head. "You don't get it, Sam. I feel it coming. Remember what I told you? Well, it's worse now. It's *here*. I saw it..."

"Saw it? What are you talking about?"

"The Devil."

"*Peter...*"

"It's waiting. And tonight... Tonight, I just *know* it's going to try and take me."

Sam sighed. "Well I won't let it. We'll be together tonight. *All* of us. So there's nothing to be afraid of."

Peter sniffled. Wiping his nose on the back of his hand, he released a shaky breath. One Sam could hear.

"I just know it's inevitable," he said. "I keep telling myself it would be so much easier if I just accepted it. Took fate into my own hands. Ended it myself."

"*Don't say that.*" Sam snapped.

"But what if I'm right?"

"Peter..."

"What *if*, Sam?"

There was silence. In the background of Sam's line, hushed voices could be heard. Chewing his lip, Peter whimpered.

"I'm just so scared..."

"I'll be with you," Sam replied. "You know that, right? You're *not* alone. You're not going to *be* alone. We're all going out together to have a good night. And I *won't* leave you. No matter what."

"Promise?"

"Promise."

Rustling sounds came through Sam's end of the phone. There was muffled speaking, Sam answering the voices before returning to Peter.

"Hey, my sister just got home. We're carving pumpkins. I'll see you tonight, okay?"

"Okay..."

"Wanna meet at seven? We can talk more before Ritchie and Theo show up."

"Sure."

"See you later."

"Later."

The call ended. Setting his phone aside, Peter laid on his bed, staring at the ceiling. His chest ached, full of fear and anxiety and sorrow. The weight of the month pressed down on him heavily. His eyes grew vacant as the late afternoon shadows slipped across his room. It wasn't long before most of the light dispersed, lost to the gloom of evening.

Peter sat up, glancing to his desk beside the window. The Light-and-Glow Pumpkin Mask his father had given him weeks prior sat atop it, pathetically staring at him from across the room. He sighed, getting to his feet and shuffling over to the desk. Looking the mask over in disdain.

"This is so stupid." Peter grumbled.

Picking it up, he slid it over his head. The rubber and latex were cool and smooth, air circulation impeccable. No condensation built up from his breathing, and the mask fit just right. There was no constriction. No discomfort. Reaching to the back of the mask, Peter pressed the switch, illuminating the eyes and mouth. Bright light poured from them—giving him a realistic jack-o'-lantern look. As he turned side to side, searching for the mirror to get a glimpse of how he looked, he snorted.

"I can't see *shit* in this thing."

Peter yanked it off, running his fingers through his mussed hair and sneering at the mask.

"Great product, *Dad*. Thanks a lot."

He clenched the mask, glancing out the window. The evening shadows were thick now, streetlights turning on as the sound of children hurrying from their homes echoed inside. With a deep breath, he left the quiet of his bedroom, heading to the living room to finish preparing for the night.

176

Jim watched in concern as Peter kneeled beside the front door, tying the laces of his worn and mud-stained Converse. Above him, a large black fly buzzed. Jim waved it away when it came to circle him, landing on the doorframe. He kept his gaze on it as he returned his attention to Peter, clearing his throat.

"Heading somewhere?" he asked softly.

"Out," Peter replied, straightening himself. "It's Halloween."

"Well, yes, I know that..."

Jim glanced at the pumpkin mask gripped in Peter's hand. The latex crumpled in his grasp.

"Are you wearing that mask?"

"Uh, yeah. I guess?"

"Maybe...maybe you shouldn't."

"Why not? Isn't that what you *wanted*?"

"Yes, but..."

Jim took a deep breath, closing his eyes. Peter stared at him, pursing his lips. Waiting for an explanation. But Jim changed the subject.

"Where are you going?"

"Just out. I already said that."

Peter flashed his father a quick, annoyed glance as he shuffled for the door. But before he could leave, Jim blocked his way. His expression became stark as his eyes met Peter's.

"Clearly," Jim replied. "But *where* exactly are you going?"

"Why does it matter?"

"It matters because I *say* it does, Peter," Jim replied, shoulders tensing. "Now, I'm not going to ask you again. *Where* are you going?"

"To a party."

"With?"

"My friends."

Jim motioned him to go on. "And where's this party at?"

"What is this? 50 Questions?"

"I don't like the sarcasm, Peter." Jim's voice grew stern.

"And I don't like that you're up my *ass* all of a sudden, *Dad*," Peter snapped back. "What's your deal?"

"Watch your tone." Jim jabbed a finger at his son. "You know what my *deal* is. We've been over this, Peter. Strange things are happening in this town. Kids are going missing. And tonight, with everyone out on the streets, everyone in *costume*... The police have already recommended staying in, if possible."

"So, what? You want me to stay *home*?"

"I just want to know where you are, Peter," Jim implored.

"And who I'm with. Where I'm going. What I'm doing." Peter rolled his eyes. "Why are you interrogating me?"

"I don't want you to get *hurt*. Or *worse*."

"I'm going out with my friends to a party." Peter threw his hands up. "I shouldn't have to tell you *everything*, Dad."

"No. But when I ask you these things, I shouldn't be lied to."

Peter scowled. "*Lied to*? I didn't lie to you."

"Well, it's getting hard for me to know for sure anymore."

"What does *that* mean?"

Jim hesitated, sighing as he shook his head. "I'm worried, Peter."

"About *what*?"

"A lot of things."

Jim took a deep breath. Pinching the bridge of his nose, he remained silent. It grew thick through the living room as Peter's frustrated stares became vacant.

"The police were here, Peter."

"*What*?"

"They were asking questions about you. Wanting to know the same sort of thing *I'm* asking. Where you've been. Who you've been with. What you've been doing. Where you've been going."

Hot tears pricked at Peter's eyes. "*Why*? Why were they even *here*?"

"Why don't *you* tell *me*, Peter," Jim said, crossing his arms. "In *your* words."

"I don't *know*," Peter said. "I didn't *do* anything."

Again, Jim sighed. He leaned against the doorframe, disturbing the fly. It buzzed away, circling the two of them. Jim's lips drew into a disappointed frown.

"Here's your chance to tell the truth," he said. "I already know what's going on, so don't lie to me."

"I already told you, *I didn't do anything*."

"Oh, cut the shit, Peter." Jim shook his head, brow furrowed. "You already confessed that you snuck out to the cemetery earlier this month. That the cat followed you home from there—*not* school, like you originally told me. And I got confirmation that yes, you *were* up there that night. You and your friends got busted. You're *lucky* you didn't get charged with trespassing."

"We already *talked* about this," Peter replied, backing away. "Look, I'm sorry, okay? I shouldn't have even gone up there in the first place."

"*Exactly*," Jim said. "However, the police tell me that's not the *only* time you've been up there."

Peter stiffened. He was expecting to hear Horace Johnson's reports of him dropping the cat off early in the morning, and of spending the afternoon with his friends on the grounds. But when his father shook his head, eyes dark, he knew there was more.

"The police said you've been going up there almost *nightly*, Peter. Wandering around. Lighting fires. *Sacrificing animals*."

"*What*?" Peter snapped, chest going cold.

"They said you *killed* that cat," Jim said, concern etched deep on his face. "You complained about it *every goddamn morning*. Said you didn't know *what else to do* about it. You told me you took it back where you found it. And you *lied* to me about where it came from."

"That doesn't mean I *killed* it," Peter shot back. "Come on. Don't you believe me?"

"It's hard when things aren't adding up, Peter," Jim said, digging his fingers into his forehead in frustration. "Or, really, when they add up *too* well."

With a heavy sigh, Jim gestured to his son's Converse. Though old and worn, they hadn't been nearly as muddy the day prior. The once white rubber toes were scuffed and covered in streaks of dried mud—dotted with fragments of decaying leaves. Jim shook his head.

"Your shoes are filthy. Your *sheets* were filthy. Covered in mud."

The color drained from Peter's face, lips parting. His eyes became worried as he stared at his father.

"I found blood on one of your shirts. Blood on your sheets. Your *pillowcase*."

"I had a *nosebleed*!"

179

Jim shook his head. "They said you brought that cat up there stuffed in a pillowcase..."

"*Really*, Dad? Do you *really* think—"

"What do you *expect* me to think, Peter? You're not sleeping. And then you're either awake before dawn, or you end up staying in your room napping until noon. It's everything the police said. The fact there was a witness... And how do you explain the bugs? All the flies and ants getting all over this house the last week or so?"

"*You* said they were coming in from the rain."

"I *thought* they were coming in from the rain," Jim corrected him. "Until I started realizing when I'd get up in the morning, the front door was ajar. Letting anything that wanted to come in, in. Or, in this case, letting whatever wanted *out*, out."

"Are you saying I'm *sleepwalking*?"

"What else do you *want* me to say, Peter?"

"*That I didn't do it*!"

"Stop *lying* to me."

"I'm *not lying*!"

"I *hear* you, Peter." Jim sourly stared at his son. "Every goddamn night. In your room. I *hear* you walking around. Pacing. Talking out loud—having a conversation with the air. Rambling incoherent things."

Peter was taken aback. His eyes widened in disbelief.

"I *know* what sleepwalking is," Jim said. "This is *exactly* what your mother started to do before she went downhill. Before things got *really* bad."

Peter tightened his grip on the pumpkin mask. His lips drew together, eyes narrowing. Before he could speak, however, Jim continued lowly.

"Do we need to make an appointment with your doctor?"

"No."

"I *really* think we should."

"*No*."

"I'm *worried*, Peter. You're becoming just like her. Only...*she* didn't brutally murder a cat."

"*And neither did I*!" Peter shouted.

"*Tone*."

"I'm *telling* you, Dad. I *didn't do it*. I didn't do *anything*."

Jim shook his head. "I'm *at least* calling your therapist in the morning. Maybe you need new medication. *Something*."

"*Dad*!"

180

"It's *scaring* me, Peter. Things are getting out of control around here," Jim said. "You're spiraling, falling back into bad habits. Failing classes. I've stood by and I've tried to help the best I can, but you're clearly not talking to me. *Something* is wrong. *Very* wrong. I can only help as much as you let me, and you're *not* letting me."

"I *can't* talk about it."

"Why not?"

Peter frowned, glancing away. "Because..."

"Because *why*?"

"You won't believe me."

"I would if you tried."

"No."

"Just *try*."

"I *don't* want to talk about it!"

"And *that's* the problem, Peter. You keep everything bottled up inside. You wait until things get *so bad* that you let them boil over. Take them out on those around you." Jim motioned at his son. "Like *that cat* for instance. You know, with all that's going on in this town, now *really* isn't the time for you to be doing this. Do you want them accusing you of being involved with all the missing kids, too?"

"*That's not me*!" Peter wailed, throwing up his hands. "*Fine*. You want me to talk? I'll talk. You want to know where the kids are, Dad? Why don't you go ask that crazy old hermit who lives out by the quarry, hm? *Go ask her*."

"*What*?"

"Her herbs. They're all buried with her herbs. They've got pumpkins growing from their heads. Why don't you have the police go out there and dig it up? They'll find a whole *garden* of bodies."

Jim's face went pale. Swallowing hard, he backed away from the door, eyes wide.

"How...how do you know where the bodies are, Peter?"

"Because I went over there to give my condolences for her cat," Peter said. "She *drugged* me. Gave me this soup that made me trip *balls*. I saw them when I managed to escape. Buried out by her house. I *saw them*."

"So *that's* where you were..."

Peter chewed his lip. His father looked him over, chest heavy with fear and disappointment. Tears stung his eyes. Peter gritted his teeth, eyes wet with his own angry tears.

"Why are you afraid of me, Dad?"

Jim didn't answer. He replayed what his son just said in his head over again. Bodies buried in the herbs, sprouting pumpkins from their heads. It was unreal. After a moment, he spoke, voice low.

"You need *help*, Peter…"

"*Help*? Why? What for?"

"You need to get back on your medication," Jim said, shaking his head. "You're not well."

"What are you *talking about*?"

"How do you know where the bodies are? Don't *lie* to me, Peter. *How do you know*?"

Peter quivered, balling his hands into fists. "What are you trying to say?"

"*Answer me*! *How*, Peter?"

"See? This is why I don't tell you things. You don't believe me. You just blame me. Treat me like I'm *sick*. But I didn't do it, Dad. I didn't do *fucking shit*!"

Jim stepped towards him. "*Watch your mouth*!"

"You're *not* listening to me." Peter snapped. "*Why won't you believe me*?"

"Are you even listening to *yourself*, Peter? You're *not* making sense. I've *seen* this before. I've *seen* it with Mom. Now I'm *seeing* it with *you*. This isn't something we can just brush off. Say, oh, Petey just had a bad day. What don't you understand about the *police were here*? This is *serious*."

"Yes. Yes it *fucking* is! You don't give a shit that I *saw dead kids*. I *know where they are*. And you don't even care that the one responsible *fucking drugged me*. She tried to kill *me too*, Dad. She's *still* trying. *She's* the reason I'm having nightmares. The reason all this is happening. She wants me dead so she can grow her *fucking pumpkins*. But *you* don't believe me. If I went missing tonight, you wouldn't even give a *shit*."

"Stop that right now. You *know* that's not true. *Why* do you think we're having this conversation? I *love* you, Peter."

"No you don't."

"*Peter*."

"No! If you loved me, you'd *fucking believe* me. But you *don't*. You *never* do. *This* is why I don't tell you things. You don't give a shit. You don't give a *fucking shit*!"

Peter's exhausted eyes narrowed. His lips drew into a hard frown as he glared at his father. His heart pounded in his chest, full of fear.

Disappointment. The grip on his mask tightened more as his shoulders trembled.

"You're out of control. You see all this pent up rage? *This* is what your mother couldn't stand," Jim said. "The lying. The sneaking around. The cursing. The yelling. The *attitude*."

"Shut up..."

"*This* is what she worried about *constantly*. What *I* worry about constantly. That you were going to get yourself into trouble someday. That you'd never apply yourself. Never have a *goddamn future*. Yes, she was *sick*. But all this constant worry about *you* made her *worse*. It was *killing* her."

"Shut *up*."

"*This* is why she chose to leave."

"*Shut the fuck up!*"

A loud slap echoed across the living room as Jim's open palm collided with Peter's left cheek. He stumbled from the blow, face stinging. Touching a hand to his cheek, Peter's eyes widened—welling with tears. His mouth fell open in shock as he stared at his father. Immediately, Jim regretted it. Tears of his own built in his eyes as he took a step towards Peter, holding his hand out.

"Petey..."

"*Don't* touch me."

"Petey, I'm *sorry*. I didn't mean—"

"Stay away from me."

"Petey, please... You need to calm—"

"*Stay the fuck away from me!*"

Peter shoved his father away from the door. Yanking it open, he ran down the front steps and across the lawn. Jim leaned out of the house, calling for him. But Peter didn't look back.

He crossed the street, disappearing into the shadows and the growing crowd of trick-or-treaters. Their boisterous laughter echoed down the block as Jim stood in the doorway, tears clouding his vision. He swallowed a sob as he turned the porch light on. It flooded the yard, leaving a beacon for his son to find later that night after curfew. When the other children had gone home, and the darkness set in heavy.

The orange and purple string lights adorning porches sparkled in the shadows of early evening, lighting homes and yards as children hurried from house to house for candy. By the time 7 p.m. rolled around, the streets were packed. Symphonies of "*Trick-or-Treat*" echoed down the block as Peter made his way to the corner of Hemlock Avenue.

He glanced at the pumpkin mask in his hand, feeling disdain for it stronger than ever. But as he shifted his eyes through the costumed crowd around him, he sighed. Slipping the mask over his head, he flicked the switch on the back of the neck—light pouring from the eyes and mouth. He still struggled to see clearly, but he'd rather deal with the blurriness than the prying eyes of passing trick-or-treaters.

As he rounded the corner, he grunted as a young girl collided with him. He could barely make out her witch costume from behind his mask—or the two boys accompanying her. Shoving him away, she spat at his feet.

"Watch where you're going, *dipshit*."

Shouldering past him, she continued on her way, the boys trailing at her heels. The heavy stench of sulfur lingered on them and even through his mask, Peter could smell it. He scrunched his nose at the odor, giving them one final glance. The heavier set of the boys, dressed in a white and black striped prison uniform, looked back at him, throwing his arms up threateningly.

"What are *you* looking at, Pumpkin Head?"

Peter didn't waste his time with them. Lowering his head, he shoved his hands into his pockets, venturing down the block towards Sam's neighborhood.

The night air was cool as Peter found a seat upon an old garden wall. It was covered in ivy, snaking down the stones like curtains. His shoulders slouched as he swung his legs, gazing across the dark streets. Yellow light poured from his mask, illuminating the sorrowful expression of the jack-o'-lantern. One that mirrored himself beneath the latex. He sniffled, cheek still warm and stinging, as he went to flick the switch off. Before he could, however, a soft voice stopped him.

"Is that you, Peter?"

He raised his head, trying to focus on the figure approaching him. He squinted, making out a dark shape, but not much more. He grabbed the sides of the mask, attempting to work it off as it clung to his neck.

"Here, let me help."

A soft pair of hands overlaid his, giving the extra strength he needed to pull the mask over his head. He turned the glow feature off, letting his eyes adjust to the evening. Blinking back tears, he was relieved as Sam came into view. She was dressed in a simple black dress with flowing sleeves. A matching witch's hat sat on her head, violet hair bright beneath the streetlamps. With a smile, she held her arms out to her sides, showing off her outfit.

"What do you think?" she asked. "It's not much, but it's comfy."

"It looks great," Peter said, wiping his nose on his sleeve.

Sam tilted her head as she looked him over. His eyes were dark with heavy bags, puffy and tearful. Beneath the faint light, she could see the redness flushing his cheek. Biting her lip, she reached out, gently resting her fingertips against it. Peter flinched.

"What happened?"

He didn't respond. His gaze remained fixed on the ground as a lone tear ran down his cheek. It fell against Sam's fingers, causing her to brush it away gently with her thumb.

"Peter..."

185

"Everything's my fault..."

Peter choked back a whimper. He squeezed his eyes shut, trying to hold back his tears. A few rolled down his cheeks. Sam did her best wiping them away, careful of his red, tender skin.

"No it's not," she said.

She took a seat beside him on the wall. With a deep breath, she touched his knee, giving it a squeeze. He tensed.

"Talk to me."

"The cops showed up at my house." Peter stared into the shadows of the neighborhoods, lost in the orange lights. "They interrogated my dad. Said I've been up in the cemetery at night, and that I killed that cat. All the shit everyone's been blaming me for lately."

"What did your dad say?"

"He didn't believe me, of course," Peter said. "He *never* does. And he wouldn't listen. He just thinks I'm crazy. That I need to be put on *more* medication. That I'm turning into my mother. That...all this is why she left. That she left because of *me*."

"That's *not true*," Sam replied sternly, turning to face him.

Peter shook his head. "It *is*, though, Sam. I've been nothing but a burden to everyone. Literally *everyone*."

"You are *not* a burden, Peter. You have to stop saying that," Sam said, taking his hand into hers. "Your mom *adored* you. At least every time *I* recall her being around she did."

"She told me she *hated* me," Peter said. "That was the last thing she ever said to me. In the living room. I'll never forget it. I was by the bookshelf, she was at the door. Her bags were packed and I just kept apologizing. Begging her to stop. To *stay*. But she didn't. She just told me I was a waste. A failure. A *fool*. She told me she hated me. And then she left."

Peter pulled his hand out of Sam's grasp. He swallowed the lump in his throat, placing his head in his hands. Sam rubbed his back soothingly, eyes softening.

"The worst thing is..." Peter blubbered. "I can't even remember what she was mad about."

"Your mom wasn't herself after the tumor," Sam said. "She was losing touch with reality. She saw things that weren't there and she was short with everyone. She took her anger out on you and your dad over trivial things. She didn't know what she was saying or doing anymore."

Peter was silent. He kept his face burrowed into his hands as he sniffled.

 186

"I know what she said at the end hurt. Those are words that she can never take back, and I know they haunt you. They sting. They're *always* going to," Sam said. "But, you also need to remember who your mom was *before* she got sick. She loved you unconditionally... She was the mom who always made sure your lunches were packed and the crusts cut off your sandwiches. The mom who drove back to school after hours, demanding to get into the classroom because you forgot your coat in the middle of winter. The mom who always brought in a huge batch of cupcakes on your birthday. The mom who, every single time you stepped out the door or into the school, would tell you she loved you. Literally announce it to the *whole* parking lot... The mom who called and demanded lefty desks be in *every one* of your classrooms. So you would be comfortable taking notes and tests. So you didn't associate learning with discomfort. So you could *succeed*. The last thing she ever wanted was to see you fail. Because she *loved* you."

Peter released a soft sob. Leaning in, Sam nuzzled her cheek against his shoulder, still rubbing his back. Closing her eyes, she sighed.

"*That's* your mom, Peter," she continued. "*Not* the woman at the end whose mind was deteriorating. Who didn't know what she was doing or saying. There was never any hate. Only love. And maybe her way of showing that love to you in the end, when words clearly didn't work, was to leave. So you didn't have to remember her that way. So you wouldn't forget who she *really* was. So you didn't have to watch her become someone she wasn't. Lost to the darkness of her mind. Sometimes the best thing we can do for someone we love is leave, no matter how much it hurts."

"I don't want *you* to leave, Sam..."

She lifted her head, watching Peter's hands fall to his lap. Streaks of tears stained his cheeks, his eyes empty. Sam tucked a strand of hair behind her ear as she frowned.

"I'm not leaving for a while, Peter," she said. "Not until August *at least*. And even so, that's not going to change *anything*. We'll still call."

"We won't even be in the same time zone..."

"Well, then I'll text you. Every day."

"But how long will *that* last?"

"What do you mean?" Sam tilted her head.

"How long until you don't anymore? Until those daily texts become weekly. Monthly. *Yearly*. And then, not at all."

Another tear fell as Peter stared across the street. The orange lights down the block reflected in his dark brown eyes. Sam's frown became more prominent as she scooted closer to him.

187

"That's something only time knows, Peter. And that's saying if that even happens at all."

"Will it?"

"I hope not. But it may," Sam said honestly. "That's life, unfortunately. That's growing up. The years we've all spent together are nothing in comparison to what's ahead. We're *seventeen*, Peter. We've barely begun to live our lives. When we've lived another seventeen years, this is going to seem like a lifetime ago. In fact, it *will* be a lifetime ago."

A heavy breath slipped from Peter's lips, shoulders trembling again. Deep in his chest, he felt the burn. The painful ache of understanding.

"And if we count lifetimes by seventeen...we've got so many more to live, Peter. Who knows what we'll be doing. Who we'll become. We're not going to be who we are today. We'll *never* be who we are today again. And that's just the thing. So many people drift apart and find each other after many years—many lifetimes. But, when they *do* meet again, they're strangers. Because that's how life is. We change. We grow. And there's nothing to be afraid of about that."

Peter sniffled loudly as a stream of tears returned. He blubbered, gritting his teeth.

"But I *am* afraid, Sam."

"Why?"

He turned to her slowly, eyes puffy. "I'm afraid I'll have to remember you so much longer than I ever knew you. But I don't want to *remember* you, Sam. I want you *here*. Making memories with me. Not *leaving* them for me. I don't want you to leave me..."

"And I want you making memories with me, too, Peter. I really do. But it's not practical to sit here and make promises I can't keep. I'd *never* do that to you," Sam said. "I'm moving to New York after graduation. I need to follow *my* dreams. I don't know where they'll take me from there. I could be in New York a year. Maybe ten. Maybe the rest of my life. I don't know, I can't tell you. But, no matter what, I'll come visit, you know? I'm not going to just leave and never come back."

"You'll visit your mom and sister," Peter said. "Your *family*. As you should. But...you'll only be here a short time. You won't have time to visit me."

"I'll make time."

Peter swallowed around the hot lump in his throat. "What if your family moves away? You'll have no reason to come here ever again. I won't *ever see you again*."

Sam was silent. She frowned as she searched for what to say. Peter sniffled again, breaths becoming unsteady. Sighing softly, Sam turned to him.

"I'll visit you, Peter," she said. "Even if it's every few years. I *promise*. But until that time comes...until things become too busy, too complicated...I *will* text you every day. To let you know I'm still here. I'll *always* be here. Even if we're not face to face."

"But I *like* being face to face..."

Sam's fingers laced with his. The streetlamp above them flickered as they stared out across the neighborhood—taking in the darkness. The porch lights in the distance. The sound of children squealing. Reminiscing their own years trick-or-treating down those same streets, laughing beneath the lights. Bags full of candy. Giving his hand a squeeze, Sam whispered against his ear.

"The beautiful thing about memories is that we'll *always* be seventeen. We never have to grow up. We'll stay this way until the end of time. In this night. In this moment," Sam said. "The future is full of endless possibilities, so many roads to take. So many outcomes. We'll never know how it ends until we get there."

Sam closed her eyes. She could feel Peter trembling, causing her to tighten her grip on his hand. Running her thumb against his knuckles, she smiled sadly.

"No matter what happens, I'm never going to forget you, Peter. No matter what. You will *always* have a place in my heart. Forever."

"*Forever...*"

"I promise."

Peter let the last tear fall. It rolled down his cheek, dripping from his chin as he sniffled. His focus remained on the distant lights—twinkling at the end of the block.

"I miss you already, Sam..."

Peter and Sam sat in silence for the rest of the hour. They huddled close together, fingers still laced. Eventually, Sam pulled away, straightening herself and smiling. She stared affectionately at Peter—the tear stains on his cheeks now faded along with the redness. Pressing her lips together in thought, she swung her legs.

"So," she began slowly, "Homecoming. That's next week already... You going?"

"Huh?" Peter asked, turning his attention to her. "Sorry. Homecoming? Ah, well, I don't know, I..."

"Do you *wanna* go?"

"I mean, it's not really my th—" Peter stopped short, blinking. "Wait. You're *asking* me? Like, if I wanna go with you? As in, *together*?"

Sam nodded. "*Duh.*"

Peter kept his gaze on her, a soft smile tugging at his lips. Running his fingers across the back of his neck, he shrugged.

"Sure. I mean, of course. *Yes.*"

Sam grinned. "Good."

"You know it's just a jock and prep party though, right?" Peter said, leaning back on his palms.

Sam chuckled, adjusting her witch hat. "Trust me, I know. It's going to *suck* big time. But, that's okay because *you'll* be there. That's all that matters."

Peter managed a smirk, slowly leaning towards Sam. He closed his eyes, parting his lips to lock them with hers. But he was quickly drawn away by the sound of crunching leaves coming up beside them. Startled, he glanced over his shoulder, spotting Theo approaching—pillowcase stuffed with candy swinging at his side.

"Happy Halloween, guys!"

Once beneath the streetlights, Peter and Sam could make out his costume. He wore his varsity jacket, unbuttoned over a flannel shirt. Much of his look was no different, aside from the makeup applied to his face. Dark shadows circled his eyes, lining his cheekbones—accentuating them. A set of cheap vampire teeth protruded from his mouth, prosthetics attached to his ears to make them pointed. Tufts of dark, patchy costume fur lined his jaw. He flashed his friends a plastic grin.

"Awesome costume, Theo," Sam said. "You look great."

"Thanks." He popped the fangs from his mouth. "I was hung up on what I wanted to do, but you know how much I love that song they play this time of year. You know the creature from the movie in the music video? I just had to."

"It's really cool," Peter said.

"Hey, where's Ritchie? Wasn't he the one that was in such a hurry to go to this party?" Sam asked.

Theo pursed his lips. Holding his hands up placatingly, he kept his voice low.

"He'll be here any second. And, I'm just giving you the head's up right now... I had *nothing* to do with it. That's all I'm going to say."

"Nothing to do with *what*?" Sam raised an eyebrow.

Down the sidewalk, Ritchie's boisterous hoots and hollers drifted to them. Theo exhaled a deep breath, shaking his head. The tinny sound of jingle bells echoed as Ritchie drew nearer, catching the attention of the friends. Once he, too, was beneath the lights, his costume became apparent.

The jingling came from the jester hat upon his head, situated neatly atop his auburn locks. Over one arm, he draped his varsity jacket—wearing a worn, unbuttoned flannel over a white t-shirt. He held a baseball bat against his other shoulder, pillowcase tied around the end in a makeshift bindle. An ugly prosthetic hooked nose was attached over his own, and a large, fake mole dotted his upper left cheek. Flashing a toothy grin, he held his arms out, showing off his chosen outfit.

"Whaddaya think?" he asked, waggling his eyebrows. "Pretty great, huh?"

"What the fuck are *you* supposed to be?" Sam asked, crossing her arms.

"Can't you tell?" Ritchie asked with a shrug. "I'm Peter. Just like on that card."

He stuck his upper teeth out, hooting again as he swung his head in circles, jingling the bells on his hat wildly. Theo gave him a sharp elbow in the ribs. Ritchie winced at the impact, straightening himself up as he glanced between Sam and Peter.

"Oh, wait! I forgot." Snapping his fingers, he reached into his pocket, pulling out a bubblegum cigarette. "Here. How about this?"

He stuck it between his lips, walking over to the stone wall and giving it a blow. A puff of sugar powder blasted into Peter's face. Ritchie cackled as Sam clenched her fists, hopping down from the wall. She shoved him hard as he staggered backwards, still grinning.

"You're an *asshole*." Sam spat.

"Oh, come on. It's just a joke. Peter doesn't give a shit. Right, Peter?"

Peter didn't say anything. His lips were drawn into a frown as he stared at Ritchie. Sam glared at him, getting into his face.

"Take it off."

"Lighten up, Sam."

"No. Ritchie. Take it off, *now*."

When he didn't budge, she ripped the fake nose from his face. Ritchie hollered as it snapped away. She tossed it over the garden wall angrily.

"What was *that* for?" Ritchie barked in alarm.

"You're a *fool*, Ritchie."

"Well, *obviously*."

Letting out a chuckle, he flashed a grin and held his arms out again. Then, he turned his attention to Peter, still seated on the wall. Unwrapping the stick of gum, he popped it into his mouth, chewing audibly and gesturing to his friend.

"So, what are *you* supposed to be, Peter?"

Peter remained silent. Picking up his mask, he slipped it over his head, flicking the switch at the back of his neck. Golden light blazed behind the sorrowful expression of the pumpkin—bright and blinding. Ritchie suppressed a snort.

"A *pumpkin*?" he asked. "You could have literally been anything, and you went with a *pumpkin*?"

"My dad's company gave it to me," Peter replied dryly.

"*I* think it's awesome," Theo said. "Definitely high quality."

Ritchie scoffed, pushing up on his nose tauntingly as he sang. "*Peter, Peter pumpkin-eater.*"

Peter's heart stopped. A lump swelled in his throat as the hair on the back of his neck rose. He furrowed his brow at Ritchie, voice cracking beneath his mask.

"W-what?"

"You know, that old nursery rhyme," Ritchie said. "How'd it go? *Peter, Peter pumpkin-eater. Had a wife, but couldn't keep her. He put her in a pumpkin-shell, and there he kept her very well.*"

Peter tensed as Ritchie's laughter echoed down the block again. He jabbed a thumb towards the wall.

"You know. I never really thought too much about that rhyme before," he said. "But that Peter, Peter has abandonment issues out the *ass*."

"Shut the fuck up, Ritchie," Sam growled.

193

"*What?* I'm just saying. His wife ran off and he got depressed, so he chased her down and locked her up so she'd never leave again. That's some messed up shit, man."

Sam rolled her eyes. Turning her attention to Peter, the face of his mask was all she was met with. Glinting in the darkness. He, however, was silent. Stiff.

"Come on," Theo finally interjected. "If we're going to this party, we better get a move on."

"Yeah, no *way* we're missing the good stuff," Ritchie said, starting off down the street without them.

Theo trailed along, motioning for Sam and Peter to follow. They stayed behind for a moment, waiting until their friends were just out of sight. With a sigh, Sam shook her head.

"Fuck Ritchie."

Peter slid down from the wall, light pouring from his mask. The miserable face of the jack-o'-lantern made Sam frown.

"Are you okay, Peter?"

"Yeah, it's fine," he said. "That's just how Ritchie is. It's his weird way of showing he cares. I've gotten used to it."

"He doesn't have to be a *dick* to you, though."

"He's a dick to *everyone*."

"You promise you're okay?"

"Yeah."

Sam reached out and took Peter's hand. Their fingers laced as they began down the dark sidewalk—trailing far enough behind their friends so they couldn't see them. Overhead, the full moon shone—huge and orange—guiding their way to the party at the edge of town.

XIV.

LAUGHTER ECHOED THROUGHOUT THE NEIGHBORHOOD as evening fell into night. The streets were crowded with children and teens, hurrying from door to door for the last scraps of Halloween candy before curfew. The luminescent glow of lights lit up the block—shining from streetlamps and porch lights. The brightest house on the block, however, was at the far end of the cul-de-sac. The Trenchards'—bustling with music and costumed partygoers.

Ritchie unwrapped a lollipop, sticking it in his mouth as he walked. The bells on his jester hat jingled with each step. His friends trailed closely behind, unwrapping candy of their own.

"If you need more, I've got plenty," Theo said, shaking his pillowcase full of sweets. "I usually just give what I get to my brother and sister, so everything's free game."

"Where'd you even manage to get *that* much," Ritchie asked, lollipop bobbing in his mouth.

"Over on Sugar Maple." Theo smirked. "Literally every house gives out handfuls."

"Damn. I've been missing out all these years," Ritchie said.

Sam raised her half-eaten chocolate bar. "Thank you for sharing with us, Theo."

"Of course."

He turned his attention to her, dark eyes falling to her fingers—still laced with Peter's. His gaze lingered for a moment until Peter noticed. He cleared his throat, quickly pulling his hand from Sam's grasp. He tucked it against the soft sleeve of his flannel shirt, popping his knuckles nervously. Sam took another bite of her chocolate, face flushing beneath the dim streetlights. Theo gave them a soft smile before returning his attention to the sidewalk. Once they were sure there were no more prying eyes, Peter and Sam released deep breaths—this time, keeping their hands apart.

"I'm surprised your dad actually agreed to let you go out." Theo glanced at Ritchie. "Wasn't he insistent that Halloween be canceled?"

Ritchie pulled the lollipop from his mouth with a scoff. "Still is. But the chief decided that canceling it would just cause backlash. They didn't want to deal with the complaints and drama. So they just upped the number of officers on patrol tonight."

"And he's fine with you going to the party?" Theo raised an eyebrow.

"He knows I'll be at Trenchard's," Ritchie said. "My mom gave him an earful about it. She said it's a crowded place and they know *exactly* where I'm at. If anything happens, the cops will have it covered. He knows better than to argue with her, so here we are."

The leaves crunched beneath their feet as they rounded the corner, down the long stretch of road to the Trenchards' house. The homes that lined the street were far larger and more extravagant than those adjacent— indicating the start of the wealthier neighborhoods. Ritchie whistled as he looked them up and down, admiring their yards fully decked out for the holiday.

"Damn, this place really *is* snob hill, huh?"

"I've never been over here before," Sam said, adjusting her hat and glancing around curiously.

"I'm pretty sure this neighborhood is all high up corporate people," Theo replied. "At least, that's what my dad said."

Ritchie sneered. "Why isn't *your* house on this street then, Peter? Your dad works at the same place Trenchard's does."

Peter turned towards Ritchie. The softly glowing, sad expression of his pumpkin mask was all his friends could see.

"My dad's not *that* high up there," he said, voice muffled beneath the latex. "And besides, we've got a lot of bills..."

"I *like* your street," Sam came to his defense. "It's quiet and cozy. Full of cute little ranch houses. You don't need something massive to have a nice home."

She shot a glare at Ritchie, who waved her off with a scoff. Peter remained silent, head bowed. Slipping an arm through his, Sam tugged him close. As they headed further down the street, towards the lights and music, a pungent odor began to waft through the night air. Theo was the first to smell it, grimacing at the scent.

"Oh, man," he gagged. "Do you guys *smell* that?"

"*Fucking pew.*" Ritchie fanned the air, coughing. "What *is* that?"

"Probably some kids playing a prank," Sam said, burying her nose in the crook of her elbow. "Eggs, shaving cream, and stink bombs are the big sellers on Halloween."

"That's no regular *stink bomb*," Ritchie hissed. "That shit's *nuclear*."

Behind his mask, Peter scrunched his nose. The foul odor pierced through the latex, heavy and lingering. He choked as it stung the back of his throat.

"Really, though," he said, "what *is* that?"

From the lawn beside them, hoots and hollers rose in the night. Three pre-teens stood in the center of the yard, dressed in Halloween costumes: a witch, a prisoner, and a zombie. Their candy bags were tossed aside as they rummaged through a backpack, retrieving large, spoiled duck eggs. Without hesitation, the witch launched the first one. It splattered against the oak door of the pristine house. As soon as the shell cracked, revealing the rotten yolk within, the smell grew stronger. Rancid.

"*Oh shit*," the prisoner retched. "That's *toxic*, Emily."

"I told you it would be, *dipshit*," the witch snapped. "Now come on. Help me plaster this place before—"

The porch light flared on. The witch cursed aloud, quickly grabbing the backpack and her sack of candy. She shouted for the boys to follow, scampering down the block as a figure stepped into the doorway. Catching a whiff of the rotten duck egg, he hissed, yelling obscenities into the street. The heavy-set prisoner struggled to keep up with his friends, calling ahead to the witch.

"It's all over my *hands*. God*damn* it, Emily!"

The group of friends backed away as the pre-teens hurried past them, disappearing into the dark of the street. Ritchie waved off the nasty smell, turning his attention to the house that had been targeted. The silhouetted figure loomed in the doorway a moment longer before turning the porch light off, dissolving into the shadows of the house.

"Isn't that Harold Trapp's house?" Ritchie whispered aloud.

"Who?" Theo raised an eyebrow.

"Harold Trapp. The guy who owns that big toy company in the city." Ritchie gestured to Peter. "Where Peter and Trenchard's dads work."

"Oh, right." Theo gazed at the house, engulfed in the dimness of night. "Is he *always* a recluse? Everyone else has their lights on, handing out candy..."

"Maybe he ran out." Sam suggested.

"*Trapp*?" Ritchie scoffed. "No, he just hates *everyone*. All he cares about is himself and his money. He's the literal definition of a *scrooge*."

"Then I guess it serves him right," Theo said.

"Yeah. Happy Halloween, *asshole*."

Ritchie flashed his middle finger to the dark house before heading down the rest of the block. The friends followed, shuffling through a mob of excited trick-or-treaters, hopeful for any extra candy they could get before the night ended.

The Trenchards' porch was lit up in orange and purple string lights. Polyester cobwebs hung between the pillars, dried corn stalks tied against them. The steps were lined with carved pumpkins—simple and shakily done. As the friends approached the front door, Ritchie elbowed his way inside—through the costumed crowd already gathered around.

"Geez, this place is *hopping*." He grunted, stepping into the foyer.

"Alex invited the whole senior class," Theo reminded him.

"True," Ritchie replied. "And anyone stupid enough to turn *this* one down is just lame."

It was nearly impossible to move into the living room. Every inch of the house was packed with teenagers, laughing and singing along to the blaring music. More cobwebs lined the interior of the home, paper bats dotting the walls. Antique candelabras flickered in the corners. Tables of snacks were scattered throughout, leaving a sweet and savory aroma between the scent of latex and colored hair spray.

Peter's shoulders tensed as he pushed his way through the crowd. The thumping bass shook the floor, loud hip-hop reverberating off the walls. His mask made it difficult to see—eliminating his peripheral vision—and the muffled music was disorienting. He took Sam's hand as he broke into the living room, breathing rapidly. Sam glanced at him worriedly as his grip tightened.

"Are you okay?"

Her voice sounded rooms away. Peter nodded weakly, scanning the room for Ritchie and Theo. They had already cut through the sea of costumed teens, heading to the stairwell where Alex Trenchard stood. He was dressed as a gothic vampire—perfect for a party host. His chestnut hair was slicked back, face powdered to appear pale. As Ritchie and Theo approached him, he smiled—flashing a pair of high-quality acrylic fangs.

"Hey!" he called, making his way down the stairs. "So glad you guys could make it."

Alex clapped Ritchie on the shoulder, smiling at Theo. He motioned around the room, to the various tables overflowing with food and drinks. He had to shout to be heard over the deafening music.

"There's plenty to eat and drink, so help yourselves," he said.

"Thanks, man." Theo gave a thumbs up.

Ritchie held a finger up as he slid his makeshift bindle from over his shoulder, untying the pillowcase. Reaching inside, he hoisted out a six pack of cheap beer, waggling his eyebrows at Alex with a toothy grin.

"If you need a *real* drink, I've got you covered," he said.

A weak smirk slipped across Alex's lips as he shook his head. "I don't drink, but you do you, man. Just make sure to take your trash with you when you leave. My dad's not okay with having alcohol here."

"No problem." Ritchie nodded. "Where's he at anyway?"

"Upstairs. He's got a big project due for work, so he probably won't be coming down."

"What about your mom?" Theo asked.

"She's out trick-or-treating with my little brother," Alex said. "I'm sure they'll be home soon, but knowing Andy, he'll be exhausted. They won't be hanging around down here either."

Alex sipped punch from the glass in his hand. Across the way, a voice carried, calling out for him. Pressing his lips together, he dipped his head to Ritchie and Theo.

"Have a good time. I'll see you later."

Theo nodded. "Thanks again for the invite."

As he and Ritchie pushed back through the sea of teens, Sam and Peter stood off to the side. The crowd was growing thicker now, bodies bopping along to the beat—crushing them against the wall. Peter held the sides of his mask, keeping it as straight as possible so he could see. The blazing strobe lights and blaring music seared through his skull. Everything was so loud, yet stifled at the same time. Incoherent. Sam took his arm gently as he felt himself growing dizzy. She motioned towards one of the couches in the corner—lightly occupied and away from the rowdy cluster closing in on them.

"Let's go over there," she said, shouting so Peter could hear.

He nodded, letting her guide him across the room. Once they reached the couch, Sam glanced at the group already seated there, chatting.

"Mind if we sit?" she asked.

One of the girls, dressed as a nurse, looked up and shook her head. "Not at all."

Peter dropped onto the cushion at the edge, tugging the mask off his head. He took a deep breath, relieved to be free of the sweaty latex. Running his fingers through his messy hair, he glanced at Sam.

"Thanks," he said. "I was getting really overstimulated."

"I could tell," she said, resting a hand atop his. "You *sure* you're okay?"

"Yeah." He nodded. "But I could use a drink."

As if on cue, Ritchie appeared from the crowd and slid beside him on the couch. He held up the pack of beer he brought—two cans already missing.

"Did someone say *drink*?" He dangled the remaining cans in front of Peter with a smirk.

Peter held his hand up. "No thanks. I'm not feeling *that* kind of drink tonight."

"Since *when*?" Ritchie snorted in offense. "It's Hallo-*fucking*-ween. *Drink*."

He popped one of the cans from the plastic ring, pressing it to Peter's chest. With reluctance, he took it.

"He said *no*, Ritchie," Sam snapped.

"Well what about *you*, then?"

"You know I don't drink."

"Bunch of wusses."

Ritchie took a swig from his open can. Peter glanced down at the beer, turning his lip up as Sam tightened her grip on his hand.

"You *don't* have to drink that," she said. "Do you want me to get you some water instead?"

He nodded silently. As Sam headed to the refreshments table, the group that had already been seated began speaking again. Their voices were muted by the thumping music, but Peter was able to catch some of their conversation. They spoke of pumpkins and werewolves. Vampires. Ghosts. He tuned them out, until their stories turned to the old cemetery on Chapel Hill. Peter barely noticed Sam's return from the drink table, pushing the water cup into his hands as his eyes locked on the girl in the nurse's outfit.

"You ever hear about all the stuff that's happened up there on Halloween night?" she asked, shaking her head slowly. "*So* crazy."

A boy in a banana costume beside her stuffed his mouth with chips. "Oh yeah? Like what?"

"I've heard about the witches," one of the other girls, dressed as an angel, chimed in. "How they were hanged from one of the trees on the hill. People said they would light bonfires out there and dance around it under the moonlight, playing instruments. Calling on the Devil. When the constable would patrol through there, they'd turn into cats and hide in the shadows."

"Isn't that where the whole 'cats have nine lives' thing comes from?" another girl, a fairy, asked. "That they could only change nine times, and after that they'd be stuck as a cat forever?"

The angel girl shrugged. "Could be. It definitely explains why people were so afraid of black cats. They thought they were witches, out doing the Devil's work. Looking for sacrifices."

Peter tensed. He shakily raised his cup, taking a sip. The water was cold against his tongue.

"*Speaking* of the Devil," another girl, dressed in a fawn costume, began, "how about the legend of Poor George?"

"Poor George?" The banana boy raised an eyebrow.

"Yeah," the fawn girl continued, "that fool who sold his soul to the Devil so his daughter wouldn't lose her eyesight."

The group went silent. She sipped her punch before picking up a cookie, shaped like a pumpkin. Taking a bite, she smirked.

"No doctor had been able to help his daughter, who was rapidly going blind. And no prayers ever worked. So, George did the last thing he could think of. He sought out the Devil," the fawn girl said. "He'd heard the rumors of sitting on the throne in the cemetery at midnight. Having wishes granted. So, one night in mid-October, he sat beneath the moonlight, begging to save sight. She was too young to lose it. And, sure enough, the Devil appeared. He promised George he would spare his daughter's eyes—in exchange for his soul. Having no other choice, he agreed, like the fool he was."

"Did the Devil actually keep his end of the bargain?" one of the boys, dressed like an astronaut, asked.

"He did. But it drove George mad," the fawn girl continued. "He started seeing things in the shadows at night. Started hearing voices calling his name. It went on for a couple of weeks, until he couldn't take it anymore. On Halloween night, he went back to the cemetery and lit a fire beneath that old tree. The tree they say the witches were hanged from. Using a sturdy rope, he chose to end the suffering himself. So he no longer could be plagued by the figures that haunted him in the dark."

Peter listened, stiff as a board. His hands quivered, the water inside his cup sloshing violently. Sam gently touched his knee with a concerned expression, giving it a squeeze as the fawn girl continued with her story.

"When they found him the next morning, swinging from a limb, silhouetted in the fog, they took his eyes. They were the perfect match for his daughter, *exactly* what was needed to save her sight. And all it cost Poor George was his soul."

"I've heard something similar," the girl in the nurse costume said. "Not *George* or anything about sight...but I did hear a story about Old Tom."

"Old Tom?"

The nurse girl nodded. "Yeah. His son had passed away from an incurable illness. He and his wife were devastated. He'd also heard the legend

about the throne and the Devil, and he went up to the cemetery in early autumn to plead for a deal."

Now, Ritchie and Theo were tuned in. At the mention of the Devil, Ritchie rolled his eyes, mouthing each word the girl spoke mockingly. Sam nudged him in the ribs as she kept her attention on the story.

"The Devil asked him what he desired, and he told him there was nothing he wanted more than his son back. He had been far too young to die. Taking pity, the Devil promised he would return Tom's son to him—in exchange for another's life. So, Tom found one of the local stray cats. He offered it as a sacrifice to the Devil, hanging it from the branches of that same old tree. But the Devil wasn't pleased. He told Tom that the life given had to be an *equal* sacrifice. A cat simply couldn't bring back a little boy."

Theo pursed his lips, glancing at Peter. He watched the grip on his cup continue to grow tighter, the plastic bending beneath his fingertips.

"Tom told the Devil he couldn't kill a man. He begged and pleaded for another way, but the Devil wouldn't have it. He told Tom if he truly wanted his son back, he would do whatever it took. Mortified, Tom returned home, forgetting about the Devil. Trying to flee the deal he had already made. But he couldn't. Over the next month, he was haunted by nightmares. Shapes in the darkness. Flies on his walls. Cats at his window. The town began to say he was cursed—that he had made a dark pact. A large blemish grew on his forearm, practically overnight. People said it was the mark of the Devil. *Proof* he had made a deal. They taunted him, threatened him. Blamed him for the misfortunes that befell the town. Terrified, Tom returned to the cemetery— alone. And there, he demanded the Devil show himself."

Peter swallowed hard, doing his best to calm his racing heart. His gaze darted frantically between the group on the couch. From the fawn girl dipping a celery stick in dressing, to the banana boy crunching loudly into a chip. His vision began to swim, thoughts clouding over with all the stories. All the other foolish, pitiful souls that had been tricked by the Devil. Across the table, another girl was mindlessly pulling tarot cards. He watched nervously as she turned them over, revealing their painted faces.

THE HANGED MAN.

THE DEVIL.

THE TOWER.

THE FOOL.

Gathering them up, she shuffled them back into her deck, pulling a new set of cards. Peter tried to slow his breathing, forcing his focus to return to the nurse girl. She continued with her story, leaning in closer.

"When the Devil finally appeared, he told Old Tom the same thing as before. He couldn't keep his end of the bargain unless equal exchange was given. And so, ashamed of his choice and overburdened by nightmares, he took his own life. Hanged himself in the tree. Legend has it that his son was found wandering around town the next day, lost and disoriented. But, that's just what *some* people say."

"I've heard the story of Old John," Sam chimed in, gesturing to Ritchie, Theo, and Peter. "I told it to my friends not too long ago. I find it fascinating that there are so many versions of the same story. They're all similar, but the names and circumstances have changed."

"I guess that's how legends go." The girl in the nurse costume shrugged. "They change over time. Some details are lost, but others are never forgotten."

"Like a game of telephone," the banana boy remarked.

"I guess so," Sam replied with a smile.

As she returned her attention to Peter, she noticed his ashen expression. Her lips drew into a quick frown as she tilted her head, grasping his shoulder. When he didn't react, she leaned in, whispering in concern.

"Peter?"

His eyes remained on the cup of water in his hands, still trembling. Sam gently took it from him and placed it on the table. Taking his cold, pale hands in hers, she gave them a squeeze.

"I think it's interesting, all the things people used to believe marked someone as being a witch, or having made a deal with the Devil," one of the boys said after a moment. "Like owning a black cat. Being a healer. Being *educated*. Left-handed. Also, having *any* sort of blemish. Warts, moles. It's insane people *actually* believed all that."

"Superstition was no joke," the fawn girl shook her head.

Ritchie took another gulp from his can of beer, emptying it. He crushed it in his fist, leaning across the couch towards Peter.

"Well, *shit*," he mocked, pinching Peter's cheek—just below his mole. "Looks like you really *did* make a deal with the Devil, then."

"Shut *up*, Ritchie," Sam seethed, glaring at him.

He ignored her, tipsy gaze fixed on Peter. "Is *that* why you killed that cat? Strung it up in the cemetery, just like Old Tom? To uphold the promise you made at birth?"

The group gathered around the couch went silent, watching in concern and confusion. Peter's lips quivered, turning into a deep frown. His

dark eyes welled with tears, shoulders violently trembling. His breaths became short and quick. Labored. Shaking his head, he fumbled for words.

"I...I didn't...I didn't..."

Sam placed her hands on Ritchie's shoulders, shoving him back into the couch, away from Peter. "Get the fuck out of here, asshole. You're *drunk*."

Ritchie rolled his eyes, snorting before getting to his feet. Peeling the fake mole from his cheek, he flicked it across the room. Then, turning to Peter one last time, he leaned down into his face. The bells on his jester hat jingled as their noses touched. Peter's eyebrows furrowed at Ritchie's whispered breath—reeking of alcohol.

"I hope what you wished for was worth it."

Pulling away, Ritchie snapped his fingers. Grabbing Theo's arm, he loudly commented on his boredom of legends and lore before ushering him towards the crowd. The bass shook the floor as they disappeared between bodies—lost to the flashing strobe lights and glow bracelets. Once they were out of sight, Peter snatched the can of beer Ritchie had given him, cracking it open and chugging it. Sam grabbed his upper arm, shaking him as he lowered the can.

"Peter, *stop*."

He refused to look at her. Sam took a deep breath as she yanked the beer from his hand, setting it beside the cup of water. She pushed her fingers through his tangled hair, watching his expression soften.

"*Don't* listen to Ritchie," she said. "He's clearly drunk. I don't know what his issue is tonight, but he's been a massive *dick* to you."

"What if he's right?" Peter breathed.

"He's *not*," Sam insisted. "The Devil *isn't real*, Peter. How many times do I have to tell you that?"

"But what *if*, Sam?" Peter's voice cracked. "What if I really *am* marked?"

"*How*?" Sam asked. "Those old superstitions they mentioned? That's ridiculous, Peter."

"But..."

"Okay, you're left-handed. So is ten percent of the world. That's just *how you are*. How your *brain is wired*. And your beauty spot? You were *born* with that. Literally *everyone* has one *somewhere*. Don't you *dare* let him make you feel bad for being *how you were intended to be*."

"What if *that* was the intent, though, Sam? What if that's my fate? If I was chosen from birth. If I—"

Sam took his face in her hands, shaking him lightly. "It's *not*. Stop letting him get to you. He's a fool."

Peter lowered his head. The music grew heavier, pounding him down into the couch. With a whimper, he wept.

"So am I…"

"*No*," Sam pressed, tilting his chin up. "You're *not*."

Peter gnashed his teeth, sniffling as fresh tears rolled down his cheeks. He shook his head, pulling away from Sam's gentle touch.

"I'm scared…"

Sam wrapped her arms around him, hugging him tight. He shut his eyes, releasing a sob—one that broke over the music. She ran her fingers through his hair again, silent as she let him pour himself out.

"I'm scared, Sam. I'm *so scared*. And no one believes me," he bawled. "Everyone is against me. *Everyone*. They all think I killed that cat…"

"*I* don't," Sam said sharply.

Peter sobbed heavily. Sam pressed his head to her chest, taking a deep breath as she waited. Slowly, Peter's sharp gasps became steadier. He stared across the room, flashing strobes reflecting in his dark eyes.

"Tonight's the night," he said absently. "It's Halloween… He's going to take me, Sam. Just like in the other legends…"

"No one is going to take you, Peter," Sam replied vehemently. "Not the police. Not the Devil. *No one*. I promise."

Peter let his eyes fall closed. He swallowed around the lump in his throat, digging his nails into his palms. He remained on the couch with Sam for a long while, quieting his thoughts and calming his nerves. Once she was certain Peter had relaxed, Sam cast her gaze across the crowd of teenagers. The house thundered as they bobbed to the beat of the blaring pop music, twirling glow sticks. Shouting the lyrics. Biting her lip, she glanced at Peter, whispering into his ear.

"Do you want to dance?"

"It's too crowded," Peter muttered. "And…that's not my type of music *at all*."

"I know," Sam replied. "It's total trash."

She smiled softly, eyes meeting his. The strobes flashed behind her, illuminating her violet hair in the dark. Taking Peter's hands, she stood, urging him to follow.

"But we can't let Ritchie and Theo have all the fun, right?"

Peter was hesitant, but as Sam continued to gaze affectionately at him, he gave in. Getting to his feet, he took a deep breath.

"Alright…"

The speakers vibrated as the music switched over to classic Halloween party jams. Yet, the teenagers on the floor didn't stop dancing. Their laughter echoed through the living room, into the foyer, and onto the front porch. It was nearing 10 p.m. and everyone was still full of energy. Showing no signs of stopping.

Fog machines sprayed thick vapor onto the impromptu dance floor, hanging low and heavy on the ground. Within the crowd, Peter and Sam stood close together, jostled by the dancing bodies all around them. Sam swayed with the beat, holding on to her witch hat as she smiled at Peter. He remained stiff, eyeing the other teens. As he scanned the room, he caught sight of Ritchie and Theo, gathered with a group of their fellow varsity players.

Ritchie twirled around with a couple of cheerleaders, face flushed from his second drink. His boisterous laughter echoed above the music. They fawned over him, leaning in and whispering gossip in his ear before he turned to Theo, spreading it again. Frowning, Peter averted his gaze, leaving Ritchie and Theo to their entourage of popular kids.

Sam's hands took his, drawing his attention back to the moment. She swayed, coaxing him to loosen up and dance. Peter licked his lips, leaning down and whispering against her ear so she could hear him through the noise.

"I'm going to get a drink," he said. "I'll be right back."

Sam nodded, releasing him. She watched as he pushed his way through the crowd, shoulders hunched as he went. Running her fingers along the black velvet sleeve of her dress, she chewed her lip. Waiting patiently for Peter to return.

207

The line at the punch bowl was minimal. Most of the teens had moved away from appetizers and salty snacks, sprawling out on the couches or dancing for the rest of the night. Peter slunk over to the table, grabbing a cup. He swirled the ladle around the punch bowl, the lime green color shimmering with edible glitter. The sherbet had mostly melted by now, leaving only a few frothy mounds behind. Careful to avoid the plastic eyeballs floating as décor, Peter began to fill his cup. As he went for another scoop, something small and black floated up with a chunk of sherbert. A dead fly. Peter grimaced, returning the ladle to the bowl. As he did, his elbow bumped against another's—grabbing a bottle of water beside him.

"Sorry..." Peter stammered.

He looked at the teen standing beside him, dressed as a scarecrow. Fake straw poked between the buttonholes of his red flannel shirt, painted face shadowed beneath the brim of his straw hat. Peter stared at him for a moment, eyes widening when he recognized who it was.

"*Doug*?"

The scarecrow turned. Behind the cheerful face paint, he looked weary. Distant. Peter frowned, taking a sip of punch.

"I haven't seen you around school the last week or so. Is everything okay?" he asked.

Doug pushed his glasses up on his triangular painted nose, averting his gaze. "Yeah..."

"Did you manage to get one of those masks for your brother?"

Doug's eyes darkened, lips drawing into a hard frown. He tightened his grip on the water bottle, ignoring Peter and heading to a dimly lit corner, away from the crowd. Peter stood still, watching in confusion. He took another sip of punch before returning to the center of the living room, trying to shake off the strange interaction.

Holding his cup above his head, he grimaced as he stumbled through the bodies, making his way back to Sam. Releasing a heavy breath, he shook his head.

"It's like fighting for your *life* getting in and out of here," he said.

He raised the cup once more, taking a long drink. Sam tucked a strand of hair behind her ear as she looked him over. Drawing nearer, she took his hand, giving it a squeeze.

"Who were you talking to over there?" she asked.

"Doug Feeney," Peter said. "I'm...actually surprised he's here."

"Doug?"

Peter nodded. "He...doesn't seem like himself, though..."

"Hasn't he been out of school lately?"

"Yeah."

Sam sought him out over the heads of the crowd, face falling as she found him tucked away in the corner. "I hope everything's okay."

Peter shrugged. Finishing what was left of the glittering green punch, he set the empty cup on an end table. The beat thumped heavier than before, shaking the whole house. It vibrated through Peter's chest, rising into his throat. Feeling Sam's grip become tighter, he glanced down at her.

"So," she said, "you ready to dance now?"

It took a long while of easing into it, but eventually, Peter let himself go. Sam's bright laughter brought a smile to his face—a genuine one. The strobe lights flashed as they jumped up and down, becoming one with the sea of costumes around them. Shimmers of green and orange and purple twirled from glow sticks—piercing through the faux fog. Everything felt stuck in slow motion as Peter glanced around the room, staring at the cobwebs on the walls and the rubber spiders on strings, bopping from the boosted bass.

Sam reached up, tangling her fingers in the hair that fell at the base of his neck. Even in the dim lit room, Peter could make out her bright hazel eyes

—fixed on him. His smile drew wider, dimples prominent in his cheeks. They were swept away in the thick of the teenagers around them, senses hazy. Outside of the beat, all was muffled. Lost within the creeping, low fog. Within the strobing lights. Peter gazed down at Sam affectionately, heart beginning to race as he tuned out the room. Tuned out the thought of prying stares. Closing his eyes, he locked his lips with hers.

Her fingers tightened in his hair as she leaned into the kiss. The heavy taste of stale cigarettes still lingered in his mouth, accompanied now by alcohol and kiwi lime. But to Sam, it was inviting. Bittersweet. They stayed there, between the lights and the music, the bouncing bodies and laughter, for what felt like eternity. Peter hesitantly pulled away, pressing his forehead to hers with trembling breath. Sam watched him closely, cupping his cheeks. Drawing a finger down his jawline, she smiled. After a long moment she pulled him back towards her, taking his bottom lip between hers—locking them together once again.

From across the room, Ritchie and Theo caught a glimpse of them through the crowd. Ritchie's boisterous laughter and dancing died down at the sight. He grabbed hold of Theo's sleeve, tugging it as he pointed to them. A soft smile slipped across Theo's lips.

"It's about time," he remarked approvingly.

Ritchie snorted, scrunching up his nose. Theo chuckled, nudging him teasingly. Ritchie's buzz was beginning to wear off, but his freckled cheeks were still flushed. He pouted as Theo shook his head.

"Leave them be."

Ritchie stiffened at the high-pitched giggling of the cheerleaders behind them. From the corner of his eye, he could see them waiting patiently for their turn to dance with him. Individually. Theo cleared his throat. Offering his arm, he smirked.

"Come on."

Ritchie blinked, narrowing his eyes. "What?"

Wiggling his elbow, Theo smirked. "Don't tell me you're shy all of a sudden."

Ritchie passed an uneasy glance to the cheerleaders. They still gathered, watching him closely. Flashing them a toothy grin, Ritchie waved them off.

"You ladies are next," he said with a wink. "Don't go *anywhere*."

Their anticipatory laughter filled the air as Theo pulled Ritchie to a less crowded spot. He jumped up and down with those around him, moving to the beat. Ritchie peered through the crowd before finally giving in and

doing the same. They swayed with the others, singing along to the overplayed pop lyrics blasting from the speakers. Ritchie twirled a green glow stick over his head, shoes squeaking on the hardwood floor with each step. Lights strobed around them as their laughter became one with the melody—lost in the crowd.

After a while, Ritchie slowed, peering over his shoulder to where the cheer squad still waited. Pursing his lips, he clapped Theo on the shoulder, motioning their way.

"We should head back," he said sadly. "I promised them each a dance."

Theo pressed his lips together, nodding. He followed behind Ritchie, only reaching out and touching his arm to stop him once.

"This isn't Homecoming," he said softly. "You don't have to put on an act, you know..."

Ritchie was silent for a moment. His eyes dropped to the floor, managing a weak nod before he looked back at Theo.

"I know..."

Across the dance floor, Peter pulled away from Sam. He rested his head against hers, breathing softly. The music around them had become slower—soothing. Her hands slid down to his arms, holding him tight. The white light caught in her violet hair, igniting it like purple flames that framed her face.

"Sam..." He choked out, lips brushing against hers. "I-I love you..."

Sam's grip tensed. She pulled back slightly, gaze fixed on him—on his deep brown eyes, full of sincerity. But she remained silent. Cupping his cheek, she watched him nuzzle against her hand, eyes falling closed. Kissing her palm. With a gentle smile, she parted her lips to speak.

Just as she leaned in, a loud, whooping holler broke her focus. Two boys, dressed as a hotdog and a chicken, bolted across the floor, bumping into them. Cold punch sloshed from one of their cups, splashing down the front of Sam's dress. She gasped in alarm, shaking the wetness from her sleeves as she cursed aloud.

"*Watch where you're going, morons!*"

Peter frowned, hesitantly reaching out, wanting to help. He stammered as he watched her readjust her witch hat.

"A-are you okay?"

"I'm fine," Sam said. "Just a little wet, but I'll dry."

Peter nodded slowly. Shifting on his feet, he cleared his throat nervously before gazing through the crowd. Sam bit her lip, watching him in silence as her eyes fell to the pumpkin mask halfway stuffed into his pocket. Reaching out, she patted it, catching Peter's attention.

"Oh, hey! Your mask," she said. "It's dark enough in here, you should put it back on. It'll look cool lit up."

Peter hesitated before pulling out the mask. Gazing at its sorrowful expression, he pressed the switch, illuminating it. With a sigh, he slid it over his head. The light poured from within, golden and bright. He stood out on the floor—a distinguishable sad jack-o'-lantern among colorful glow sticks and fog. Sam smiled.

"It looks so good."

Behind the miserable pumpkin head, Peter smiled back. The joyful laughter of the cheer squad lifted above the music once again, catching his attention. He turned to where they were gathered, watching as they twirled beside Ritchie. Peter clenched his jaw.

"We should probably head over there," Sam said softly. "It's past ten. I don't know how late they want to stay."

Peter nodded reluctantly. The loud dance music returned through the speakers, vibrating off the walls. Heavier than ever. Shuffling through the crowd, he and Sam made their way over to Ritchie and Theo.

Doug Feeney sat in the dim corner, eyes dark and vacant as he stared across the room. Though his face was painted up in a cheery, stitched smile, his lips were drawn into a hard frown. He clenched his fist at his sides, digging his nails into his palms. The music and lights were becoming too much. Grating on him.

He pushed his glasses up, searching every face in the crowd. Looking for Alex Trenchard. Yet, he hadn't found him for the entirety of the night. Alex had been too busy hosting—flitting from room to room, refilling drinks and snacks. Scowling, Doug was about to give up. It was nearing 10:30 p.m. and he knew his parents would be worried if he stayed out much longer.

He didn't dare make them believe there would be a second empty seat at the dinner table.

Setting his water bottle down, he stood. As he gazed back across the sea of costumes and lights one last time, he spotted one he hadn't seen before. A jack-o'-lantern. Its sad expression burned bright in the hazy darkness. Doug's chest tightened, a hot lump swelling in his throat. He stared at it, watching it mingling within the crowd as his breaths grew short and heavy. Angry.

With a trembling hand, Doug reached into the pocket of his jeans. Beneath the strobing lights, a switchblade snapped open—tight in his grasp.

"What time do you want to bounce?" Sam turned to Theo, adjusting her witch hat.

The partygoers showed no signs of stopping. A few of them bumped into her as she waited for a reply.

"I'm down to leave in the next half hour or so," he shouted back to be heard over the music. "Did Trenchard ever say how late this thing's going?"

Sam shook her head. "Not sure."

She turned to Peter, who was staring in the direction of Ritchie and the cheerleaders. His laughter lingered, even as he bid them farewell, returning to the company of his friends. Sam pursed her lips as she glared at him, brows furrowing at the bells jingling on his hat.

"We're thinking of wrapping things up at eleven," Theo filled him in.

"*Eleven*?" Ritchie scoffed. "The party's only just getting good!"

"I'd rather be *home* by midnight," Sam snapped. "My mom and stepdad are going to be up waiting for me. I don't want them to worry."

Theo nodded. "Same, man."

"*Fine*." Ritchie rolled his eyes. "But only on one condition."

"And what's *that*?" Sam crossed her arms.

"*You* guys party with me," he smirked. "I've been stuck with the cheer squad all night. Let's at least end it *together*."

Sam passed a glance to Peter. He remained silent—just a hollow, glowing pumpkin head. Narrowing her eyes, she returned her stern gaze to Ritchie.

"No more bullshit?"

He nodded fervently. "Yeah, yeah."

With a sigh, Sam unfolded her arms. "Fine. But I *mean* it, Ritchie. No more."

The synthwave beats pounded across the floor, in sync with the strobe lights. As the crowd around them jumped and swayed, they too joined in. Lost in growing laughter and flashing lights. They seemed to surge faster as the song played on, slowing the movement of the room. Everything became dreamlike, wavering. Flickers of a moment.

It was even more disorienting beneath the pumpkin mask. Peter struggled to see clearly, just barely able to make out his friends in the dimly lit crowd. His head spun, overstimulated. Attempting to shift his focus across the room, he squinted as he spotted a figure slipping through the crowd. Heading his way. Doug Feeney's scarecrow face became recognizable between the flashes. However, it was quickly lost amongst the strobing lights and writhing bodies.

A wave of teens hooting along to the music crushed him from all sides. His mask jostled, covering his eyes, blocking his line of sight. Light still poured from the eyes and mouth as he grunted, feeling the weight of the crowd press against him. He staggered, struggling to readjust the mask. Finally pulling it snug, back into position, Peter paused to orient himself in the pulsing environment.

Something sharp dragged across his right bicep, slicing it open. Peter grunted, slapping a hand over the tear in his shirt sleeve—feeling the slippery wetness of blood as the slash began to sting. His trembling fingers came away

214

coated in crimson, from where it was beginning to blossom darkly through his flannel. Classmates dancing nearby pulled themselves to a halt, staring. When Peter looked up, he found the scarecrow standing right before him, the straight-edge of a switchblade glinting in his hand.

Doug slashed again—this time towards the neck. Peter's eyes widened as he raised his arms in self-defense. The blade through the soft flannel of his shirt, digging a second gash into his right forearm—this one deeper than the first. Peter felt his heartbeat in the wound as he gritted his teeth, hissing in pain. He backed as far as he could into the crowd, squeezing his bleeding wounds. Trying to put as much space between himself and Doug. But Doug was right on him. Peter's throat grew hot and heavy with panic—feeling as though it were filled with cotton. Unable to call for help. As Doug raised the knife above his head, Theo noticed the commotion from the corner of his eye.

"*Hey!*"

He shoved himself between them, spreading his arms defensively. Doug managed to stop himself, keeping the blade high and visible. The strobe lights glimmered across its bloodstained surface, catching the curious attention of the room.

"What the *fuck* are you doing, man!" Theo shouted.

Finally realizing what was happening, Sam and Ritchie hurried to Peter's side, pulling him away from danger. His knees buckled beneath him, audible whimpers and panicked gasps stifled beneath his mask. Sam pressed her hands over the cuts, warm blood pulsing across her fingertips.

Two boys from the football team quickly pushed through the crowd, grabbing Doug and forcing his arms to his sides. He struggled, cursing and thrashing as he tried to swing the blade at them, but they were too strong. Ritchie gripped Peter's right shoulder in concern.

"Holy *fuck*," he breathed. "Are you alright, Peter?"

"We have to get him outside," Sam demanded.

Ritchie turned on his heels, snapping his fingers. He shouted to the crowd, voice echoing above the music.

"*Get Alex now!*"

The sea of teens broke apart. Theo pressed his lips together tightly as he glared at Doug, feeling the hate that radiated from his eyes. Eyes that didn't look away from Peter, murmuring incoherent detest beneath his breath. Of masks. Of blood.

Turning back to his friends, Theo shook his head. "Let's get the hell out of here."

215

None of them hesitated. All three took hold of Peter, helping him towards the foyer. The crowded room parted as they passed through, concerned whispers lingering heavily in the air.

Ritchie and Sam pulled the sweaty latex mask off Peter's head. His tousled hair hung in damp ringlets, eyes wide and empty. Even with the restricting mask removed, he still couldn't catch his breath. Each inhale he took was shallow. Wheezy. Theo placed a hand against his back, rubbing it softly while Sam slid his arm free of his flannel.

The sleeve of his t-shirt was torn, stained bright red. While the first laceration was minimal, the second was jagged. Deep. Sam cursed as she opened her water bottle, pouring it over the wound. Bloody water ran down Peter's arm as he flinched, still struggling for air.

"Is he going to be alright?" Ritchie asked, voice quivering. "*Shit*. What *happened* in there?"

"Doug lost his fucking mind, *that's* what happened," Theo replied bitterly, still caressing Peter's back.

"That's not like him at all," Sam said, tears welling in her eyes. "What the *fuck*."

"It was...the Devil..." Peter panted between gasps. "He's here... He's going to take me..."

Sam clapped a hand against his cheek gently. "*No he's not*. Stop saying that."

Ritchie slipped the worn flannel shirt from his shoulders. He tore it along the seam, managing to peel a strip of soft fabric free. Holding out to Sam, he gestured to Peter's arm.

"Here."

Sam took it, wrapping it around the rinsed gashes and tying it tight. Helping Peter slide his arm back into his own shirt, she looked him over carefully. His cheeks were pale and stained with tears, eyes still wide. Breaths

trembling with dread. Drool dripped from his bottom lip as he stared off—lost. Only the dark of night reflected in his eyes.

Taking a seat beside him on the porch steps, Sam gently drew his chin to face her. Tilting it up, she stroked his hair back, brushing his tangled bangs out of his eyes. With a heavy breath, she held up four fingers.

"Pretend my fingers are candles," she said softly. "I want you to blow them out. One at a time. Okay?"

Peter's head dipped into a weak nod. Sam returned the gesture, positioning her hand close enough to feel his fragile breaths. The first was barely a puff of air. Sam bit her lip, lowering her pinky as she kept her other fingers raised. Peter kept his gaze on them, this time exhaling a little stronger. Down went the next finger. Sam could feel his next breath—a cool breeze against her middle finger. She put it down, leaving only one. Peter inhaled long and deep, blowing a steady breath against her. Folding her finger down and balling her hand, she nodded.

"Again."

Ritchie and Theo watched curiously as she held up her fingers again, Peter blowing against them—his breaths returning to normal. When her final finger folded against her palm, she leaned in, wrapping her arms around his neck gently.

"Good job, Peter," she whispered in reassurance.

Ritchie slid his varsity jacket over his shoulders, shaking off the chill of night. Scrunching his face, he turned to his friends.

"We need to get my dad," he said.

"So call him then," Sam replied, running her fingertips over Peter's ear.

Ritchie shook his head. "I'll never get a hold of him. It's Halloween. Tonight and New Year's Eve are the two busiest nights of the year for cops. Do you know how many calls they get? For the stupidest shit? Toilet paper in people's trees. Shaving cream. Silly string. It would take *forever* to get him here."

"Then what are we supposed to do?" Theo asked. "I know it doesn't look that bad, but Peter really should get to the hospital."

Peter shook his head. "No. No, I'm fine..."

"*Peter.*" Sam was stern.

"They'll call my dad," he said, averting his gaze. "Please. I can't... I can't burden him any more."

"You're *hurt*," Sam pressed, staring at him. "You *have* to. And knowing your dad, he'd be more upset knowing you *didn't* go."

Peter shook his head again, forcibly this time. "I *can't.*"

"Look. Let's just go get *my* dad," Ritchie interjected. "He's stationed at Chapel Hill tonight. It's not that far from here. If we go up there and tell him Doug Feeney lost his fucking shit and *stabbed* Peter...he'll bust this place wide open."

"*Chapel Hill...*" Peter's voice was hollow.

"Yeah," Ritchie replied. "You know how overrun it gets on Halloween. And this year, I'll bet that greaseball Johnson requested *extra* backup."

Peter tensed. The images from his nightmares once again played on repeat in his mind. The stories his classmates had told at the party. The threats of Grýla. His stomach churned as the color drained from his face. Shaking his head, he shut his eyes.

"We'll be quick," Ritchie said. "Just to get my dad."

"For real, man," Theo replied, gesturing to Peter. "Then we can get you to the hospital to get those cuts looked at."

"*No*," Peter stated flatly.

"We'll take you *home*, then," Sam insisted, taking his hand.

"I don't *want* to go home..."

"Why not?" Theo raised an eyebrow.

Hot tears stung his eyes as Peter stared down the dark street, trying to drown out the ever-growing dread looming over him. Lowering his head, he choked out a weak response.

"I just don't..."

His friends fell into an uncomfortable silence. Sam placed a hand on his undamaged arm, squeezing it gently. Pursing his lips, Ritchie glanced out at the thickening shadows. The approaching midnight hour. Porch lights had already been turned off, trick-or-treaters returned home. Only silent stillness crept across the distant neighborhoods now. Inside the house behind them, however, the thumping hip-hop still reverberated. As if nothing had happened. With an impatient sigh, he turned to his friends.

"Come on." Ritchie gestured into the darkness. "Before it gets any later."

Theo and Sam helped Peter to his feet, supporting him as they made their way down the front steps of the Trenchards'. Leaving the party lights and sounds behind, they crossed the street, heading into the night—towards Chapel Hill.

Alex Trenchard pushed through the sea of guests, making his way into the living room. The music still played, but the volume had dropped substantially since his attention was gathered. Hushed whispers filled the room as he came upon the scene. His eyes widened, mouth drawing agape as he looked at the two football players restraining Doug Feeney. Then, his gaze fell to the floor. A small pool of blood stained the hardwood.

"What happened in here?"

A girl in a bee costume stepped forward, voice trembling as she pointed directly at Doug. "Doug attacked Peter..."

"*What?*" Alex asked, whirling on his heel.

The knife in Doug's hand gleamed in the party lights. His straw hat shaded his eyes, but his mouth was drawn into a vivid frown. Tensing, Alex slowly approached him.

"Doug?" he asked in concern. "What's going on?"

Doug didn't answer. His expression remained dark as his classmates held him back. He stared bitterly at Alex, flashes of Greg and his parents' inconsolable wails flooding his mind. The weak apology Paul Trenchard had spewed to him on the sidewalk. Curling his lips down even more, his breathing became shallow. Hot hate burned his soul as the words of the old woman rang loud in his ears. *An eye for an eye.* Tightening his grip on the handle of his switchblade, he snarled.

"A *son* for a *son*..."

With a burst of adrenaline, he tore out of the restraining grip of his classmates. He jabbed the blade deep into Alex's stomach, twisting. Alex gasped, eyes wide as Doug continued to turn it. Hot, sticky blood gushed from the wound as he ripped the knife out, plunging it to the handle into Alex's ribcage.

The makeshift dance floor was no longer silent. Screams broke out as partygoers stampeded for the door. Their bodies clashed together, shoving Doug and Alex violently as they panicked. Alex pressed a palm to Doug's

chest in a weak attempt to save himself. Doug jerked upward on the handle, slicing through muscle. Cracking bone. Blood sputtered from Alex's mouth as he wheezed labored breaths, softly begging Doug to stop.

Doug leaned in, twisting the knife harder as he whispered against Alex's ear. "Not yet. There's someone who needs to see this."

Even behind his closed office door, Paul Trenchard could hear the screams. They trilled above the music, floor shaking as a horde of feet pounded against it. He leaned back in his chair with a sigh, rubbing his tired eyes. The light from his lamp bathed the paperwork and blueprints spread out across it—design ideas for potential products for the upcoming Christmas season. The only attempt at making a comeback from the further rut Trapp & Co. had found itself in.

His eyes scanned the pages titled *Hans and Heidi*. They were lined with concept sketches of interactive dolls and notes on potential features. Something simple. Safe. As the high-pitched wails continued, Paul rose to his feet. Tugging the office door open, he headed into the hall and towards the stairwell.

The lights still strobed as he descended, making out blurred bodies as they tore for the doorway. He narrowed his eyes as he reached the bottom step, scanning the room. The panicked, fleeing faces. Only when his gaze fell upon the scene in the center of the living room did his heart drop.

A teenager dressed like a scarecrow plunged a knife into Alex's side, blood spraying from his son's mouth, adding to the tide of crimson already pouring down his frilled shirt. He slumped against the scarecrow, his whispers barely audible. Paul's throat swelled shut, rooted to the spot. Unable to scream. From the corner of his eye, the scarecrow spotted him. His glasses were flecked with Alex's blood as he turned to the stairwell, lips drawing up into a cruel grin—mirroring the stitched, painted mouth of his makeup.

Grabbing a handful of Alex's slicked chestnut hair, he pulled his head back. Pressing the sharp edge of the blade to his throat, the scarecrow sneered.

"*This* is for Greg..."

He drew the blade quick and sharp—slitting Alex's throat open in a clean line. Blood rained in curtains from the pulsing wound as Alex gurgled. The scarecrow shoved him forward, watching mercilessly as he hit the ground in a limp pile. Thick crimson pooled around him, soaking into the hardwood and Persian accent carpet. Paul released a pained whimper, knees threatening to buckle as he gripped the balustrade with white knuckles. Watching as his son breathed his last at the bottom of the stairs.

The strobing lights shimmered across the blood-soaked blade as the scarecrow turned his full attention on Paul. They flashed across his face, creating hollow shadows. His grin drew wider—more malicious—as he charged.

Paul turned on his heels, staggering as he climbed. His heart raced as the teen's heavy steps thundered up behind him. As he made it to the hallway, he hurried for his office. But before he could close the door behind him, the scarecrow had caught up to him, breaking through. Paul backed away towards his desk, holding his hands up. His breathing drew labored as he kept his eyes on the intruder, not daring to look away.

"Please," Paul sniveled, tears rolling down his face. "Please *stop*."

The teen brandished the blade in Paul's direction, smile still sinister on his lips. Paul bumped against his desk—cornered—as he shook his head. More tears came as he sobbed.

"*Why*?" he asked.

The light of the lamp caught in the scarecrow's blood speckled glasses as his look of cruel joy diminished. Darkness coated his face as he glared at Paul, grip tightening on the handle of the switchblade.

"You needed to know what it felt like," he spat bitterly. "To stand by and watch as your loved one...your *child* suffered. Bled out. *Helpless*."

"I-I don't understand," Paul choked.

"You said you'd give anything to make it right. To take the pain away."

Paul stiffened. His mouth fell open as he stared upon the teen's painted up face. Behind the scarecrow, he abruptly recognized him. The boy from the day of the mask recall. The one who stopped him outside his car.

Doug Feeney.

"Your hush money may have been enough to silence my parents, but it's *not* going to bring my little brother back." Doug hissed.

"D-Doug..." Paul stammered.

"I'd offer the same to *you* for Alex," Doug said. "Unfortunately, though, I don't have corporate backing. I don't have a lobby of lawyers and clowns to throw money at *you* to keep *you* quiet."

His gaze fell to the knife in his hand. Blood sparkled against the surface, like polished rubies. Narrowing his eyes, he returned his attention to Paul.

"So, I'll have to silence you myself."

Doug lunged. Instinctively, Paul grabbed his office chair, holding it up. The blade pierced harmlessly through the leather, causing Doug to curse aloud. He continued to swing frantically, repeatedly stabbing into the barrier. The sheer force of the jabs made Paul's arms tremble. He tried to keep the chair steady, but when the blade made contact with his knuckles, he dropped it.

Paul let out a shrill cry as blood ran down his fingers. He gripped his wound with a hiss as Doug approached again. The knife came down swift and hard, lodging itself into Paul's sternum. He released another pained wail as Doug pulled it free, stabbing again. And again. Over and over. Quick and sharp. Blood sloshed across his face and costume with every jab—driving the knife in and out. Harder and faster. Eventually, Paul's weak gasps and cries died into pathetic gurgles.

Stepping back, admiring his work, a smile slipped across Doug's bloodstained lips. He watched the blood pool across the floor, dotting the walls and desk. The blueprints splayed across it. Wiping the blade off on his pants, he retracted it, satisfied his revenge had been served.

The gurgling stopped. The room fell still. Silent. With a contented sigh, Doug embraced it. Admiring its sweetness. The hushed silence he had longed for.

XV.

THE AMBER LIGHT OF THE HUNTER'S MOON radiated as midnight approached. It caught on bare branches, illuminating them softly beneath the gentle glow, like old bone. Reaching up towards the dark skies. A chilling breeze carried down from the mountainside—sweeping through the valley, whistling like hollow echoes of ghosts in the night.

The group of friends tried to shake the cold as they made it to the old iron gates of Chapel Hill Cemetery. Several unoccupied police cars lined the curb, lights flashing. Despite this, however, the interior lawn was nothing but shadow. Reminiscent of the night they had arrived weeks prior. When all had been calm.

Ritchie exhaled, a thick cloud of condensation billowing from his lips. He reached into his pocket, pulling out his cell phone and turning the flashlight on. A bright ray of white light cut through the darkness, into the depths of the cemetery. Into the stillness that crept between the headstones.

"Come on." He gestured to his friends. "The sooner we find my dad, the sooner we can go home. There's a pretty decent crew here tonight. It shouldn't take long."

Peter stiffened, staring up at the iron gate. The wind rattled through it, emitting a creaky groan. His throat began to tighten again, head spinning with the sounds that echoed from the cemetery grounds. The wind, the scattered leaves, the crickets. And somewhere out there, deep in the back of his mind, the whispering of his name. Calling from the treetops.

Peter, Peter...

He took a step backwards, away from the gate. His friends glanced at him, waiting for him to follow. But he remained frozen, knees trembling as he dropped his gaze to the ground.

"What's wrong?" Sam asked, gently resting a hand on his shoulder.

Peter shook his head. "I don't want to go in there, Sam..."

"We have to find Ritchie's dad," she said. "As soon as we do, I *promise* we'll leave."

"Not tonight..." Peter murmured. "*Please* not *tonight*."

He shrugged away from her touch. His slash wounds stung down to his fingertips, causing him to wince. With a frown, Sam looked up at him.

"I'll be right here with you," she whispered. "We *all* will. Nothing's going to happen to you tonight."

Peter began to shake his head again, but was stopped as Sam took hold of his face. She cupped his cheeks, forcing him to turn his fearful gaze to her.

"Once we find him, we'll go home," she promised.

Peter parted his lips to speak, but she pressed a finger to them, hushing him. Already knowing what his interjection would be. With a sad smile, she ran her fingers down his cheek.

"You can stay at my house if you don't want to go home," she said. "We have the pull-out couch in the den. I can set you up there for the night. My mom and stepdad won't mind."

She took his hands, giving them a firm squeeze. Pursing her lips, she inhaled deeply—gazing sternly into his eyes.

226

"Just...make sure you text your dad," Sam said. "So he at least knows you're safe. Please."

Peter's shoulders tensed. He looked away from her, back to the shadows on the pavement. The flitting leaves.

"I know it's sometimes hard for you to see it, Peter, but he loves you, you know..."

"I know..." Peter muttered.

He lifted his head, gazing out across the dark emptiness. The thick blackness of night. His chest tightened, tears threatening to run from his eyes. They stung in the bitter air as his lips drew into a pensive frown.

"I just wish he *liked* me..."

Before Sam could respond, Ritchie's voice echoed from inside the gate. The bright light of his cell phone flashed, catching their attention.

"Let's *go*!" he called impatiently.

Peter began to shove his hands into his pockets, but Sam stopped him. Taking hold of him, she laced their fingers together. His skin was cold, trembling beneath her touch. Giving him an encouraging squeeze, she nodded towards the gate. Towards the dark pathways within. Keeping his shoulders hunched in caution, he allowed Sam to lead him into the shadows of Chapel Hill.

Fog hung heavy amongst the graves. Ritchie's light reflected against the white, making it hard to see beyond the pathways. The tree branches were nearly bare now—no longer full of vibrant leaves as they had been earlier in the month. Most had collected in piles against the headstones, scattering with the rush of wind. Only the sound of the friends' footsteps echoed through the silent cemetery—crunching the gravel beneath them.

"It sure is quiet," Theo remarked, shrugging the chill from his shoulders.

"Well, I'd hope so. No one's stupid enough to come up here tonight," Ritchie replied.

"Only us." Theo shrugged with a smirk.

"Hey." Ritchie jabbed the end of his baseball bat against Theo's side. "If Johnson sees us out here and wants to start shit, my dad will shut him right up. Don't worry about it."

He swung the bat up, resting it against his shoulder as he continued on the pathway. The cool night air stung his cheeks as he peered through the darkness, searching for any sign of his father and the other officers. But all was still. Pursing his lips, Ritchie snorted.

"You know, it actually wouldn't surprise me if it was fucking *Doug* that killed that cat and strung it up in the tree," he said.

"Let's not talk about this, please," Sam interjected.

"I'm just saying," Ritchie replied. "He always gave me serial killer vibes. Crazy smart, a loner. I don't know. Hell, maybe he's behind all the kids going missing, too. Didn't something happen to his little brother recently?"

"*Enough.*" Sam's voice was stern now.

"It's *not* Doug," Peter said softly. "Didn't Sam tell you?"

"Tell me *what*?" Ritchie asked, cocking an eyebrow. "Oh, you mean about that old hag on the mountain?"

He snorted, turning back to the pathways, the bells on his jester hat jingling. Peter tensed, staring at his friend.

"I told my dad about it," Ritchie said after a moment. "He basically laughed the whole thing off. They've gotten plenty of calls about her in the past. People are concerned—more for her wellbeing than anything else, I guess. My dad's been up there before and he's found nothing. Just a bunch of overfed cats, that's all. She's just a lonely old lady. She means no harm."

"But...did they *check*?" Peter pressed. "*Recently*?"

"They're *not* going to waste their time with her," Ritchie said. "They're busy enough as it is this time of year. Going back up there would be doing a disservice to *everyone*."

"You don't believe me..." Peter mumbled.

"I'm *just* telling you what my dad said." Ritchie snapped. "There's *nothing* up there."

Peter's gaze fell to his feet, lips quivering as they drew into a hard frown. His stomach churned heavily. Sam gently stroked his arm, turning back to the others with a sigh.

"Speaking of the police... Where *are* they, Ritchie?" she pressed.

"For real, man," Theo said, "it's hella late. Shouldn't they have been with their cars?"

"Maybe they're busting someone out here." Ritchie shrugged. "I don't know."

His brow furrowed as he stopped at the forking path. The path all too familiar to him and his friends. He shone the light down each direction, eyeing them carefully. In the distance, up the hill, he could make out the faint flickering of amber light through the fog. Pinpricks scattered amongst the upper cemetery. Clearing his throat, he motioned ahead.

"This way," he said. "There's light. Looks like they're up at the chapel."

Ritchie continued onward. The others hesitated, watching until he vanished into the white haze—only the light of his phone reflecting back to them. Theo sighed heavily, pushing his hands into his jacket pockets. Before he could follow, however, the distant chime of the chapel bell echoed down the hill, across the empty cemetery. He bristled, turning to Peter and Sam. Both were just as stunned, eyes wide as they stared through the shadows— towards the flickering lights upon the hilltop.

"Is that...?" Theo began.

"The chapel," Sam said quietly. "It must be midnight."

"I thought that place was abandoned..." Peter breathed.

"Maybe Ritchie's right." Sam gave his hand a squeeze. "The police probably *are* up there. Someone must have broken in."

"You know what they say about a church bell tolling at midnight on Halloween..." Theo chuckled weakly. "Death is near. Someone will die by sunrise."

Peter's hand went clammy in Sam's grasp. His chest tightened, breathing becoming shallow. He focused on the fog, the shadows stretching across the hill. Again, the bell tolled ominously. Heavy in the night.

"That's just an old legend," Sam brushed Theo off, running her thumb across Peter's knuckles. "No truer than Grims or Devils."

The branches above them creaked. Shifting their gaze to the trees, they could make out bulbous black bodies perched in the branches. Stark beneath the moonlight. Vultures ruffled their feathers as they peered down, hissing in aggravation. Peter stared up at them, gazing into their beady black eyes, words whispering off their tongues with each hiss.

Peter, Peter...

Sam gripped his shoulder. His muscles tensed as he continued to stare into the trees. Chewing her lip, she gently urged him forward, up the hill.

229

Ritchie's voice carried down from ahead, once again impatiently calling his friends to follow. Peter hesitated, but finally gave in. Yet, even as he and the others ascended the path before them, he kept watch over his shoulder. Eyes fixed on the hungry vultures.

"What took you so long?" Ritchie snorted once his friends joined him.

"We had to rest a minute," Theo said. "We're exhausted, man. And Peter really needs his arm looked at."

"Well I'm *trying*," Ritchie snapped. "If you guys would just keep up with me..."

"Whoa..."

Sam's astonished voice caught the boys' attention. They turned to where she was facing, staring out at the flickering lights across the hill. Through the shroud of fog, they could make out shapes—faces—blazing beside the old headstones. Jack-o'-lanterns, carved out of the plump pumpkins that filled the cemetery on their last visit. Every single one was lit, burning brightly in the night. Releasing Peter's hand, Sam made her way farther up the path—entranced.

"Who carved all of these?" she asked aloud, eyes wide in wonder.

"It must have taken forever," Theo replied. "There's *thousands* of these things."

"They're beautiful," Sam said. "But, I don't understand. This place is off limits on Halloween. Why carve and light all these pumpkins if no one is going to see them?"

"It was probably the groundskeeper," Ritchie sneered. "So he could blame it on *trespassers* and waste everyone's time again."

As the friends continued up the path, they scanned the sea of glinting jack-o'-lanterns. Ritchie turned the light on his phone off, letting the soft amber glow illuminate the way. From the treetops, feathers rustled—more vultures landing and watching. The group slowed as they stared back, curious

and uneasy. The scavengers hissed, opening their wings wide in welcome. Admiring the precession along the jack-o'-lantern lit paths.

"I want to leave..." Peter whispered, gripping his stinging wounds.

His eyes frantically darted from tree to tree, feeling the prying gaze of the vultures. The gaze he had known well from his nightmares.

"We're almost to the chapel," Ritchie said. "After that, we can get the hell out of here, okay?"

"*Please*, Ritchie..."

The vultures shifted, branches creaking beneath their weight. Their necks craned low in a mocking bow, eyes fixated on Peter. He trembled, swallowing around the lump forming in his throat.

"*I'm scared...*" He whimpered.

Sam turned to the flickering patch of jack-o'-lanterns. She studied their glowing faces, stopping when her eyes met one that looked familiar. A pathetic frown had been carved into it, eyes weary. It was practically identical to the mask Peter had worn earlier that night. Walking over to it, she inspected the vine. It had been damaged—almost severed all the way through. Biting her lip, she took hold of the stem, twisting as hard as she could until the pumpkin broke free. Its sad face glinted through the shadows as she held it out to Peter.

"Here," she said softly. "It's not much, but it's light. We're almost there. And then we'll all go home, okay?"

Peter hesitantly took the pumpkin, hugging it tight to his chest. His nails dug into the thick, orange flesh as he tried to steady his breathing. Counting slowly to himself.

One...two...three...

Sam returned to the patch of pumpkins, removing two more and carrying them over to Theo and Ritchie. One was carved with a goofy spiral pattern, the other a traditional terrifying grin. She held them out, encouraging the boys to take them.

"What's this for?" Ritchie asked, sneering.

"Light," Sam said, pressing the jack-o'-lantern to his chest.

"We don't *need* light," Ritchie retorted, staring down at the silly carved face. "It's bright up here with all these jack o' lanterns lit. And besides, we have our phones."

"In case their batteries die," Sam quipped back, handing Theo the other pumpkin.

"They're *not* going—"

231

"For *comfort* then," Sam interrupted him, rolling her eyes. "*Please*, Ritchie."

She gestured to Peter. His eyes were still wide as he worked on steadying his breath. His fingertips twitched against the pumpkin as he continued counting.

Four...five...six...

Bending down again, Sam tugged a cheerful jack-o'-lantern from the bunch. She held it tight as she glanced ahead through the fog. In the distance, the dark silhouette of the chapel loomed at the top of the hill. From its windows, she could see amber light—feeble and flickering. Like that of the jack-o'-lanterns surrounding them.

Seven...eight...nine...

Peter, Peter...

Peter's grip tightened further against the gourd, gaze returning to the trees. Still, the vultures stared down at him. His heart pounded, breaths coming in erratic pants. Their bloodstained beaks glimmered in the jack-o'-lantern's glow—hissing in hate.

Peter, Peter pumpkin-eater...

The hair on the back of his neck rose, nails digging deep into the pumpkin—leaving crescent moon shaped marks. He stifled a cry, turning to his friends.

"Do you hear that?"

"Hear *what*?" Theo asked, raising an eyebrow.

The others stared curiously as Peter trembled, tears stinging his eyes at the realization they couldn't. Gritting his teeth, he looked to the trees. To the bulbous bodies mocking him.

From his head, he fed the seeder...

"*That!*" Peter cried.

But once again, he was met with confused silence. Ritchie shook his head, motioning towards the chapel.

"Come on. Enough dragging our feet already," he scoffed.

"Please..." Peter begged. "Please just *listen*. Tell me you can hear it..."

They crowned him with a pumpkin-shell...

"I don't hear anything, Peter," Sam said truthfully. "Just the wind and the leaves."

Peter hugged the pumpkin, letting a few tears fall. They rolled down his cheeks as he stared across the flickering landscape. Out beyond the graves. And sure enough, he heard what Sam had mentioned. The wind whistling through bare branches, creaking barren limbs. The scuttling of leaves across

the pathways. The vultures shifting in the trees, ruffling their feathers. But then, somewhere out there, he also heard the light footfalls of padded feet. The crunching of leaves beneath them.

Peter stiffened, feeling eyes on his back. Not the eyes of the vultures; something different. Something he had sensed the night they first snuck out to the cemetery. The ever-watching gaze amongst the headstones. Exhaling a shaky breath, he glanced over his shoulder—into the thick shadows stirring.

And dragged him off to rot in Hell...

A low growl rose from the center of the path. Between the rolling fog, a pair of red eyes shone—burning like candlelight. Peter's mouth fell open in fear. He stiffened—petrified—as the dark silhouette took shape. It became a large black dog, with hackles raised and tail low. Its jowls were turned up, exposing bloodstained fangs. Slobber dripped from its jaws as its blazing eyes locked on the group, throat rumbling in rage.

"*The Grim...*" Peter quavered.

His friends turned, seeing the figure on the path. Just as Peter had, they froze, hearts racing. The dog lowered its head, snapping its jaws with a snarling bark. Theo hugged his pumpkin to his chest, glancing quickly at Ritchie.

"Is that one of the K-9 units?" he whispered frantically.

Ritchie's blue eyes grew wide. The glowing red pair met his as the dog growled again, sticky saliva dripping from its bottom jaw. Its snout wrinkled as it bared its fangs, pointed ears flattening against its head. Tightening the grip on his bat, Ritchie shook his head slowly.

"N-no..."

"It's the Grim," Peter breathed.

"*Fuck.*" Theo cursed.

"It *can't* be," Ritchie said, voice trembling. "Right? It can't be. This shit's not real. You said so yourself, Sam. It's just superstition. Right? *Right*, Sam?"

Sam didn't respond. Her lips were pressed together tightly, focused on the wispy silhouette before them. It seemed to pay her no mind—looking between the boys before stopping on Peter. A low snarl emitted from its chest as its fur prickled—standing higher on the back of its neck.

"What was it you said about Grims, Sam?" Theo swallowed.

"They protect graveyards." Sam whispered.

"Yes, but...from *what*, exactly?"

"Trespassers," Ritchie spat. "*Shit.*"

"And the Devil..." Sam exhaled.

"Yeah, but the Devil *isn't* real," Ritchie snapped. "So, then, the *Grim* shouldn't be real, either, right?"

Sam's fingernails dug into her jack-o'-lantern, burying themselves into its thick orange flesh. The candle within flickered in the gentle breeze that picked up down the path. She steadied her breaths, keeping still, not daring to look away from the shadowy hound.

"*Fucking right, Sam?*" Ritchie's voice cracked.

"I-I don't know..."

"The *fuck* do you mean you don't know!"

"If it protects against the Devil...it won't hurt *us*, right?" Theo asked softly. "It'll protect us."

"Supposedly," Sam said. "But, if it sees us as trespassers..."

"If it sees us as *trespassers*...?" Ritchie urged her to continue.

"It'll chase us into an early grave," she finished shakily. "That's how legend goes."

"We should have just gone to the *hospital*, man." Theo groaned.

The Grim sniffed heavily, tasting the air. Inhaling the scent blowing towards it on the wind. Again, its burning red eyes locked with Peter's, jaws dripping hungrily. Gaze full of hate.

Noticing the dog had fixated on Peter, Sam turned to him. He was frozen in place, shoulders quivering as he gripped his jack-o'-lantern with white knuckles. More tears stained his face as he panted, trembling uncontrollably. Too terrified to look away. Her gaze fell upon the torn, bloodstained fabric of his shirt, the gashes left behind from the attack at the party. Inhaling sharply in realization, she fought to keep her voice low.

"Peter..."

He didn't answer. His knees buckled as he whimpered—staring deep into the blazing eyes of the Grim. It stared back, searching his soul. Then, with a snort, it bolted forward. Sam let out a shrill scream as its paws pounded against the gravel—claws raking the earth.

"*Run, Peter!*"

Without hesitation, he turned on his heels, hurrying behind his friends. They sprinted up the hill, pumpkins tight in their grasps. Their feet slapped against the pathways, echoing off the crumbling headstones. Behind them, the snarls and snaps of the Grim closely trailed—its body breaking through the fog. From the treetops, the vultures looked on in amusement, wings spread wide as they bobbed their heads.

"What do we *do*, man?" Theo asked between pants.

From the front of the group, Ritchie's eyes flitted across the cemetery. He searched through the jack-o'-lantern filled grounds for any sign of escape. Any possible way to lose the Grim. But all seemed futile. The land was too overgrown with vines and old, weathered headstones. Drawing a labored breath, he fixed his attention on the chapel, slowly coming into view at the top of the hill.

Flickering light poured from its windows and doors—thrown wide open and inviting. Through his adrenaline-filled gasps, he managed a sigh of relief. His father and the other officers were clearly nearby. With a swift flick of his head, he motioned towards it.

"The chapel!" Ritchie hollered. "Come on!"

Theo picked up his pace, mere inches behind Ritchie. Sam trailed close after, continually glancing over her shoulder to Peter. He fell behind, wheezing in uneasy, panicked breaths. Sam called for him to hurry, over his shaky, wet coughs breaking through the air. The Grim snapped at his heels, jaws dripping hungrily.

Peter's vision grew hazy as he ascended the rest of the hill, watching Ritchie disappear into the well-lit chapel. Theo was the next inside. He and Ritchie took hold of the heavy doors, Sam scampering through the entryway. She turned back as Peter skidded inside. Using all their strength, Ritchie and Theo slammed the doors shut—just before the Grim could reach them.

The hound threw itself against the old wood, snarling and barking. The weight of its body shook the chapel, rattling the handles and locks. Ritchie released a quivering breath as he stared. Waiting. Eventually, the pounding stopped. A low, disappointed growl drew from beneath the door. Then, after a moment, it shuffled away—leaves crunching as it disappeared into the shadows of the cemetery.

Ritchie sighed heavily as he slumped against the doorway. He used his bat as a crutch, shaking his head as he turned to Theo. He, too, was struggling to catch his breath, hand gripping his chest as he blew a long exhale from his lips. Peter leaned against the wall of the vestibule, gasping. He hacked, throat rattling with phlegm as his shoulders trembled.

"Are you okay?" Sam asked him once she had gathered herself.

Peter's eyelids fluttered weakly as he looked at her. He coughed one last time, straightening himself up before nodding.

"I'm fine," he wheezed. "I just...need a minute."

"I think it's time you lay off the cigs, man." Theo chuckled between his own shaky breaths. "What about you guys? Everyone else alright?"

"Surviving," Ritchie replied, sliding the jester hat from his head as he stepped away from the door.

Sam flashed him a quick smirk. "Well, you finally got that scare you wanted when we came up here weeks ago. Happy now?"

Ritchie waved her off. "Sure. But one's enough. I'd rather *not* do that again, thanks."

"Is it...still out there?" Peter asked worriedly.

"No." Sam shook her head. "I'm almost positive it left."

"What if it comes back?"

Peter's gaze fell to the floor. His dark eyes were wide with fear and exhaustion. Again, his fingers pressed against his pumpkin, feeling the grooves left behind by his nails. As Sam chewed her lip, thinking of what to say to comfort him, Ritchie's astonished voice drew her attention away.

"What the...?"

The others followed his gaze, staring out across the chapel as he stepped into the nave. Every sconce and candelabra was aglow with dripping white candles—the shimmering gold flames reflecting in his blue eyes. And just as the gravesites had been, every pew was filled with jack-o'-lanterns. Their wide, grinning faces stared forward towards the altar—adorned in its own barrage of carved pumpkins.

Withered leaves were scattered across it, candles blazing within the jack-o'-lanterns. Dried corn stalks decorated the reredos, hay bales stacked neatly beside them. Vines snaked their way up and down the walls, overtaking the stained glass windows.

The others followed behind Ritchie, making their way up the aisle as they curiously scanned their surroundings. Taking in the colorful ambers and browns of a perfect autumn harvest around them. Beautiful, but unsettling.

"Ritchie..." Sam whispered. "Where's your—?"

She stopped short. As her eyes met the scene before her, her heart dropped.

The three scarecrows they had discovered amongst the plots were propped up in the choir. Flies buzzed about their heads, maggots churning inside their burlap faces. Only now, the fabric had been peeled back. Gnawed away by the weather and hungry insects. A putrid stench lingered in the air, drifting over the pews as the group stared in disgust. Even from a distance, they could make out the rotten flesh—graying and pulled tight against the bone, smeared with pumpkin guts. Black blood lined their cheeks and stained their opened mouths, jaws cracked and twisted. Ritchie's face contorted as he

looked on in repulsion, staring hard at the corpse stuffed into the middle scarecrow.

"Linda…" He retched. "*I fucking knew* that was *Linda*!"

"Holy shit." Theo covered his mouth. "Then that must mean…"

"Chrissy and Tasha." Ritchie tensed. "*Fuck*."

The sound of flies grew louder as they swarmed the rotting bodies, draped in damp burlap and leaves. Sam's mouth fell open as she blinked back tears. The stench of decay stung her nostrils as she backed away, digging her nails into the flesh of her pumpkin. She pressed against Peter, turning to him for comfort. But he merely stared forward—brown eyes wide, lips parted and quivering.

He, however, wasn't focused on the scarecrows.

The large, once upright cross behind the altar had been tilted—turned upside down into a Petrine cross. Blood-soaked vines snaked their way around it, binding tight the body that hung upon it. The throat had been torn open, thick blood drenching the face and head. Hay burst from its mouth, tinged red. The eyes had been gouged out, hollow sockets stuffed with the same straw. Both arms were tied together behind the corpse's back, right leg bent at the knee and positioned at an angle behind the left. Peter's heart dropped as he recognized the pose. One he had seen at the party just hours before while seated on the couch, watching the girl pulling tarot cards.

The Hanged Man.

He released a shallow breath as he backed away, hugging his jack-o'-lantern tight to his chest. Its flesh cracked beneath the force, light inside sputtering. Tears blurred his vision as he panted, staring helplessly at the face of the man on the cross. Beneath the caked blood and fear-stricken features, he could see the hardness. The bitter resentment.

"It's the groundskeeper…" Peter gasped.

Before the others could respond, they were startled by a loud hiss echoing across the choir. A large vulture perched on the pulpit, cocking its head to the side as it inspected them, feathers ruffling. Its bloodied beak parted, emitting a low, raspy breath.

Peter, Peter…

The friends stiffened, hugging their jack o' lanterns closer.

"Did…did that thing just…?" Theo stammered.

"No way, man," Ritchie said stiffly. "It couldn't have. Right?"

Peter, Peter pumpkin-eater…

This time, the voice didn't come from the vulture. It was raspy, higher-pitched. Human. The friends turned to the priest's door, tucked away in the

corner of the chancel. An elderly woman stood there, a plump, ripe pumpkin in her calloused hands. She grinned at the group, exposing crooked yellow teeth. Peter inhaled sharply at the sight of her. Turning to the others, he fought back tears that continued to well in his eyes.

"It's *her*," he breathed. "The old woman from the mountain..."

His gaze fell on Ritchie. He was stiff as stone, the grip on his bat tight as he tucked his jack-o'-lantern under one arm. His chest fell, eyes flashing with guilt as Peter's lower lip trembled.

"I *told* you..."

Grýla hushed him as she made her way across the sanctuary, coming to stand behind the altar. Setting the pumpkin down in the center, surrounded by smaller jack-o'-lanterns and candles, she sneered.

"So nice seeing you again, Peter." Her lips curled at his name. "I knew you wouldn't miss such a special occasion."

"*Occasion*?" Ritchie spat.

"What is she *talking* about?" Theo whispered, glancing at Peter.

But he didn't answer. Peter pursed his lips, shoulders tight and tense. His fingertips twitched against his pumpkin as he stifled a terrified sob. The candlelight was starting to become too bright, the smell of decaying leaves and rotting flesh too strong. The sounds of the vulture shifting on the pulpit too loud. His eyes fell to his feet, staring at the muddied toes of his shoes.

"Oh, he didn't tell you?" Grýla jeered. "Tonight's a *very* special night. It's the night the veil between the living and the dead is at its thinnest. The night spirits return to roam the earth; some searching for loved ones, others for a host to give them new life. It's a homecoming for lost souls. A triumph for the dead."

A soft mewl came from behind the altar. A sleek black cat leapt upon it with a chirp, trotting over and seating himself beside one of the lit jack-o'-lanterns. His tail thumped the surface as he blinked his yellow eyes slowly, staring at Peter. His whiskers twitched as he let out a low growl, ears flattening against his head. Peter's stomach turned as the cat hissed, revealing a tongueless mouth.

"And tonight, we're here to celebrate one soul's return in particular," Grýla said, reaching out and stroking the cat. "Dear old Jack."

"Jack?" Ritchie raised an eyebrow. "Who the *fuck* is *Jack*?"

"Old John..." Peter murmured.

Sam shook her head, looking him hard in the face.

"*No*, Peter," she said quietly. "You know that story isn't true. You *know* it."

"Hold up," Ritchie interrupted. "*You* said the *Devil* wasn't real. Not that *John* wasn't. In fact, you told us *that* part *was* true. So which *is* it, Sam?"

"It's *all* true, my dears." Grýla smirked. "Every last bit. John was a town outcast. A *fool*. Down on his luck and looking for a way out. A quick way to gain respect. And so, he wandered out here late one Halloween night, drunk and rambling to the night air. Wishing the town could see him for what he was worth. What he *believed* he was worth. In his stupor, he found himself seated upon the throne, seeking the Devil. And sure enough, he conjured him. Told him he wanted the admiration of a King, and all the earthly pleasures that came with such a title. Of course, the Devil obliged. But, you all know the rest of *that* story."

"That he hanged himself from the old tree to try and trick the Devil, but he got tricked himself," Ritchie said. "Yeah, yeah. We've heard it. So *what*?"

"Ah, but you never heard what comes *after* that, have you?"

The boys glared at Sam. She gave them a nervous look, shaking her head and shrugging her shoulders. Grýla's grin grew wider as she brushed her hand through the decaying leaves upon the altar, retrieving a silver dagger. She plunged it into the top of the plump pumpkin, sawing away in a jagged motion. Cutting up and down, hollowing it out.

"The Devil kept his promise. But, all promises come with a price—and that price is *more* than just a soul."

The top half of the pumpkin broke free. Wet, stringy guts clung to it, slimy pumpkin seeds protruding between them. Grýla carefully removed them with the blade before continuing to carve away at her creation. More pieces of pumpkin fell atop the altar. The cat twitched its tail in interest as it watched, sniffing the fragments left behind. Grýla's eyes grew dark as she sliced away another chunk.

"When one sells their soul, the Devil does more than just claim it. He inhabits the body, the shell left behind. Uses it to take form, seeking out the next naïve victim. One foolish enough to come up here on a cold autumn night and sit upon his throne. Speak wishes to the wind. The Devil doesn't just take your soul. He takes *you*."

Grýla jabbed the tip of the dagger directly at Peter. His brown eyes went wide, tears running down his face. Her lips drew up into a crooked smile as she continued brandishing the blade at him.

"There was George. And there was Tom. And then, it was poor old John," Grýla sneered. "And now, it'll be *you*, Peter."

239

He shook his head, gritting his teeth. Grýla sliced another chunk of pumpkin, nearly finished with her creation. She hummed aloud the tune that haunted Peter so heavily throughout the month, causing him to quiver.

"Oh, Peter, Peter..." she cooed. "If only you hadn't been so foolish as to sit upon the throne. So *needy*. So *desperate*. And for what? Go on. We're all here. You might as well share what your deepest desires are. What you *really* asked the Devil for."

"A Chemistry grade," Ritchie scoffed. "We already know. And he *failed*. So, there. The deal's off."

Grýla wagged a finger at him, clicking her tongue. "Now, now. Of *course* he didn't wish for a silly *grade*. Did you, Peter? Go on, now."

Peter squeezed his pumpkin against his chest harder than ever. Its sad expression folded in, the light inside fading. Tears poured down his cheeks as he released a soft sob. His friends stared at him, mouths parted in worry.

"Peter..." Sam gently touched his arm. "Did...did you really make a wish?"

A tear fell from his chin, landing on top of the jack-o'-lantern in his arms. Theo's eyes widened as he shook his head.

"You *didn't*, man..."

"It was supposed to only be a story..." Peter sobbed. "I didn't mean to..."

"You made a *wish*? An *actual* wish?" Ritchie snapped.

"Wouldn't *anyone*?" Sam defended him. "Yeah, Peter joked about his Chemistry grade...but if that were *you*, wouldn't *your* heart answer for you? You can't tell me it wouldn't."

Ritchie fell silent. His eyes softened as he turned to Peter again, this time with sympathy. Parting his lips, he spoke softly.

"Well, what'd you wish for, Peter?"

"The floor's yours." Grýla spread her hands, gesturing across the chapel.

Peter could feel the grinning faces of the jack-o'-lanterns in the pews staring at him. Each flicker like knives in his back. But still, he didn't answer. After a moment, Grýla shook her head.

"Well, then. If *you* won't share, I'd be *glad* to."

She sliced another sharp ridge in the pumpkin. Running her fingertips across the smooth flesh, she smirked. The cat beside her shifted on his paws, glaring at Peter.

"You wished to never be alone, never be forgotten. They're your biggest fears, yes? Is that why you cry yourself to sleep? Why you gave up

240

trying to succeed? So you don't have to move on? My deary told me all about it. Told me all about *you*. Your trauma. Your grief. Your *fear*." Grýla stroked the head of the black cat, listening to him purr. "All those nights you spent up here, sitting on that cold stone. Pouring your poor little heart out. Begging for someone to hear you. To make your desires come true. If I'm honest, I've heard some pathetic requests over the centuries, Peter. But *yours*... You really *are* the biggest fool of them all."

The vulture on the pulpit bobbed its head up and down, hissing with laughter. Peter's face flushed as his lips drew into a pained frown. Sam stepped closer to him, caressing his arm and resting her head against his shoulder. But he didn't move.

"George and Tom at least weren't selfish. Their wishes were made for loved ones. Jack at least was given a court. But *your* wish, Peter... Why, its fulfillment is as simple as death."

Grýla set the dagger down. Using her fingers, she cleaned the rough edges left behind on her carved pumpkin.

"After all, the dead are never alone," she sneered. "That's why cemeteries are so vast. Endless."

She raised her creation, the flickering light around her reflecting off its flesh. The whole pumpkin had been hollowed out, carved into a crown. Its pointed spikes were jagged, shaky from her old hands. She held it out to Peter.

"We all know how this story ends, Peter," she said. "It's the same as all the legends do. Go to the tree. Do what is expected of you. You made a deal, after all."

Peter's mouth fell open as he shook his head. "*No...*"

Peter, Peter pumpkin-eater...

The vulture's wings opened wide. The cat's yellow eyes gleamed as it crouched, gaze searing through Peter.

"And, how appropriate might I add." Grýla gestured to the jack-o'-lanterns in each of their arms. "You all brought offerings. Gifts for the new King."

From his head, he fed the seeder...

The friends shared nervous glances as the light inside their pumpkins flashed. Again, the vulture hissed out a cackle as Grýla smirked.

"The pumpkins want their new King, Peter. Don't keep them waiting."

They crowned him with a pumpkin-shell...

The words became heavier. Louder. As if spoken by a choir of voices. Another teardrop rolled down Peter's cheek as his friends closed in around

241

him, gripping their jack-o'-lanterns tight. They glared at Grýla, watching helplessly as she outstretched her arms, the candlelight violently flickering across the chapel.

And dragged him off to rot in Hell...

The front doors flew open. A heavy gust of wind blasted through the chapel, sputtering the candles. The group whirled to face the entryway as a low growl drifted across the nave. In the dim lit vestibule stood the Grim, hackles raised and red eyes blazing. Its white fangs were exposed, dripping hot saliva. It remained still for only a moment before barking and bounding up the aisle.

Before the friends could react, however, the cat upon the altar wailed. His tail flared as he bared his own fangs, pouncing from his position and landing before the Grim. It stopped in its tracks as the cat hissed, unsheathing his claws and swiping at the hound. They raked across the Grim's snout, drawing a pained yowl. It snapped its jaws at the cat, but he was too quick. He leapt onto the Grim's back, sinking his fangs into its nape, tearing away flesh and fur with his claws. The hound thrashed as it attempted to shake the cat, slamming into pews. A symphony of yelps and screams overtook the chapel as Ritchie dropped his jack-o'-lantern to the floor.

"Come on!" he shouted. "We gotta go. *Now!*"

The others didn't hesitate. They released their jack-o'-lanterns, letting them crack and split across the cold stone floor as they hurried down the aisle, keeping careful watch on the Grim. But it was too distracted by the cat. It threw itself against the wall, yipping and snarling as the cat continued to claw, tongueless mouth opened wide and snapping.

The crisp night air was refreshing as the friends pounded down the steps, hearts racing as they ran back down the hill towards the entrance. Looking out across the jack-o'-lantern lit landscape, Theo called out to Ritchie.

"Which way?"

"*Not* past the tree," Ritchie demanded. "We'll take the side trail. Through the modern plots."

"Isn't that *longer*?" Theo pressed.

"Longer, but *safer*," Ritchie hollered back. "Now *come on!*"

As the friends disappeared down the lesser traveled dirt path, dissolving into shadow, Grýla frowned. The vulture took off from its perch, circling the Grim. The cat didn't give in, still attacking with all its strength—holding the hound off. Pressing her fingers firmly against the pumpkin-shell crown, Grýla scowled.

"Go on!" she called out into the night. "You can't run from the Devil. You can't hide from fate!"

The path the friends took was blanketed with decaying leaves—not tended to like the rest of the cemetery. And while the glow of the jack-o'-lanterns was bright, it barely reached the vacant headstones that dotted the newer plots. Ritchie led the way, the light from his phone guiding them, reminding them every so often to watch where they stepped. To be careful not to trip. Roots from nearby trees snaked across the path, concealed by the leaves. Yet, while it was a longer route, it was quiet. There were no vultures or shifting leaves or growling Grims. All was still. Peaceful.

"I've never been in this section before," Theo said, gazing out across the newer headstones.

"I think these are the cheaper plots," Ritchie whispered. "Tucked away in the corner up here. They rarely get visitors."

Peter's head hung low as he caught his breath. Though no longer running, his heart still pounded, hands trembling. Sam watched him from the corner of her eye, reaching out and gently taking his hand. She laced her fingers with his, looking sincerely into his eyes.

"I'm sorry I didn't believe you," she said sadly. "When you mentioned the woman on the mountain...I-I didn't know you meant *her*..."

"That woman's *batshit*, okay?" Ritchie scoffed. "She's completely talking out of her ass, you know? *Obviously* she's heard the town legends, too."

"She's probably been around long enough to have *seen* them happen," Theo remarked dryly.

Ritchie smirked. "*Legit*. But, for all we know, it's all a crock of shit. She just wants to scare us because it's Halloween."

Peter grimaced. Feeling his grip tighten, Sam ran her thumb over his knuckles. Smiling sadly, she coaxed him to look at her.

"I won't let anything happen to you tonight," she said. "I promise."

He didn't respond. His eyes scanned the dark plots, searching the headstones. A sense of familiarity began to overtake him as his mouth drew open.

"I *know* this section…" he whispered.

Sam turned to him as his hand slipped from hers. He walked ahead, brushing past Ritchie as he surveyed the stones. His friends watched as he continued along the path, before stopping abruptly.

"Peter?" Sam asked, joining him at his side.

His eyes were wide, fixed on a lonely headstone set apart from the others—nestled into a corner plot, near the edge of the tree line. Peter inhaled sharply as the light from Ritchie's phone grazed the marble, catching on the large, block letters engraved across its face.

HARLOW.

Peter's shoulders slouched as he swallowed around the lump in his throat. His mind became static, buzzing with empty thoughts. His mouth drew into a deep frown as he approached, wringing his hands. The others stood back, keeping the light on him as they watched. Silent.

The marble was ice cold beneath Peter's fingers as he reached out, running them through the engravement. Tracing each letter. H. A. R. L. O. W. His eyes glazed over with fresh tears as his hand slid down to the name etched into the stone. He let it linger there, fingertips pressed lightly into the grooves. A single tear fell down his cheek as he read the name over and over: Judith Harlow.

Peter slowly shook his head. Shadows of memory crept upon him. Things he had drowned out. Kept locked away. His breaths grew heavy as he sniveled, collapsing to his knees at the base of the stone. His friends hurried over, gently resting their hands against his back as they hushed him.

"Hey…Peter, hey…it's alright." Ritchie squeezed his shoulder.

Again, Peter shook his head. This time, however, it was more forceful. Tears spilled from his eyes as a sob broke from his throat. It was heavy and hoarse, causing his body to tremble uncontrollably. Theo and Sam wrapped their arms around him, pulling him close. He leaned his head against them, howling relentlessly. Sam hushed him again, pressing her face against his as she stroked his hair back.

"It's okay," she whispered. "We're here."

"I-I didn't know…" Peter choked. "I…"

But he *did* know. The looks of confusion on his friends' faces reminded him of that. Again, flashes of memory resurfaced, taunting him.

HARLOW

He remembered the phone call; hospice informing his father of the news. He remembered Jim's wails of grief as he watched from the corner of the living room—too afraid to speak. Too consumed by guilt. Shame. Sorrow. He remembered sobbing into his pillow, screaming and weeping and begging. Begging harder than he had the day she left. *Praying* that she come home. That it all be a dream—a nightmare. But it wasn't. He remembered picking out the flowers—daylilies. Her favorite. He remembered shakily writing on the card attached: *I'm sorry my love wasn't enough for you to stay. Please forgive me - Petey.* He remembered the sweet scent as he buried his face into them on the way to the funeral home, hiding his tears amongst the soft white petals. He remembered his suit was too big, the sleeves too long, but it was all his father could afford. He remembered fiddling with his tie, wringing it into knots in his hands. He remembered Jim's touch as he told him to relax. That it was okay.

But it wasn't okay.

He remembered her body lying in the casket—done up pretty. She wore her favorite necklace and earrings, lips painted a light rose. He remembered all the sympathy. All the *I'm sorries.* All the pats on his back and the handshakes and the hugs. All the people he hardly knew—all the people who hardly knew *him.* Hardly knew his grief. He remembered pressing his face to her, weeping against her burial gown. He remembered spewing his own slew of *I'm sorries.* Staining her clothes in tears. He remembered kissing her forehead. How cold her skin was. How stiff. It didn't feel like his mother. But he *knew* it was his mother. He remembered his father prying him away, hushing him. Holding him. Petting him. He remembered the casket being sealed. And the wail that broke from his chest with the knowing he would never see her again.

He remembered the graveside, the burial. How sick the scent of roses made him. How they reeked not of beauty, but of death. He remembered tossing the one he was given onto her casket as it was lowered into the ground. And he remembered the rain. How heavy it fell, turning the dirt into thick mud. But he stood there alongside his father, soaked all the way through. He didn't mind it, though. The raindrops dripping from his tousled hair, running down his cheeks, hid his tears. He remembered the cars pulling away, leaving one by one. He and his father were the last to go—and he remembered that, too. Looking in the rearview mirror as the rain filled the freshly dug grave. As he silently said goodbye for the last time.

Then, he remembered the bills. All the phone calls that came after. All the stress his father endured. His bawling. His lack of sleep. Peter

remembered all the nights he found him with a bottle of sleeping pills—dozing in his armchair. He'd cover him with a quilt, kissing his cheek, and then go to his bedroom, crying himself to sleep. Alone. Uncomforted. He remembered how he wished he could take the pain away. Away from himself and away from his father. He remembered sitting in his therapy sessions after that—no longer able to voice his feelings. His hurt. He'd just sit on the couch and stare out the window, until it came the day he did speak again. *You can't help me anymore. You can't fix me. I'm sorry.*

I'm sorry...

But most of all, he remembered that night. The night she left. The night he begged her to stay. Pleaded with her not to go. He remembered arguing with her, telling her she was okay. That she was going to *be* okay. He didn't understand then. Maybe, he never really did. But her words stung. Words she didn't mean. Still, they ate away at him. Sent his mind to a dark place. Drowning out any other memory he had. Any other he would make. He remembered her stepping out the front door—into the night. Into the heavy rainfall. He remembered his father chasing after her, begging her to wait. Not to go. He remembered being alone. In shock. Weeping. Collapsing to his knees on the living room floor, rocking as he sobbed. Blubbering words.

I'm sorry...

"I'm sorry..."

Peter pressed his head against the marble. His friends continued to hold him, keeping him secure. The tears didn't stop. He sniffled, shaking his head as he apologized again.

"*I forgot...*"

The guilt grew heavy again. But this time, with understanding. The lifting of blame. Of forgiveness. Slowly raising his head, he stared at her name.

"You weren't sick of me," he choked. "You were just *sick*."

He placed his hand against the stone again. Tracing the letters with his fingertips, Peter shook his head. A tear rolled down his nose as he inhaled sharply.

"I-I *forgot*... I'm so sorry I forgot."

His friends tightened their embrace. Shakily pulling away from the headstone, he held them back. Their warmth calmed him. Steadied his breathing. Peter frowned, wetting his lips.

"You didn't leave me," he whispered. "You didn't forget. *I* did. *I* left you. And I *forgot* you..."

He closed his eyes. Gritting his teeth, he squeezed the last tears from his eyes. They fell against the base of the headstone as he whimpered.

"I'm sorry..."

Resting his head one last time against the marble, he sighed. The night air brushed across his face—chilled and haunting. He gently pressed his lips to the cold stone, warm breath whispering against it.

"I love you, Mom..."

The leaves crunched beneath the friends' feet as they silently made their way down the hill. The amber moon slipped behind a sea of clouds, darkening the night sky. Ritchie kept the light on the makeshift path ahead, cursing under his breath at the low battery notification displaying on the screen. He tapped it away, glancing over his shoulder to the others. They wearily trailed behind, scuffing along through the leaves.

"Hey, let's *go*," he urged. "My phone's dying."

Sam cocked an eyebrow. "*Oh?*"

Ritchie waved her off. He shone the light across the vast darkness before heaving a sigh. Everything in the newer section looked the same. As he was about to continue onward, a sharp hiss from Peter stopped him. Sam released his hand as he held pressure to the gashes in his arm. Though hours old, they still pulsed beneath his fingers—stinging violently. Pursing his lips, Ritchie opened the call icon on his phone.

"What are you doing?" Theo asked, joining his side.

"Calling my dad," Ritchie said. "*If* I can get through. Service sucks up here."

"You should have just done that to begin with, man," Theo huffed.

"I doubt he would have answered."

"Then what makes you think he will *now*?"

Ritchie looked down at the time displayed across his phone: 2:11 a.m. Pressing *call*, he held the phone to his ear. Silence met him on the other end as it searched for service.

"His shift just ended," Ritchie said. "With any luck, they're still up here."

The dial tone finally echoed from Ritchie's phone. His eyes lit up in relief as he held it close, waiting for an answer. Again it rang—this time, however, rising from the distance. The others slowly turned their attention across the cemetery—back towards the flickering lights of the jack-o'-lantern filled plots. Ritchie pulled the phone away from his ear, hearing both the ringing in his device and from afar. Sucking in a hard breath, a smile met his lips.

"*I knew it*!" he exclaimed. "He's still here. *Come on!*"

Ritchie took off through the shadows, straying from the pathway. He staggered through the grass, nearly tripping over low grave markers. Theo called out to him, urging him to wait. But Ritchie continued on, running towards the familiar ring of his father's cell phone—echoing through the night. Hesitating, the others followed along, stumbling through the darkness.

"Something's not right," Sam said as they made it back to the main pathway, just before the fork. "Why isn't he answering?"

"He's probably finishing up with something," Ritchie replied hopefully. "Maybe he busted that old bitch."

The ringing was louder now. Closer. When the call disconnected, Ritchie redialed, gritting his teeth impatiently.

"Come on, Dad... Pick *up*."

In the distance, the old barren tree came into view. Flashes of light shone off the trunk, coming from the flickering jack-o'-lanterns and bonfire beneath it. Again, the ringtone blared across the pathway as Ritchie pulled himself to a stop. His stomach dropped as he stared, eyes fixed on the dark branches. Silhouetted in shadow, he could make out bodies strung up by the neck. Swaying in the night.

"The witches," Theo whispered. "Didn't they say on Halloween night you could see them?"

"I-I think so," Ritchie stammered.

His father's phone rang again, clearly coming from the tree. Exhaling heavily, he began towards it. His friends followed close behind. Peter still gripped his injured arm, eyes narrowing as he stared ahead. His heart raced as Grýla's words burned in his head—her command to go to the tree. He fell behind, carefully taking in the sounds around him. Cautious.

"Dad?" Ritchie's voice trailed as he made his way towards the tree.

There was no response. The call disconnected again—unanswered. Cursing beneath his breath, Ritchie approached, wary of the figures lingering

in the branches. As he stepped into the light of the bonfire, he went pale. His blue eyes widened in terror as his mouth fell open, trembling uncontrollably.

They weren't witches strung up from the branches. Nor were they ghosts. The freshly hanged bodies all wore uniforms embellished with the Oakridge Police Department emblem. All seven officers' necks were crushed, bound in thick pumpkin vines. Their eyes bulged from the sockets, mouths pried open and bloody—tongues cut out. Ritchie released a shrill scream when his gaze fell upon the corpse of his father, still swaying in the wind.

"*Fuck*!"

Tears poured down his freckled cheeks as he tightened the grip on his bat. His stomach twisted, churning into heavy knots. And while he gasped for air, blubbering between his horrified sobs, he cursed.

"I'll kill her," he spat. "I'll *fucking* kill that *bitch myself*!"

The friends clasped hands over their mouths at the sight. Ritchie swore again, taking the bat and beating it against the trunk of the tree. He burst into tears as he swung over and over again, splitting the bark in a weak spot. Theo approached him slowly, reaching out and placing a hand upon his shoulder.

"Ritchie..." He tried to calm him. "Hey, man. It's okay."

"*No*! Don't touch me, man!" Ritchie wailed. "It's *not* okay. It's *fucking not okay*!"

He went to swing the bat again, but Theo grabbed his wrist. Taking a deep breath, he wrapped his arms around Ritchie, pulling him in close. Ritchie's shoulders eased at the touch, eyes spilling over as he gnashed his teeth. Lowering the bat, he rested his head against Theo's chest, listening to his breathing. His rapid heartbeat.

"I'll kill that bitch. I'll fucking *kill her*..."

"What do we do now?" Peter asked, voice quivering. "The police are dead. They can't help us. *No one* can help us..."

"We *have* to get out of here," Sam said. "We can't stay any longer."

Once his breaths were steady, Ritchie scrunched his face in anger. Pulling away from Theo, he returned to the base of the tree, staring up at the limp body of his father. Then, an idea struck him.

"His radio," Ritchie said. "If I can get his radio, I can call for help. Get the rest of the unit out here."

"There's no *time*, Ritchie," Sam urged. "We *need* to go."

"Sam's right, man," Theo replied. "Let's just get home and call the station from there. If *this* is what that woman's capable of..."

"I *told* you," Peter said again. "I warned everyone."

250

His friends turned to him. His hand remained pressed against his wounds, eyes falling to the bonfire. The flames reflected in his dark brown eyes as his lips drew into a frown.

"I *said* she was the one killing those missing kids. Turning them into pumpkins in her garden. But no one listened to me. No one believed me." He chuckled, holding back tears. "Not the police...not my dad..."

"*We* believe you, Peter," Sam said. "And we're going to get out of here. She's never going to hurt anyone ever again."

As Peter parted his lips to speak, a low growl emerged from the path behind them. Leaves scuttled, crunching beneath a heavy weight. Peering over their shoulders, the friends were once again met with the Grim. Its body trembled as it tried to stand, bite marks and deep gashes lining its back and head. Peter backed away towards the fire, cursing beneath his breath. The Grim took a shaky step forward, hackles rising.

"*Shit*," Theo cursed. "What do we do?"

"Run." Sam breathed. "It's hurt. If we run, we can—"

"*No*," Ritchie interrupted.

He reached up, taking hold of the legs of his father's swaying corpse. He grimaced at the body's stiffness, fumbling for the holster strapped to his hip. Grunting, he retrieved the loaded Glock. His eyes stung from tears that still clouded them as he turned back to his friends. The Grim stared at them, snarls erupting into vicious roars. Raising the gun, Ritchie violently gestured for the others to move.

"*Get back*!" he hollered.

His friends didn't hesitate. They sprinted to the tree, getting behind him as he aimed the handgun at the hound. The muzzle exploded as he pulled the trigger, firing a bullet towards the Grim. But it harmlessly passed through it. Ritchie's mouth fell open as another snarl rose from the throat of the hound, creeping closer.

"*No*..." He shook his head. "That's impossible..."

Clenching his teeth, he aimed again, firing another shot. Just as before, the bullet whizzed through the body—as if it weren't there at all. Ritchie spat, breaths becoming heavy as he fired again, and again. This time, the bullets strayed. His arms trembled as fear overtook him, watching the Grim shift into shadow—airy like the fog.

"*Fuck*!"

Theo took hold of his arms, lowering them—an attempt to save what bullets were left. The Grim staggered nearer, red eyes burning through the darkness—flickering like the fire before it. It bared its fangs, jaws dripping in

251

hate fueled hunger. But as it approached, it suddenly stopped in its tracks. Its ears raised in alertness, frantically surveying the cemetery. Its tail lowered, tucking between its hind legs as it shied away—whining in fear. The friends watched in confusion as it yelped, taking off up the hill, back towards the chapel.

"What was *that* about?" Theo asked.

"I don't know..." Sam whispered. "Something must have spooked it."

"Yeah," Ritchie sneered. "Probably the *gun*. Hopefully it stays away. Now come on, let's get the fuck out of here."

Theo looked worried. "I don't think it was the gun, Ritchie... Sam, what are Grims afraid of?"

She shook her head and shrugged. "I-I don't know. I didn't think they were afraid of *anything*, based on legend. If they're brave enough to guard the grounds from trespassers and witches and—"

"The Devil," Peter said flatly.

"My, my... You are *such* a clever one..."

The high-pitched, raspy voice met their ears. Peter held his breath, turning towards it. Grýla stood amongst the flickering jack-o'-lanterns, grinning widely. She gripped the pumpkin-shell crown in one hand, a thick rope in the other. Peter glared at her bitterly as she approached the tree, the black cat trailing at her heels.

"It's a wonder you're failing school," she sneered. "If only you applied yourself..."

"Fuck you, *bitch*!" Ritchie shouted through misty eyes, raising the handgun.

Once more, Theo grabbed his arms, forcing him to lower it. "*Stop*, man. Stop."

"*No!*" Ritchie retorted, shrugging him off. "She killed my dad! She killed the *whole fucking unit*!"

Grýla clicked her tongue, sneering. The cat chirped as he leapt atop a nearby headstone, tail beating against it. His yellow eyes gleamed in the firelight, whiskers erect as he stared at the friends—inspecting them.

"So quick to pass blame, aren't you?" Grýla hissed. "*I* wasn't the one to kill them. They happened to wander into their own fate, like pathetic pigs to slaughter."

Ritchie stiffened. "*You're lying.*"

"I wouldn't dream of taking credit for such a thing," she said, gesturing to the jack-o'-lanterns surrounding them. "It was the pumpkins, leaving an offering for their new King. Ensuring the ritual goes on without

252

fail. We couldn't have them squealing and bringing reinforcements, now, could we?"

"You're crazy." Ritchie snarled. "*Pumpkins* can't do *that*!"

"Don't underestimate them," Grýla warned. "They can possess far more than just a candle's light."

Out amongst the graves, leaves began to shift. The light inside the jack-o'-lanterns flickered rapidly. Ritchie swallowed hard, gazing out across the dim grounds. Listening to the creaking and twisting in the soil.

Grýla turned her attention to Peter, who had backed closer to the tree. His breaths were shallow, gaze flitting between the fire, the old woman, and the cat. He tried hard to ignore the bodies hanging above him in the branches —their legs swaying inches from his head. With a smirk, Grýla approached, offering the thick rope.

"Now, now, Peter... It's time," she cooed. "You know how the story goes. There's no sense dragging it on any longer. Dear Jack's been waiting for so long to be free. And the Devil needs his due."

Peter shook his head, tears burning his eyes. "N-no..."

"Come now, Peter," Grýla coaxed again, stepping closer. "Don't you want your wishes to come true? You don't want to be all alone, do you? Unloved? Forgotten?"

A tear rolled down his cheek. His mouth drew into a hard frown as the firelight danced in his dark eyes, glinting bright in their wetness. The old woman pursed her lips with a sneer.

"You know that's what will happen, don't you? After graduation, everyone will go their separate ways. Live their own lives. They'll be too busy to think of *you*, left behind in this small town," Grýla said. "They'll have new jobs, new homes. Live far, far from here. Far from *any* thought of *you*. They'll have new friends. New *loved ones*. You'll barely be a memory, Peter. But you already know that. You already know how unfortunate life is. How *painful*."

"Don't listen to her, Peter," Sam urged, voice trembling.

"You can end that pain right now," Grýla encouraged. "You just have to do what all the others before you did. Go on, now."

She stepped to Peter's side, holding out the rope. His shoulders trembled as his gaze fell to it. The lump in his throat became thicker—tighter.

"Get *away* from him..." Ritchie growled threateningly, taking aim with the gun.

Grýla ignored him, keeping her focus on Peter. With a smirk, she tilted her head, watching another set of tears roll down his cheeks.

"And just think..." Grýla said softly. "You'll be with your dear mother again."

Peter stared into her milky eyes, face contorting in anguish.

"Oh, I struck a nerve, didn't I?" Grýla asked. "But isn't that what you want? Isn't that what would make you happy? Being reunited with her?"

"*Don't listen*, Peter!" Sam cried.

"It'll be quick," Grýla promised. "Just a little *snap* and a twitch. And then it's all over."

She brandished the rope again. He stared at its thickness, how tightly the fibers were coiled. How tense. Grýla pressed it into his hand, closing his fingers around the thick braid with an encouraging smile. His eyes drifted off to the bonfire, watching sparks ascend into the night air. Reaching up, she tangled her calloused hands in his dark hair, patting his cheek gently.

"Go on," she purred. "Be a good boy. Don't keep your mother waiting."

"*Peter*!" Theo shouted.

"Don't do it, Peter!" Sam wept. "*Please* don't do it!"

Peter's fingers tightened around the rope. It was heavy and roughspun—sturdy. He was silent for a moment, lost deep in thought. Replaying Grýla's words, but also Sam's promises. Her pleas for his happiness. His future. Peter swallowed around the lump in his throat. Pressing his lips together, his dark eyes narrowed.

"No..."

"What did you say?" Grýla's grin vanished.

"I said *no*!" Peter shouted.

He threw the rope into the bonfire. It crackled as it ignited, licked by the flames. Grýla's eyes widened in distress. Growling, she turned back to Peter, hatred heavy on her face.

"I won't do it," Peter said. "I *won't*... It wouldn't solve anything. It wouldn't prevent the pain. Wouldn't end it. I *know* what pain is. I live with it every day. In my heart, in my chest. In my head. Life *fucking sucks*. And there are plenty of times I've thought about easing that pain. About lessening the burden on everyone else."

Peter shook his head. He sniffled as he wiped the tears from his eyes. His bottom lip quivered as he took a deep breath, glaring at Grýla.

"I know what it's like being left behind. Feeling like you weren't enough. Like you could have been there. Could have *done something*. Like maybe you could have prevented what happened from happening. I know how much that hurts. And I wouldn't *ever* put that on someone else..." He

glanced at his friends. "I wouldn't ever put that on those I love. Those that *love me*. I made a promise... A promise to my dad that I'd be safe. A promise to my mom that I wouldn't forget. A promise to Sam that I'll stay. And a promise to myself... A promise that I'll get better. That I'll find my happiness. That I'll have a future. I *want* a future. And if that future is to never leave this town...to be stuck here forever and rot...I'll rot while living. Not while left behind in the dirt."

"You really *are* a fool, aren't you, child?" Grýla laughed. "You act as though you have a *choice*. There is no choice, boy. You *made* your choice when you sat on the throne. Now, it's fate. And no matter what you do, the end is always the same."

The sounds of earth moving echoed between the graves nearby. Leaves shifted again, vines snapping. Stone crumbling. Peter tensed, scanning the cemetery. Stabbing a long, crooked finger to his nose, Grýla hissed.

"Either you do it yourself," she said, "or have it done *for you*."

Before Peter could respond, the sounds from the graves grew louder. He was drawn away as he focused on movement in the shadows—the violent flickering of jack-o'-lantern light. In the dim night, he could see vines snaking up from the soil, pumpkins shifting as their carved expressions faced the tree. All were grinning. Staring straight at him. Grýla smirked as she stepped away.

"*That* is the only choice you get to make."

"For fuck's sake..." Ritchie's hands shook, still holding the raised gun. "*Move*, Peter!"

He waited for Peter to be out of the line of fire before taking aim at Grýla. Gnashing his teeth, his arms trembled as he tried to steady himself for a clear shot. His finger teased the trigger. As he was about to squeeze it, however, something sharp drove into his lower leg. Ritchie yelped in pain, glancing down. His eyes widened in horror at the sight of a plump jack-o'-lantern—its carved teeth sunk into his skin.

"*Shit!*"

He pointed the handgun at it, firing. The pressure released from his leg as the pumpkin exploded into a shower of orange flesh. A few strands of stringy guts sloshed from inside—left behind from carving. With a hiss, Ritchie reached down and touched his leg. Fresh blood coated his fingertips, gushing from his punctured and torn jeans. He cursed aloud, turning to the graves behind him.

The faces of the jack-o'-lanterns shifted in their luminous light—grins wider than ever. Tensing, Ritchie aimed the gun towards them. Their vines twisted as they rose from the dirt—thick and billowing. They slithered across

255

the plots, making their way towards the tree. The pumpkins rolled after, tugged by the vines as their mouths snapped open and closed—flashing their sharp cut teeth. The friends' eyes widened in disbelief as the jack-o'-lanterns drew nearer, surrounding them.

"Since you were too much of a coward to fulfill your destiny yourself," Grýla began, backing away into the shadows, "I'll leave you to the mercy of your court."

Peter swallowed hard, staring out across the pumpkin filled landscape. Their hollowed and sinister grins were filled with anticipation. His breathing grew rapid as he frantically looked for an escape. A clear-cut path to break free—head towards the cemetery gates. But with each second, the jack-o'-lanterns inched closer.

"This isn't possible," Theo stammered, scanning the horde around them. "They're *pumpkins*! They can't come to life."

"The veil's thin," Sam said, cautiously taking a step backwards. "Maybe it's the spirits of the dead returned...using their shells as vessels."

Ritchie held his leg with a hiss, shooting her a hard look. "I thought jack-o'-lanterns were supposed to keep spirits *away. Not invite* them in!"

"Seems a lot of legends got things wrong, huh?" Theo breathed.

His gaze fell to Ritchie's bat, discarded beneath the tree. Inhaling deeply, he rushed over to it, grasping it firmly. His eyes narrowed as he glared out across the landscape—the pumpkins practically on top of them now.

"*Why* though?" Peter whimpered. "Why leave things out?"

"It's like a game of telephone," Sam said sadly. "Like that kid said at the party. Things change over time. They get lost, left out. Forgotten."

Ritchie shook his head, clenching his teeth. "Maybe it's not so much that things are forgotten...but left out on *purpose*. So that the legend *wouldn't* be forgotten."

His friends turned to him as he released his leg. He stood up straight, wincing. Passing his gaze to Peter, he frowned.

"A legend can't die if it keeps being fed," he said. "*Of course* the important parts are left out. So fools go looking for them. So the story can go on."

Theo tightened his grip on the bat. "Well, that ends tonight."

He raised it over his head, hammering it down hard onto one of the pumpkins. It split down the center, the light inside extinguishing. Wasting no time, he turned to the next, beating it with the bat. Ritchie stiffened, drawing his mouth into a hard frown as he took aim with the handgun again before firing. The bullet tore through multiple pumpkins—their shells exploding

across the headstones. He fired again, taking out another few as their grins began to fade into sinister anger.

"Come on!" Theo hollered to the others.

Again he swung the bat, splitting another in half. Sam balled her hands into fists, kicking at the ones surrounding her. Their faces caved in from the force of her heavy boots. Peter watched as a plump jack-o'-lantern rolled his way. Gritting his teeth, he took hold of his injured arm, cursing. When it was close enough, staring up at him with fiery eyes, he raised his left foot, stomping it over and over until it was nothing more than a pile of flesh.

The jack-o'-lanterns didn't stop coming. From atop the hill they rolled, closing in around the tree. But with each wave, the friends used what strength they had to smash them. Beat them. Stomp them. Saving what few bullets were left in the gun, Ritchie punted a smaller pumpkin. It flew through the air, landing within the flames of the bonfire. It sizzled as it shriveled from the heat—coiling in on itself.

Theo smirked. "Three points! It's *good*!"

Ritchie flashed him a toothy grin before turning back to the horde, kicking and stomping. As Sam split another down the center, she glanced over to Peter—still near the trunk of the tree. He pounded what he could beneath his feet, juice and guts staining the rubber toes of his Converse in an orange tint.

"How many *are* there?" Peter panted, chest rattling as he kicked another one.

"*Thousands*," Theo said, beating another to bits. "We're never going to get rid of them all."

"Let's hold them off then," Ritchie huffed. "Once we see a break, we run."

A large pumpkin rolled up beside Peter, vines snapping. They slithered across the ground, sneaking up behind him. He spun around to face the blazing jack-o'-lantern as its vines snaked up his legs. It watched him with eager eyes, squeezing tight, causing Peter to flinch. He tried to kick the pumpkin, but its grip was too firm. Peter yelped in pain as the vines crawled up his torso to his arms, crushing his wounds. Fresh, warm blood oozed from the cuts beneath the pressure. Using what strength he had, Peter reached into his pocket. Removing his pocket knife, he snapped it open. Traces of old, dried blood lined the blade, glinting in the light of the bonfire. Gritting his teeth, Peter sawed away at the vines.

The pumpkin hissed as its grip lessened, leaves withering and falling with each cut. Harder and faster Peter hacked, severing them enough to slide his injured arm free. Then, he worked his way down, cutting through the rest and slipping from their grasp. He wheezed a heavy breath as he rammed his foot into the mouth of the pumpkin, stomping its light out. Panting, he glanced over to his friends, watching as the horde began to fall back. Coming in slower than before.

"Alright!" Ritchie hollered. "This is our chance. Let's go!"

He and Theo took off towards the path. Sam hurried to Peter's side, grabbing his wounded arm tenderly as he winced. He still struggled for breath as she leaned against him, whispering softly.

"Come on," she urged. "The exit isn't that far. We can make it... We'll *make* it."

With a weak nod, Peter pushed forward, grasping Sam's hand. He pulled her through the rising wave of jack-o'-lanterns, back to the darkness of the pathways. Their feet thundered against the earth as they trailed behind Ritchie and Theo, towards the flashing lights of the cop cars in the distance. The cemetery gates. The promise of escape.

XVI.

Fog hung heavy near the lower plots as the friends hurried through the dark cemetery. The light of the jack-o'-lanterns faded behind them, leaving only the amber moon to guide them. As they reached the fork in the path, at the center of the cemetery, they stopped to catch their breath. Ritchie winced, pressing his hands to the still bleeding wounds on the back of his leg. They burned beneath the pressure, causing him to hiss in pain. Theo gently placed a hand on his shoulder.

"You okay?"

"It's just a little puncture," Ritchie snorted. "I'll survive."

Theo pursed his lips in disagreement. Before he could say anything further, however, Ritchie waved him off, stepping away from his touch. His blue eyes scanned the shadows, catching the sign ahead: THIS WAY OUT. Glancing over his shoulder, he turned his attention to Peter and Sam—still easing themselves. Peter held his knees as he leaned forward, wheezing rattling breaths. A line of drool dripped from his bottom lip as he fought to steady himself. With a hoarse, phlegmy cough, he straightened. Sam touched his arm as he turned to her, managing a weak smile.

"You know how...Coach Donohue is always...up my ass...and threatening to flunk me?" Peter hacked. "He should...give me a pass for the rest of the semester from...all this cardio."

"The *semester*?" Theo laughed. "He should give an *A* for effort and let you sit out the whole *year*."

"He'd *already* sit out the whole year either way. The only time I've ever seen Peter in the locker room during Phys Ed is when he's hiding in the bathroom stall lighting up." Ritchie smirked, clearing his throat and imitating the coach's dry voice. "*You joining us today, Smokey? Or are you using my class as a crutch for your bad habits again?*"

"Coach Donohue's a *dick*, man." Theo scoffed.

"How's your arm?" Sam asked Peter after a moment, her eyes softening as they remained fixed on the gashes.

Peter shrugged his right shoulder, wincing. "Sore."

"We really need to get out of here," Sam said, voice trembling. "You need a doctor...and Ritchie should see one, too."

"That's the *least* of my concerns right now," Ritchie huffed.

His gaze fell to the flashing lights of the cop cars through the dense fog. The red and blue rays were hazy. Distorted. In the distance, the sound of footsteps through leaves rose up—shifting and crunching. Ritchie scrunched his nose, tightening his grip on the handgun as he motioned the others to follow.

"Come on. We don't have much farther," he said. "Let's go before that bitch shows up again."

He winced as he took a step. Shaking his leg, he exhaled heavily before continuing on at a hastened pace. Theo nodded in agreement, following. As Peter was about to do the same, Sam took his hand—lacing her their fingers. Her gaze fell to the ground, watching the leaves scatter across the pathway. Her mouth drew into a pained frown.

"I'm so sorry, Peter," she whispered.

"What for?" he asked.

"Making you come up here," she said sadly. "I never should have..."

A tear rolled down her cheek. Blinking back the wetness in her eyes, she dabbed her face, trying not to smear her mascara. Peter frowned as she shook her head.

"I'm sorry," she choked.

"Hey..." Peter squeezed her hand. "It's not your fault, Sam. It was supposed to just be for fun. A *story*... You didn't know..."

"I know...but I just..."

Peter gently took her chin, tilting it upward. His brown eyes still carried traces of fear, but he did his best to allow them to soften.

"*None* of us knew," Peter said. "And besides, you didn't *make* us, Sam. We *all wanted* to come up here anyway. Please don't blame yourself."

"They're after you because of *me*," Sam said. "If we hadn't come up here... If I hadn't suggested it..."

"It *wasn't* your fault. If *anyone's* fault, it's *mine*. *I'm* the fool who sat on the throne, Sam..."

Sam reached up and touched his cheek. "You're *not* a fool, Peter..."

He nuzzled against her palm. They stood there, silent, until Peter finally pulled away. The night air was growing colder—frosting his throat with each breath.

"Let's get out of here." A cloud of condensation billowed from his lips. "I'm *exhausted*. If...the offer still stands, I'll definitely take you up on staying on the couch."

Sam smiled softly. Her gaze fell to his pocket and the outline of his phone pressed against his hip. Noticing, Peter chewed his lip, retrieving it. The screen flashed on, warning that the signal was poor. His heart panged when he read the notification behind the alert.

Dad

3 Missed Calls

Peter tensed, swallowing around the lump in his throat. Locking his phone, he lowered it to his side. He exhaled deeply, returning his gaze to Sam.

"I'll text my dad when we get out of here..."

He pushed his hands into his pockets, shoulders slumping before continuing on the path. Sam remained still for a moment, eyes fixed on the iron gate in the distance—hidden in the shadows and mist. Exhaling a heavy breath, she began behind him, listening to the sounds of the night echoing from atop the hill.

The closer the friends drew to the gate, the thicker the fog became. It coated the headstones and lawn, making it impossible to see anything beyond the pathway. They remained silent, wary of their steps—taking in the sounds around them. The wind rattled the bare branches of the trees, scattering leaves across the earth. Crickets chirped at the far end of the cemetery, rejoicing in night song. Above, feathers rustled, accompanied by avian hisses. The vultures were returning.

Peter's heart raced as he became aware of them. His shaky breath released in a burst of condensation, eyes scanning the fog. Faintly, he could make out flickers of light low to the ground—more jack-o'-lanterns. Clenching his jaw, he carried onward, whispers from the trees searing through him.

Peter, Peter pumpkin-eater...

There was mockery behind the words now. The branches above creaked as the bodies shifted, wings stretching open. From the corners of his eyes, through the darkness and mist, he could see them swaying. Taunting him with their haunting dance.

Bound in vines, he was a bleeder...

His friends didn't react. While he tried to push the fear rising in his throat back down, he kept quiet, not wanting to draw attention to the watchful eyes. Not wanting to delay any longer. A withered leaf crunched beneath his shoe as he pressed on, the chill of the night biting through him.

They spoke the words and read the spell...

Something shifted amongst the graves. Peter inhaled sharply, puffing a cloud of condensation with each shallow breath. In the faint light of the autumn moon, he could see it. A tall, dark figure looming in the shifting white. It was cloaked in black, features indistinguishable in the darkness. But there were flickers. Distant glints of light. One was held in the figure's grasp —dancing like the flame of a candle. The other two were positioned just

under the hood of the cloak—a deep amber. Bright, hollow eyes watching him. Searching his soul.

And crowned the Fool to rule in Hell...

The vultures took off from the treetops. The heavy sound of their wings beating the night air echoed off of headstones as they returned up the hill. Peter released a quivering breath, stopping in his tracks. The figure was gone now—as if it had evaporated into the fog. But still, he felt the eyes watching. From the trees, from the graves, and from the mist. He closed his eyes, focusing on his breathing. He imagined candles before him, slowly blowing each one out—drowning his growing anxiety. Ritchie's voice pulled him back, however. Peter's eyes snapped open, the panic-filled words of his friend becoming clear. His mouth drew into a trembling frown as he stepped through the fog, the silhouettes around him taking form.

The gate of the cemetery was blocked. The large, black Grim stood shakily before it, eyes blazing through the shadows. Hot drool dripped from its jaws, coated in blood. Its hackles were raised, tail low as it stared at the friends. They stepped back slowly, not removing their gaze from the burning red eyes before them. A low growl rumbled in the Grim's throat.

"*Shit*," Ritchie cursed.

He raised the handgun, hands trembling. But before he could fire a shot, Theo called out to him.

"Don't waste it!" he hollered. "It won't work, remember?"

Spitting, Ritchie lowered the gun. The Grim stared at him, baring its fangs and snarling. Taking another step back, Ritchie cursed again beneath his breath. He stumbled, leg throbbing as he hissed. Theo reached out, grasping his shoulder for support.

"What do we do?" Sam whispered.

"*That's* the only way out," Ritchie said. "We're going to have to try and get through. That's all we *can* do."

"You're *sure* there's not another exit?" Theo asked.

"I mean, *maybe* back up the hill..." Ritchie winced. "Through the tree line up there beyond the chapel. I don't think it's fenced in. But..."

He shook his head. The growls from the Grim grew louder as it inched forward, the fog churning around it. Ritchie swallowed hard.

"We'll never make it."

"And what makes you think we will if we try through *here*?" Theo asked sternly, panic beginning to tinge his voice.

"There's four of us," Ritchie said, "there's only one of it. It can't take us all at once."

263

"So, we split up?" Theo raised an eyebrow.

"That's literally the *stupidest* thing we could do," Sam said angrily.

"*No*," Ritchie snapped. "It's like when Coach Harrison has us do a split back. It confuses the other team, right?"

"You're talking *football*." Sam sneered. "We're not passing *pigskin* off to one another here. And *besides*, you and Peter are *hurt*. Do you really think you can outrun that thing long enough?"

Ritchie pursed his lips. The Grim continued closer, claws scraping the dirt. As it snarled again, his eyes lit up in thought.

"We just need one person," he said. "Someone to be bait. Get it to chase them. Then the rest of us make a run for it."

"Oh, *great*." Sam threw her arms up. "So just *leave* one of us behind to be its *chew toy*?"

"Look. The cars' lights are still on out there. They've *got* to have the keys in the ignition," Ritchie said. "We get out, get in a *fucking car*, grab whoever's bait, and *bam*! Hit the gas and *go*."

"It won't work, Ritchie," Sam said, shaking her head. "Those cars have been running *all night*. Do you really think they're going to last? The batteries are probably *near dead* and tanks out of gas. It *won't work*..."

"I've helped my dad jump a car before. If we need to—"

"We don't have *time*."

"Well, we have to try *something*."

"Ritchie's plan *could* work," Theo said after a moment, turning to Sam. "The Grim is bound to the cemetery grounds, right?"

"According to legend, yes," she replied.

"So, then all we need to do is get through the gates," Theo replied confidently. "Once we set foot outside of them, it can't follow us. We just have to be quick."

"We can make it," Ritchie agreed.

Sam glanced at Peter. His gaze remained fixed on the shadowy figure of the Grim, fingers tugging against the soft flannel sleeves of his shirt. Sam's eyes fell on the blood-soaked fabric of his right arm. She watched his chest rise and fall in anxious breaths, still rattling from overexertion.

"*I* can be the bait," Ritchie said, garnering his friends' attention. "You guys run to the car. Once you're through the gates, I'll be right behind you."

"Absolutely not. You're *hurt*. There's *no* way you'll outrun it," Sam said.

"I've played football on a busted ankle before. When adrenaline kicks in, I'm—"

"*No*, Ritchie," Sam pressed sternly.

"I'm with Sam on this... Besides, man," Theo added, "*you're* the only one who can *drive*. *You* need to get to the cars."

"*Fine*. Then which one of you is volunteering?" Ritchie snorted.

The Grim took another step forward, eyes gleaming through the fog. Peter bristled, parting his lips. Before he could speak, however, Sam shook her head.

"*Not Peter*," she urged. "He's hurt, too."

"Then *I'll* do it," Theo said.

"*Theo*," Sam pleaded.

"Look, next to Ritchie, I'm the fastest one here. And I'm *not* hurt," he said. "I can lure that thing away from the gates to give you guys enough time to get out. As soon as you cross over the cemetery grounds, I'll follow you."

"We can *do* this," Ritchie repeated. "We'll make it."

The Grim growled, eying the group. Its hair rose higher on the back of its neck as it bared its fangs, lowering its head. Peter gripped his right arm, inhaling sharply.

"Let's go!"

Theo broke away from his friends, sprinting up the pathway they had just come from. The Grim charged, claws scraping the dirt beneath them, tearing after him. It barked its high-pitched, chilling cry, echoing across the fog-cloaked stones.

"*Now!*" Ritchie hollered.

Sam bolted to the left, Ritchie following as fast as he could without staggering. Peter rushed the opposite way, lungs giving out. He gasped for air, sharp pains of overexertion stabbing into his ribs. Sam and Ritchie drew further ahead toward the gates as exhaustion began to take hold of him. The Grim ascended the hill after Theo, drawing to a halt as it caught sight of Peter struggling. Without hesitation it turned, bolting back across the lawn. Realizing it had diverted its path, Theo skidded to a stop, eyes wide.

"*Peter!*" he shouted.

Peter glanced over his shoulder, seeing the black hound closing in. He gasped in panic, sprinting with what little energy he had left. His shoes clapped against the pavement leading to the gates—feet sliding on the gravel. He cursed beneath his labored breath, the Grim at his heels. From the pathway, Theo thumped the baseball bat hard against the ground, hollering to get the dog's attention. But it no longer had interest in him. Its focus was solely on Peter.

It smelled the blood beneath Peter's shirt. Smelled the fear that poured out. And smelled the long, lingering scent of something dark. Something it was drawn to. Something it swore to keep out.

It was mere inches from him as the gates drew nearer. Peter panted shallowly as he reached the threshold—the familiar iron CHAPEL HILL CEMETERY overhead. As Peter stumbled beneath them, the Grim's jaws snapped at his ankles—barely missing. The dog snarled as Peter collapsed onto the pavement, wheezing and hacking on phlegm coating his throat. His arms trembled as he slowly raised himself, glancing over his shoulder into the shadow and fog of the cemetery. The Grim's eyes gleamed from within, backing away in defeat as it snorted.

Peter released a whimpering chuckle, tears pricking his eyes. He was free. *Safe.* His legs trembled violently as he got to his feet, knees scuffed beneath the tears in his jeans. He waited until the Grim disappeared into the darkness before turning to the cop car parked beside the gate. Sam waved him over to it, holding onto the opened passenger side door. He hobbled to the vehicle, climbing into the back seat.

Ritchie cursed as he turned the key in the ignition, engine sputtering. The dashboard lights illuminated, check engine and low fuel signals burning boldly. He scrunched his nose, pumping the gas pedal as he tried to start the car again. Once more, the engine fought to turn over before failing.

"*Shit.*" Ritchie slumped back in his seat.

"I *told* you," Sam hissed, pulling her witch hat from her head.

Ritchie waved her off. Sitting up, he tried once more, leaning over the steering wheel as the engine jittered. Peter slouched against the door, watching from the back seat in silence. The inside of the car carried a trace of warmth, breaking the chill of the night. He held his injured arm, the gashes stinging from his cold sweat. Closing his eyes, he leaned his head against the window, exhaustion taking over.

Again, Ritchie turned the key. The engine jolted, rattling as it had before, but then it started up. His eyes widened in relief as he hooted, bouncing in the driver's seat. Sam glanced at the dashboard. The warning lights were still bright.

"We're not going to get very far," she pointed out.

"We'll get far *enough*," Ritchie sneered, staring towards the cemetery gates. "Where the hell is Theo?"

Peter opened one eye, sitting up. The car was silent as the three friends gazed through the rolling fog. But aside from the shifting shadows and white, there was nothing but stillness. No sign of Theo. No sign of the Grim. Ritchie huffed, frowning as he shifted the car into drive.

"What are you *doing*?" Sam asked.

"Something's wrong," Ritchie said lowly. "Theo should have been out by now. He should have been *right* behind us."

Peter and Sam remained silent. Worry lined their faces as they continued staring through the windshield. Waiting. But still, their friend never came. After another moment, Ritchie shook his head.

"We have to go get him."

"We're going *back in*?" Peter breathed, gripping the headrest of the passenger's seat.

"We *have* to," Ritchie stated flatly. "I'm *not* leaving Theo behind."

Sam turned in her seat, touching Peter's hand gently. "It'll be quick..."

Peter flopped against the back seat, shrinking down. He swallowed the returning anxiety rising in his throat, wringing his hands in his lap. Ritchie gently pressed his foot to the gas pedal, the car rolling steadily towards the iron gates. Gravel crunched beneath the tires as it pulled through the entrance of Chapel Hill, headlights reflecting nothing but a bright glare of white. It blinded them as they searched for any sign of Theo. The blue and red lights atop the car swirled, adding splashes of color to the dense fog.

"I can't see shit," Ritchie grumbled.

The car maneuvered farther into the cemetery, beginning up the dirt path. The engine rattled shakily, causing Peter to sit up. He glanced at the dashboard lights—the multiple failure warnings still lit up. Taking a nervous breath, he leaned forward again, peering out into the white. Only when the car jolted, trembling with a loud *bang* did he fall back.

"What the *fuck*, Ritchie?" Sam shouted, jostled in her seat.

Through the fog, she could see a headstone shoved against the front passenger side. Ritchie slammed his foot against the brakes, gripping the steering wheel tight as he gritted his teeth. He threw the car into reverse,

267

slowly backing away as the stone grazed the exterior of the car once again. Peter winced, pressing himself further into the back seat.

"I *told you* I can't see *shit*," Ritchie repeated.

He put the car in park, exhaling heavily and watching the white swirl around him—tinted in the flashing lights. *Red. Blue. Red. Blue. White. Red. Blue.*

BAM!

The friends jumped as Theo appeared through the mist, falling hard against the hood of the car. His breathing was labored as he pushed himself up, hobbling to the back seat as quickly as he could. Peter scooted over as Theo yanked the door open, collapsing into the car. He winced as he slammed it behind him, sweat pouring down his face.

"What took you so long, man?" Ritchie demanded, whirling in his seat.

Theo hissed in pain, gripping his thigh. Fresh blood coated his hands, jeans torn and stained deep red. Applying pressure to the jagged wounds, he cried out—pain searing through him.

"Holy *shit*," Ritchie breathed, eyes widening. "What *happened*?"

"That thing *bit* me." Theo grimaced.

"*What*?" Sam gasped.

"I managed to beat it away with the bat," Theo said. "But I don't understand how. The bullets went right through it…"

"Maybe it's getting tired," Sam suggested. "It's spectral, but also physical. Right? Maybe it takes too much energy to shift between the two."

"I don't know, man." Theo closed his eyes, gnashing his teeth. "After half the shit we've seen tonight, I'm not even going to question it anymore."

"Are you okay?" Peter quivered.

"I'm alive." Theo gave a pained chuckle. "I don't think it's *too* bad… just hurts like hell."

"*Don't think it's too bad*?" Ritchie pitched. "*Theo*! You're *bleeding*."

"It's just a little puncture. I'll survive."

He flashed Ritchie a weak smile. But Ritchie didn't return the gesture. His worried gaze remained fixed on the gashes in Theo's leg, blood soaking through the denim. Turning away, he shifted the car into drive.

"We're going to the hospital," he said sternly.

"About *time*," Sam replied.

Ritchie stepped on the gas, the engine revving angrily. But the car didn't move. Frowning, he tried again, pushing the pedal to the floor. Ominous clicking echoed throughout the car as it attempted to turn itself

over. It sputtered once or twice more as Ritchie pumped his foot, and then, all went silent.

"*Fuck!*" Ritchie hollered, slamming his fist against the steering wheel.

The red and blue lights atop the car continued to twirl, headlights still bright in the fog. Pursing her lips, Sam glanced at the dashboard warnings and then to Ritchie.

"I bet the battery's near dead," she said. "It's got enough juice to keep us lit up, but not enough to move."

"How *convenient*," Ritchie quipped, turning to the back seats. "How far do you think you can make it, Theo?"

Theo winced, gingerly gripping his thigh again. "If we go slowly, I can at least make it to the gates."

Ritchie nodded. "There's another car there. It's probably just as low on power, but if we can get to it, we'll take it as far as it'll go. Then we can get help. You okay with that?"

Theo didn't answer. He and Peter stared ahead, eyes wide and mouths falling open. The color drained from Peter's face. Ritchie raised an eyebrow, about to question them, until he felt Sam's fingers dig into his arm. He turned to her.

"*What?*"

That's when he saw it. The black body of the Grim stood stark against the fog, illuminated in the headlights. Its fur was coated in blood, staining its chest and snout. It snarled, ears drawing back and hackles raising. Ritchie's throat swelled with panic as it bared its fangs, jowls turning up and into a crescent moon grin. He reached for the door, hitting the locks before pressing himself back against his seat.

"What do we do?" Sam whispered, keeping her gaze locked on the Grim.

"We're *trapped*." Peter whimpered.

"It's *fine*," Ritchie forced himself to exhale. "We're in the car. It can't get us."

"But what if it doesn't leave?" Peter asked, lips coiling into a hard frown. "What if we're *stuck* here?"

No one dared to speak or move. The police lights flashed across the Grim, glinting in the wet blood matting its thick fur. Its red eyes gleamed as it lowered its head, roaring in anger. With a vicious bark, it sprang forward.

Its heavy body landed on the hood, denting the steel. It began to slam its head into the windshield, fangs scraping and snapping against the glass, smearing blood in dirty red streaks across its expanse.

Peter sagged in the back seat, panicked breaths heavy. Tears poured from his wide eyes as the entire car rocked beneath the Grim's force. His gasps became audible, drool seeping from his lips as he sobbed. Sam reached her hand into the back seat—feeling for Peter. Her fingertips brushed against his torn jeans, touching his exposed knee. His shallow breaths grew wheezy as the snarling grew louder. More violent.

"*Shit*, man," Theo cursed.

The Grim pounded the windshield with its paws, claws leaving deep scrapes in the glass. Tiny cracks began forming, spider webbing beneath each ferocious strike. Swallowing hard, Ritchie sat up, pounding both his fists against the horn. A high-pitched, elongated *beep* drifted through the fog— echoing off the headstones surrounding them. The Grim's ears flattened against its head. With a snort, it leapt from the hood, vanishing into the white fog. Even after it had disappeared, Ritchie laid on the horn, letting the noise reverberate before releasing it.

All fell silent once more.

Ritchie fought to catch his breath as he glared through the cracked and bloodstained windshield. His mouth pressed into a hardened frown as he slouched in his seat. Sam sighed shakily, patting Peter's knee. He still gasped for air—whimpers breaking through the silence.

"Candles," Sam said softly. "Remember the candles, Peter."

His breathing remained shallow and panting. Sam gave his knee a squeeze as she closed her eyes. In the stillness, the group rested. Peter flopped his head against the window, letting his gaze linger on the fog. The rolling white peppered with flashing reds and blues was somehow soothing. *Red. Blue. Red. Blue. White. Red. Blue. Red. Blue. White.* He steadied his breath with each flicker, watching the colors twirl. *Red. Blue. Red. Blue. White. Red. Red. Red.*

Peter lifted his head. The bright crimson glow bled through the glass, no longer flashing. His lip quivered as he scooted towards Theo, an unearthly snarl tearing through the silence. The eyes of Grim stared through the glass— fixated on Peter. The car jolted as its body rammed into the passenger side, rocking the friends within.

Theo cursed as he held onto the seat in front of him. Ritchie grasped the steering wheel, Sam buckling herself in with a shriek. Peter sobbed as the Grim pummeled the car again, knocking him against Theo. The hound howled, clawing the back door and window as it continued to bash against it —stronger each time.

"*Make it stop!*" Peter wailed.

Harder and harder it hit, the car rising up and tilting towards the driver's side. Ritchie tightened his grip on the wheel as he cursed, pounding the horn again. But this time, the Grim ignored it. It barreled against the door, denting it in as Peter fell into Theo's lap, screaming.

"We gotta do something, man!" Theo shouted.

Ritchie scanned the dashboard and glove compartment, looking for anything to use as a distraction. Anything to deter the Grim long enough for them to break away. But there was nothing. He punched the wheel in frustration, glaring out at the fog in defeat. *Red. Blue. Red. Blue. White.*

The car lurched under the force once again. Sam winced, gripping the seat belt strapped across her torso. Another shrill cry broke from Peter's throat as the car tipped—this time, almost completely rolling over. As the Grim pulled back to lunge again, Ritchie turned the black knob beneath the stereo, gnashing his teeth. An earsplitting siren blared through the night, stopping the hound in its tracks.

Peter covered his ears, lowering his head between his knees as he bawled. The wailing sirens grew deafening as Ritchie toggled between them. The Grim's ears flattened as its tail lowered. It backed away from the screeching alarms, whining. Then, it took off into the fog. Ritchie unlocked the car, popping the door open as he grabbed the handgun. He aimed it in the direction the dog had run off, firing a single shot. A final threat to keep it away. Slumping back into the seat, he waited a moment before silencing the sirens.

Ritchie heaved a sigh of relief. As he turned to the others, Sam quickly unbuckled herself, shoving her door open. She shakily stepped out into the night, the cold air nipping through her velvet witch dress. Her boots crunched through the gravel as she grabbed the damaged handle of the back passenger door. Most of it had been caved in, severely dented and scratched— smeared with blood. Inhaling sharply, she tugged the door open, watching as Peter scooted closer to Theo.

"It's okay," Sam whispered, holding her hand out. "It's just me."

Tears rolled down Peter's cheek as he fought for breath. He reached out a trembling hand, taking hold of hers. She carefully pulled him across the seat, helping him out of the car. His knees buckled as he struggled to stand.

"It's okay," Sam repeated. "You're okay."

"What are you doing?" Ritchie asked, stepping out of the car again.

Sam made her way to the back driver's side door, pulling it open. "Getting the *hell* out of here before that thing decides to come back. Now come on, give me a hand with Theo."

271

Ritchie tensed as he headed to her side, reaching in and taking hold of Theo's arms. Sam assisted him, guiding their friend up from his seat, careful of his leg. Theo hissed in pain, falling against the car as he emerged. His leg still oozed blood. He attempted to put weight on it, crying out at the slightest bit of pressure.

"Shit's busted, man." He winced.

"You can't put *any* weight on it?" Ritchie asked.

Theo shook his head. "I think the ligaments are torn. *Fuck.*"

Sam wrapped one of his arms around her shoulders for support. Nodding to Ritchie, she instructed him to do the same. Once they had him situated, held upright with his leg dangling, they tried to walk forward.

"You got this?" Sam asked softly as Theo hopped along between them.

"Yeah," he stammered through gritted teeth. "It hurts, but it's better than the alternative."

Ritchie smirked. "Guess your football season's over, huh?"

"I could say the same for you." Theo chuckled weakly.

Ritchie managed a snort. He took a shaky step forward, his own leg trembling from the added weight of Theo. Sam worked to steady them both, barely taking a step. Even with help, Theo could barely stand. It would take far longer to make it back to the cemetery gates than before.

While his friends continued to assist Theo, Peter leaned against the passenger side of the police car. His shoulders trembled as he quelled his panicked breaths, watching condensation billow from his lips. The tears had dried on his cheeks, cold in the night air. He kept his gaze on the fog. While all had fallen silent, he swore he heard something rise up from atop the hill. Out there in the white mist.

Peter...

Drawing a quick breath, he pressed himself against the car. The stillness surrounded him, swirling in the chilled haze. He paused, listening, until he heard it again.

Peter...

It was a voice he knew. One he had heard many times before. One, however, he couldn't quite pinpoint. It wasn't raspy like the vultures. Nor breathy like the cats. It didn't chatter like the ants. And it wasn't scratchy like the old woman's. It was soft. Feminine. Sweet. His shoulders eased as it carried down from the hill again—fluttering in a sing-song tone.

Petey...

Peter's eyes softened. The familiar voice brushed his ears in the gentle breeze. His chest tightened as he parted his lips, exhaling a shaky breath.

272

Through the white of the mist, he could see a shape taking form. The silhouette of a woman, wearing a flowing gown. Peter stepped away from the car as his name was called again. Honeyed. Light.

Petey...

"M-Mom?"

His voice trembled as it answered back. His mind grew fuzzy, replaying the words of the old woman—the words of Sam. *The veil is thin.* He took another step forward, entranced by the flowing shape in the night. The loving voice he had longed to hear again. His eyes fell vacant as he took another step. And then another. Steadily making his way back up the hill.

Petey...

"Peter?"

Sam noticed him ascending the pathway to the upper cemetery. When he didn't acknowledge her, she called out again, louder this time. But her voice fell on deaf ears. He paid her no mind—oblivious to all around him. Sam stepped forward, pulling Theo with her. He grunted, trying to steady himself.

"Peter!" Sam cried out again. "Peter, stop! *Wait!*"

He disappeared through the dense fog. Her chest rose and fell in frantic breaths as she moved forward again, trying to stay mindful of the pace Theo was able to walk at. He slid his arm from her shoulders, adjusting himself against Ritchie and gesturing up the hill.

"Go on," he said. "We'll catch up."

Sam nodded, taking off up the dirt path before her. The mist swirled in endless white the farther she ascended—swallowing her whole. Bracing together for support, Ritchie and Theo slowly followed behind, one step at a time.

The upper cemetery was dark as Peter passed through the fog. The light of the moon no longer reached the grounds—obscured behind billowing

273

clouds. The chill of the night bit hard, temperatures steeply dropping the closer dawn approached. Around him, he heard the shifting of feathered bodies in the trees, their eyes watching. He heard the scampering of tiny padded paws, chirps rising with them. And he heard his name being called, still so sweet.

Petey…

Peter removed the lighter from his pocket. Giving it a flick, the feeble flame ignited—dancing through the darkness. It wasn't much, but it allowed him to see close by, giving him a sense of security. His gaze strayed to the crumbling headstones, silhouettes of vultures perched upon some of them. They hissed raspy taunts at him, but he ignored them. His focus was solely on the figure he had seen in the mist. The voice calling for him.

Petey…

"Mom?"

The fog stirred. From the corner of his eye, he could see the shape forming again. Standing amongst the graves. Light. Airy. Its gown fluttered in the breeze, leaves scattering at the hem. Peter turned towards the silhouette, holding his lighter out. Again, the voice called—closer this time. Peter veered from the path, feet sinking softly in the wet grass around the ancient plots. Fragments of leaves and mud speckled the once white toes of his shoes as he ventured further into the mist. Approaching the figure. His lighter sputtered as he drew near, chest panging with longing.

"M-Mom?"

When the flickering flame illuminated the figure's features, however, Peter was taken aback. The gown was tattered and torn—worn with time. It was smattered in dirt, gnawed away by maggots. They writhed beneath gray flesh pulled tight to the bone, wriggling through empty eye sockets. Ants erupted from rotten and cracked lips, pouring between the teeth. Flies swarmed its head, clinging to the thick, dark curls that fell against its shoulders. Peter's eyes widened in terror as he backed away, a hollow cry escaping from his throat. The figure stepped towards him, jaw cracking as it dislodged—swaying loosely. More insects dropped from the gaping hole: centipedes, earthworms, roaches. The sounds of their bodies writhing and hissing brought fearful tears to his eyes. Peter staggered backwards, feet sliding on the muddy ground. A voice slithered from the figure's mouth again, this time bitter. Raspy. Deep.

Peter, Peter…

Within the cavernous eye sockets, a spark of amber light flared, mirroring the feeble flame dancing on Peter's lighter. Sunken eyes, full of

274

hate. Peter hastened his steps as he turned back towards the path, the figure at his heels. As he reached the edge of the grass, it sneered, rotten flesh convulsing. The maggots and flies beneath churned, piercing through the skin. Black fluid wept from the opened pores, spilling into a heap of ants. And then the body burst, dispersing into a swarm of buzzing flies, circling Peter. He released a pitiful whimper, stumbling onto the path. Without hesitation, he took off, running through the fog. Away from the horde of insects. The haunting image of his mother—eaten away by time. By pests.

As he hurried through the grass, he stumbled, foot catching in the crack of an old, low headstone. Peter hit the ground hard, elbow first. Searing pain tore through his leg as his snagged ankle twisted with a *snap*. He cried out in pain as he rolled onto his side, grasping his already wounded arm, elbow now aching. Pulling his foot free with another yelp, he attempted to sit up. His ankle burned as he squeezed it, feeling his pulse throb through the swelling. Peter hissed as he grabbed hold of a headstone, pulling himself back to his feet. He gingerly put weight on his damaged ankle, wincing at the sharp pain shooting through his foot. But he was able to take a hobbling step. Then another. He let go of the headstone, limping forward as he heard his name again. This time, however, it was from a voice he was *certain* he knew. One he couldn't mistake.

Sam hurried up the hill, searching through the fog. When her silhouette became visible, Peter called out to her, flicking his lighter on again. He waved the flame back and forth, high above his head. Once she spotted it, she sprinted across the lawn towards him.

"Be careful!" Peter warned. "There's low stones here."

Sam safely made it to his side, looking him over in worry when she saw his trembling knees. His awkward stance—favoring his left ankle.

"Peter..." She breathed. "What *happened*?"

"I twisted my ankle," he admitted. "But I'm okay. Really."

"Why did you come up here?"

Peter averted his gaze. "I...thought I saw something."

"*Saw* something? What was it, Peter?"

He shook his head. "Nothing. I just... I just want to get out of here. *Please*. I want to go home..."

"We will." Sam nodded. "Come on."

She took his arm, wrapping it around her shoulder for support. Peter hopped forward, removing the weight from his pained foot. He hobbled ahead, Sam keeping up with each of his labored steps.

"That's it," she said. "Easy..."

As he took another step, he heard the shifting of feathered bodies again. The scurrying of paws. Peter froze in place, feeling eyes fix heavily upon him. The clouds above lifted, revealing the bright light of the moon. It bathed the cemetery grounds once more, casting amber light across the headstones and up the twisted trunk of the old, decaying tree. Peter's breath caught in his throat when he saw its branches—the limp corpses of the Oakridge Police Department still swaying from them.

"No..." He shook his head. "No, we *can't* be back up here...We didn't come this way..."

From behind the tree, a raspy cackle echoed. Peter shifted onto his good leg, turning towards it. Grýla stepped out of the fog, a clowder of cats at her feet. They chirped and mewled as they surrounded the trunk, yellow and green eyes glinting. The old woman wagged a crooked finger at him as she approached, clicking her tongue.

"When will you fools learn you can't outrun fate?"

Peter tensed, feeling Sam's grip tighten. Grýla smirked as she looked him over, her attention drawn to the ankle he was favoring. One of the cats at her feet mewled, tail thumping the ground impatiently.

"The Devil doesn't take kindly to cheats, you know," Grýla hissed. "No matter where you run, no matter where you hide, he'll find you. He *always* finds you."

Peter's lips pressed into a hard frown as the old woman stepped closer. Her yellowed teeth were exposed in a drawn up grin, crooked and rotten.

"The Devil's always watching," she said. "He knows everything we do. Everything we desire. He takes the shape of the things you love. The things you fear. You cannot escape him. *No one* can."

She gestured across the cemetery—to her cats and the vultures perched in the treetops. Upon the headstones. The breeze rattled through the branches again, scuttling leaves across the pathways.

"Insects. Shadows. Vultures. *Cats*..."

A chill fingered Peter's spine, the feeling of watchful eyes returning. But not just from beyond the graves and in the trees. They were the eyes between the cedar and hemlock on the mountain. Eyes outside his bedroom window. The dark corner of the street. The shadows of the boxcar. Eyes both seen and unseen. The black cat. The ants. The darkness. The fog. A passerby —one whose glance lingered on him longer than usual. His stomach churned into knots as Grýla jeered.

"He's there. He's *always* been there... He's the fly on your wall. Miniscule, but observant. Easily overlooked. Watching every step you take.

Every page you turn. Infesting your mind. Infesting your dreams. Infesting your *body*. Feeding off your misfortune. Your woe. Waiting for you to break. To be foolish enough to make a deal. Desperate enough to demand your desires. To *beg*."

She took another step forward, brandishing a thick rope weaved from fresh pumpkin vines. Peter's eyes fell to it, a heavy lump forming in his throat.

"But he's grown tired of watching. Tired of *waiting*. It's time to pay up," Grýla sneered. "Either do it yourself, right *now*, or let it be done to you. It's inevitable either way. It'd be easier on *all* of us if you just stopped being a *coward*."

"Peter's *not a coward*!" Sam shouted angrily.

Her hazel eyes were wet with tears. The old woman turned to her, grin quickly fading. Sam shook her head, her grip on Peter tightening.

"He's *not* a coward..."

The vultures surrounding them hissed in mockery. Grýla's lips curled back up into a sneer. She extended the vine rope once more.

"Then let him *prove it*."

Peter's arm slid limply from Sam's shoulders. She turned to him, eyes widening. He shifted on his feet, grimacing as he put weight on his injured ankle. But still, he stood, straight and firm, chest rising and falling heavily. Grýla tilted her head, looking him up and down.

"Come now, Peter," she cooed. "It's only a brief moment of pain. And then, sweet release. All the worries of the world will be gone. All burdens lifted from your shoulders. All hurt drained from your heart. All the others did it. All of them were given what they wanted. All of them are *free*."

"Don't listen, Peter..." Sam wept. "Please don't let her do this..."

"You'll never have to stress about a failed test again. Never have to worry about graduation. About your so-called friends moving on. Forgetting you. *Abandoning* you."

"*Don't listen to her*!"

"You'll never have to suffer another restless night. Never have to cry yourself to sleep, alone in your room." Grýla drew nearer. "You'll never have to see those prescriptions again. Never have to spend your mornings popping pills. You *know* they don't work. They just make you feel worse, don't they? *Sick*."

Tears burned Peter's eyes as each of Grýla's words pounded down on him. His knees trembled harder, heart aching. He desperately tried to convince himself she was wrong. But the truth stung like the lump in his throat.

277

"You'll never have to sit in a cold office, pressured to speak your sorrows. Confessing to so-called *doctors* who are only there for the money. They don't really care about you. They don't really listen. But then again...no one does, do they?"

Grýla cupped Peter's left cheek, caressing it with her thumb. Her milky eyes stared into his, which had grown lost and vacant. Welling with tears on the verge of spilling over.

"It hurts, doesn't it?" she cooed. "The redness may be gone, but I know you still feel the sting. How devastating it must be, knowing not even your own *father* wants to listen to you."

Grýla took Peter's chin, forcing him to look upon her. His lips parted as he released a shaky breath, tears rolling down his face.

"But the *Devil* listens," Grýla purred. "He hears your pleas. Your hurt. *He* cares. *He* offers comfort. *Relief*."

In the dark around him, the flickers of light began to shift. Flecks of amber within the fog. A bonfire flared to life beneath the tree, crackling violently. In its glow, the shadows of the police officers swayed against the bark, twisting Peter's gut.

"Give yourself to him," Grýla whispered. "Keep your end of the bargain. *End your suffering*."

She pressed the thick vine to his chest. It twitched beneath her fingers as she grinned, watching the firelight dance in his dark eyes.

"Why be a Fool when you can be a *King*?"

The sound of heavy feet scuffing through the dirt rose up behind them. Ritchie and Theo appeared from the fog, staggering over to Sam. As Ritchie's gaze fell upon the old woman, his eyes narrowed, face contorting in hate. His expression grew worried, however, as the shadows began to shift. The distant pinpricks of light became brighter as the horde of jack-o'-lanterns rolled from out of the fog—surrounding the tree. Their carved grins grew wider as they stared up at Peter, vines thumping the earth in anticipation.

Peter shook his head. His tears fell heavy as he whimpered, attempting to back away. Hot pain rushed through his ankle, but he bit it back. One hobbling step at a time.

"I-I can't," Peter uttered. "Please..."

"*Leave him alone!*" Sam screamed.

"Last chance," Grýla growled bitterly, eyes narrowing.

Another tear rolled down Peter's cheek. "*N-no...*"

"So be it."

The thick vine snapped to life, snaking its way up Peter's torso. It wound itself around his neck as he cried out, grabbing at the leaves. The vine squeezed tight—crushing his throat. Peter gasped for air, digging his nails into the plant's flesh.

"*Let him go!*" Theo shouted.

Before the friends could move, the jack-o'-lanterns swarmed them, forging a wall of blazing light. Blocking them off from Peter. They watched helplessly as he ripped the leaves free from the pulsating vine, saliva sputtering between his bluing lips.

"*Why are you doing this?*" Sam sobbed.

Grýla turned to her, lips curling. "Don't play dumb, my dear. You *know* the legend. You told it to your friends. *You* brought them up here."

"*You* told me to bring them up here!"

Ritchie and Theo turned to Sam. Their eyes widened and mouths dropped, expressions of shock quickly recoiling into ones of anger.

"*What?*" Ritchie seethed. "What do you *mean* she *told you to bring us up here?*"

"I ran into her at the grocery store," Sam confessed, tears spilling from her eyes. "I was there picking out pumpkins to carve with my family. She approached me and complimented my outfit. She told me I looked very *Halloween*. I thanked her...what *else* was I supposed to do?"

"I don't know," Ritchie snapped. "Don't talk to *crazy old bitches?*"

"*I didn't know she was crazy!*" Sam shrieked back.

"How the *fuck* did you not know?" Ritchie glared at her. "*Everyone* in town knows about her!"

"I knew *about* her," Sam said. "I didn't know *who she was*. Besides, *you* said yourself that she's *harmless*. Even your *dad* thought so, Ritchie. So don't you *dare* come after me!"

Behind the wall of pumpkins, Peter had managed to retrieve his pocket knife, sawing away at the vine. With each stroke of the blade, it loosened with a hiss. Before long, he was able to pull it away from his neck, fresh air finally rushing down his throat. Rattling coughs erupted from his chest as he attempted to hack away what was left.

"She seemed like a sweet old lady," Sam continued, swiping at her tears. "She was talking about carving pumpkins and baking for Halloween. She told me it was her favorite time of year. About things she used to do with her friends when *she* was younger. That's when she asked if I'd heard of Old John and the Devil. The story behind the jack-o'-lanterns."

Peter slipped free of the vine, trying to run back to his friends. His ankle burned, causing him to cry out and stumble. His chest rose and fell in shaky breaths, stopped by the barrier of jack-o'-lanterns. He could do nothing but watch. Listen.

"She told me all of that happened here in town," Sam explained. "She said teenagers for generations came up here and recited it. Brought carved pumpkins. Took turns daring each other to sit on the throne. She said it was just a fun scare for the season. Nothing more."

"Well she *lied*," Ritchie hissed.

"She set us up…" Theo muttered in shock.

"It was our last Halloween together. She said it would be perfect. *Fun*. Something we'd never forget…"

"Oh, *trust me*," Ritchie spat nastily. "I'll *never* forget this."

"So *she* left out all the important bits," Theo surmised.

"*Why?*" Sam choked, turning back to the old woman.

"To keep the fools coming, of course," Grýla replied simply.

"But why *us?*" Sam clenched her fists. "Why tell *me?*"

"I'd seen you around town," Grýla admitted. "Walking home from school with your boy friends. It was the quickest way to fulfill what needed to be done. I knew if I told *you*, you would tell *them*. Boys are gullible. They'll do anything a pretty girl tells them to. Just look at Peter…"

The vines had begun to snake their way back up his body, digging into his legs and arms. He continued to slash away with the pocket knife—but he was growing weaker. Exhaustion was kicking in from all the weeks he had gone without proper sleep. And the pain from his injuries—his ankle, his elbow, his arm—slowed him even further. He yelped as more vines slithered from the plump bodies of the jack-o'-lanterns, wrapping around his ankles, holding him in place. They wound their way around his arms and wrists— stopping him from hacking at them. He struggled, trying to break free, but it was no use. He was tethered in place, like a living scarecrow. A fearful howl broke from his throat.

"He would have done *anything* to impress you, my dear." Grýla sneered at Sam. "That's why he sat on the throne. To prove he was brave. To get your attention. To *please* you."

A tear rolled down Sam's cheek as she shook her head. "It wasn't supposed to be *Peter*…"

"What do you *mean?*" Theo demanded, raising an eyebrow.

Sam stifled a sob, keeping her gaze averted.. "Peter wasn't supposed to sit on the throne. *Ritchie* was."

"What the *fuck*, Sam!" Ritchie roared.

"It was supposed to be *just a story*. Something fun to do. A scare..." Sam said hoarsely.

"So you were going to offer *me* to the *Devil*?"

Sam turned a hot glare on him, eyes flooded with tears. "You've been such an *asshole* lately, Ritchie. Picking on Peter. Being a snob. A *fool*. You were the one who wanted to do something scary, so I figured this was a way to *scare you*. To teach you a lesson. Peter was never even supposed to *come*! But then *you* opened your *big mouth*!"

She sobbed uncontrollably, shoulders quaking. Mascara ran down her cheeks in thick, dark smears.

"I was just planning to scare you, Ritchie... When you sat down, I was going to *scare* you. I didn't know it was *real*. I *never* would have brought *any* of you up here if I knew."

Peter's wails of pain only broke her more. She turned to find the vines had slithered under his shirt, ripping his skin as he flailed. He sunk his teeth into one of them, yanking at the leaves. But they were too firm. Too strong. They fought back, winding around his neck to hold his head in place.

"Let him go!" Sam screamed. "Fucking *let him go right now*!"

"You know I can't do that, my dear," Grýla said. "A deal has been made. A promise for a soul. A body. The Devil needs his due."

"Then take *me*!" Sam pleaded desperately. "This is all *my* fault. It wasn't supposed to be Peter. It was *never* supposed to be *Peter*. Take me instead!"

A sharp chuckle erupted from Grýla's throat. "*You*? Oh, sweet child... The Devil doesn't want *you*."

Sam's shoulders fell as she watched Grýla circle the bonfire. The cats followed at her heels, making their way over to Peter. He grunted as he struggled, no longer able to move. Reaching into the pocket of her skirt, the old woman produced a handful of pumpkin seeds. The vultures hissed and croaked, spreading their wings in the branches above. Peter whimpered, tears wetting his face.

"You see," Grýla continued, "women are too smart. Too *wise*. The Devil knows he can hold no power over them, for he'd be tricked. Made to bend to their will."

She caressed Peter's cheek with the back of her wrinkled hand. Pursing her lips, she shushed him.

"Men, however, are fools. They'll sell their souls so easily. You can promise them *anything*. Fortune. Glory. Love. Power. How gullible they are. History has proven that since the dawn of time."

"Find another man, then!" Sam begged. "Just *not* Peter... *Not Peter*..."

"It's too late for that," Grýla said. "The Devil can't wait any longer. John's body is becoming useless—worn away by time. It's been far too long since someone new has come along. Longer than ever before, in fact. It's only a matter of time before that bag of bones crumbles, turns to dust. He needs a fresh body. And Peter promised *his*."

Taking two small pumpkin seeds between her fingers, Grýla forced Peter's mouth open. He struggled within the vines, attempting to break free, but they held too tightly. He sobbed as her calloused fingers pressed down on his tongue, placing the seeds upon it. Then, she pressed up on his chin, shutting his mouth. Tears streamed down his face as he retched, struggling to keep the seeds from sliding down his throat. Pushing them forward on his tongue, he used what strength he had to spit them out.

Grýla flinched as the stream of saliva and seeds hit her in the face. She growled in disgust, wiping away the wetness before glaring at Peter. He heaved a breath, drool dripping from his lips as she hissed, drawing her hand back. It slammed against Peter's cheek—the heavy *smack* echoing off the headstones. He cried out at the blow, skin reddening. His breaths turned into pained whimpers as Grýla rubbed her hand, yellowed teeth gritted tightly.

"Why are you doing this?" Peter wept.

"To keep a promise," Grýla hissed. "You're not the only one who made a deal, boy."

"What do you mean?" Sam questioned, blinking back tears.

After a long, silent pause, Grýla turned to face her.

"My son," she replied softly. "Long ago... so, so very long ago. We came here looking for a new life. A future. Back then, there was nothing but wilderness. Only a few small townships cropping up within the valley. Things were hard, but we managed. We always had a warm fire and pelts. Fresh meat. And all was well, until the evening my son didn't return home."

Grýla smoothed the wrinkles from her skirt. Her once bitter demeanor vanished, overtaken by guilt. Sorrow. She stared into the bonfire beside the tree, the flames pale in her milky eyes.

"I found him strung up in an old tree. *This* tree. Lifeless, but still warm. And I begged and pleaded that Death take *me*. That he return my boy. But it wasn't Death that answered me. It was the Devil—from the hollow in the bark. He told me of my son's doing. His bargain for a kill on each of his hunts. It was why we didn't struggle. Why we didn't perish when winter came, like so many of the others—lost to the mountains." She sighed. "The Devil told me my son had promised him his soul—his *body*—in exchange for our survival. But I told him he couldn't have it. That boy was *mine*. And I wasn't going to let the Devil have him. I begged he take me instead. But the Devil refused. Women are too wise, he said. He knew I would have found a way to trick him. So I made a bargain with him instead. A trade."

The cats at Grýla's feet chirped sadly as they looked up at her. She gripped her shawl tight, lips pressing together as her eyes narrowed. The firelight gleamed across her skin, shadows dancing across the bark of the tree.

"He promised to set my son free if I found him another soul. Another body. And so, I agreed. I lured a foolish gold panner, spinning him stories of riches buried here. Like I said, you can tell a man anything, and they'll follow. The Devil had a new body, and he was pleased. He let my son's soul go free," Grýla continued. "But, it didn't take long for the body to rot. The Devil threatened to take my son back if I didn't keep searching for him. Didn't keep *serving* him. Finding him fresh flesh. New fools to claim. And so, that's what I did..."

She rubbed her fingertips against the sleek pumpkin seeds in her hand. Her lips drew up into a wicked smile again, gaze passing between Sam, Theo, and Ritchie. They stood, silent beyond the barrier of jack-o'-lanterns. Watching in fear.

"When the old body began to decay, become useless, I would seek out another. Telling the story of the one who came before. Luring the next desperate fool up here—seeking their desires. Searching for the truth in legends. It was the only way to keep the cycle going. Keep the Devil from claiming my son," Grýla said. "And I won't *ever* let him."

She turned back to Peter, watching the shadows cast by the fire flicker across his face. The light reflected in the wet tear stains that lined his cheeks as she approached again. She shook the pumpkin seeds in her hand, gazing into his fearful dark eyes.

"Only when the veil thins does the Devil need the body. When the days become shorter and the nights become longer... Every Halloween, he'll return to it. Use its shell to wander the earth. To be among the living. But with each passing year, the body becomes less useful. Eaten away by worms. Maggots. By time. There's only so many years the Devil can make use of it," she said. "And when the time comes for him to claim a new one, it's a glorious celebration. The crowning of a new King. And *this time*, the release of a lost, wandering soul."

283

Grýla took a handful of Peter's hair, yanking his head back. He hissed, whimpering beneath her touch. She shook her head, clicking her tongue as she jostled the seeds in her hand.

"It's a shame you won't be attending *your* Homecoming next week," she jeered. "But, at least you'll get to experience *Jack's*."

"Please..." Peter begged. "I wanna go home... My dad...he's waiting for me. *Please...*"

Snot dripped from his nose as he wept, harder than before. From behind the wall of jack-o'-lanterns, his friends called out to him. Pleading that Grýla release him. That she find someone else. Call off the Devil. But she paid them no mind. Her grip tightened in Peter's hair as she held him firmly in place, watching his bottom lip tremble as he choked out weak words.

"I just wanna go home to my *dad...*"

Smirking, Grýla leaned in. Her cheek brushed against his as she whispered into his ear—her breath hot.

"There's nothing but the dark void ahead for you, child," she uttered. "If *home* is what you seek, you best pray someone leaves a light to guide you there..."

Once again, Grýla forced Peter's mouth open. He fought to pull away, to bite down, but her grip was too strong. Her fingers pressed against his tongue, pushing the pile of seeds inside. This time, she aimed for the throat. Peter gagged as she emptied her hand, snapping his mouth shut. Her fingertips squeezed his jaw, locking it closed. He whined in terror as he struggled to release himself, but there was no use.

"Swallow," Grýla commanded. "Don't cry. It'll all be over soon."

Drool oozed from between his lips as he broke, the seeds sliding down his throat. Burrowing deep into his gut. Grýla released his face, eyes wide as she grinned.

"*Peter*!" Sam cried out.

His stomach began to churn, twisting and burning. Sweat beaded across his forehead, dampening his dark hair. A low moan escaped his chest as more saliva dripped from his mouth—thick and heavy. Then his throat began to sting. Tightening. He coughed hoarsely, gagging on a thick sensation swelling it shut, leaving him gasping for air. Grýla smirked, gently clapping a hand against his cheek.

"That's a good boy," she crooned.

"*Peter*!"

Sam's desperate scream rang throughout the cemetery. Heavy sobs broke from her chest as she lashed out at the jack-o'-lanterns, kicking down as

many as she could. But they kept closing in. Rebuilding their wall. Making sure nothing could be foiled.

Peter hacked and retched, the burn rising through his stomach and chest. Everything felt like it was on fire—searing his insides. Tearing his organs apart. He choked, spitting up fragments of leaves. Bits of vine. His head throbbed, pulsing with painful twinges that surged through his body. Sam's cry reached him through the agony, ringing in his ears. Using what strength he had left, he turned his head towards her voice. She, Ritchie, and Theo looked on in horror, faces stained with tears.

"I-I'm sorry..." Peter rasped. "I'm *so sorry*..."

He sputtered again, another wad of leaves erupting from his throat. A stream of orange pumpkin guts and seeds spewed from his mouth, staining his lips. Fragments of vines filled the putrid smelling bile—laced with flecks of blood. Pain shot through his skull, radiating down the right side of his face and into his orbital socket. His eye began to pulse, feeling as though it were going to burst.

"We gotta get the hell out of here," Ritchie wept. "*Now.*"

"*No!*" Sam hollered. "We *can't leave him.*"

"Come *on*, Sam," Ritchie urged. "It's too *late.*"

He grabbed Theo, pulling him back towards the pathway. In the trees above, the vultures hissed with laughter. Their wings spread wide as they danced, words slipping from their tongues.

Peter, Peter, pumpkin-eater,
Bound in vines, he was a bleeder...

"S-Sam?" Peter's voice was weak now. "Don't go... *Please* don't go... Don't leave me..."

"I'm *not* leaving..." she choked.

A frail cry broke from this throat, heavy in the fog. "*Please don't leave me.*"

"I won't leave you," Sam sobbed pitifully. "I *promise...*"

Another stream of vomit spewed from Peter's mouth. Froth foamed at his lips as he choked, sharp vines beginning to protrude from his skin. They tore through his flesh, snaking out of his arms and back as he gargled saliva and blood. The crimson fluid dripped down his chin, staining his white t-shirt. Each breath he took became more labored. His right eye bulged as pain seared through his skull—putting pressure on his temple. Peter howled in agony.

From beside the bonfire, Grýla watched. The light gleamed across the wet blood on his skin and fear in his eyes. The cats looked on, jowls drawn up into grins as they waited, ears twitching with each of Peter's cries.

"It's gone to your head, hasn't it?" Grýla asked. "Like a tumor, I'd assume. You can feel it growing, can't you?"

Peter couldn't answer. Blood sputtered from his lips as he coughed. Darkness swam at the corners of his eyes, only the flickering fire before him visible. His head drooped beneath the pressure, feeling as though it were ready to explode. Another stream of blood ran down his chin as his eyelids fluttered shut. He tried to ease the pain by thinking of somewhere outside the cemetery. Somewhere safe. *Happy.*

He thought of the back seat of Ritchie's father's car. The booth at the diner. He thought of the noisy cafeteria. The cramped bathroom stall in the locker room. He thought of the hot bleachers beside the football field. The cold steel of the broken down trains. He thought of the soft carpet on Sam's bedroom floor. The warmth of his bed.

He thought of the smell of rain, the sweet scent of cedar. He thought of the mountain air, the morning fog. The taste of ash on his tongue. The lingering odor of cigarette smoke—coating his clothes, his hair, his room. He thought of the sound his bike tires made as they rode through the gravel. The heavy metalcore blasting through his headphones. Ritchie's high-pitched laughter. Theo's encouraging words.

He thought of Sam's soft lips. The sweet taste they left behind. Her gentle hands, holding his. Her bright hazel eyes. Her violet hair, blazing in the autumn sun. He thought of his father, waiting at the kitchen table, sipping a cup of overly sweet coffee. His burnt toast. Orange juice with too much pulp. He thought of his hugs. His daily whispered *love yous.*

And then he thought of his mother, her sweet words. The comforting scent of a home cooked meal—made with love. Marionberry pie. Her tender arms, holding him. Tucking him into bed. Kissing him goodnight, with promises to see him in the morning. Promises to see him again...

They spoke the words and read the spell,
And crowned the Fool to rule in Hell...

The vultures took off from the treetops, circling the blazing bonfire. The air became heavy—cold. Puffs of condensation billowed from Peter's lips with each of his frail breaths, the night growing darker than ever. He gradually opened his eyes, vision hazy as he tried to focus on the shapes around him. Flitting through the fog. Only one in particular was bolder than the others, however. Standing out amongst the graves.

"He's here..." Grýla grinned.

Peter watched as it approached, the buzzing of flies growing loud. It wore a hooded cloak, candle flickering faintly in its grasp. Peter panted a fearful breath, bloody drool rolling from his lip. He had seen the figure before—and not just amongst the headstones. He'd seen it in his dreams, offering him candlelight. Prying for his desires. He'd seen it in the corners of his bedroom. Standing over his bed. Looming. Watching. Waiting. As it stepped into the light of the bonfire, its features finally became visible.

It was a walking corpse. What little flesh was left on its face was pulled tight across the bone. Its eye sockets were hollow, but somewhere deep within them, there was light. An amber glow, dancing like candlelight. Searing into his soul.

Grýla bowed her head to the figure as it walked past, the cats doing the same. The jack-o'-lanterns turned away from the path, facing the entity. It slipped silently over to Peter, teeth drawn into a wide grin. Extending one of its long, crooked fingers, it raised Peter's chin, forcing him to look upon it. He wheezed weakly as his eyes met the dark void of the corpse's skull. The glowing amber eyes deep within. The hot flames. He fell entranced by their flickers, staring into them. Lost.

Sam's cries carried across the cemetery again, begging and pleading more than ever before. She tried to grab the figure's attention, but it didn't pay her any mind. She had nothing it desired.

Keeping Peter under its trance, the figure pressed the dripping white candle into his vine-wrapped hand, urging him to take it. But he had no strength left. Peter's fingers trembled, frozen in the night air. His grip on the candle failed, and it fell to the ground before him—flame extinguishing. The figure hissed in displeasure. Leaning in close, its decaying flesh pressed against Peter's nose.

The amber light within flashed. With a crack, the jaw of the corpse unhinged, releasing a stream of angry flies. They buzzed deafeningly, swarming Peter's head. As he went to scream in terror, they poured into his mouth. Down his throat. Sam wailed at the sight.

"Holy *shit*," Theo cursed from the path.

More flies billowed from the corpse's body. Peter's dark eyes became vacant as the insects infested his throat, filling his lungs. As the last of the flies escaped the decay, maneuvering its way up Peter's nostril, the corpse disintegrated. Bone crumbled into a cloud of dust—an empty shell. Peter's head flopped forward, hanging limply as the vines that bound him loosened their grip—finally releasing him.

287

His eyes remained vacant for a moment. Empty. But then, they lit up, reflecting the amber firelight. His lips pressed together tightly as he steadily raised his head. The vines that protruded from his flesh shuddered as he straightened himself, taking in the cold of the night. Shrugging his shoulders, the joints cracked, allowing them to relax. He was silent, staring across the cemetery. Across the darkness.

The jack-o'-lanterns rolled towards Peter, gathering around the bonfire. Once they had dispersed, Sam hurried across the lawn—keeping her distance, but drawing nearer. Tears welled in her eyes as she exhaled softly, staring through the fire at her friend.

"P-Peter?"

His brown eyes flashed amber. Sam backed away as they slowly turned on her. Eyes she didn't recognize. Eyes that weren't Peter's. Grýla staggered over to Sam's side, shaking her head with a grin.

"Peter's no longer here," she said. "He's in a better place now, if you can consider it that. A place free of pain. Of sorrow. A place he never has to fear being alone. What you see now is just a hollow shell. The vessel left behind."

Sam's mouth fell open as tears streamed down her face. She shook her head, watching as the vines sprouting from Peter's body twisted, coiling themselves gently around his limbs and torso.

"Gaze upon him, child." Grýla beamed as Peter raised a hand to his face. "Gaze in awe and admiration. It's not every day that you stand before the Devil."

Peter dug his nails into the flesh of his right cheek. He burrowed them deep, piercing the skin—blood pouring down his face. He raked away, ripping off bits of skin. Then, he reached for his scalp. The hairline. Pressing his fingernails into his temple, he tore again. This time, peeling away the outer layer of flesh. He pulled it slowly, stripping it clean from the bone. What should have *been* bone.

In its place, however, was a plump pumpkin. Freshly grown from the enchanted seeds. Peter dug away at the thick orange flesh, clawing out a hole for the eye and half a jagged smile. A perfect pumpkin grin. As his arm fell back to his side, the layer of flesh that had peeled away sagged—tissue still connected—hanging like a wet curtain from his chin.

Sam fought the urge to vomit as she collapsed to her knees in the grass. Her eyes went wide as Ritchie and Theo hobbled over to her, staring at Peter's mutilated body. A sob erupted from Sam's throat as she leaned forward, pressing her face to the damp ground. Her cries turned into angry,

tormented screams as Grýla retrieved the pumpkin crown she had carved. The boys stood beside Sam, their own tears staining their faces as they watched in terror. In the trees, the vultures returned—spreading their wings wide in their haunting dance. The tongueless black cat trotted beside Grýla, standing before Peter's body. It chirped as it gazed up at him in admiration.

"Peter, Peter pumpkin-eater..." Grýla recited.

The cemetery became alive with the words as they drifted across the graves. Echoing on the wind. They slipped from the beaks of the vultures, from the mouths of the cats. They poured from the carved jack-o'-lanterns. Sam shook her head as they billowed—grating against her ears.

From his head, he fed the seeder;
They crowned him with a pumpkin-shell;
And dragged him off to rot in Hell.

Grýla raised the pumpkin-shell crown, gently resting it atop Peter's tousled hair. Voices carried across the graves. Hushed whispers of awe. Peter stood still, amber eyes glinting in the firelight. Drawing her lips into a smirk, Grýla motioned to the jack-o'-lanterns surrounding him.

"It's been so long since you've had a new vessel," she said. "So much so, the spirits of those indebted to you have chosen to inhabit the pumpkins this Halloween night. A faithful court you have, no?"

Peter's gaze slowly acknowledged the grinning jack-o'-lanterns lining the lawn. Their carved expressions were ones of admiration. He kept his lips tight as Grýla bowed to him once more.

"They've grown fond of you. They revere you as their King. Peter may not have asked for glory as John had, but it's fitting. It's only right that we continue the tradition."

The candles within the pumpkins flashed as the cemetery came to life again. The voices of the vultures and cats rang out, swirling in the night air. Sam glanced up, weeping as she stared upon the scene before her.

Peter, Peter, pumpkin-eater,
Bound in vines, he was a bleeder;
They spoke the words and read the spell,
And crowned the Fool to rule in Hell.

"All hail the King!" Grýla exclaimed.

The cemetery erupted, echoing her words. "*All hail the King*!"

XVII.

The bright, tinny sounds of instruments echoed throughout the cemetery, bouncing off crumbling headstones. Patches of light flickered along the pathways, from the jack-o'-lanterns lining the lawn. Their carved grins were wide, glowing brighter than before. Overhead, the vultures soared—circling the chapel and upper portion of the cemetery. Their jovial hisses joined the music ascending the hill. In the faint firelight, the shadows danced.

Grýla's thirteen cats pranced on their hind legs, blowing tiny horns and flutes. They banged upon small drums and rattled little bells. And while

joyful, there was an air of unease to the sound. It drifted through the night, vibrating across the plots. Up the hill the cats marched, tooting and banging and jingling. Leading the procession.

Peter sauntered behind them, chin dipped low as he kept his lips pressed tight into a frown. His eyes reflected the amber jack-o'-lantern light as he followed the parade, remaining fixed ahead—never straying. The pumpkin crown weighed heavy on his head. With each step he took, the peeled skin swung from his face, dripping blood onto the collar of his flannel.

Grýla brought up the end of the line, clapping her hands to the beat of the cats' music. Her lips were curled up in thrill, exposing her yellowed teeth. Her gaze shifted across the hilltop, to the dark graves set upon it, then back on Peter's body. As the procession approached the chapel—glowing brightly with candlelight—she bowed her head.

"It's not much further, my lord," she said.

Peter remained silent. His empty eyes were set on the shadows ahead, where he knew the stone throne awaited him. The cats carried on with their melody, prancing as they played, the sound distorting the deeper into the cemetery they went. And while it carried down to the lower plots on the wind, it was nothing more than a dull drone. Echoing like lost phantoms in the night.

Sam gripped a fistful of damp grass and leaves as she pressed her forehead to the ground. Her sobs had died down, but her chest still heaved in heartbreak. Ritchie and Theo stood beside her, trembling from the chill and fright. They stared off through the fog—where Grýla and the cats had ushered Peter.

"It's all my fault..." Sam whimpered. "It's all *my fault*..."

Theo winced as he managed to kneel beside her. His damaged thigh throbbed as he shifted onto his good leg, placing a hand on her back. He caressed her soothingly, lips drawn into a pitiful frown as he shook his head.

"No it isn't, Sam..."

She lifted her head. Her hazel eyes were red and puffy from tears, dark mascara streaking down her cheeks. She glanced towards the flickering light up the hill, the gathering of jack-o'-lanterns.

"I *promised* him," she wept. "I promised him I wouldn't let anything happen to him. That I wouldn't let her hurt him."

She squeezed her eyes shut, gnashing her teeth. Leaning back, she wrapped her arms around herself—for comfort from the cold.

"*I promised him...*"

"There was nothing you could have done," Theo reassured her softly. "There was nothing *any* of us could have done..."

"He was so scared..." Sam's voice was hollow. "He'd *been so scared*. For *weeks...*"

She wiped her face, smearing her mascara further. Her gaze rose to the hill again, to the distant sounds of celebration. Swallowing around the lump in her throat, she tried to stifle the next wave of tears.

"He was so scared of *dying*."

"Aren't we all?" Ritchie asked weakly from behind her.

Sam and Theo turned, eyes narrowed. His arms were crossed, keeping out the chill as he shivered. In the faint light of the bonfire, the wetness on his face shone. He sniffled, eyes dropping to his feet.

"No one *wants* to die," he continued. "And *Peter* sure as hell wouldn't want *us* to. That bitch got what she wanted. Now's our chance to get out of here."

"No." Sam stated flatly.

"*What?*"

"Not without Peter."

"Sam..." Ritchie's eyes softened.

"*No.*" Sam heaved a breath. "I already broke too many promises to him. I'm *not* breaking another."

Theo grasped her shoulder, giving it a gentle squeeze. Tears stung his eyes as he shook his head again, mouth turning into a hard frown.

"Sam..." Theo began, searching for words. "Peter's..."

"He's still in there," Sam snapped, biting back tears. "I *know it*. He's *still there*. I *can't* leave him. *I promised.*"

She couldn't fight it anymore. A lone tear spilled from her eye, running down her cheek. Her black painted lips trembled as she stared—lost and empty—into the stirring shadows. The flickering firelight. After a moment, she turned back to her friends.

"What if it were *you*...?"

The boys remained silent. With a deep exhale, Theo eventually nodded. Ritchie, however, continued to stand still. Stiff. Keeping his arms tight around himself.

"Peter's been your friend since *Kindergarten*," Sam admonished him. "The *first friend* you *ever had*. You've known him longer than *either* of us."

She shakily got to her feet, helping Theo stand. Holding his arm to keep him steady, she turned back to Ritchie. His lips had drawn into a broken frown, tears welling in his blue eyes. Softening her voice, Sam sniffled.

"He *loves* you, Ritchie. He loves *all* of us. And he wouldn't leave *you* behind..."

A whimper broke from Ritchie's throat. He quickly covered his face, wiping the falling tears on the sleeve of his varsity jacket. Blinking back the rest, he snorted another wad of snot. With a trembling breath, he finally nodded.

"Okay..." he said weakly. "Okay. But we have to move *quickly*."

The brassy fanfare grew louder as Peter approached the throne. Jack-o'-lanterns were piled high in stacks beside it, vines snaking up the stone. They weaved between the cracks and grooves, draped like curtains from the seat. Though the darkness lay thick across the throne, engulfed by the chapel's towering shadow, pinpricks of light danced at the base. Small, lit candles— what appeared to be hundreds of them. Their flames flickered atop the wicks, shifting in the gentle breeze. Peter gazed at the twinkling display, feebly reflected in his dark, empty eyes.

"What do you think?" Grýla leaned into his shoulder, breath hot against his ear.

The music blared around him, vibrating off the stone. But Peter kept his focus on the candlelight. As the cats surrounded the throne, continuing their pageantry, Grýla adjusted the crown over Peter's tousled hair. Once it was situated firmly, she bowed her head.

"Go on." She gestured towards the throne. "Your subjects are waiting."

Peter's feet scuffed through the decaying leaves scattered along the pathway, the candles sputtering with each step. As he slowly approached the ancient chair, the music dissolved. The cats put down their instruments, lowering their heads in respect. Peter's gaze fell upon each of them, watching the candlelight shimmer off their sleek fur. Still, he said not a word as he stepped onto the base, taking his seat upon the cold stone.

The cemetery fell into a deep silence. The breeze died down, leaving nothing but stillness across the plots. Peter looked out across the fog—its thick white tendrils tinged with shadow. In the distance, patches of jack-o'-lantern light could still be seen. The cats settled on their haunches as they chirped up at him, but he didn't acknowledge them.

"It took far longer than expected," Grýla said as she approached, "but we finally found you a new vessel. How does it feel?"

Peter's shoulders rolled forward, joints cracking. The vines jutting from his skin writhed, wrapping themselves around him securely. His blank stare caught the candlelight as Grýla beamed—flashing her rotten teeth.

"This body is young," she said. "We searched for someone older, but every attempt failed. I suppose superstition isn't as sought after as it once was by the older generations. *Children*, however... They're gullible. *Foolish*. And I know you don't discriminate. A body is a body. You'll claim whatever's offered—young or old."

She gestured to him. Peter clenched his fingers against the rough stone, knuckles popping. He remained silent as Grýla continued.

"The pumpkins left an offering at your tree," she said. "Sizeable, I must say. They truly do admire you."

The jack-o'-lanterns' faces grinned up at him. Peter dropped his gaze to them, watching the faint light trapped inside their shells flicker. Feeble souls yearning for praise. Keeping his lips tight, he lifted his chin to them in acknowledgement. The leaves sprouting from their vines eagerly rustled. From beside Grýla, the cats trilled happily.

"We *all* do," Grýla added with a grin.

The candlelight glistened in Peter's eyes as he sat, unmoved. Their dark brown hues burned with amber sparks—the only signs of life within them. In the distance, crickets began to chirp. The wafting breeze returned. Peter straightened against the stone as Grýla raised her arms to the cloud covered skies.

"All hail the King!"

Her voice echoed off the nearby headstones and trees. The vultures above spread their wings, necks craning as they gazed down upon Peter. The cats rose to their hind legs again, instruments once more in their grasp. As before, the cemetery vibrated in the joyous cry of unison.

"*All hail the King*!"

The roar of music erupted from the cats as they tooted their horns and banged their drums once again. They pranced in merriment, circling the throne. Peter stiffened as the fanfare droned on, a low buzzing blending with the bright, tinny sounds. From the pumpkin-shell crown, a fly emerged, crawling across the orange flesh and burrowing itself into Peter's thick ringlets of hair. As the sound of vultures stirring in distant trees rose up across the hill, he drew his attention back to the path. Within the fog, a dark figure appeared. He remained still as the silhouette emerged from the swirling mist.

Sam's shoulders trembled as she made her way up the hill, candlelight gleaming in her wet eyes. The cats nor the vultures noticed as she approached. Nor did Grýla. She happily clapped along with the music of the clowder, lost in the rhythm. But Peter saw her. The closer she drew, he lowered his head, mouth pressing into a harder frown.

"*Let him go!*"

Her voice was stern, breaking over the cats' tune. They drew to a halt, lowering their instruments. Silence overtook the cemetery again, hanging heavy in the cold early morning. Returning to all fours, they hissed and glared at Sam, who continued her approach. But before she could get any closer, Grýla blocked her path.

"It's *too late*, my dear," she cooed. "I've already told you; your friend is gone. Lost to the shadows."

"*No*," Sam argued, fighting back tears. "No... He's still *in* there."

Her gaze never wavered from Peter's dark eyes. While illuminated with a tinge of unfamiliar rust, she looked deeper. Beyond the feeble reflection. Searching for any sign of life. Any sign of Peter.

"There's no use living in denial," Grýla said. "It only makes the grieving worse. Why, you should know that. Your little friend lived in denial *every day*. Look what that did for his grief. Look what it did to *him*."

She gestured towards the throne. The cats surrounded it now, backs arched and tails puffed as they growled. Peter merely stared, crown slipping forward on his head.

"It made him a *fool*. Consumed him in sorrow. Desperation. Don't let his failures bleed onto *you*, my dear. Accept the truth."

"He's still there…" Sam breathed. "I *know he's still there*. Let him *go*, goddamnit!"

"He belongs to the Devil now," Grýla jeered. "He willingly offered his soul. A pitiful exchange out of fear of abandonment. But don't you worry… the Devil will take good care of him. He always does. Why, look how pleased his audience is. Come next Halloween, Peter will be among them. A plump little gourd. *Grinning. Happy.* Isn't that what you wanted for him? *Happiness*?"

Sam clenched her fists as the jack-o'-lanterns turned to her. She glared at them, taking in each of their faces. Feeling the heaviness of their souls. Trapped. Lost. Clinging desperately to the little light flickering inside them, all that had been left to guide their way. She thought of Old John, weaving between the graves, searching for peace. For a place to rest. Turned away by the Devil. Mocked by the weak flame he had been given. Waiting for new light to bring him home. Tensing, Sam turned her gaze to Grýla.

"John…erm, *Jack*…" she began. "You said this was his homecoming. You said he'd be set free."

"That's right," Grýla replied confidently.

"How?" Sam asked.

Grýla chuckled. "What do you mean, *how*? Clearly you saw it for yourself."

"It's not because of the new body," Sam said. "Peter had nothing to do with Jack's freedom…"

She faced Peter. His jaw clenched as she took a step closer, the breeze chilling her spine. The cats hissed at his feet as a vulture swooped from the branches above, perching itself behind his left shoulder. Its beady black eyes glinted in the firelight, staring Sam down.

"*The Devil* is the one who needs a body. To walk among man on Halloween night. To tempt them," she recalled. "The legend said that Jack tricked the Devil. Was able to bargain for his soul. But…that doesn't seem right. The Devil wouldn't go back on his word."

Sam furrowed her brow in thought. She replayed the legend she had been told, and the different variations of it. And she remembered what Grýla had told them—how she begged and pleaded for her son to be spared. How she had made a bargain so his soul could be set free.

"It was *you*, wasn't it?" Sam asked. "*Jack* was your son."

Grýla breathed a weak chuckle, curling her lips. "A clever one you are…"

"But that happened so long ago," Sam said. "Old John…"

297

"Is *not* my son," Grýla stated. "He was another simple-minded fool out looking for riches. Looking for worldly desires. *Jack*, however, yes. And it was, indeed, so very long ago."

"I don't understand," Sam murmured, shaking her head. "You said you've been bringing bodies for the Devil so he would keep your son's soul free. You've been doing this for *ages*... Why *now*? Why *Peter*?"

"It has nothing to do with *Peter*, like you said. He simply was the fool. The one to take Old John's place. The next to offer his body and soul. His only role in this was to keep *my* end of the deal. Delivering another body to the Devil, to ensure my son's safety," Grýla said. "What freed *Jack*, however, was *light*."

The candles surrounding the throne spat and sputtered. Sam looked on, perplexed. From the corner of her eye, she caught Peter staring at her. The amber glow in his eyes grew bright, like candle flames themselves.

"When I made *my* bargain, the Devil set Jack free. He gave him a candle—told my son it would guide him through the shadows. Through the empty, dark void. Help him search for home as he wandered aimlessly, longing for rest. But he warned him, should I not keep my end of the deal, should a fresh body not be delivered before the last turns to dust, he would take his soul back. After all, the light that guided him was a gift from the Devil. It was Hellfire that burned at the wick. And until new light—*pure* light—was offered, his soul walked the wire between peace and Hell. Until someone else claimed him, he was never truly free," Grýla continued.

"So why didn't *you* claim him?" Sam asked. "He was *your son*."

Grýla's jaw tightened. "The Devil is wise. He doesn't like to lose. His deals are crooked. *Binding*. Since I was the one who made the bargain, begged for Jack's freedom, I *couldn't* be the one to claim him. I tried. Believe me, child...I *tried*."

Peter's lips grew tighter. He shifted heavily on the throne, the vulture beside him hissing. The pumpkins at his feet flashed, shaken by the breeze.

"It had to be someone else. But not just *anyone*," Grýla explained. "They had to *know* my son. Had to be familiar with him. Have interest. Care. *Believe*. It was only us in the mountains then. Only *us* in the snowclad valley. After the bargain was made, there was no one else *to* claim him. No one who knew him. So I had to keep bringing bodies, biding time. Chasing the Devil off while my son wandered helplessly in the shadows between realms. Lost. *Forgotten*."

She inhaled as one of the cats approached her. It chirped sadly, stretching a paw up at her, tapping her leg. She reached down, gently scratching behind its ears as she turned back to Sam.

"And so, just like the other legends—George and Tom and John—I also told that of Jack. *Wanderin' Jack*. To make people care. To make people *believe*," Grýla said sadly. "It took generations. Countless children attempting to call upon him in mirrors, offer him their candle's flame. *Claim* him. But all were cowards. They'd end the ritual before it could be completed. Before Jack could take his fresh light. *This* time, however, it was a success."

From down the pathway, leaves scuttled, the heavy sounds of labored breathing rising. Sam turned, catching a glimpse of Ritchie and Theo hobbling up the hill through the fog. They supported each other's steps, dragging their injured legs along.

"Three girls completed the summoning. Called Jack home. Offered him their light. *They* believed. *They* set him free," Grýla jeered. "Unfortunately, Jack left them as sacrifices to the Devil. An appeasement, if you will. A gift for his freedom. I'll admit, they *did* make such lovely scarecrows..."

"Why do you need *Peter* then?" Sam's voice raised. "Your son was *freed*. You got what you wanted."

"Old John's body was giving out," Grýla explained. "I needed one *final* body to complete my end of the deal, delivered to the Devil before the first light of dawn. That's why I had to work quickly, find a new fool early in the month. I couldn't afford to wait."

Again, the cat at her feet stretched up, gently digging its claws into her skirt. Grýla lifted the plump tabby into her arms, scratching beneath its chin. The cat's tail flicked as it stared at Sam with bright green eyes—searching deep into her soul.

"Someday you'll understand, child. You'd do *anything* for those you love," Grýla said. "We *all* did."

The cats stepped away from the base of the throne, joining Grýla at her feet. The candlelight shone against their fur—gleaming in their eyes. For once, they weren't angry. They were sorrowful. Helpless. Grýla sighed as she lowered the cat in her arms back to the ground.

"When townsfolk go missing, they blame the witches," she said. "And when they come knocking on your door, you best learn how to hide. How to *shift*. But that only works a handful of times. After that, you're bound to the body you chose to inhabit. *Vultures. Cats.* The greatest tragedy, however, is no one will follow a cat to the throne, or listen to a vulture. No one will know to sit and speak their desires. *Their* loved ones were lost. Returned to the Devil. *Damned*. And they, too, paid a price."

Grýla balled her shaky hands into fists. Her milky eyes narrowed as the cats rubbed against her leg, offering comfort. On the back of her neck, she could feel Peter's eyes searing. Hateful. With a heavy exhale, Grýla gritted her teeth.

"I wasn't going to let that be *our* fate."

"Sam!" Ritchie's voice trailed across the plots, drawing the attention of all gathered.

He stepped forward through the fog, clinging to Theo. His blue eyes burned in the candlelight as he scanned the scene before him. When his gaze fell upon Peter, staring back at him bitterly, he swallowed.

"What the hell is going on?"

Sam didn't reply. She looked between the cats at Grýla's feet, then to the vulture perched beside Peter. It craned its neck, nuzzling his cheek as its feathers ruffled. Her hands shook as she pressed her lips together, taking a step towards the throne. Again, Ritchie called out to her, Theo's voice now joining his. But she remained silent. Her focus was on Peter, on the amber light in his eyes. The light she knew wasn't his.

"Let *me* make a bargain, then."

Her words were confident, unwavering. She continued to stare upon the mutilated face of her best friend, directly into his eyes. Peter leaned forward in interest. Listening. Sam inhaled sharply as the candles at his feet sputtered violently, but she didn't dare show any fear. She kept her back straight and her chest high, brow furrowed.

"Sam!" Ritchie shouted. "What the *fuck* are you doing?"

She ignored his pleas, inching closer to the base of the throne. The sound of buzzing grew louder the closer she approached, finding black flies swarming Peter's head. They crawled in and out of the crown, tangled in his hair. A few landed on the right side of his face, where the pumpkin flesh broke through. They hovered around the wet, drooping skin at his chin, sucking on droplets of blood. Peter rested his elbows on his knees as he gazed upon her, the light behind his eyes flashing.

"Let him *go*," Sam demanded firmly. "Let him go and let *me* make a deal instead."

"Don't be foolish, my dear," Grýla spat. "Making a bargain over a stupid boy."

Sam turned to the old woman. Her hazel eyes were wet with tears as she pressed her lips together, shaking her head.

"You said you'd do anything for those you love," she said softly. "Well, *I love Peter.* He's my *best friend.* And I'm *not* going to let him be damned."

She faced the throne again, taking in the bitterness radiating from Peter. More flies had gathered now, feasting on the gashes in his arm. Swallowing back her fear and disgust, she spoke, voice trembling.

"It was *my* fault," Sam confessed. "*I* brought Peter up here. *I* let him sit. But it was *never* supposed to be him. He wasn't even supposed to *be* here. So, *please.* Let him go. I'll do anything."

Peter sat at the edge of the throne. Steadily raising his arm, he beckoned her closer with his finger. She hesitated for a moment, but then found the courage to walk forward. Leaves crunched beneath her boots with each step, until she stopped at the base of the throne. Standing before Peter.

"*Sam!*" Theo called out. "Don't do it!"

Tears grew heavy in her eyes as she tuned her friends' voices out. Now mere inches from Peter, she could see deep into his eyes. Beyond the familiar brown, amber flecks crackled. Sparking like candlelight. They were beautiful, alluring—but Sam knew they were anything but pure. With a shaky breath, she bowed her head.

"I can bring you a body," she whimpered. "Lure someone else up here for you. Just please... *Please* promise me that Peter will be okay. That you'll set him free. *Please...*"

A tear rolled down her cheek as Peter's gaze hardened. She pressed her lips together tightly, biting back a sob and shaking her head.

"Let him go home..."

Peter reached a hand out to her. Beneath the sleeve of his flannel, a vine protruded, slithering between his fingers. His eyes flashed, urging her to take it—accepting the offer she had made. Inhaling sharply, she shakily extended her arm, taking hold of Peter's hand.

"*Sam!*" Ritchie shouted desperately, voice cracking.

Peter's skin was cold. Ashen. And his grip was heavy—no longer soft and kind. Sam flinched as the vine shot from his fingertips, winding around hers. She did her best to smother her fear as it crawled around her, tightening against her skin. Only when one of the leaves pricked her did she cry out. At the first bubble of blood, the vine retreated. Sam winced as Peter ran his thumb across her wound, smearing the blood upon his own hand. Pulling away, he glanced down at the sticky red stain coating his skin, shimmering in the candlelight.

Peter's lips curled up on the left side of his face, baring his teeth. They were still tinted with flecks of the blood that had erupted from his throat. On

301

the right side of his face, the carved pumpkin grin stretched wider. Within the hollow, a light flashed, illuminating bloody tendons and mangled flesh inside. Sam fought back a wail as flies buzzed from between his teeth. In the trees above, the vultures rejoiced, ruffling their feathers and opening their wings wide as they danced. The temperature dropped, Sam exhaling a quivering pant—billowing a cloud of condensation.

"You're a *foolish* child," Grýla uttered. "You have no idea what you've done."

"I saved my friend," Sam said sternly. "That's all that matters to me."

"It's much more than just finding a new fool to trick," Grýla hissed. "It comes with sacrifice. Offerings that *you* must make."

Sam tensed. Peter's eyes burned into the back of her neck as she stared at Grýla. The old woman shook her head.

"There's no backing out of it," she said. "You're bound to him now. A servant to his will."

The cats mewled as they scurried around her feet. Sam inhaled sharply as Grýla pointed a crooked finger at her.

"Just *remember*, dear," she said, "someone needs to claim him. Someone needs to leave him light—and it *cannot* be *you*. Only then will he truly be free. Will *you* be free."

"Peter has people who care about him," Sam replied confidently. "*Someone* will claim him."

She faced the throne again. Peter sat upright, wide grin still etched across his lips. The vulture behind him was perched to his right now, beak buried in the pumpkin flesh of his face. It hissed hungrily as it tore through, removing stringy pumpkin guts and seeds—dripping in blood. Sam took a shaky breath, eyes watering.

"Only *one*," she said. "*One* body. That's all I'll give."

Peter remained unmoved. He stared at Sam, the light inside the pumpkin half of his head flashing. The vulture turned away from its meal, craning its neck towards her as it hissed again. Its beak was covered in blood. The vines around Peter rustled, snaking down the stone. Sam winced as they slithered up her legs, wrapping themselves tight about her arms and waist. She fought against the rising fear in her chest as they tugged hard, pulling her to her knees. Once she was kneeled before Peter they released her, skittering back through the fallen leaves.

"I've had *enough* of this..." Ritchie growled.

He made sure Theo was steady before pulling away, limping across the lawn. With each step, the pain in the back of his leg dwindled, giving him the

strength to move faster. As he approached the throne, however, the jack-o'-lanterns rolled forward—blocking him.

"Get out of my way," he hissed.

They remained fixed in place, grins wide and eyes narrowed. Ritchie scoffed, bringing his foot up and smashing it into their faces. Their bodies collapsed, splitting into fleshy piles of cracked shell and guts. Peter's grin faded—slipping back into a hard, bitter frown.

"Stop it, Ritchie!" Sam called.

Ritchie didn't listen. He continued tearing through the horde of pumpkins, punting them and crushing their shells. As another wave rolled in, Theo hollered to him.

"Leave them alone, man!"

He staggered forward, up the remainder of the hill as fast as he could. The pain searing through his leg was unbearable. He hissed with each step, calling for his friend again. Ritchie drove his foot through a plump pumpkin, splitting it in half. Orange flesh and guts stained his white shoes as he pulled away, sweat forming on his brow. He panted, auburn strands falling from his neatly styled hair, hanging into his eyes. Passing a glance to the throne, he scowled.

"Get out of Peter, you *fuck*," he snarled viciously.

The vulture perched beside Peter grunted. Its beady black gaze pierced through Ritchie as he straightened himself. He kept his focus on Peter, whose head was now lowered—eyes blazing.

"Ritchie..." Sam breathed. "Please..."

"*No*, Sam," he shot back. "It's almost dawn. We've been out here *all fucking night*. We're exhausted. We're *hurt*. And I'm *done*. It's time to go *home*."

Sam stayed on the ground, kneeling before the throne. She reached a hand for Ritchie as he punted another pumpkin, storming past her. His feet crunched through the decaying leaves scattered across the lawn as he stopped before Peter. Clenching his fists, he glowered at him.

"You say *Peter's* a coward," he spat. "But the only coward I see here is *you*."

Peter's chin dipped, eyes narrowing upward at Ritchie. The vines sprouting from his body writhed, rustling at his sides. He kept his lips tight, merely watching. Listening.

"The Devil's supposed to be big and scary. Supposed to strike fear in the hearts of mortal men. But there's *nothing* scary about you," Ritchie snorted. "Look at yourself. *You're* a coward. Hiding inside a shell. A *kid*. What's the matter? Too afraid to show who you *really* are?"

Peter's shoulders slumped. The vulture beside him grunted again, spreading its wings wide before taking off into the night. Leaves scuttled across the pathways and lawn, tossed by the growing breeze. It tousled Peter's hair, disturbing the flies. They buzzed, swarming around his crown as his mouth drew into a deeper frown.

"*Ritchie...*" Sam breathed. "*Shut up...*"

"Come on," Ritchie taunted. "Show me what you got. *Scare* me."

"Shut *up*, man!" Theo yelled, gripping his wounded thigh.

Ritchie gritted his teeth, peering at Sam from the corner of his eye. He tipped his head towards the pathway leading down the hill. Towards Theo. Urging her to go. But she remained kneeling—heart pounding in her chest. Again, she whispered his name, trying to silence him.

"That's why we all came up here in the first place, right?" Ritchie asked with a shrug. "Sam wanted to scare me. So, go on. *Scare* me. Show me what you've got. Because, quite frankly, a bunch of shitty pumpkins aren't scary. Nor are *stupid birds*. Or *cats*, for that matter. And Peter... *definitely* not Peter. So why are you hiding behind *him*, hm? I thought you wanted men to cower before you."

"That's *enough*, Ritchie!" Theo bellowed.

Ritchie quickly silenced him with a sharp wave of his hand. He kept his eyes locked with Peter's, feeling the heat of the fire within them.

"Do it. *Scare me, bitch*!"

Peter didn't move. He stayed in place, still as the stone he sat upon, glaring into Ritchie's soul. With a snort, Ritchie leaned forward, pressing his nose to Peter's. The wet blood from the torn away flesh was ice cold.

"I see no King here. Only a *Fool*."

The vines growing from Peter snapped forward. They slithered up Ritchie's legs and torso, constricting him. Ritchie hissed as they tore at the wounds in his leg, wrapping their way up his body. He struggled, flinching as the leaves grazed his skin, drawing blood. From the ground, Sam screamed, tears spilling from her eyes. Theo hobbled quickly towards the throne, steps laden with pain. But just as they had before, the pumpkins stopped him. Grinning up at him with hateful glee.

Peter retrieved his pocket knife, flipping it open. The dried blood on the blade glinted in the candlelight as he rose to his feet. Ritchie gasped in terror as Peter sneered, flies pouring from the hollows of his face. The vines wove through Ritchie's auburn hair, jerking his head back. As Peter

approached, he shoved his fingers into Ritchie's mouth, pulling his tongue out as far as it would go. Then, pressing the blade to its wriggling base, he mercilessly began to saw away.

Ritchie sputtered blood as he flailed, struggling to break free of the vines. But they were too tight. They held him in place as he gargled a weak scream, overtaken by those erupting from Sam and Theo. Once the muscle was completely severed, Peter tugged the limp tongue from Ritchie's mouth. Blood poured from his lips as he gasped, blue eyes wide in shock. Sam let out another sob-filled scream as she fell back onto her elbows, crawling away.

"*Ritchie!*" Theo shrieked.

Peter's lips curled on the left side, admiring the tongue in his grip. He wagged it teasingly in Ritchie's face before tossing it aside—scraps for the scavengers.

"*You talk too much.*" A hollow voice rattled from deep within Peter's throat.

Ritchie gurgled blood, flinching at the voice. It wasn't Peter. It was too deep, too raspy. Too distant. It was a voice he'd never heard before. One that numbed the mind, chilled the blood. Sent fear pulsing through the veins. Peter leaned forward, flies swarming angrier than ever now. They darted from the carved features on his face, crawling from the damp hair beneath the crown. At the scent of fresh blood, they flew to Ritchie, landing on his lips. Sucking at his blood-coated chin. Crawling into his mouth. He whimpered weakly as the light behind Peter's eyes blazed, deep like Hellfire.

"*Are you scared now?*"

Another curtain of blood rained from Ritchie's mouth. Peter dropped the pocket knife, wrapping both hands around Ritchie's neck. His fingers pressed tight, crushing the airway closed. Ritchie thrashed with what little strength he had left. He gagged on the blood filling his throat, eyes bulging as Peter's grip grew tighter. His fingernails dug deep into Ritchie's flesh, streams of crimson running from beneath them. Peter smirked, feeling fear seeping from the skin as he twisted. With a loud *crack*, Ritchie's neck snapped.

"*No!*" Theo wailed, crumpling to his knees. "*Ritchie!*"

Sam crawled over to Theo, breaths full of panic as she wrapped her trembling arms around him. Her face was stained in fresh tears, makeup smudged and running. She broke as Theo shoved his head to her chest, sobbing pitifully. He pounded his fist against the ground, chest rattling as he bawled.

"Not Ritchie," he wept. "*Not fucking Ritchie!*"

305

Peter twisted Ritchie's limp neck side to side. Back and forth. The vines burrowed beneath the skin, cutting away at ligaments and muscle. Using all his strength, Peter wrenched Ritchie's head upward. With a sickening *pop*, it tore away from his collarbone, spraying a cloud of blood into the air. Ritchie's body collapsed to the ground as Peter beamed, holding up his prize. Bloody fragments of flesh hung from where the neck had been severed. The crimson wetness gleamed in the firelight, splashed across Ritchie's freckled cheeks. With a sneer, Peter gazed upon the lifeless expression.

"Who's the Fool now?"

Peter tossed the bloody head over his shoulder. It landed amongst the nearby headstones with a *squelch*. The vultures hissed gleefully, diving from the trees and surrounding it. Their sharp beaks tore through the flesh and hair, plucking at the eye sockets. Digging for brain matter.

The wind howled through barren branches as Peter turned to Sam and Theo, huddled together on the lawn. His eyes blazed in hate as he lowered his head, stepping towards them. Vines rattled around him, the ground trembling beneath their wake. From the dirt, more pumpkins protruded, larger than the others. Sam panted in horror as she pressed Theo's head to her chest. Only when she noticed the cats retreating, tails puffed and ears lowered, did she look away from the horde rising from the soil.

One by one, the cats took off down the hill, yowling. They were terrified, no longer eagerly praising Peter. As he drew nearer, the light inside the jack-o'-lanterns snuffed out altogether, blanketing the cemetery in deep shadow. Sam whimpered as Theo pulled away from her, staring across the dark landscape. Only the amber light of Peter's eyes shone.

"Go!" Grýla urged from the shadows. "You've given him an offering. A *sacrifice*."

Sam turned to her, voice quivering. "What do you mean?"

"The more he's given, the stronger he becomes. You must *hurry*."

"But..." Sam whimpered. "How will we—?"

"Sunrise," Grýla replied. "He only has until sunrise. Get to the gates. Go *home*!"

In the heavy shadows, her body shifted. She hunched forward, bones twisting and cracking as she changed shape. Her once milky eyes glinted gold in the fading moonlight, white hair now black and sleek. As the darkness dissolved, all that was left in her place was a black cat. It turned to Sam, whiskers twitching as it mewled.

"And don't forget. Bring a body. Pray someone leaves a light. For Peter's sake..."

The cat took off after the others. Sam called out to it, but it disappeared into the shadows. Whimpering, she glanced back at Peter. The vines tearing through his skin coiled around him, scurrying across the ground. The flesh that hung from his face drooped lower now, catching on the collar of his flannel. Behind the carved pumpkin flesh, light poured—flaring angrily.

"Come on, Theo," Sam urged, tugging on the sleeves of his varsity jacket.

He shook his head vehemently. With another sob, he rammed his first against the earth again. Sam took his face into her hands, forcing him to look at her. His dark eyes were puffy, overflowing with tears.

"He took my best friend," Theo wept. "That *motherfucker....*"

Sam swallowed around the lump in her throat. "He took *my* best friend, too..."

"I *loved* him, Sam," Theo choked.

His cheeks were wet, lips trembling as he tried to bite back another sob. He pressed his face to Sam's shoulder, inhaling sharply as he wailed.

"I *fucking loved him.*"

"I know, Theo..." Sam whimpered, cupping a hand against his face. "I know..."

The leaves beside them rustled. Sam raised her head, looking up into the fiery eyes of Peter. She stifled a scream as she backed away, pulling Theo with her. He winced as he crawled, his mangled leg dragging behind. Peter followed, vines slithering through the grass, creeping towards Sam and Theo. They continued to back away, stopping only when they collided with a crumbling headstone. Sam winced as her head thumped against it, heart racing. Peter shuffled slowly through the leaves, glaring down at them as a smile tugged at his lips.

Sam stared at him, looking deep into his eyes. Beyond the flickering light, she searched for anything familiar—for the dark brown she knew. The dark brown she loved. Her knees trembled as she pulled herself to her feet, brushing away the leaves that clung to her velvet dress and legs. Her tights were torn, chilling her legs, but she ignored it. Wetting her lips, she sucked in a deep breath.

"I know you're in there," she called. "I *know* you are, Peter..."

The vines curled around Peter's body, pulsating. His grin drew wider, exposing his bloodstained teeth. A heavy chuckle rattled from his throat—deep and hollow. Yet Sam stood firm, displaying her courage.

"I know you can hear me," she continued. "And I know you're tired. I know you're scared. But I need you to *fight*. I need you to *remember*."

Another snicker slipped between his teeth, buzzing with flies. Sam sniffled, clenching her fists as Peter took another step forward. Shaking her head, she broke.

"I love you, Peter," she wept. "I *love you*."

Peter stopped in his tracks. His shoes scuffed beneath the leaves, grin quickly fading. His lips fell open, vacant; and the light behind his eyes dimmed. The warm, familiar darkness filled them as his body tensed. The vines recoiled sharply, slithering up his body. Sam breathed a puff of condensation, watching his gaze settle on something behind her. As she slowly turned her head, a low growl rose from the hillside—drifting on the wind.

From the low fog that still clung to the headstones, the Grim emerged. Its red eyes blazed through the white, snorting hot clouds of mist with each breath. Its back was arched, head low as it snarled, baring its fangs. Peter gritted his teeth, knees buckling as he stared at the hound. Saliva dripped from its jaws as it crept across the lawn, gaze never wavering from Peter.

"*Shit*," Theo cursed, dragging himself closer to the headstone for cover.

The Grim brushed against him, snout wrinkling. But it paid Theo no mind. Making its way to Sam, it stood before her, hackles raised as it glared up at Peter. A deep rumble rattled in his throat as he stepped back, bristling at the sight of the hound. Sam froze, gaze passing between Peter and the Grim, breaths shallow.

"Sam," Theo whispered, "what do we *do*?"

"It's not going to hurt us," she replied. "We're not what it wants..."

Peter took another step back, the Grim inching forward. Its tail lowered as it roared, red eyes blazing in hate. Biting her lip, Sam looked on, watching as the dog steadily forced Peter away. One slow step at a time.

"Remember the legend?" Sam breathed. "A Grim's purpose is to protect the souls of the dead. To guard them. To keep the Devil out..."

The hound lunged at Peter, snarling wildly. He hissed, taking refuge behind the building wall of jack-o'-lanterns and freshly sprouted plump pumpkins. The Grim's teeth came down upon the gourds, tearing through their orange flesh. Their vines snapped, whipping at the beast. But it didn't

stop. Its claws raked through the shattered shells and guts as it gnawed away, howling in rage.

"This is our chance," Theo called to Sam. "Let's get out of here."

Sam shook her head adamantly. "We can't leave Peter..."

"We'll go get help," Theo pressed. "You heard that old woman... We need to go. *Now*."

Sam remained in place, watching the leaves shift in the breeze. The growls of the Grim tore through the air as it worked its way through the horde of pumpkins. In the distance, she could make out the faint hues of morning—dawn breaking on the horizon. The dark black of night bled into a navy blue, still dotted with stars. Inhaling sharply, Sam's eyes widened.

"*Sunrise*," she breathed, turning to Theo.

"What about it?" he asked.

"The Devil only has until sunrise," she said. "Remember the legend... The *throne*..."

Theo tilted his head, realization dawning on his face. Across the lawn, the Grim yowled, leaping back as the jack-o'-lanterns rolled towards it. They snapped their sharp teeth, chomping at the hound's paws. Yipping in pain, it recoiled, but then lunged forward again. Swallowed by the mass of orange gourds.

"If you're seated on the throne and the first light of day reaches it..." Sam began.

"You'll be dragged down to Hell with the Devil," Theo finished.

"Right," Sam nodded. "*That's* what we have to do."

"What?"

"We need to get Peter back onto the throne," she said quickly.

Theo shook his head. "But...wouldn't that mean sending Peter to Hell, too?"

"The Devil doesn't own him," Sam said confidently. "I made a bargain. He *can't* take Peter."

Across the cemetery, the distant sound of crows echoed. Stirring in the branches. Awaking to greet the new day. Sam pressed her lips together, turning back to the Grim. Back to the jack-o'-lanterns. Back to the throne. Peter stood behind the horde, stiff with fear as the dog chomped through orange flesh—cracking shells. Taking a deep breath, she nodded.

"I'll be right back," she said to Theo. "Dawn is coming..."

Sam crouched behind a headstone, keeping her focus on the pumpkins and the Grim. The larger gourds that had unearthed lashed out with heavy vines, winding around the legs of the hound. It barked ferociously as it struggled to break away, teeth tearing at the restraints and shredding leaves. Once she was certain all were distracted, she made a run for it, breaking past the mass. Heading towards Peter.

His eyes were burning amber again. Sam's shoulders trembled as she panted, strands of violet hair hanging into her face. She blew them away, focusing on Peter. The vines that snaked around him hissed, stretching towards her. Clenching her fists to quell her fear, she parted her lips. Tears stung her eyes as she approached, bowing her head.

"You've been given your sacrifice, my lord," she said, pushing through the words—hoping they sounded convincing. "I pray it pleased you."

Peter tilted his head, eyes narrowing. Inspecting her. Flies buzzed around him, darting to the splotches of blood staining his face and clothes. Sam glanced up, feigning admiration. Her cheeks were flushed, still streaked in mascara, but she did her best to appear awed.

"I'll bring you a new body," she promised. "In exchange for Peter. But, I won't make you wait until *his* body rots away. I'll make it soon. So it's fresh again for next year."

She took a step forward. Behind her, the snarls of the Grim grew louder, the number of jack-o'-lanterns dwindling. Peter's eyes flashed, amber sparks reflecting within Sam's as she stood before him. Her boots pressed against the white rubber toes of his shoes as she swallowed, leaning against him.

"The world is full of Fools," she whispered. "They're so easy to find..."

The crows cawed in the surrounding trees. Biting her lip, Sam glanced towards the chapel. The sky bled royal blue. Returning her gaze to Peter, she smirked.

"Sometimes," she breathed into his ear, "they're right under our noses..."

Using what strength she had left, Sam planted her palms against his chest and shoved. Peter stumbled, caught up in the vines wrapped around his body. Unable to catch himself, he fell backwards, hard against the seat of the throne. The vines writhed as he landed on them, leaves tearing. Peter winced as his head collided with the cold stone, the pumpkin-shell crown toppling forward. It landed on the hard ground below, splitting in half. As Peter sat up, eyes flashing in rage, dread set upon him. His lips parted, mouth falling open as his eyes widened—fixed on the sky.

From over the chapel's steeple, the sun rose. Its gleaming orb of light broke through the fog, faintly illuminating the cemetery. A single ray streamed through the spire, streaking across the base of the throne. Peter cowered as it crept up the seat, burning away the shadows of night. A shrill screech tore from his throat as it engulfed his body, offering him to the dawn.

A pile of insects poured from Peter's head. They flew from the carved eye and mouth holes, from his nostrils, from between his lips. They slithered from his ears, crawling from his hair. In a black cloud, they dispersed, broken by daylight. Sam watched as the swarm burst into flame—vanishing into the early morning. Then, with a final shudder, Peter's body slumped heavily against the throne. Motionless.

The snarls of the Grim died down as the light inside the jack-o'-lanterns faded. Their wide, happy grins shriveled—turning in on themselves. Burned out. They were no longer animated—only still and simple, as pumpkins should be. The Grim panted, sniffing the lifeless gourds before wagging its tail. With a cheerful bark, it took off towards the chapel, becoming an airy apparition. One with the mist.

Sam shakily turned her attention back to the throne, to the body of Peter sagging within it. Tears welled in her eyes as she hurried forward, voice cracking.

"*Peter!*"

She knelt beside the stone. Peter's face was still torn, exposing orange pumpkin flesh beneath. She grimaced at the carnage, gently tilting his chin up. His head flopped over, revealing only the left side of his face. The intact side. With trembling fingers, she reached out, softly touching his cheek.

"Peter?" she whispered.

But there was no answer. His skin was cold beneath her touch. Pallid. Her chest ached, throat swelling and eyes burning with tears as she stroked his hair, shaking her head.

"No..."

A sob tore from her throat as she pressed her head to his, wrapping her arms around his shoulders. The dead vines that protruded from his skin swayed as she wailed, her sorrow carrying across the silent cemetery. Theo pulled himself to his feet, hobbling across the lawn towards her. He pursed his lips tight as he watched, eyes brimming with tears.

Sam buried her face into Peter's shoulder, tangling her fingers in his thick, tousled ringlets. Damp and matted, but still soft. Her chest rattled with each sob, leaving her gasping for air.

"I'm sorry," she wept. "I'm *so sorry*, Peter..."

Theo's hand gripped her shoulder tight. His breath quivered as he stared down at Peter's lifeless body.

"I promised I wouldn't let them hurt you..." Sam sputtered. "I *promised...*"

She slowly pulled away, gazing down at his face through falling tears. They stained his cheek, dappling his hair. Her lips quivered as she looked him over, gazing into his open eyes. They were vacant and dark. Glazed over. Sam inhaled sharply, her stomach heavy with guilt. She touched his cheek again, running her thumb from the corner of his eye to his chin. Hoping for a twitch. A sign of life. But when he remained still and stiff, a pained squeak slipped from her lips. Sliding her hands down his arms, she gripped his flannel sleeves, giving them a rough shake. Her sobs became a hollow scream.

"Don't leave me. Don't you *fucking leave me, goddamnit*!"

Theo hushed her, caressing her back as she wept bitterly.

"Sam..."

She gasped for breath between each pitiful whimper. Her eyes ached as they grew puffier, head throbbing. Tracing his jawline, she parted her lips, voice cracking.

"Please don't leave me, Peter... I *love* you..."

She ran her fingers up and down his face, attempting to warm his skin. But as the morning fog lifted, it only grew colder. Eventually, Theo patted her back, motioning her away.

"Come on," he whispered. "We gotta go, Sam..."

"*No*," she choked.

Theo stared at her sadly. With a trembling breath, she lowered her head, pushing her fingers through Peter's hair again. Another wave of tears fell as she looked upon his face, taking in all of his features. Burning them into her memory.

"I won't leave you," she uttered against his ear. "I'll come back for you. I'll come back…"

She nuzzled against him again, swallowing back the heavy lump in her throat. The even heavier one in her chest.

"I'll get your dad… And I'll come back. I *promise*."

She kissed his cheek, the cold cruel against her lips. She heaved a sob, brushing the mussed bangs from his face as she gazed into his empty eyes.

"I won't forget you, Peter. I won't *ever* forget you."

A single tear fell from her chin, landing against his pale lips. She wiped it away with her thumb.

"I won't let *anyone* ever forget you… I *promise*."

Birdsong fluttered across the cemetery, the faint rays of morning sun breaking the chill of night. Leaning down one last time, Sam pressed her lips to his cheek again—hard. She held there for a moment, before finally pulling away with a heavy sob.

Sam shakily got to her feet. Theo held onto her shoulder for support, giving her a gentle squeeze. She looked down at Peter, slumped across the throne, one final time. Backing away, she sighed heavily into the morning air.

"I *promise*…"

Leaves crunched beneath Sam and Theo's feet as they made their way back through Chapel Hill. The early morning was alive with activity. Crows cawed from the treetops, squirrels scurrying through the brush. Tiny songbirds chirped their greetings, the breeze carrying each note across the expanse of graves.

Near the lower plots, fog still hung—light and wispy. Catching sunlight. Sam kept her head down as she walked, slow and solemn. Only when she saw movement among the mist did she stop and look—gazing out across the tendrils of white.

It was only for a split second, but she swore she saw it. A figure standing amongst the graves—shrouded in the soft haze—airy and light.

Peter. Though fleeting, Sam was certain he smiled at her, a jack-o'-lantern held tightly to his chest. And within, a flickering candle. A ray of sunlight. But just as soon as she had seen it, he was gone. Leaving nothing but the stirring fog once more.

As Sam and Theo stepped out of the iron gates, the heaviness of the night vanished. The sun streaked across the blacktop, bringing with it the bustle of morning. Down the block, children laughed. Cars honked. Life went on. Sam tightened her grip on Theo's shoulder as they stepped down the sidewalk. But before they could cross the street, a gentle voice echoed—from beside the gates of Chapel Hill.

"Are you okay?"

Sam turned, gazing down at a young girl. She looked no older than ten, standing on the sidewalk with three boys her age. They picked away at candy—spoils from their night of trick-or-treating. Sniffling, Sam nodded.

"Yeah," she said softly. "Just had...one hell of a Halloween is all."

The little girl could sense the fear in her eyes. Gazing off through the gates, she gripped her lollipop tight. The fog was still thick within, making it hard to see anything beyond the glimmering white.

"What's *in* there?" she asked.

Sam hesitated. Tightening her jaw, she released a trembling breath. Then, she turned back to the children, voice sincere.

"The Devil."

The boys booed at her as they waved her off, spewing that the Devil wasn't real. That she was making it up. Just trying to scare them. The little girl, however, stood wide-eyed. Listening intently. Sam wet her lips.

"Have you ever heard the story of Lonely Peter?" she asked softly.

The children shook their heads. Theo tensed as Sam pressed her lips into a hard frown, fighting back tears. She swallowed around the lump in her throat, pushing on. Confidently telling her tale.

"Peter thought he was all alone. He thought no one cared about him. Thought he was a burden. That everyone was better off without him. That, someday, they would all forget him." Sam paused, inhaling shakily. "One night, Peter and his friends came up to this cemetery. They sat around the old tree with jack-o'-lanterns at midnight, telling scary stories. Stories about the Devil. His throne. It's up there, you know? At the top of the hill. Just beyond the chapel."

Sam wiped her nose on the back of her hand, sniffling again.

"Peter sat on the throne that night, and he made a wish. A wish to never be forgotten. To never be alone. The Devil heard his cries and offered him a deal. But, all deals come with a price..."

Biting her lip, Sam looked down at the little girl one last time. She could see the wonder in her eyes. The fear. Sam laid a heavy hand upon the child's shoulder.

"Tell your friends," she said, forcing a smile. "It's a fun scare this time of year, when the veil is thin. When the days get darker. I promise. It'll be a memory you'll *never* forget."

It took Theo a long while to hobble through the neighborhoods. His leg ached, but he pressed on, clinging to Sam. She didn't speak a word after they had crossed the street, leaving the cemetery behind. Her eyes only remained fixed on the sidewalk.

As they headed through the wealthy neighborhood, they could see a squad car parked outside the Trenchards' house at the end of the street. They ignored it, shuffling along, back through the quiet, familiar streets. Streets that only hours before were full of laughter. Full of life.

Harold Trapp stood in his driveway, cursing aloud. He scrubbed away at the remnants of rotten duck eggs, splattered across the hood of his Mercedes-Benz. Sam and Theo paid him no mind as they staggered along, but as they passed his property, he stopped, glancing at them. He scrunched his nose with a snort, muttered beneath his breath. As he plunged the sponge

back into his soapy bucket of water, he noticed something at the end of his drive. Two cats. A plump tabby and a skinny black one. They stared at him, tails beating against the pavement as he grunted, ignoring them. Returning to his cleaning.

Sam and Theo crossed into the next neighborhood, pausing as they reached Cedar Street. The tiny ranch houses dotted the road, residents still sleeping soundly in the early morning. Sam squeezed Theo's shoulder as she heaved a shaky breath, starting down the sidewalk.

On the left-hand side, the familiar tan house appeared, curtains drawn. She recognized the mountain bike sloppily tossed beside the garage, and the old black car in the driveway. Her heart ached as she looked upon the window at the far end of the house, still cracked open, curtains fluttering. But what she noticed more than anything else was the porch. Even in the morning light, she could see it. The porch light—softly glowing. Left on overnight.

Sam took a deep breath, fresh tears coming on as she stood before the lawn. Theo reached down, squeezing her hand. Nodding once. Finding strength, she approached the porch, making her way through the damp grass. Up the front steps. And as her knuckles softly rapped against the front door, her eyes remained fixed only on the light.

A pale beacon of love, never turned out. Still offered.

A light to guide the lonely home.

THE END

317

THANKS
FOR
READING!

Dorian J. Sinnott is the author of numerous works of horror and dark fiction. His stories have appeared in over 300 publications around the world and have been nominated for the Best of the Net and Eric Hoffer Book Award. Many of his works have been adapted into audio productions, as well as graphic novels. He is the recipient of the 2023 Chronogrammies Readers' Choice Awards for Best Local Author. A graduate of Emerson College's Writing, Literature, and Publishing program, Dorian currently lives in New York with his two cats.

Find out more at: www.doriansinnott.com

ADDITIONAL WORKS

It Came Upon a Midnight Clear
Wicked Little Things
Into the Uncanny: 12 Tales of Terror
Return to the Uncanny
Watercolors: A Selection of Poetry

MORE INCLUDED IN

Horrorscope: Volume II
Zombacon
Bloodlust: Drabbles 2
Summer Terrors
Forest of Fear
Alcyone Issue IV
Legends of Night
Winter Shocks
Well, This is Tense
Eldritch and Ether
Run Rabbit Run
New Tales of Old: Volumes 1 and 2
Forest of Fear: Volumes 1 and 3
Planetside
Maelstroms
Dark Stars